Greek
Secret

OTHER TITLES
BY FRANCESCA CATLOW

The Little Blue Door

Behind the Olive Trees

Chasing Greek Dreams

Found in Corfu

The Last Christmas Promise

Another Greek Summer

Greek
Secret

Francesca
Catlow

LAKE UNION
PUBLISHING

Text copyright © 2023, 2025 by Francesca Catlow. Previously self-published in 2023. This edition contains editorial revisions.

Published by Lake Union Publishing, Seattle

www.apub.com

Amazon, the Amazon logo, and Lake Union Publishing are trademarks of Amazon.com, Inc., or its affiliates.

EU Product Safety contact:
Amazon Publishing, Amazon Media EU S.à r.l.
38, avenue John F. Kennedy, L-1855 Luxembourg
amazonpublishing-gpsr@amazon.com

ISBN-13: 9781662526275
eISBN: 9781662526268

Cover design by Emma Rogers
Cover image: © Giacomo Augugliaro / Getty; © high fliers © Dewin ID
© Ann Rudova © ForestDigital / Shutterstock

Printed in the United States of America

I dedicate this book to my children. The driving force behind everything I do.
M, you told me to hurry up and write more books . . . you can't say I'm not trying.
Love you both always.

Chapter One

Now

People swarm around me, pushing to make sure their holiday starts before anyone else's does.

I don't need to worry about that. I'm going to be enjoying this heat for six months and I'm not here for a holiday.

My bags are among the first to appear on the carousel, ironically, so I make my way into the arrivals area in good time.

The airport in Corfu is only very small – it's a matter of steps until I'm faced with a crowd of taxi drivers with names scrawled on paper. It's slow going with two suitcases and my backpack, but this gives me time to look over the faces of waiting people, and their signs.

One catches my eye: *Ruby*.

I know it's not for me though, as Aunt Hazel is meeting me in person.

I see other names too, but it amuses me that there's another Ruby being picked up, as it isn't the most common name. Not that uncommon either, I suppose.

The driver's head is bowed, and his face is hidden under a mass of hair while he looks at his phone. Momentarily, I glance about, wondering who this other Ruby might be that he's waiting for.

I stand on tiptoe in my ballet pumps to see over people's heads, but there's no sign of Aunt Hazel.

She's not in here.

I make my way through the glass doors and stand on the pavement, watching taxis, minibuses and cars filter past. People casually step out in front of them, expecting that they will stop in time as they cross the road.

My entire body shudders at their confidence.

Even with a zebra crossing, I can't do that. Not for a long time, anyway. Perhaps when I was a teen; I can't remember now. Maybe.

As it is, I have to turn away and avert my eyes. I lock them on to the pavement, focusing on its dull shade of grey and the heat from the sun beating down on my head.

A thudding begins in my chest, as though there's a fire burning behind my ribs and my heart has been tasked with stamping it out. Where could she be?

The flight was a little late, so she should be here by now. I glance at my phone again, but there are no messages and no missed calls coming up. Nothing.

Another fifteen minutes go by. I type out a message to Hazel to say I have arrived, and I'm worried, so I'll get a taxi and meet her at their restaurant. That way, if she's forgotten me I'm on my way, or if something worse has happened I've put forward my intentions, or if she's late she'll arrive, see my message and turn around.

Hopefully.

Better to be dropped in a seaside resort with tourists meandering around, because someone will be able to point me in the right direction for Aunt Hazel's restaurant. If I get dropped off in a little village with only people who *actually* live in Corfu, it might be harder to find where I need to be.

Stupidly, I didn't bother to take down the address of Hazel and Pericles' house, only the name of the village. What would have been the point when Hazel was meant to be picking me up?

Apparently, the point was in case I was left at the airport.

I drop my phone back into the pocket of my wide-leg trousers and anxiety stabs at me as my brain pulses with two little words: *what if.*

What if something has happened to her on the way to the airport? What if she's stuck somewhere?

Scenes of her car tumbling off the road and colliding with olive trees slide across my eyes and I can almost feel the loose items in the car bouncing around her as she falls, hear the call of sirens when she's found.

No.

She must have got the time wrong or has just been held up. I've known her to be late for things, although maybe not important things. Usually, she sends a message to say what's happening, but there must be a valid reason.

The pressure of my cases leaning against my legs begins to weigh me down.

Desperately, I scan the faces of anyone who comes near me, and I can't help but compulsively circle the ring on my right hand with my right thumb.

My fingers wrap around each other, hoping this will somehow bring luck. If something's happened to Hazel, I don't know how I'll cope. It would be my fault – she's coming to get *me*, after all.

Taking my phone out of my pocket, I stare at the selfie of me and my best friend, Amara, taken only a matter of days ago at our farewell picnic. Still no message from Aunt Hazel.

This is ridiculous.

Seeing an empty taxi pull up to the kerb, I thrust my phone into my pocket and walk towards the immaculate Mercedes. A woman gets out to help with my two large suitcases, and asks, 'Where you go?'

'San Stefanos, north-west. It's also called Agios Stefanos.' I smile, but only briefly as a man passing by turns abruptly to face me.

He's taller than me, with a mass of wavy hair that grazes his broad shoulders, and a fine layer of stubble crosses his face.

'San Stef? North-west?' he says. 'You are Ruby?' He lifts the sign with *Ruby* scrawled on it in front of his chest, then taps it with his right index finger.

Apparently, there is no other Ruby, and he really *has* been waiting for me.

Turning to the first taxi driver, I do my best to apologise because it seems I'll be needing my cases back out from her boot. 'I'm so sorry. I had no idea. Thank you. *Efcharistó.*'

She shrugs and seems OK about it.

The other driver, the man with all the hair, says something to her too. She replies with a smile as she unloads my bags from her car.

On long legs, he strides towards the traffic. Only, this guy actually takes a second to glance before leaving me trotting to keep up with his pace.

'I was looking for my auntie. I guess she's the one that booked you. She was meant to be collecting me herself.'

'I know.' He yanks my luggage up on to the high kerb and keeps walking through the car park. Sweat starts to collect on my upper lip from all the trotting.

'Well, *I* didn't. I saw your sign, I just thought there was another Ruby. Shame you didn't put the last name.'

He turns to me with his eyebrows hunched over his eyes.

'You didn't think it was a good idea to ask? To check?'

His grumpy face irritates me. It isn't as though I did it on purpose. 'I'm sorry, but I would have thought my aunt would text or call. You don't know her. This is very unusual.'

He pulls a set of keys from his pocket and presses the button. The indicators on a Ford Focus flash.

He laughs a little. Not a big booming laugh. More like a little snort.

'That is funny. Living with someone for many years and not knowing them. I suppose it is possible.'

Now it's my turn to frown. What is he blabbering about? I watch as he lifts one suitcase into the boot then places his hands on his hips and eyes the next case. He settles on opening the rear door and shuffling it on to the back seat.

I open my mouth to speak, but I'm struck by the realisation that this car doesn't look like any of the other taxis at the airport. He turns to me, and his face lifts slightly.

'Am I missing something?' I look from the mass of wavy hair back to the car.

He points at his chest. 'Yianni. We have met. I am Hazel's stepson.'

I shake my head in disbelief.

How could this tall man in tight-fitting jeans and with wild, almost shoulder-length hair be the boy from the wedding I met years ago?

My heart skips – this attractive Greek man can't be that kid. I can't marry the two images in my brain at all. He had short hair, *maybe* curly on top? I can barely picture him back then.

Now he's muscular and holds himself with confidence, the sort of man you can't help but watch out of the corner of your eye to check they actually look that good.

'Are you sure?' It's a ridiculous question, which I realise as I'm asking it, even before he's vaguely struck by mirth. 'No, I mean, you don't look at all how I remember you.'

'Good. You look about the same.'

'Do I?'

Yianni pushes his lips out, tilts his head and inspects me for changes before shrugging. 'Yes.' He turns towards the car. He must be lying, because back then I had my natural long dark hair, instead of my textured blonde bob with only my roots giving me away. 'And she did text you – Hazel. I saw it send.'

To stop my mouth from hanging open, I pull my phone from the pocket of my playsuit.

'Here.' Yianni turns to me, his face so damn smug that I thrust the phone towards it to wipe the look right off him. 'No message,' I add for good measure.

He takes the phone out of my hand and studies it. He looks at me with a raised eyebrow.

'It's still on flight mode.'

Chapter Two

Now

'I don't know why Hazel sends me and does not come herself to get you. I could have helped with the food.' Gripping the steering wheel with his left hand, Yianni pushes his hair back off his face with the right.

If the journey wasn't being peppered with the awkwardness between Yianni and me, it would be idyllic. Huge birds of prey, at times not too far overhead, circle outside the car window as we meander from inland villages to mountain roads.

Giant cypress trees protrude like thin green party hats on top of all the other trees and the sky is the brightest aqua blue I think I have ever seen. I want to breathe it all in, absorb it into my forever memory, because it's the most beautiful road I've ever been along.

All types of trees hug the roads, from olives to lemons and many I don't recognise.

The landscape is scattered with darling hamlets of whitewashed buildings, all of which seem silent and still. It's as though even the breeze has decided it's too hot out to bother rustling the leaves in the trees.

'How about, instead of dropping me back at the house, we go straight to the taverna? That should catch up some time, right?'

Honestly, anything to shut him up. For someone so pretty, he really can sulk his face into a heavy scowl. It isn't as if I have intentionally missed messages and calls. Of course, he was right – I'd left my phone on flight mode.

I thought I was relaxed and ready for this adventure, but when I thought something had happened to Hazel, I guess I spiralled a little and got my thoughts in a tangle. Times like that, I think I'm the only person to get such stupid ideas.

As soon as Yianni took the phone off flight mode on my behalf, three messages came through from Hazel, plus one from Yianni and about five missed calls from him too, including voicemails.

Yianni looks me up and down in a nanosecond.

I feel it.

I feel the presence of his eyes flicking over me. Perhaps it's more obvious to me because his thick black eyelashes emphasise the motion.

'Are you sure?' He angles his watch towards his face for the hundredth time.

'Of course.' I stifle a yawn. It's creeping into late afternoon and straddling the point of evening. I was awake half the night travelling to the airport, making sure I was dropped off by the taxi hours in advance of the flight. I gently twist my body as much as I can to ease my muscles. 'It'll be fine,' I confirm. 'Under one condition.'

'Condition?'

'Yep. No more sulking about the fact I accidentally left my phone on flight mode.' I make sure to elongate the word *accidentally*, so he can't miss its presence in the sentence.

Yianni tuts and mutters in Greek before taking a deep breath, pushing it out to vibrate his lips. His fingers fidget on the wheel.

I'm starting to think I've asked the impossible here. He might never agree to the terms.

'I am not sulking. I am late for work. This is all.'

'Should I assume you're not agreeing to my terms then?'

I stop avoiding looking directly at him and shift in my seat, folding my arms over my chest, as he sucks in his cheeks.

'How can I stop sulking, when I am not sulking? This is impossible, no?'

He glances at me, doing his best to smile briefly in my direction.

'Fine. You're not sulking. In that case, can we start afresh? Can you forgive me for making you late in the first place?' There might be a slightly sarcastic tone to my voice.

Why did I even agree to move here for six months?

I snatch a breath and look out of the window. *You work with this knob now, Ruby*, I remind myself. He has no idea how much this means to me. No idea about my dreams of running my own restaurant one day. He doesn't care. No one does. They don't need to, either. My dreams are my own.

At least the view out of the window is enticing. Better than the rain in England. Even when it isn't raining there, to me it's been raining for the past two years.

Yianni manoeuvres a winding bend that lets me see right over an edge and down into the sea of green below. It stretches out, away from us, until it merges with the sky in the curve of the earth.

I let out a breath as pointedly as Yianni had earlier. Just because we are going to be working – and living – together doesn't mean I can't ignore him. Hopefully.

I gave up trying to please people after Jonathan. I learnt the hard way that it is better to just do what makes *you* happy and not worry if someone else wants to be miserable. However hard that can be.

I also decided never to let anyone else distract me from my own narrative on my life. This is the fresh start I need to get back my dreams.

'Fine, fine. We can go straight to the restaurant. If we make it on time, I forgive you.'

My skin prickles with bad memories.

Old wounds throb like they've been reopened, and I wish I could be swallowed up by the pretty view and spat out at home in my bed.

Yianni exhales next to me, and he almost laughs.

'I'm sorry I seem . . . sulky. This season is a big deal for me. More responsibility and . . . You know, it doesn't matter. I'm sorry for my sulk face. We all make mistakes.'

I'm completely perplexed by this shift. It's not something I'm used to seeing. I watch Yianni as he watches the road ahead.

A smile inches across his face. 'I should be used to it anyway. I didn't realise you would be as bad as Hazel. She is useless with her phone.'

I don't respond, but I do share in Yianni's smile.

He pulls the car into a small dusty car park that has two other cars in it. The restaurant is almost all terrace, with a wooden framework around it in lieu of solid walls.

Pericles is standing at the entrance, holding a menu. Above him, on a metal chain, is a sweeping wooden sign that reads: Greek Secret.

The words are baby blue, and the sign looks as traditional as it could possibly get.

To the right of the restaurant there's a trellis hung with grapevines. On the left side there is a bar with high wooden stools, then at the back is the main building where the kitchen and toilets are situated.

I'm leaning towards the windscreen and taking it all in again, having only a very vague memory of being here when we visited for Aunt Hazel and Pericles' wedding.

It hasn't changed much, only a fresh lick of paint perhaps.

Yianni jumps out of the car before I've even managed to undo my seat belt.

'Bye then,' I whisper as I get out of the car.

He's jogging into the restaurant and well out of earshot.

Only a handful of tables are taken. I have no idea what all the fuss to get back was about.

Pericles grips Yianni's arm, smiling under a quiff of thick slate-grey hair that has a wave to it.

I wonder if that's where Yianni got his curly hair from, or if it's from his mother's side.

As I slam the car door, Pericles looks across at me and his face changes to a frown. He looks at his son, then hits him on the arm with the navy leather menu.

They have a heated micro-conversation in Greek before Pericles turns towards the restaurant's interior and calls Hazel's name. He jogs down the few steps towards me with open arms.

'Ruby! It has been so long. *Kalispera*.'

Pericles is a sizeable guy, almost six feet, with broad shoulders and a little too much weight balancing around his middle. His big hands grab my shoulders, and he kisses my cheeks four times before releasing me.

Behind him I hear a squeal and the tapping of feet running down the wooden steps as Hazel comes and embraces me too. Garlic and dill permeate the air around her, which only makes me realise how hungry I am, having not eaten since a big fried breakfast at the airport many hours ago.

'Look at you!' She cups my face with her garlicky fingers. 'I am so happy you decided to come. I thought you were going straight

11

to the house, though, to unpack and rest. I left food in the fridge for you.'

She takes my hand and begins to walk me at a quick pace towards the restaurant.

'There was a little misunderstanding. I accidentally left my phone on flight mode and made us late.'

We reach the steps, where Yianni has installed himself with his feet slightly apart and his hands behind his back, ready to greet anyone coming into the restaurant. His fitted black jeans and shirt are obviously his work clothes, and he looks like he was born ready to start work.

'Yianni was very good about it though,' I tell Hazel. 'Didn't sulk or anything.'

He looks at me from the corner of his eye as I say his name. There's perhaps a tug to his lips – a spasm, or the ghost of a smile?

I smile at him through pursed lips. I expect him to mirror my sarcasm, but instead his lips seem to twitch again with a suppressed smile before he returns his gaze towards the street.

'Well,' Pericles says, 'you are here now. That is what matters, yes?'

'I bet you're hungry, aren't you? Why don't you put your feet up for tonight, just as we intended? I'll get Natalia to bring you some food over. Look, there she is.' Hazel points as my cousin, Natalia, comes out of the kitchen balancing two huge plates with whole fish on them.

As soon as she sees me, a grin spreads across her face. She can't stop and say hello with her hands so full, but she mouths *Kalispera* from a distance.

Hazel wraps her arm around me. 'Ooh, you feel lovely and cold.'

'Yianni likes to keep a cold atmosphere in his car.' I grin, playing it off like I'm talking about the air-con.

'I can't blame him, it's already much hotter than usual. Are you excited to be here? I know when I suggested this you had your reservations, but I think this could be a welcome change of scene. Time to heal, away from all the old reminders.'

'Yeah.' I twist the ring on my finger, pulsing it up and down, wishing she didn't have that look in her eye.

My mum's stopped doing it so much now, but seeing Hazel's brows drawn together and her lips slightly turned down at the corners is almost enough to make me scream with frustration and run all the way back to England.

'I know, I know, you don't want to talk about it. I know you well enough, but I'm here if you ever fancy a chat.' She almost physically sits me down at a square table for two and slides into the chair opposite mine.

'I've also heard you're a workaholic. A little bird tells me that's all you ever seem to do now. I bet you're itching to get to work, but I still think you need to take a moment to rest after all that travelling.'

'It's OK, I'm interested to sit and watch you all work. You know, you shouldn't call Mum a bird – it sounds sexist.'

Hazel's face lights up like a beacon of joy and the creases between her eyebrows vanish.

'Oh, you silly thing.' Hazel stands and moves to kiss my cheek. 'I'm so happy you're here. I'm excited to get some time with my beautiful niece. I really hope you like it here. It's where I found my peace, my happiness. I so hope it brings you peace too. You're in paradise, how could it not?'

At last, excitement ripples over me. She's right, I'm in paradise.

Chapter Three

Now

'Come here, you!' I push back my chair as Natalia puts down a plate filled with a whole sea bass and roasted potatoes.

She barely has the plate out of her hands and on the table before I'm squeezing her.

'Mama says as it's not too busy I can have a break to say a proper hello. What drink would you like?'

'Well, this is one of the few evenings I won't be working, so a glass of white wine, please.'

She trots off behind the bar, where Pericles is making drinks for one of the tables, and I carefully begin to fillet the fish on my plate while it eyeballs me.

Over the past ten years, I've spent my life circulating through every type of restaurant job. Therefore, filleting a fish isn't an issue in the slightest. Before I get my own restaurant, I want to know the ins and outs of every single job so I can have the place running perfectly.

Hazel hasn't mentioned what role I will take on while I'm working in Greek Secret – whether I'll be serving, in the kitchen, mixing cocktails, or playing a statue like Yianni on the front door.

Natalia makes her way back to my little table and sits down opposite me.

She's somehow a plain but pretty girl. The sort of girl that anything could be moulded on to. The right make-up could make her a model, or she could be forgotten in an instant. The thing that makes her striking without effort, though, is her hair. It's a mass of curls, much more so than Yianni's. Hers is much longer and in better shape. Even with it wrapped up and fastened in a big claw clip, curls playfully poke out in defiance to show the beauty of it all.

'*Yamas*,' we chime as my bulbous wine glass clinks against her lemonade.

There's a pause as we both sip. I close my eyes and let out an involuntary hum of satisfaction. The wine is cool on my palate, sharp and refreshing against the warmth of the evening. The temperature isn't quite sweaty-hot, but it is only a few steps away from it.

'How's school?' Placing down the glass, I slip a forkful of fish into my mouth.

Natalia lifts her eyes to the ceiling and complains that a teacher still hasn't been replaced at the school and how she can't wait to go to university in England when she is older.

'At least it's only Greek history we have no teacher for. I could not care much for the subject. And how have you been? I have not seen you since—'

I wave my hand to stop her. I can't bear to hear the end of the sentence, but I have a mouth full of lemony sea bass and can only interject with my hands.

Eventually, I manage to say 'I'm fine', before swallowing the remainder of my food. 'Seriously. Please don't pull that face at me. I don't want to see it.'

She goes from the pathetic sympathy face to opening and closing her mouth to gulp back unsaid words, or just empty air, as she tries to load herself with new words.

It doesn't matter which it might be – if she is trying to escape words or create them – as I continue talking to prevent her letting out any either way.

'It was a strange time, and we really don't need to talk about it. I really don't *want* to talk about it. So don't feel like you *need* to acknowledge it or even bring it up. I'm just really excited to be here and ready to learn anything and everything I can. Fresh start.'

'Learn? You have been doing this longer than me!'

I shrug as I stab my fork into a piece of potato. 'That doesn't mean I won't learn something new. I hope I get to learn something new.'

She has no idea how much it means to me. In the comfort of family, I'm hoping to gain the confidence to finally take the next step and find a way to run my own place somewhere.

'Perhaps you can learn how to fish?'

I let out a little snort. 'I think I'll stick to filleting.'

Natalia is soon called back into the kitchen, and once I have finished my meal, I'm already itching to be useful.

My fingers smooth the ripples out of the white paper tablecloth that has been carefully placed over a blue cloth one.

I bide my time, watching the other diners in the restaurant. I'm not sure what Yianni was fussing about. It isn't as though it is high season and out-of-control busy. There are only three tables with customers and all he is doing is standing at the door . . . Waiting.

A breeze rolls through the restaurant, and I let myself take a lungful of the warm air.

Greek Secret has a rustic vibe and the air is filled with the aroma of warm bread, grilled lamb, fresh fish. All, of course, with the distinct notes of garlic and dill and thyme.

After sending off a message to Mum with an update, I can't sit about people-watching a moment more. I scoop up my plate and head towards the kitchen door. Yianni catches my elbow.

'Where are you off to?'

He is so hard to read. I can't tell if he is irritated or just curious.

'The kitchen.' I indicate with my head as my hands are full. 'I thought I would help by taking my plate back.'

'Tonight, you are the guest. Hazel's orders. Let me take this.'

His hands edge towards the plate, but I step back, pulling it just outside of his reach.

His jaw tightens and his brow lowers, casting a shadow over his eyes, making them look like cups of black coffee – no sugar, though.

'Ruby, you are our guest. Hazel's orders. Now please, come sit.'

He edges towards the plate again, but I ignore him and keep on walking towards the kitchen at the back of the restaurant.

I can hear a distinct hissing sound emanating from him, but I ignore it and march on.

There's no actual door to the kitchen, although there is a doorway and, behind it, a staggered entrance, so it isn't easy to just look in from the restaurant. It's a good way to get some air into the room too.

Everything's modern in the kitchen. More so than the restaurant. In here, it's all stainless steel and expanses of worktop space. The sort that's easy to work in and keep clean. The sort I want one day.

'I brought these,' I announce, lifting my plate and glass.

Hazel's glasses are being used to push her hair back from her face and she's wrapped in a black apron. Her cheeks and chest are rosy as she gently jiggles a frying pan with eggs in it.

'You naughty thing. I told Yianni there is no work for you today. Didn't he say?'

I slip the plate down on to one of the surfaces near Natalia, who is scraping a used plate over a bin.

As I try to tell Hazel that yes, he told me, but I'm actually hoping to help, she continues, 'Yianni, you let her take her own plate. I said she isn't to do any work today.'

Hazel's lips purse and she seems to be genuinely disappointed in him.

I turn to see Yianni looming behind me, pushing his hair back off his face. Although I can still see tension in him – even in his biceps, which seem to contract under his short sleeves – he dips his head to Hazel.

'I am so sorry, Hazel. I did not catch her in time. Ruby, please.' He gestures towards the entrance of the kitchen, and I apologise before stepping out ahead of him.

'Why not sit here?' He indicates the bar, and this time I don't argue.

I sort of feel like I've got him in some kind of unintentional trouble.

For the rest of the evening, I nurse another glass of wine and have a sensible conversation with Pericles about the business.

This is why I'm here. This is what I want. To soak it all in. To have as many sensible conversations as I can, subtly asking how he's been running things all these years, to glean the secret to his success.

Other than the obvious nature of the setting and a captive audience of people here on holiday.

No one here knows my true intentions. The true reason why, after initial concerns about the logistics of living here and what to do with all my things, I grabbed Aunt Hazel's offer of work and booked plane tickets right away.

My whole family thinks I just needed another job after losing mine at La Salle à Manger.

I was always worried I only got promoted to maître d' there because the owner, Charles, thought I was attractive and was open about his thoughts on my *luscious full lips*, among other things.

That's as far as it ever went. Comments that he saw as compliments. The difference being, his compliments made me feel sick, burning at the back of my throat, and they came all too often.

Here, I know I've only got the job because I'm family, but maybe I can exceed their expectations, maybe I can learn what it is to make a business fly instead of dying at the bottom of the ocean, the way my parents' beautiful bakery did when I was a child.

I loved that bakery, running around and pretending I was helping. But it's the biggest reason I've never told anyone my ambitions of owning a place. That failure hurt my parents so much. People loved their baked goods, but the overheads were too high and they hadn't saved enough to prepare.

That's all I know. They don't like to talk about it much, and I don't like to ask.

Here, I have all the freedom to ask things about success, instead of the pain of failing.

Pericles tells me there are two other people who work at Greek Secret on a regular basis, Nico and Gaia.

The man, Nico, works behind the bar during the busier parts of the summer and the girl, Gaia, comes in to help clear plates and sometimes take dishes out to tables. Gaia's one of Natalia's best friends and is also only fifteen.

I begin to calculate how much it must cost to pay all these people and who exactly works here, a cleaner, another cook, bar staff, wait staff. Here, I might eventually be able to get my hands on the books, instead of trying to glance over Charles's shoulder when he would look at his iPad in the evenings.

Between our conversations, I watch Yianni. He's a mystery. That and his obvious good looks draw the eye completely unintentionally.

He's nothing like the boy I vaguely remember from all those years ago.

As Pericles makes drinks, I try to squeeze the memory of him out from the depths of my mind. He didn't say much to me back then. I barely remember him.

He is the only one not to give me the famous Greek welcome.

I try not to dwell on it, but it nags at me.

It's as though something has caught between my teeth and, without anyone noticing, I have to get it out. I have to be clear of it and know what it is. What he is. It'll be the only way I can concentrate here.

I sip my now-warm wine and wonder if he'll be this enigmatic all summer.

Chapter Four

Now

At the end of everyone's shift, we all sit down together to discuss the plan.

This is it. What I've been waiting for. To find my place in the world for the next six months.

At the end of the summer, I might've saved enough money to put towards something of my own, and hopefully I'll feel ready to take the next steps towards my dream of owning my own restaurant.

I'll start small, something where people can come and enjoy a night away from other distractions, a place of luxury that's still accessible. Somewhere people want to get dressed up a little and escape their reality for a few hours.

Somewhere I can escape in the happy faces of those around me. That's what I love about working in hospitality, the smiles. The joys of good food and a sumptuous atmosphere.

The thought of it makes me tingle with delight. I have to make this dream come true. If I can't make it happen by the end of this year, then it never will.

The tables have been cleared and cleaned and we gather to one side of the taverna near the bar, where it's a little more sheltered from the view of the road. Yianni and Pericles push two square tables together for us to sit round.

Everyone else has either been wearing long sleeves or has slipped something light over their tops. I guess the May nights hold a mild chill for them; to me, it's delightfully warm still after the drizzle back in England.

Hazel's glasses slide down to the tip of her nose, back to where I'm so used to seeing them. Her blonde hair is tied up in a way I have never seen it before, though. I suppose I'm used to seeing Hazel-on-holiday and this is work-Hazel.

It seems so backwards, for England to be the holiday destination when paradise is home. But I suppose it is what it is.

'As we have discussed, we will pay your wage at the end of the month, and you will get free meals and have your own room in our home. Our home is your home. Now, I know you were enjoying your work as a maître d', but after lots of debate' – Hazel's eyes flick towards Yianni in a micro-move that I catch nonetheless – 'we think perhaps you will start here with work behind the bar. If you are happy with that.'

'That's perfect. I'm just happy I can help.'

Hazel's cheeks lift; she doesn't smile as such, but she visibly relaxes. She sits back in her chair instead of pressing her forearms into the table, and the lines around her eyes soften. Perhaps she was worried I would be disappointed and that's why she particularly wanted to talk about it before I started work. Maybe she thought I would make a fuss after coming out of a job where I was of a higher rank.

What the role is doesn't matter; I'm happy to have a job again after a month of feeling useless. I loved being a maître d', but there was always that itch that I only got the job because the owner wanted to sleep with me.

Not that I would ever have slept with Charles. Yuck.

Then, when the place was failing, I was first to be cut.

It's left me with more worries than ever about whether I'm even able to run or own a place of my own.

Hazel doesn't know how much this means to me. How could she? I've never had the courage to tell anyone. Just in case I fail before even getting to that point. Or worse, make it fail when I get my dream, like my parents with their bakery.

It's like throwing a coin in a wishing well. If I say my wish out loud, it might never come true.

To have the chance to spend a whole summer picking Hazel's and Pericles' brains about how to run every last aspect of their very own taverna is amazing. To find out whether they took out loans to do it all up, whether they rent the place or own it all outright. This is exactly what I need.

I've learnt that there's very little in life we truly have control of, if anything. Dreams can be just that. Dreams.

But I can do my best to learn as much as I can wherever I can, and this is a great opportunity. And I can hope that it'll bring me one step closer to my dream being my reality.

I couldn't stay jobless in England. The idea of munching my way through more of my savings would break me.

I've already eaten into my dreams for my future far too much, one way or another.

With my meals and accommodation paid for, everything I earn here can be saved, all while finding out if I can do this. In six months, I guess I'll know, one way or another.

Either I'll be in a position to start my own business or I'll have to rethink everything, and likely give up on my dreams altogether.

Now that my place in Greek Secret has been established, Yianni seems lighter and a smile tickles his full lips more than once. He makes the odd witty remark, actually, and is sarcastically funny as the family exchange chatter over drinks. He wraps his arm around his half-sister, Natalia, as he teases her about her boyfriend.

Maybe he had seen me as a threat to his job, and that making him late might make him look worse. It has been such a long day, since getting up early to travel. I can't suppress my yawns any longer.

It's skirting midnight when Hazel says we should make a move. Everyone stands and begins to kiss Yianni goodbye.

For some reason, I thought he still lived in the family home. Without more than a nod to this thought, I follow suit and edge round the table to say goodnight to him.

'Thank you for picking me up from the airport today. I really am sorry for the confusion.'

He shrugs, but not in the sulky way he did earlier. He seems more relaxed. Almost like he barely remembers the misunderstanding.

I lean in to kiss his cheek. It's stubbled against my lips.

I hadn't meant to kiss him, not really. It was going to be an air kiss, close enough to almost seem real but with no lasting sensation.

Instead, my lips find his cheek and the smell of warm citrus and a note of burnt wood charm my senses.

I don't want to, but something under my ribs can't help but note the feel of him.

The shape of his mouth as his lips briefly imprint my cheek.

As I pull away, I smile, and can't resist the urge to subtly suck my lower lip.

The taste of salt from his skin lingers.

My forehead buckles under the weight of my action, and I can feel a frown crease it.

My pulse quickens and embarrassment touches my cheeks at the thoughts of his taste crossing my mind.

Yianni's eyes sweep over me as we step back.

His eyebrow arches and alarm pricks at the base of my spine that he might say something about the look on my face.

He doesn't.

He just says, 'Sleep well, Ruby. *Kalinikta.*'

'*Kalinikta*, Yianni.'

Chapter Five

'One salmon en croûte, one mussels in champagne. Can I get you anything else?' I press a smile into my face and wish my hands would stop shaking.

The couple barely acknowledge me as they shake their heads and continue their conversation over the dim candlelight.

The whole room is dark, with the exposed brickwork painted charcoal and black-and-white photos scattered on the walls.

I've waited on tables since I was fourteen. Today is no different.

I've waited in dark restaurants and bright cafés. This is no different.

Except that it is.

It is, because I care more about this job. This is my first job outside of my home county of Suffolk. My first big-city London job.

If I'm really lucky, maybe I could work my way up from waitress and get some hands-on experience of the different roles in a restaurant.

This is the perfect place too. A busy restaurant in Shoreditch is bound to be better than a little café in a market town not far from where I grew up.

I just have to stay focused and my drive will shine through.

Politely, I nod, even though the couple are still not looking at me, and I turn to move away.

Another waiter almost spins to serve his table. He has the posture of someone who knows their worth and the looks to back it up.

Our eyes meet as I stride back towards the kitchen.

It might be my first day, but I thought I'd met all the other wait staff at the induction. Not him. I'd have remembered him.

He catches me up and whispers in my ear, 'Are you an actress?'

'No.' A smile grazes my lips, and I do my best to suck in the laughter that's swelling inside me.

He doesn't laugh.

He's serious.

Before the kitchen doors, there's space to walk side by side.

This beautiful man is watching me. Brazenly watching me as he keeps in step.

I could do without this distraction. I'm still coursing with first-day nerves – first-minute nerves, almost – and this guy's asking what I am before he even knows who I am.

'A model then? You have to be a model. Not runway, but commercial, right?'

'No. I'm a waitress.' My hands smooth the black bow that hangs from my neck.

We all look the same here. Everyone has to gel their hair back in the same way and wear the same clothes.

No. We don't all look the same.

He wears it differently to everyone else. On him, it looks good.

I do my best to undercut his comment. 'And why not runway?' Not that I think I'm any kind of model material, but he doesn't need to know that.

Together, we swing the doors open to the kitchen. Its explosion of heat and sounds. Hissing pans, bubbling water and voices calling from one person to the next. I love the community. The hubbub.

'New girl!' Rob interjects across the room.

Rob's sweating red face is there, over one of those sizzling pans.

I march away from this man who thinks I'm some sort of model, to seek out the comfort of my old friend Rob. The one kind enough to get me this job and a place to stay. I really owe him.

'Yes, chef.'

'Never, and I mean *never*, date an actor,' he warns as he glances over my shoulder. 'Even if they're as tasty as this steak.' He flips the steak, making fat hiss and spit. Smoke fuses with steam as it fills the room with greasy air.

'I have no idea what you're talking about. I'm here to work. To learn. That's all.'

Rob clicks his tongue, shaking his head.

Someone shouts *service!* and I head back to where I'm supposed to be, next to a hot, blinding lamp above a chrome surface that reflects the burning glare back into my eyes.

'Because you're too short. You're definitely stunning enough. Just too short for runway.' His chest skims my arm as he grabs a plate from the counter, and he flashes me a broad smile with deep dimples. 'Have you had work done?'

'What sort of question is that?' Laughter bubbles over my confusion. 'No, of course not.'

'Wow.' He holds my gaze for a moment too long.

Then he picks up plates and he's gone.

'Same table as Jonathan, new girl. Table six.' Two plates are thrust in my direction.

Jonathan. Now I have this mystery man's name.

I pick up the plates and move towards the door and out to table six.

Jonathan is only just placing his plates down as I arrive.

'I have . . .' I look at the plate in my left hand, suddenly unsure of what the hell I'm looking at.

Jonathan steps in. 'Vegetable soufflé.'

'That's mine.' A round lady with perfect eyeliner smiles at me.

I place it down, followed by the second plate to the only person still waiting.

We move off. Jonathan and me.

'Thanks.'

'Don't worry about it, model. I just want one thing from you. No. Two things.' He stops just shy of the kitchen door.

'OK? What are they?'

'Your name, and a date.'

Chapter Six

Now

The car pulls up and we get out to the sound of cicadas. Without their song I'm sure we would be in complete silence, but they fill the air so densely it can barely carry any other sound.

The house is a little out of the way, still in the village but on the edge of it.

I can't see my surroundings fully, but I can feel the life around me in the same way I can feel the life of the air in the breeze. I tilt my head to the sky and the light of a million stars punctures the night with devastating brightness and definition.

I don't have time to hover, though, as everyone is making their way towards the house.

A sound manages to push against the cicadas and the headlights of another car creep up behind me. I shade my eyes against it, and I can hear Pericles speaking in Greek with a gruff tone.

He steps forward and is in front of me, feet crunching along the ground, calling a name. *Yianni.*

Yianni gets out, a shadow over the headlights, says something to his father, slams his door and goes to the boot.

That's when it hits me.

My bags.

We'd forgotten to take my bags with us. My hand presses to my forehead as I make my way towards the car.

'Yianni, I'm so sorry.'

He doesn't look at me as he passes the first suitcase over to Pericles, who smiles and reassures me before taking the bag inside.

'It is OK. Lucky I remembered, no?'

'I'm so sorry. Were you on your way home when you noticed? I hope you hadn't got far.'

His eyes lock on to mine and a half-smile lingers on his lips. 'No,' he says slowly. 'I had not got far.' Then he swings open the back door of his car and tugs out the second suitcase.

'I'll take that. Sorry again. *Kalinikta.*'

'*Kalinikta*, Ruby. Try not to forget more of your things.' And with that, he is back in his car.

As I step into the house, it doesn't matter that it's late and my eyes can hardly stay open, Aunt Hazel begins to offer me drinks, food, and pretty much everything under the roof.

After I politely decline, Natalia shows me to my room.

She flicks a switch and illuminates a room that is not what I expected.

It looks masculine.

There's a single bed with a charcoal-coloured sheet and a chalk-white blanket. The furniture is plain wood and a white reading lamp is on the bedside table.

Then there's the centrepiece to it all. A collage of photos hanging above the bed.

All the photos feature Yianni.

'I'm so happy you are here for the summer,' Natalia says. 'It's like I now have an older sister as well as a brother! *Kalinikta*, Ruby. Sleep well.'

I kiss Natalia on both cheeks before she gives me a tight squeeze.

Closing the door behind me, I stand for a moment with my back pressed against the door.

Is this Yianni's old bedroom? Why would he leave all those photos behind?

I creep along, glad the floor is tiled and not creaky wood. My feet make it to a shaggy black rug before I climb to stand on the bed.

Although the floor isn't squeaky, the bed is.

It's impossible to move quietly or elegantly to the photos and I wobble along the bed.

I study the pictures.

I have to.

Something about them is like gravity, pulling me in.

There are family photos, of Yianni holding his baby sister in the hospital and what I guess must be his mum and him when he was young. But most of the photos are with friends.

Days at the beach, beers, smiles, topless in swim shorts, dressed up in full pirate costume and one as a fairy princess with a wand in one hand and a beer in the other. His toned abs clad in a pink leotard.

It's the life of a vibrant twenty-something played out in thirty or so photos.

Why, when he moved out, wouldn't he take these with him? It doesn't make sense.

I crumple down on to the bed.

I put most of my photos and bits away when I left my house to come here. Even though it's being sublet by my best friend and her boyfriend, I still didn't leave out loads of personal things.

I can't understand it.

In a daze, I plod through my night-time routine. I'm lucky my room has its own small en suite with a shower. I can continue my tired thoughts of Yianni and his photos uninterrupted by anyone else.

All I want to do is fall into bed, but I can't help but take one last gawp at the photos that will live above my head for the next six months.

Yianni's bright smile shines in all the photos and at every age.

I can see it now, just about, the kid I met in passing and the man he has become.

The smile, the one that's so bold, that I'm yet to see in person.

I ease myself under the sheet and the blanket.

They smell of Yianni's aftershave mixed with freshly washed linens.

It has to be his current room, no question. Why else leave photos behind? This can't be a room he *once* lived in ages ago. These are sheets that he has used and which have been washed ready for my stay.

I take in another lungful of the deep citrus with that same note of pine. No, not pine; something woody though. Something darker.

I take one last deep breath of him before closing my eyes to a pang of guilt.

It's rolling across me twofold.

Firstly, the idea that I might have kicked Yianni out of his own bed makes me wonder if that is the reason he is being standoffish with me, and I don't want him to hate me.

Secondly, there is a feeling I want to ignore, a feeling that has crept up on me over the afternoon and that I have intentionally refused to notice.

Everyone being too nice to me, as always. Apart from Yianni. It was actually refreshing to be around someone not overreacting to my past.

Even Natalia was actively wanting to point out how much I've been through. It was there on the edge of her lips.

I saw the moments her eyes welled with pity, and I had to quickly divert it.

I don't want anyone's pity.

I want to move on.

I want to live my life for me.

Anger rises up above it all, and however much I try to ignore my feelings about my past, they collide in my mind with my present.

We are all a product of the past.

I hate that.

Squeezing my eyes tightly shut, I expel a small tear on to Yianni's pillow in the dark.

Chapter Seven

Now

Being exhausted doesn't prevent me from being up early.

I roll to the right side of the bed and sit on the edge of it. The light is already cascading under the curtains.

In the dark, I was aware of driving down a narrow road with shadows the shape of trees, but I have no idea what it's really like out there.

Before I wash or get myself ready for the day, I rush to peek out of the window.

With great ceremony, I tug the curtains open, and it's all I can do not to press myself against the glass.

My lips part and I whisper 'Oh my' to the window. To the view.

Undulations of every shade of green roll in every direction. Dark points of tall trees tower above others in clusters. Olive trees are scattered about and there are runs of drying golden grasses here and there. Corfu unravels all the way to my feet in a glorious carpet of vibrancy.

There's even a lemon tree not far from my window.

I feel as though I have officially arrived at last. As though yesterday was just a dry run for the view out of my window.

It makes me want to put some trainers on and walk. I want to explore everything, to immerse myself in it all. It's so long since I've been abroad.

The last time I went away was with Jonathan, back when we were happy and life seemed to be coming together for us.

We had a week in Spain to celebrate one of our anniversaries. I snatch a deep breath, filling my lungs until they burn a little, before exhaling any thoughts of Jonathan.

There's no point going over the past.

There is no way I can go back and change it or improve it.

Dragging myself away from the view, I pull the curtains closed again before showering and dressing.

I run a little mousse through my damp hair and sit down on the edge of my bed.

Yianni's bed.

I bite my cheek at the thought of kicking him out of his own bed and all the things he would have done here.

I shake the thoughts from my head, making droplets of water spray over my shoulders from the ends of my hair.

I'm sure he thinks I want to kick him out of here and his job too. He must resent me.

All the drawers are empty. I need to find out if he has left because of me or if he was moving out anyway.

I make my way down the twisting, creaky stairs.

The house looks very different in the light of day. It's older than I expected.

The kitchen has worn pine cupboard doors that are almost amber in tone, although I doubt they started that way. The surfaces are a paler wood that doesn't complement the cupboards at all.

Little round plastic handles adorn every drawer and door, and there's Hazel in the middle of it all, frying eggs again. This time on a small white oven hob. The kitchen couldn't be more different to the one in Greek Secret.

'How did you sleep?' She grins at me over her shoulder.

'Good, thanks. Where is everyone?'

I sit down on one of the four metal chairs at the round kitchen table. The room is already warm – the frying eggs only add to it with a greasy cloud.

I'm glad I'm used to a hot kitchen, but wonder how I'll feel about it in August. At least I'll mostly be making cocktails, I guess.

'Pericles is collecting more eggs from the chickens. Natalia is still in bed. Coffee?'

I nod as she points at the pot.

'And eggs?'

'Please.'

I scrunch at my hair. It's drying well enough in here, but I'm desperate to get myself out in the sun.

'I've been thinking,' Hazel begins, 'you're not going to want to rely on us to drive you places you might want to go. You had a little scooter when you were sixteen, didn't you?'

I sit back in my chair, almost blown away at the memory.

It was powder blue and I saved up for it working in a darling little independent coffee shop, washing up cups and saucers. Buzzing about on that thing gave me independence and almost gave my mother a heart attack, and working in that coffee shop kickstarted my desire to have my own place in hospitality.

'I did indeed. Feels like forever ago.'

'Well, Pericles has a little bike he never uses. I spoke to him, and he is happy for you to use it over the summer. If you'd like?'

Excitement makes my fingertips tingle in the same way they do when holding the handlebars of a running motor. 'I would love that. Thank you.'

After breakfast, Pericles takes me out to a little shed and shows me the motorcycle.

It's a bit bigger than I expected. But I'm more than happy to get behind the handlebars of this little red devil. Pericles shows me how things work, not that I need him to, and as soon as I can, I have the satnav in my earphones and a helmet on and I'm off.

I head back towards San Stefanos.

It makes sense to me to feel out the journey that I will be doing late at night on my own. I want to have it ingrained in me as soon as I can. My sense of direction is pretty good, but I want it to be part of me.

I'm easily distracted as I glide along the road next to olive groves and skies that are clearer and bluer than any I've ever encountered before.

It's not long before I'm pulling up outside the restaurant.

The bifold doors have been pulled around the bar area side of the restaurant, where there is a solid roof. All the chairs and tables that were under the terrace with the vines have been brought into the locked area overnight. There's also a little chain across the entrance that says 'Closed'.

I hope to look over the stock so that I will be ready for the evening. Maybe at lunch I can have a look.

During May, I'm only working six evenings a week. As the season progresses, I'll work lunch and dinner.

I step over the 'Closed' sign, then take a step towards the glass to press my face to it. Scanning the bottles as best I can at this distance, I make mental notes of where everything is.

'What are you here so early for? You start tonight, no?'

Yianni's voice close to my neck startles me so much I bang my forehead on the glass door.

'Shit. Yianni! You frightened the life right out of me.'

I rub my forehead and turn to look at him. He's in an unbuttoned shirt and baggy grey trousers and his lips are suppressing a laugh, presumably at my expense.

'*Syngnómi*. Sorry.'

The smell of freshly baked goodies accompanies him.

He steps around me and unlocks the door. I hear him talking in Greek as he goes in. I'm not sure whether to follow him or not.

A girl smartly dressed in black with silver pumps walks out and beams at me.

'*Kalimera*,' she says as she passes me, unhooking the 'Closed' sign and re-hooking it once she's past. An action with no thought, as though it's been done many times before.

The door has been left open.

I step towards it, only for Yianni to begin the process of unfolding the doors fully.

As I enter the bar area, he places his hand on a stool and drags it back, making a toe-curling grating noise.

'Where are your shoes?' I stare at his bare feet.

Instead of replying, he stretches. Fists and arms tense, brought out wide to display his lean muscular body and golden-brown skin.

I avert my gaze, instead looking back at the bottles behind the bar. Havana Club. Gordon's. Blue Curaçao.

'I haven't been awake long. Thought I would walk to the bakery.' He folds his arms across his chest.

Limoncello. Bacardi. Jack Daniels. Chambord. Baileys.

'Sorry if I . . . disturbed you.' A little laugh unintentionally pops out as I glance towards where the girl disappeared out of the taverna. 'Did you sleep here last night?' I turn to him, and my arms clamp themselves across my breasts and my eyebrows pull themselves together. I notice that I'm mirroring his body language, and now I want to switch position, but I know it would seem unnatural to do so.

'Yes.'

'Here?' My arms release to my sides to point at the floor.

'Yes.'

'Last night?'

'*Nai, nai, nai.*' He hops off the stool and makes his way round behind the bar. 'My bed is taken. This is my home for the summer.' A lock of hair drops in front of his face, and he pushes it behind his right ear. Then he disappears, ducking down behind the bar before popping up again shaking a carton of orange juice.

He tilts it towards me, wordlessly offering me some of the contents. I shake my head.

I was right. I'm an unintentional usurper. I've taken his bed and I bet he thinks that next I'll be after his title at the restaurant.

'I had no idea. I thought perhaps you'd moved out or—'

'I have. To here. No worries. Forget it. Why are you here? I answered your question. You still have not answered mine.'

'Oh, I want to familiarise myself with the drinks. What order they're kept in, what stock you have, what cocktails you serve. If I'd known Hazel's plan to put me behind the bar, I would have studied a bit more last night. I'll go if I'm disturbing you. Or if your friend is coming back.'

I need to stop. I don't *need* to know what the girl was doing here. It's niggling me.

Yianni smiles and casually says, 'She won't be back today.'

I'm not really sure what that means. Maybe a casual encounter?

She didn't even stay for the croissant that's hanging out of the bag on the counter next to me. Perhaps I frightened her off.

'I can still leave if you want me to.'

Yianni doesn't respond right away. Instead, he watches me while he takes a swig of his juice. He wipes his top lip with his palm, and wipes the palm on his trouser leg.

Although he is hard to read, I'm pretty sure I can give as good as I'm getting. I relax and let my face fall blank under his gaze.

Eventually, he nudges his chin upwards and says, 'You had best come here then. Better for me to show you than Nico tonight.'

Chapter Eight

Now

'Come this side, with me.' Yianni nods before picking up the croissant and taking a mouthful.

My stomach is lurching with a cocktail of emotions.

There's usually a feeling of comfort when I step behind a bar or into a restaurant kitchen. It's where I've spent all my working life. It has that sense of being home.

But being in a confined space with Yianni is less than ideal.

Not that being close to someone behind a bar would normally be something I even notice. It's second nature to skirt around people, arms becoming tendrils and slithering past each other when needed. Bodies seem to learn the dance of working behind a bar or in a kitchen.

But with Yianni it's different.

I'm letting myself feel a heat that I shouldn't.

I wish he would do up the buttons of his shirt, something, anything.

'Do you need to make notes? Or have you got the memory of a Greek?' He glances at me from the corner of his eye and I catch a cocky curl to his mouth.

'I don't think I'm that good, but I can handle myself.'

Yianni nods, stuffing another bite of flaky croissant into his mouth. A crumb falls and rests perfectly on his pec.

It's impossible to stop my eyes from rolling into the back of my head.

'You're getting crumbs' – I look over his chest, waving my hand at him – 'everywhere.'

Looking down, he casually dusts himself off, littering the floor before finishing his breakfast.

'We have ten main cocktails. Here . . .' He passes me a navy menu from under the bar. 'And they all need to be the same every time. Yes? Every Porn Star, she must look and taste the same as the last.' Yianni's eyebrows flick up and down, barely noticeable. His face doesn't crack into laughter. So neither does mine.

'That's fine. I can be consistent. Is there an ingredients list I can look at?'

Yianni turns in circles, lifting folders under the bar. Moving papers and pens from one place to the next.

Fixing my eyes on the menu he's placed in my hands helps to calm me and to keep my eyes off his shirt flapping open.

I pull my shoulders back and wait for him to continue talking me through everything. I am a professional. I'm able to maintain focus at all times.

I study the list of cocktails: Porn Star Martini, Old-Fashioned, Sexy Greek, Mojito, Cosmopolitan, Yianni's Special—

'What's a Yianni's Special?'

'That can only be made by my beautiful hands. Here.' He places a sheet of paper on top of the menu I'm holding.

Propping the menu on the bar, I pick up the ingredients list.

'There's no ingredients list for Yianni's Special.' I flip the paper to check the back but it's blank.

'I told you this. It is only made by me. If I'm not here' – he shrugs – 'no special.'

Yianni leans in close to my shoulder, looking over the paper with me. He reaches over me and stabs his finger into it. 'This. Make this one.'

'Now?'

'Yes. Let's see what you can do. I'll be the tester.'

'You know you can't replace brushing your teeth with a Mojito.'

'Who says I haven't brushed my teeth?' Yianni stands tall, folding his arms over his chest, tilting his chin to look down at me.

'Have you?'

'Why are you worried about my teeth? Worry about your cocktail.'

A childish urge bubbles up to argue and tell him I'm not bothered by his teeth, or those full lips of his. I quickly press it back down.

It's been a long time since I haven't been in charge. Yianni is in charge here. Even with Charles back in England, I was the one making sure the place ran smoothly. Charles just owned the place.

Here, I guess it's Yianni.

He stands frozen, the way he did in the doorway last night. Only last night he looked more welcoming standing in the entrance of the taverna. Now, with his arms locked over his chest, he's back to looking grumpy and harsh. It's only his hair flowing to his shoulders that softens him.

I check the list and try to commit the quantities to memory. I've made a Mojito a million times before, but there's always different nuances here and there. A different balance of flavours.

It shouldn't matter, but I need this drink to be perfect. There's an urge to impress Yianni and break down this wall he's fixed between us. It seems if I'm going to learn anything here, I might have to get it from him.

I scan the bottles behind me, picking the ones I need and pulling the shaker and glasses off the shelf before selecting the freshest-looking sprigs of mint.

Lifting lids off long trays, I turn back to him. 'There's no ice.'

My words break his frosty exterior and he jogs off towards the kitchen. I guess the container under the bar will be filled before service later.

Yianni quickly returns with a silver bowl brimming with ice.

'There. Ice.' He sits on a bar stool opposite me and studies me as I continue working.

As I put it all together, I find a thin metal stirrer to put in the tall glass, along with a circle of fresh lime to decorate the rim of it.

'One Mojito.' I slide it in his direction.

'No straw?'

'It's bad for the environment. You should bring your own reusable one.'

Yianni rolls his eyes before picking up the drink and sipping. Without a word, he sips two more times.

'Well done. It's a Mojito.'

'Is that it?' My fingers dig into my hips. 'Does it conform? Is it good enough?'

Yianni shrugs. 'I only wanted a Mojito because I couldn't be bothered with brushing my teeth.'

'Stop it.' I lean forward on the bar without thinking.

Yianni takes a deep gulp of the minty concoction.

'It's good. Same as mine, same as Nico. You fit.'

The seal of approval is always consistency. It's essential and I'm content with this compliment. If a patron enjoys a drink or a meal, they expect it to be the same the next time.

I don't dwell on it or let Yianni know my thoughts. There's no need for him to know how much power he has over my career right now. Even so, I'm secretly smug and inwardly high-fiving myself at getting it right.

It's the first step in knowing I'm good enough away from Charles's La Salle à Manger.

'What do I need to know about Nico? Seeing as we'll soon be working together.'

Yianni leans over the bar so our faces are only inches apart.

'Nothing.'

I can smell the mint on his breath. All the inappropriate feelings I've been suppressing since yesterday stir inside me more vigorously than mixing up the Mojito.

Yianni is my aunt's stepson. This heat is only inside my head. It must be ignored. I'm supposed to be focusing on myself. My goals. Not sexy Greeks . . . unless it's making the cocktail.

I step back to collect myself and hope he hasn't noticed my inward fluster.

'So what's next? The till?' I step towards it. It looks simple enough, but I'd say anything to step out of Yianni's gravitational field.

He drinks more of the cocktail.

'I can't believe you're drinking that at this time in the morning.'

'I need it' – he points at his mouth – 'for my teeth. Remember?'

There's no sign of a smile and I have no idea whether I've offended him or if he's trying to make me laugh.

I feel too hot and bothered to laugh as he gets up and makes his way back round to my side.

He scoops up a fat folder and drops it with a dull thud on to the bar.

'This is important. Very important. Come.' He opens up the folder and leans over it. His finger points at the pages.

I step closer.

'Come, come. You need to learn this.'

I'm close enough to him that I can feel the heat of his body emanating from under his shirt. I feel like a teenager again as I struggle to listen to him talk about the importance of keeping receipts and records. He goes on at length about spot checks, as they're regularly performed in Corfu, and penalties are high if books aren't in order.

The sharp smell of mint on his breath is too vivid in the air. If I close my eyes, I can taste it as though it's my own.

'Maybe I should finish this later, maybe with Hazel or your dad? I think I've got a good idea now. Actually. Or maybe Nico could help me. When I meet him?'

I try to move past Yianni, but he angles himself so I can't get through.

'You are sure? I know everything about running this place. This is my job.'

The part of me that wants to learn and absorb everything wants to stay, but the part of me that can't keep my eyes from drifting to Yianni's open shirt or thinking about the mint in his mouth knows I need to leave.

'OK, maybe you could help me later then? When you've brushed your teeth and got dressed?'

He looks down at himself and almost manages a smile.

'Fine.'

There must be something in the breeze that is messing with my head, because I can't remember the last time I felt attracted to anyone, and the timing couldn't be worse, or more inappropriate.

Chapter Nine

'So wait, while I'm still waiting tables, you're cheating on me with not one but two girls?'

I shuffle off Jonathan's mattress to grab another slice of stuffed crust pizza from the box on the floor.

'No. It's not cheating. It's acting.' Jonathan swings his slice of pizza through the air and presses his other hand dramatically to his chest. 'Anyway, these girls have nothing on you, Rubes.'

I playfully grunt into my pizza as I slide back on to the mattress.

He knows I'm proud of him for getting the part of Lysander in *A Midsummer Night's Dream*. I've told him enough times.

I've only just found out that Lysander is meant to kiss two girls in the play. I console myself with the knowledge that they're touring high schools. Which means any kissing is probably brief.

'It won't be for long anyway. Another four months touring with this company, then I'll land something bigger. Something that'll change both our lives. Doing some Shakespeare will look so good in my portfolio. You won't need to wait on tables any more when I'm rich and famous.'

Slowly, my head drifts up and down.

We've been together almost six months now and I still haven't told him *my* dreams. I've kept them guarded, the way I always do.

I was only eight when my parents' bakery closed. My mum was heartbroken. I vividly remember watching from my window as she went to the bottom of the garden to cry. That was her dream and it didn't work out.

It's left Mum and Dad cautious and me afraid to even express what I want to do. When I was working at a café when I was a teenager, I casually voiced that it would be *cool* to run somewhere one day. My comment was met with a cloud of sadness and tales of disaster.

Since that day, I've never opened up to anyone about my dreams of running my own restaurant.

I know all of Jonathan's dreams – he shares them openly and proudly. I wish I could do that.

He wants to be on TV or in films. To be taken seriously as an actor in dramas or thrillers, that sort of thing. He's willing to put the work in for it, building his way up.

When we were first dating, he told me how he wanted to go to one of the big fancy acting schools, but his mum couldn't afford the tuition, so he's been doing his best to make it without all of those connections. He says that's all the schooling is about. You can either act or you can't, but at the end of the day, it's not what you know, it's who you know.

I'm glad owning a restaurant won't be like that. I'm going to learn everything there is to know and save as much money as I can and make sure it'll be a success.

One of my parents' big problems was not understanding the business side of things and factoring the costs of every detail into the products they were selling.

I have to be different. I have to be prepared. Learning everything I can about each role will help me to do that.

I haven't told Jonathan that, like him, I'm willing to put the work in. I'm willing to build my way up from the ground all the way to my dream of owning a restaurant. Every extra penny from my job I save.

It's not much yet. Less, now that I have to travel to see Jonathan on tour.

'Your olive's going to fall off.' Jonathan's eyes bulge as the pizza slice sags in my hand. I'd forgotten I was even holding it.

I manage to catch it in my mouth before it falls.

'What's wrong?' He dusts his fingers over his jeans and twists on the mattress to face me.

I'll be glad when he has a proper bed and we don't have to sleep on a mattress on the floor.

'I wish I could watch you in your show. That's all.'

Although I do wish that, it really isn't *all* I was thinking.

'You sure that's all? You went pretty still for a minute there.'

This is it. My time to finally tell someone my dream.

I love Jonathan, and he loves me. He needs to know this to be a part of it all. How can we move towards a future together if he doesn't even know the direction I'm heading? It would be unfair to keep my dreams from him at this point.

Placing the pizza slice back in the box, I snatch a breath to prepare myself to let out the dream caught in my chest.

'It was what you said, about me giving up waiting tables. I know you always say you'll look after everything—'

'Of course. When I'm starring in movies, you won't have to work.'

A drip of fear rolls over me like a drop of rain. What if he is as negative about it as my parents? What if he thinks I'll fail?

If we are going to be together for the long haul, he needs to know my endgame the way I know his. We love each other, after all. For this to work, we need to support each other equally.

'The thing is . . . I want to . . . I mean, I want to own my own restaurant. When I was a kid, my parents owned a little bakery, and I loved being in there and helping out. Then when I was older I worked in a café, and that's when I realised that I loved working in hospitality, but I wanted to do it my own way. I love listening to everyone chatting and smiling over food they love. People are always happy when they're eating and drinking, and they go out and celebrate and, well, I want to be a part of that.'

Jonathan's frozen, unmoving. My heart pounds up in my head, waiting for a reaction.

His hand reaches to my face, smoothing his fingertips over my eyebrow and down my cheek.

'Then we'll make it happen. When I get my next part, and it's something big, I'll help save up for your dream with you. Damn, I'll buy you a place if that's what you want. Anything for you, Rubes.'

Tears sting in the back of my eyes as relief and joy swirl up, burning hot.

'Thank you.' My voice is weak and flimsy.

'What for?'

'Always saying the right thing.'

Jonathan pulls me in, and our mouths meet softly at first before we each press deeper into the other.

He pulls me on top of him and tugs off my top.

There's no real way for him to know how much his support means to me. Or maybe he does know? Maybe my constant support for him over these past months has meant a lot to him too.

'I know you're feeling jealous of all these fictional women throwing themselves at me.' Jonathan twists, rolling me on to my back and moving to be over me.

'They're real women . . .' I breathe as his soft lips press fierce kisses over my chest.

Jonathan hums with laughter before sitting up and pushing his fingers through his barley hair. I get to see those deep dimples of his as he grins.

'Well, let me show you how they're not as real as you.'

Chapter Ten

Now

'I'm sure you'll enjoy your first night.' Hazel links my arm as we walk into Greek Secret together. 'Look, there's Nico. Nico! I have someone for you to meet.'

Twisting a glass round a tea towel is a slim, good-looking guy with soft shaggy hair around his face.

Yianni hangs back like his shadow as Nico places down the glass and stretches out a hand over the bar.

'I am Nico,' he beams. 'I've heard everything about you. But no one tells me how beautiful you are. Wow, your lips, they are—'

'No, before you ask, it's not filler,' I tell him. 'Everyone asks that. I just have big lips.'

Nico dips his chin with a chuckle. 'I was saying, they are beautiful. You get your good looks with Hazel? *Naí?*'

'Firstly, I wish I had Ruby's lips, and secondly, you know I'm immune to your charm, Nico. So leave it for the girls paying for drinks.' Hazel squeezes my arm. 'Come on, sweetheart. Let's go over things.'

Nico's fingers linger on mine a moment more than a normal handshake and I have to retrieve them from his leisurely grip.

Before we can get to the working side of the bar, Yianni slips out, briefly kissing Hazel's cheek before making his way to stand at the entrance, the way he did last night.

Hazel begins to skim over a few things. All the bottom-line stuff I have to know to perform my basic tasks.

'I actually went over some of this earlier with Yianni. He promised he would continue, but . . .' I look over at him shifting his weight on his feet. 'I guess he's too busy to pick up where he left off.'

'When was that?' Hazel slides her glasses up her nose. They make her eyes look like black-rimmed saucers.

'Oh, when I took the bike for a test run. I popped in here and Yianni helped me with a few things.'

'Well, if I'm honest, I need to get back into the kitchen. Maybe Nico could pick things up? Nico?'

'Yes?' Nico flips a glass as he turns to face us.

'Could you answer any questions Ruby has for me? You must look after her until she's ready to fly on her own.' Aunt Hazel kisses my cheek and gives my face a squeeze.

This affectionate action makes me flinch and my teeth grit. I hate anyone touching my face and ruining my carefully applied make-up.

All I want to do is run to the bathroom to check my scars are still covered.

'Oh, I'm so sorry, sweetheart. I should've thought—'

I hold my hands up, praying she won't say more and her saucer eyes won't fill with pity.

'It's OK. Honestly. I'll see you later.'

She hesitates for a moment. I can't bear even a second of it, so I turn my back on her and begin my work with Nico.

He picks up an unopened bottle of vodka and sends it somersaulting through the air.

'Whatever you ask, I will provide. Maybe even a tour of the island? I know all the best places.'

'Oh really? I could use a—'

'Ruby.' Yianni cuts over our conversation. 'I promised to teach you the till.'

Unlike Nico, who is full of warmth, Yianni's presence feels like a chill breeze rolling through.

For a moment there, it was nice to be greeted by Nico's warmth. But I'm here to work.

That's my goal. My one and only goal.

Although I *am* looking forward to swimming every day. It's always been my favourite way to keep fit.

Yianni starts going through the simple motions of the till. It's so basic a child could do it.

'Ruby, would you take the drink order for the couple who have just come in.' Yianni looks down at me with his dark eyes softer than I've seen them before. 'Please.'

'Sure thing.'

I don't bother with a notepad. It's a table for two. I've taken bigger orders than that and remembered the lot when I've had a pen run out.

It's the perfect first outing from behind the bar. I guess that's why Yianni picked this minor job for me.

They're a sweet older couple, who order a bottle of wine between them. They ask straight away if I'm new, because they know everyone here and they don't know me.

They seem so pleased with themselves when I confirm it's my very first shift.

As I turn back towards the bar to get their wine and glasses, and add the wine to their bill, I notice an exchange between Yianni and Nico that's wiped the smile right off Nico's face.

'They only wanted a bottle of house red,' I relay to them both. 'All OK?'

'Yes, yes. Everything is good. Yes, Yianni?' Nico taps Yianni's shoulder.

'*Naí*. All is good. Now, Nico, you get the wine, and Ruby, you add the order to the bill how I showed you.'

With that, we all slip into the rhythm of work.

Now I just have to find a way to figure out more about the running and owning side of all this, and hopefully from Hazel.

Chapter Eleven

'Rob was so sad to see me go, he made me promise that when he has a restaurant in France, I have to be his maître d'. I'm going to miss seeing him so much.' My head slumps on to Jonathan's shoulder.

Although a big part of me will miss working with Rob in Shoreditch, it's time to move on. There was no further growth there. Not really. I've been working that same job for almost a year, and even Rob has been talking about moving on.

Jonathan has got us some work in a little pub-restaurant just outside of London. It means we can live together at last, renting a room in a house with shared facilities. Anything to be together.

It'll save loads of money too, because we'll only be paying one lot of rent and we won't have to pay to travel to see each other any more.

The only downside is I've had to use the money I'd saved to buy a car, as there's no bus to the pub where we'll be working.

'I'm sure it'll be hard for you, not seeing Rob every day. But at least you've got me.' Jonathan kisses the top of my head.

We have two full suitcases that we haven't unpacked yet. Instead, we put on the telly in the corner of the room to watch another rerun of *Friends* in each other's arms.

All my childhood things are still in my old room at my parents' house, and Jonathan's the same. Everything is at his mum's in Colchester.

'Do you think I can borrow the car to see Mum at the weekend? She's been really missing me lately. Apparently.' Jonathan sucks in a hard breath before letting out a bellowing sneeze.

'Bless you. Of course you can. Do you want me to come with you?'

'Nah. She adores you, but I can drop you at work and head over to her on Saturday.'

'OK . . . won't you be working too? I haven't seen the rota yet.'

Jonathan already works at this place. I haven't even been there yet, but they've given me a job based on Jonathan saying I'm reliable and Rob giving me the best reference humanly possible.

'It's your first day, but I'm not in. Maybe they want to suss you out without me.'

We fall into silence. Holding each other as we relax into the life we are building, one step at a time.

Although Jonathan is back to working in a restaurant, this place often hires actors and is used to working around auditions.

He's had to quit jobs in the past year where they've been too rigid. Including when we first met. We only worked together for about two weeks before he had to quit to go on tour.

Luckily, he's had so much acting work, building his profile. Including lots of extra work and walk-on parts for well-known productions and films.

With a face like his, he's bound to get noticed by the right person soon.

'I wonder where we'll be living in five years from now. Do you think you'll bring all your actor friends to my restaurant for dinners?'

'Only the very best ones. Only the megastars. You'll be able to cater for the best of the best and get three Michelin stars and stuff.'

'I'll have to make a lot more money in the next few years then. It sounds like this place will need to be pretty fancy.'

'I've told you – I'll buy it for you.'

'I know. I guess I always thought I'd have to do it all myself.'

'But we help each other. You got a car so we can get to work and so I can get to auditions so we can eventually have all the things we deserve.'

'Maybe next week we could go and see my parents? It feels like so long since I've been back to Suffolk to see them.'

'Erm, yeah. Sure. I think we are working most days though.'

'I thought the pub wasn't open on a Monday?'

'Yeah, course.' Jonathan wraps his arm around me and pulls me tighter to him. 'Oh shit, I actually have an audition on Monday. I was hoping to take the car. If that's OK? It's a good part in a touring production. Can't believe I forgot. That's OK though, right? We can go and see them next week? Yeah?'

I slide away from him and over to my suitcase, carefully laying it on the floor, ready to start the process of unpacking.

'You're not mad, are you?'

'No, not at all.'

We rented this room fully furnished, so it's just a matter of deciding what drawers to put things in.

I pick up a scarf that holds one of only two creature comforts I have from home.

It's a photo of me and my parents on a beach together. It was from when my Aunt Hazel got remarried in Corfu a few years back.

'You are, aren't you?' Jonathan shuffles to the edge of the bed. 'I can cancel it if you want? You know I always put you first, right?'

'I know.'

'I'll cancel.'

'No, honestly, we can go next week.' I begin to laugh, turning back towards the bed. It's so much nicer than his old mattress on the floor.

He's perched on the edge, his face riddled with concern as he leans forward with the weight of his body over his knees.

I edge towards him on my knees and wrap my arms around his neck.

'Don't be silly. We can see my parents anytime. We're building a life and we both have to work hard at it. They had a dream and they gave up on it. I don't want us to be like them.'

However much I miss seeing my parents, at least I get to chat to them on the phone when I'm not working. And we can get back to Suffolk another week.

Chapter Twelve

Now

Scars are like writing nightmares on flesh – silver lines that represent the darkness of pain.

I hate that.

I tell myself they're also a representation of living, because these things go hand in hand. Love and pain. Hurt and happiness.

I hate that too.

Really, my scars are the reason I come down to the beach early to swim, so I can do so unseen, without my make-up on.

I could park near the middle of the beach. But I don't.

I park high up outside a taverna called Fantasea with a view across the endless turquoise sea and the scattered buildings of bars and tavernas that skirt the shore.

I love the view. But that's not what I'm there for. I'm there to be invisible.

Each day, I spend a moment with my toes sinking into the wet sludgy sand on the water's edge as the foam traces its way further up my legs, preparing me for what is to come.

Alone.

I like to take a moment to breathe.

Letting the salty air and subtle smell of seaweed fill my lungs before I fall deep into the reflection of my life.

I spend these moments looking as far out to sea as I can, studying that place where the sky and the sea are brought together in a thin line, at times defined and at others almost impossible to make out.

The thought makes me touch the scar on my forehead.

I can feel the fine ridge under my fingers.

This is the only time of day I venture out without a scrap of make-up. I never speak to anyone; I never even get close to anyone.

The sea looks like a shadow of the sky. Or perhaps it looks like the sky's fallen comrade.

I spend so much time considering their colours, why they are the way they are and why life is the way it is; why we have to endure pain and scars.

How I love it in Corfu, but also feel myself slipping into thoughts I know I shouldn't dwell on.

I have a routine now that suits me well enough. Breakfasts with Hazel and Pericles. On weekdays – when Natalia has school – she joins us.

Yianni avoids me. Maybe he picked up on my attraction to him.

I often find myself looking at the photos he left in his room. One is from the time we first met all those years ago, at Hazel and Pericles' very own big fat Greek wedding.

All I remember from that time was worrying about my first year of uni and if I did well enough in my first year to carry on. That, and how beautiful and happy Hazel looked in her flowing white dress. I remember more of Natalia, too; she was maybe five years old and would be chatting away to me in English before slipping into Greek, still expecting me to understand every word.

I was more actively sociable back then, laughing with family, but all I remember of Yianni is that he was there, and at fourteen, to me, he was a kid.

Now, everything is the opposite to back then. It's too easy for me to put up my social front now – that is, to spend time chatting and laughing, making friends with customers who are at the restaurant for one meal or one drink, then never to be seen again. I slip the façade on, and take it off, as easily as my make-up.

I'm used to it.

Used to having friends for only a matter of hours.

Micro-friendships where I hope I've done well enough in their company to gain a tip.

This isn't where I thought I'd be when I came here to their wedding all those years ago. I thought I'd get my business degree, save up, get a business loan for the rest and have a thriving restaurant in the heart of Suffolk, or maybe by the coast if I could find something for the right price.

So much has happened, I've fallen into a black hole, and I'm hoping that one day I'll drop out the other end and land in a place where I'm happy and I'm better equipped to make real connections again.

I'm missing the grounding of my parents and my friends at home. Amara's a good one for that. She gets it.

I miss our conversations over coffee. She's the only friend I really miss. We've known each other a long time, one way or another.

That's not to say I don't love being here with Hazel and Natalia too, but they're busy so much of the time. They both make the effort when they can, and I adore it when they do.

One of the reasons I love working in hospitality is people.

Hearing stories, watching people laugh with their friends and loved ones. But lately I feel like something has slipped down the crack in the sofa, like spare change.

I do spend time with Natalia, Hazel and Pericles, at least, and it *is* refreshing to have people around me in the morning, and not just faceless figures running up- and downstairs, waking me up but not talking to me because they're behind a wall. My neighbours in Suffolk were like unseen ghosts haunting me.

Chatting over breakfast or sharing a smile to say goodnight are things I hadn't realised I'd missed, living alone for so long.

I don't see Yianni much outside of work. All he does is give me orders.

One Sexy Greek, one Sex on the Beach, one beer and a dark rum and Coke.

That's usually it.

I've spent a small amount of time with Gaia, Natalia's friend, who seems hard-working and full of questions – not quite to the point of an interrogation, but she isn't afraid to say what is in her head, and I respect that.

I like working with Nico, although after five minutes I understood why Yianni thought it was better I learnt from him and not Nico.

Nico is almost the opposite of Yianni and would flirt with a tea towel if he was bored. He is nice enough though, and honestly, I think he might be as lonely as me.

That, or I'm reflecting myself into his eyes.

He loves to chat to everyone and often stays late to help if it's needed.

I do think Hazel or Pericles must have warned him off me though.

After offering to show me around the island, he has never set a time or day or even ever mentioned the subject again. I brought it up again last week and he skimmed over it.

Maybe he has decided I'm too dull to show around.

Once I'm done considering how strangely disjointed my life is between the quiet mornings of reflection and the constant chatter of nights, and after my daily comparison of my life and my scars to the line of the blues of the sea and the sky, it's time to swim.

Each day, I wade in with my hair in a tiny knot and goggles pulled over my eyes. Then I put my face in the water until the salt makes my skin feel as taut as the strings of a violin.

I float along, catching sight of silvery fish darting about around me, carrying on until my shoulders and buttocks are warm with exertion.

When I'm done swimming, I lie on the beach reading, mostly books about manifesting my dreams.

The dreams I still haven't told anyone about – apart from Jonathan.

The ones he kept with him; I have to give him that, at least.

They are still there inside me though, burning just as hot as my muscles and my skin in the sun.

Time is ticking away, and the embers are burning with the last of their fuel.

Normally, after my mornings of tanning, I go home, have lunch and ready myself to work from six often until midnight. But all of that is about to change.

As June is edging forwards, so are the numbers of people in the resort.

People want to have a little drink or a meal in the afternoon. Beach bars are more popular for lunch, of course, or places with swimming pools. Greek Secret doesn't possess either of those attractions; it's situated on a road near hotels that are a little further out of the resort.

This means people are starting to pop in for a drink on their walk back from the beach, or they are venturing a few more steps from nearby pools for lunch.

I haven't eaten anywhere except for Greek Secret or Hazel and Pericles' house, but every person visiting says that they've never had a bad meal in San Stefanos, and one of the reasons they return year after year is the standard of the food.

Hopefully, I'll find out sooner or later if that's true.

When I have had a whole day off, I've taken the bike around the island, along the meandering roads and through the olive groves. I've loved it. I never stay in the resort.

I've got no one to go for a meal with. No one I know to talk to. So I just keep moving.

I'd rather that, though, than wasting my time with the wrong person.

Chapter Thirteen

Then

'You'll never guess what?' I can't help but bounce on my heels as I walk along the high street.

I might be surrounded by sad-looking, run-down buildings that have seen better times, but to me the world is the colour of a glowing sunrise.

'Hello? Ruby, the line isn't great. Say that again.'

I press my phone harder to my cheek, willing the words to carry through.

'I had a call from Motka at work—'

'How many other Motkas do you know?' I can hear the click of Jonathan's tongue then the laughter in his voice tickling the line.

'Listen, listen, he's said I can work as a commis chef in the kitchen! How exciting is that? I'll get to learn a whole new set of skills.' A skip leaps out of me and a mum shuffling a pushchair along looks up at me with a broad smile.

'Hey! Well done! That's big news, babe. Well done you. We should celebrate. I was just grabbing dinner – I'll get us an extra-special something and you can tell me all about it at home.'

I squeal a little at the idea of cooking up something nice in preparation for my new role in the kitchen.

'Perfect. Love you, see you in a bit.'

'Love you too.'

The line clicks off and I'm left grinning from ear to ear at absolutely no one.

I only popped into town to grab some shampoo, but I had to get the bus because Jonathan has the car for a callback.

Damn, I didn't even ask how it went. Hopefully, we'll have two things to celebrate.

There's a bus stopped as I round the corner. With my phone in one hand and my bag in the other, I sprint to catch it before it pulls off. My feet slap along the ground as my ballet pumps nearly fly off my feet.

Luckily, this driver seems to find my sprint amusing and he waits for me to get to the doors. His cracked skin rolls into a deeply lined smile.

'You're all right, love, I won't leave you behind.'

'Thank you so much!'

I pay my fare and sit on one of the hard bus seats. It's not busy. Only me and a handful of others, and I've only got to wait three stops before I'm home.

The buildings meander past me while I sing happy songs in my head and wonder what delightful ingredients Jonathan will pick up from the shop.

I write out a message in the WhatsApp group between me and my parents. I'm pretty sure they think I'm mad, getting a business degree to spend two years waitressing and living in a room with my boyfriend. But I'm happy, and this experience will get me that bit closer to my own restaurant.

They both reply with congratulations and wishes for a lovely evening celebrating.

They've never once put down my choices. They've only ever supported me, even if they don't know where it's all heading. Mum always says she's happy if I'm happy.

I'm sure if I told them I wanted my own restaurant, they would try to be supportive. I just have an underlying feeling that they would get a nervous energy about it and cite all the problems I might face, whereas I like to focus on people who have managed to run a place successfully. Like I will.

I would so love to talk to them about what I'm building up to, and get some advice about running a place. I just can't bear the sad expressions that come with the mention of the bakery and hearing about all the problems and the things that went wrong.

I need to focus on what should be done, not what shouldn't.

With bright thanks to the bus driver, I practically skip off the bus and all the way to our door.

I'm greeted by some of the quieter housemates making their dinner in the kitchen, so I head straight upstairs.

Our car was on the street outside so I guess Jonathan must be back.

I swing the bedroom door open to be greeted by a large bunch of red roses.

'Congratulations!' Jonathan's face appears behind them as he pulls them down over his chest.

Dropping everything I'm carrying, I reach out for the flowers.

'Oh my gosh, you shouldn't have—'

'And that's not all.' He raises a hand from behind the flowers to reveal a bottle. 'Champagne! The real stuff too, straight from France.'

I gasp, leaving my jaw slack behind my hands. We can't afford it, not really, but it's so lovely of him to celebrate my achievements like this.

He wraps his arm around me carefully as his hands are still full of gifts.

Our lips meet in a natural kiss.

'Wait, how did the audition go?'

'Very well. It's down to me and one other bloke. They said they'd give me a call later in the week and let me know.'

'That's fantastic! More things to celebrate.'

Jonathan places the flowers in my hands and I take a deep inhale of their velvety rouge petals. They're subtle and sweet.

We never have flowers. It'll be nice to have something to brighten up the place. There are a few little things here and there. Some photographs and a random vase I bought to store random bits and bobs in.

'Ooh, I can use that vase for flowers at last.' I tip out the contents on to our chest of drawers, ready to fill the vase with water.

'Come on, let's get some glasses for this bad boy.' Jonathan wiggles the bottle of Moët in my direction.

'Did you pay on credit card?'

With the flowers in one hand, I tuck the vase under my arm to close our door and follow Jonathan across the landing to the stairs.

'Let's not ruin the night by talking about money.'

He's right. We should enjoy the little things and worry about money tomorrow.

This pricks up my anxiety. It's not in my nature to ignore the future, but I really want to live in the now. To live how Jonathan does and enjoy what we have in this moment in front of us.

The kitchen is empty. There's only the lingering smell of coriander and coconut from Spencer's curry to give away the fact the kitchen was in recent use.

Jonathan searches all the glasses in the cupboards, while I fix the flowers.

All we have are two red-wine glasses. It doesn't matter that we don't have elegant flutes to sip from. One day we will.

'*Santé*,' we chorus as our glasses strike together.

'Will you be getting a big pay rise now you're one of the chefs?' Jonathan relaxes against the counter, sipping his champagne.

'No, sadly not.'

'Wait, I thought commis chefs got more than wait staff.'

'Yeah, but I have no experience. I only got it because they know I'm reliable. I'll show up and work hard. Motka said as much on the phone.'

'*Motka from work?*' Jonathan raises an eyebrow before hiding his sarcasm in charm and champagne-sipping.

'Yes. Motka from work.'

'I guess you won't get as much in tips now either, working in the kitchen. Shit, I really thought it would come with more money.'

'Why won't I get as much in the way of tips? We have a tip-share system . . .'

'Oh, come on. We all pocket a certain amount. Don't act like you don't.'

'I don't.' I take a bigger gulp of champagne than I mean to.

The loud chime of Jonathan's phone begins to go. He slams his glass down on the counter a little too hard as his hands race to the back pocket of his baggy jeans.

'Hello?' He leaves the room to take the call.

I take this moment to look at our shelf in the fridge to see what we are creating for dinner.

There's two ready-made steak Dianes for us to heat up. It wouldn't have been my first choice, but in a restaurant it is something we both like. In that, it was the perfect pick.

'I got the job!' Jonathan wraps his arms around my waist, our heads tipping into the fridge. 'I've got the lead in an independent film and it's going to be touring festivals. This could be it. The thing that really gets me seen.'

He spins me around and presses his lips to mine as my back digs into the shelves. I let myself be taken by him. By his zest for life and his enthusiasm.

I love it when Jonathan gets a new part. He'll be on a high for weeks about it.

I won't ask about money though. Not tonight. It's probably not a paid role, or maybe it'll be profit-share if it ever makes some money.

He's so talented, it'll make money eventually.

Chapter Fourteen

Now

'Are you ready?' Hazel pulls her handbag up on her shoulder.

'Yep. Let me just get my phone.'

I jog back up the stairs. The shower is running. Yianni's in there, although I haven't seen him.

Grabbing my phone from my bed, there's a message from Mum: *Have fun with Hazel xx*

I bound back down the stairs in the way I'm accustomed to now. This has become my new normal.

'Come on then, kid. Let's go.' Hazel claps her hands together.

There's something about Aunt Hazel that has the energy of a children's entertainer.

Even though she's perfectly polished in her crisp white linen trousers and fitted T-shirt, her hair takes on a slightly wild edge when she pushes her glasses up into it.

That slightly manic vibe is probably because she wants to make this morning fun. That, or she wants to have a serious chat.

Even though Yianni has tried to put his stamp on the fact he basically runs Greek Secret now – and even Hazel has told me to pick his brains if I'm interested – I'm sure she'll be able to mentor me about restaurants and running the kitchen or applying for loans. Anything.

I just have to get her to mentor me without knowing she's mentoring me.

Should be easy.

Hazel takes me into Corfu Town. It's quite a drive from her house, but it's nice to spend time alone together.

The town is full of people of all nationalities meandering into shops stuffed with Corfiot goods or traditional-looking dresses.

'Shall we get a drink? Or an ice cream? When you were little, you'd go nutty for a 99 Flake.' Hazel nudges into me.

'Did I?'

'Uh huh. I remember taking you up to Great Yarmouth with Tim.' I don't think about Uncle Tim much. Aunt Hazel divorced him twenty or so years ago. 'He got you one – he was OK when he wanted to be. Anyway, you squealed so much with excitement that when he put it in your hand you jumped up and down and dropped it on the floor.'

'Oh God, I actually *do* remember that. I was so upset, even though you got me another.'

'First thing you did when you got home was tell your mum about the ice cream that got away. I'll get you another one now.'

'Not a 99 Flake though.'

We both peer at tubs of gelato that could compete with the colours of the rainbow.

I stick to one scoop of vanilla to cool me off and it arrives with a biscuit with a picture of the Mona Lisa on it.

'What happened with you and Tim?' I muse, licking my ice cream as Hazel pays.

'*Efcharistó*,' Hazel says as she's handed her change. 'Since when did you stop pulling your punches? That's a big question.'

We move slowly between people dripping with sweat as our ice creams attempt to run away from us.

'He wasn't who I thought he was. When we were first married. We got married so young. He was very charming.' Hazel stops to peer into the window of a jeweller's shop and its elegantly displayed silver and gold. 'The thing about charm is, it's easy to wear. Like a necklace. And it's just as easy to take off.'

Hazel falls very still for a moment before springing back into life with an over-eager smile behind what's left of her ice cream.

'Enough of him,' she says. 'I'm interested in you.'

Only, I'm interested in her and Uncle Tim. Her words resonate in my head. Jonathan was charming, ready to glitter for those around him, but only when the lights were shining directly on him.

'I'm really not that interesting.'

'Nonsense. Have you been enjoying your time swimming? If you want a buddy to come with—'

'No. Honestly. I'm used to my space.'

'Yes, yes. Of course you are. I suppose you've been living on your own since . . . well, you must feel positively claustrophobic, living with us.'

I want to tell her that's not it at all. I want to explain that I can't stop staring out to sea and wondering what it all means, but I'm afraid it'll make me seem a little crazy.

'Not at all. I've actually loved having people to have breakfast with.'

'Aww. That's lovely.' Hazel wraps her arm around me, doing her best to avoid putting sticky fingers on my shoulder.

'Now, what's the future looking like?'

'And when did you stop pulling *your* punches?'

Hazel hides a smile behind the last bite of her cone.

'Well, I suppose you get it from me then, don't you? You've been with us a little while now. I just wondered if you were thinking of staying longer, coming back next summer, or on to the next big thing?'

I toss the last of my cone into my mouth and chew thoughtfully.

I'm still not ready to tell Hazel my plan. She might try to take over, or worse, she might tell me she doesn't think it's a viable idea and to pick something outside of running my own place.

Although I'd love a restaurant, I've been toying with the idea of a café to start me off. I could do cakes and artisan coffee.

I'm not sure where it would be yet. But I'm still trying to work out how much deposit I would need to rent a place, or maybe to buy somewhere. There's still so much to think about.

'I'd hazard a guess that you already know exactly what you want to do. You've always been a dark horse. Getting information out of you is like getting blood out of a stone sometimes. You're worse than a teenage boy. And I should know, I had to put up with Yianni.'

The thought of him is like an itch I'm determined not to scratch.

We continue weaving down a narrow street with pale-yellow walls and shops full of herbs filling the air with oregano and dill.

'What was he like? As a teenager?'

'Yianni? Gosh . . . where to start. I think he could win a medal for quiet sulking. No, not sulking. Brooding. He broods, he doesn't sulk.'

I tilt my chin down to the uneven cobbles to hide the snigger that's desperate to show itself.

'Don't laugh too hard. He wasn't the only quiet and brooding teen I've known.'

Hazel's bright-blue eyes narrow on me.

I feign insult, but she's right. I tried to hide in the quiet shadows at that age. Nice to know Yianni and I aren't so dissimilar.

'I do worry about him.'

'Really? He seems to enjoy his work, and flirting with the girls at the bar with Nico.'

'He's so driven. In the past two years, he's made some great changes to Greek Secret and business has never been better because of him. It's the girls I worry about. He had a dreadful relationship at university. I didn't take to her at all, then I saw her poking her finger so hard in his ribs at a family party. She thought no one was looking.' Hazel's eyes narrow and the muscles in her neck look drawn out. 'He never said anything, and we tried to be there for him, but he's never really opened up. Underneath it all, he takes everything in and some people will suck the light right out.'

'I had no idea.'

'Why would you? He's not one to go around advertising his emotions. I'm glad he's throwing himself into the business. It's good for him. He doesn't need another painful mistake distracting him right now.'

I know how that can go. How easy it is to fall in love and be pulled away from dreams. To build a new life with everything entwined, only for it all to fall apart one brick at a time.

It feels good to have Hazel tell me stories, instead of always feeling I have to share mine. In a strange way, it makes me feel almost like I could open up and say more.

Chapter Fifteen

Then

'Look who's come to visit!' I swing the door open to our shared house before Jonathan's key even hits the lock.

'Visit?' His hand is still floating with a key in it and a Lidl bag full of shopping rests by his leg.

I pull the door open a little wider to reveal my mum and dad.

Jonathan's face lights up and he swiftly thrusts his keys into the back pocket of his jeans so he can shake my dad's hand and kiss my mum's cheek.

'You two are always so busy working, and we haven't seen you in months, so we thought . . .' – Mum looks from Dad to Jonathan, her cheeks swelling in smiles – 'let's have a mini break!' Mum clasps her hands together loudly.

'You'll never guess where they're staying.' I pick up the abandoned shopping from the step and move towards the kitchen to fill our part of the fridge.

The old Victorian house is empty other than us, as everyone else is at work.

They all follow on behind me.

'The White Horse! Where you both work!' Mum has a bounce in her step as she makes her announcement.

Dad shrugs over her shoulder in that classic French way he always does.

Dad looks and sounds typically French. I'm not one to feed into clichés, but he really does look like he should be walking around with a beret and a striped T-shirt. These days he is as grey as a pigeon, but he used to have rich brown hair and deep dark eyes over a characterful nose.

I didn't get his nose, luckily, as I don't think it would be as attractive on a girl, but he's where my natural colouring comes from, and my hooded eyelids too.

My roots, lashes and eyebrows are chocolate brown but the ends of my hair I've bleached a sandy blonde for years. I distinctly look more like my dad's side of the family. I got his bee-stung lips too.

My mum, on the other hand, doesn't look much like me. Her skin is pinched pink and she's exceptionally fair. All I got from her is my straight nose and the smattering of freckles on it that come out in the sun.

'Are you busy today? We can understand if you have plans?' Dad directs this at Jonathan. I've already reassured them that we don't. We haven't been put on shifts today.

'Of course not, Marco. You and Fern are always welcome.' Jonathan flashes his dimples as he pats Dad's shoulder. 'Can we get you a drink? Or maybe we could take you out for lunch?'

I shoot a look in Jonathan's direction from the corner of my eye. Between rent, the cost of running a car and Jonathan rarely being at work for the past month because of endless auditions, we haven't even got enough money this month to add to my restaurant fund.

I try each month to save at least two hundred pounds. This month, we can't even stretch to that. I need enough money to prove I'm serious to get a business loan.

I've been wondering about starting small, getting a little place, maybe even a pub. There are loads going bust that I could breathe some life back into with good food and great service. I want to make people feel like they've had the most wonderful and relaxing time when they walk through my doors.

'Maybe we could take you both out? As we've sprung this on you. Have you had lunch?' Mum pulls up the sleeves on her lilac cardigan.

'I wouldn't hear of it.' Jonathan passes me a lettuce, then juice and milk for the fridge. 'We'll take you out. There's a bakery not too far. You two are the experts, though, as you used to run a bakery. You can tell us if you think this one is *really* any good. Your home-made cheese scones are still the best I've ever had.'

He's only being lovely, but Jonathan isn't thinking. If we go out and pay, it'll be more on the credit card and more I'll have to pay off with my savings.

'That's too kind of you to say, Jonathan.' Mum looks at him then shoots me an affectionate smile, as if to say, *isn't he sweet?*

I sort of wish he hadn't brought up the bakery. Mum and Dad never talk about those times much. Dad particularly feels like he failed Mum; he didn't get things right along the way and shattered their dreams.

It's why I've never told them about my dreams of owning my own place. I'm sure it would fill them with anxiety.

'And your apple tarte too, Marco. You really spoilt us when we came to stay.' Jonathan closes our allocated cupboard.

'It was my *mamie's* – my grandmother's – tarte tatin recipe. I'm sure I've said many times, she worked with my grandfather in their own patisserie.'

'I'd have loved to have met them. And tried their food. If it was even half as good as yours, I bet it was the best in France.'

'You're very welcome to stay more often, you know. You can enjoy all the baked goods you like. You know we love to host.' Mum presses her lips together as though she's said something she shouldn't.

Guilt glides over my skin and seeps in like face cream.

We've been in a cocoon for so long, Jonathan and me. We often go months without seeing friends or family from back home. We see his mum more, because she raised Jonathan as a single mum and is all on her own.

'We'd love to' – Jonathan wraps his arm over my shoulder – 'wouldn't we? Maybe we should pick out some dates over lunch? Anything to get more of those scones and that apple tarte!'

I love how well Jonathan gets on with my parents when we are all together. However busy life can get, I know that this is how it should be. All of us getting along.

I press my head into Jonathan's chest and playfully poke him in the ribs. 'You're such a charmer, aren't you?'

Chapter Sixteen

Now

Yianni comes over to the bar and lightly taps it, saying, 'Two vanilla milkshakes,' before he turns to walk away.

I make the milkshakes and walk around the bar to take them to the table.

There are only two tables of customers, one with five people whose drinks I've already made, and another with two girls, a blonde and a brunette, perhaps in their twenties.

'Here.' Yianni walks towards me and puts his hands out to take the glasses from me. 'I can take them.'

As I pass them to him, one slips through his hand and shatters on my foot, slicing it open.

Greek words swirl out of Yianni's mouth and around my head as my entire body goes tense.

For a moment, I don't even look down. My jaw locks. My fingernails penetrate the skin on the heel of my empty hand before a thin whisper slips out of my lips.

'Fuck.'

Then, as a deep pain ripples up through my body, I twist to hop towards the bar and away from the pool of milkshake that's curdling with my blood on the floor, scooping to clutch my left foot in the process.

I don't mean to, but French pours out between my teeth, literally, not just 'excuse my French' but the rich and potent force of it. '*Aïe! Putain d'enculé de bâtard! Putain de merde!*' For some reason, French swearing always comes more naturally to me than English when I'm in real pain or a temper.

Yianni momentarily stops talking to tilt his head and open his mouth as though he might ask what the hell I'm saying, but I bare my teeth at him and growl, 'Please get a cloth before I bleed out on the floor.'

'I am so sorry, Ruby.'

I can't reply.

Yianni calls over Pericles, who's been pottering around in the background.

He orders his dad to make fresh milkshakes, and to clear the mess. Or I assume that's what he is saying as Pericles starts bustling around us.

'Come. I need to get you to the back.' Yianni slides his arm around my ribs to get me to lean on him instead of the bar stool.

I hobble for a step or two before Yianni gives up and instead scoops me up like I'm made of cloth and marches me and my dripping foot towards a side room.

It's his bedroom.

I'm torn between my interest in looking around the room and my throbbing foot, which seems to ooze more blood with each and every pulse of pain.

The foot wins, of course.

Yianni presses a cloth carefully to the wound, making me scrabble away from him.

It's my left foot and my left hand has been clutching it since moments after it happened; consequently, my fingers are covered in blood. Yianni grabs what I assume is another cloth and presses it to my foot.

Hazel bursts in with all guns blazing, like a police officer called to an ongoing crime.

'What happened? Oh my God, Ruby. Let me see.'

Yianni quickly moves out of her way as she bustles past him and drops to her knees next to the bed. She carefully lifts the cloth and her eyes bulge before she firmly presses it back into my foot, making me gasp. 'What happened?' she repeats.

Yianni steps forward.

'A milkshake glass. I dropped it on her foot.' He paces the room. 'It is the bloody . . .' He clicks his fingers to draw the English word out of his Greek mind. '. . . the bloody condensation. It was wet and it slipped.'

I squirm a little as I try to blow the pain out with each breath, before giving up and pressing my lips together so tightly I'm sure they've completely disappeared in on themselves.

Hazel pulls her glasses off her face and rubs one eye with the back of her hand before replacing them. 'I'll have to take you to the health centre or something, Ruby. I can't put a plaster on it, it's much too big, and what if there's glass in it? I saw the mess on the floor.'

'No.' Yianni interrupts the plan, making my face screw up even tighter than it already is.

If he says I need to keep working and put up with it, I'm going to bloody well slap him with the back of my hand. 'I will take her. If we get stuck waiting or get sent to hospital, you, Baba, Natalia and Nico will make it work this evening. Get Natalia to ask Gaia if she can work today too.'

Hazel begins to speak to him in Greek. I've never actually heard her speak Greek the whole time I've been here. I'm taken aback by it.

Their exchange is pointed and brief.

Without further explanation, I'm scooped up again by Yianni, who has paid me more attention in the past few minutes than he has in the past few weeks.

Chapter Seventeen

Now

Yianni was gunning it until I snapped at him to drive sensibly.

I'm not going to die from a glass to the foot, but a car is a lethal weapon.

My knees are pulled up to my chest and my foot's between my hands, firmly knotted in the cloth Yianni has given me. The one that was white, but is slowly making its way to red.

It's a really long time before anything is said.

He's gripping the steering wheel so hard it looks like he might break it, and his eyes keep darting towards my foot.

Spurred on by his glances, the urge to look at it again takes over me.

I peel back the cloth to see the narrow gash running along the middle to the side of my foot. I snatch a sharp inhale through my teeth at the sight of it.

I can almost taste the sweet vanilla from the milkshake residue as I do.

My swelling flesh screams with anger at having the pressure taken off it.

It is enough to make me momentarily hold my breath while I wrap it back up. I think the bleeding is slowing, at least.

'Oh shit!' I exhale my words as I press the cloth back down.

'What? Is it worse?' Yianni's head keeps skipping between me and the road.

'Please keep your eyes on the road. You're making me nervous. And no, it's not worse. I said shit because I just realised, this is a T-shirt. I thought it was a cloth. Is it yours?'

An audible exhale falls from his lips and amusement lingers. This time, he doesn't turn to look at me but keeps his eyes locked on the road as I've instructed.

'You can keep it. I am not into tie-dye.' He briefly glances at me and smiles. 'How is it feeling?'

'Rubbish. I can't believe it's this bad.'

'I cannot believe it cut you at all. I have dropped a glass on my foot before. I've never been cut.'

'Mmm. You wear trainers to work. I don't even want to think about it.' I push my weight further back into my chair. Every position is uncomfortable. 'Remind me not to wear flip-flops to work again. Trainers only from now on.'

'Trainers? You mean sneakers?'

I guess he doesn't know all of my very English terms. 'Yeah, sneakers.'

We pull up at the health centre. It's pretty small – smaller than I expect it to be, anyway.

I let Yianni do all the talking, for obvious reasons.

I zone out and watch the ceiling and imagine I'm looking at the line where the sea and the sky come together. The haze. The complexity of life drawn in pale-blue lines and where they begin and where they end.

I probably won't be doing that as much until my foot heals.

There's no way I want to get sand in this cut.

As the wound is being cleaned with some kind of antiseptic, my mind bursts back into my body with a hiss. My hands fumble for something to grab on to and find the corner of Yianni's shirt.

'You owe me a drink for this,' I say through gritted teeth.

Four Steri-Strips, some gauze and a bandage later, and we are on our way back. Still in silence.

I need distraction from my foot throbbing in time with my pulse.

I do my best to find it in the million shades of green and the sun bouncing off people's swimming pools or imagining how half-finished buildings with their rebar and concrete platforms will eventually look.

Watching snapshots into someone else's world makes me feel more human. Silently witnessing someone else's life and world when they don't know I'm watching.

It's one of the reasons I fell in love with working in bars, restaurants and cafés. I get to be a part of so many lives. Getting to see the happy moments over a celebratory dinner or serving a glass before it's raised to a smiling face has kept me going.

Many years ago, working in a café, I was consumed by people's stories. The things they would tell each other over a coffee . . . I'm still amazed to this day at the things we all talk about in public, forgetting hospitality staff are always nearby.

Yianni breaks the spell of silence. 'What were you saying? When you hurt your foot?'

His voice is like a doorbell at my brain, trying to rouse me into a response, but I can't understand what the question is that's being asked.

'When?'

'You went into a different language. French, no?'

'Yeah. I'm half French. I mostly know how to swear and order food, a little conversation too.'

I don't like to make a big deal out of speaking French; it's nowhere near as complicated as Greek.

Yianni pushes out his bottom lip and bounces his head in thought.

'Of course, your father. That makes sense to me. These are the most important of subjects. To show anger and passion and to fill your belly. Sensible.'

'Something like that.'

A smile tugs at the corner of my mouth at his appreciation of my language skills.

'What did you say? In French?'

I know what I said. I know exactly. But I feel a little stupid translating my outburst, so instead I repeat it in the original language.

'*Putain d'enculé de bâtard. Putain de merde.*' I say it quickly, with as little emphasis as I can. Almost like it's only one long fluid word, sliding along like treacle.

'In English.' Then he quickly adds, 'Or Greek.' And glances at me with a tickle in his tone and a glint in his eye.

I'm not sure I've seen his eyes glint like that, not in my direction anyway.

I cough, as though taking ceremony in what I'm about to say.

'Roughly, I said, *Whore of a fucker of a bastard. Whore of shit.* It sounds better in French, obviously.' As soon as the words leave my mouth, I nibble back my bottom lip and my hand finds my forehead to partially cover my face.

I'm not embarrassed as such, but a certain level of cringe washes over me.

Yianni, on the other hand, is laughing. His ribcage contracts as he struggles for air. 'Good to know the French like to swear as much as the Greeks.'

'Oh, really?' I lower my hand a little off my face.

'If you had dropped the glass on me, I would say: *gamó tin poutána mou.*'

'Do I dare ask what that means?'

'It is not worse than you: *fuck my whore.*'

'I honestly feel disappointed. I thought that Greek was the origin of basically everything. Surely it's more colourful than that?'

'If you drop a glass on my foot, I guess we will find out.'

We chortle along together before silence falls over us again, but this time with a smile lingering between us.

It hovers there for a long moment.

I relax and turn back to the window, but Yianni continues, albeit with a new subject. 'I will take you back to the house. You must not work this week. Not until you have some rest.'

Within a few minutes we are back at the house to the chorus of cicadas, and I quickly get out of the car before Yianni can get to my door and scoop me up again like I'm some kind of ice cream.

It's more of a struggle than I thought it would be, so I let him take my elbow and hand to rest my weight over his fingers.

'I think you should lie down. Come on.' He keeps hold of me and walks me in the direction of the stairs as soon as we are in the house.

I sort of want to argue; I feel strange about him taking me up to his bed with no one else here.

This is one of only a handful of times I've actually seen him in the house. I know he has been in every day over the last few weeks, but our paths don't cross all that much.

He comes back for showers and some meals, but apparently not when I'm about.

After sitting me on the bed, he leaves the room and returns with pillows to put under my foot.

He hesitates.

His arms cross over his chest, making his short-sleeved black shirt constrict around his biceps.

His lips look poised to speak, but something is stopping him. Maybe he feels he shouldn't leave me alone, or perhaps he is desperate to leave and doesn't want to say.

I really don't feel like being completely alone right now. Ever since Jonathan, I have become a complete queen at filling my time. Work, gym, friends, family, and if I'm at home, I pick up any book or binge-watch TV programmes I've seen a thousand times before, all to the sounds of the neighbours, which makes it feel like someone is there chatting in the next room.

But when this house is empty, it's really empty.

'Does it seem strange? Me settled into your room as though it's mine?' Asking questions will keep him here longer, otherwise I will have to silently look at the ceiling or my phone, because I left my book at the restaurant.

He shrugs. 'Yes. But I don't want you to feel like I want you out.'

'You do though, don't you? I know I pissed you off with the whole taxi thing—'

'Not this again.' His eyes almost disappear into the back of his head, but there's a lightness in his tone that makes me think twice.

He sits himself down next to me on the bed. The edge of his leg presses against mine and I'm as aware of it as I would be if someone pressed the cold, flat edge of a blade against my leg.

'Oh, shut up. You almost broke my foot this afternoon. I think it's high time you start being nice to me.'

'When am I not nice?' He clicks his tongue. 'Well, I suppose I will be covering many of your shifts behind the bar now, so, I think this is punishment enough.'

'Oh, seriously? Shut up. I've seen you! You bloody love it. The girls only come in to chat to you and Nico.' I shake my head and catch sight of the smug look on his face. Before he can open his mouth, I know what he wants to say and correct myself before he can. 'Not that Hazel's food isn't brilliant, it is. Of course people come to the restaurant for that, and my cocktails too.' I suppress a smile. 'But you *do* seem to have a high percentage of women who come back at any excuse to linger at the bar for a chat. You and Nico are like some sort of bloody . . . tag team. You smile and chat them up over dinner and he takes over when it's time for a cocktail.'

Throughout my little rant, he is pouting under furrowed brows. Now he can't resist a chuckle.

He tries to deny my allegation, of course, but the chuckle turns into laughter, and he stops trying to hide his knowledge of such an obvious fact.

He says, without conviction, 'I do not know what you are talking about.'

'Really?'

'Really?' he mocks, pressing one hand into the mattress, leaning a little closer to me.

It's my turn to fold my arms across my chest. I put on my best tell-tale voice. That annoying little know-it-all tone that rattles around primary schools.

'So, you're telling me that my poor little foot *didn't* come about because you wanted to be the one to go to the table and chat to those two girls?' I lower one eyebrow and raise the other as much as I can, and as he suppresses laughter – poorly – I add a *hmm?* for good measure.

That last sound tips him over the edge, again.

'*Naí*, yes! You caught me. I think I will get better tips than if you take the drinks. OK?'

My cheeks are starting to ache from smiling.

There's lift in his cheekbones too. It's emphasised by the neatly thought-out stubble that defines his jaw and his cheekbones perfectly at all times.

The way his face transforms under the helium-like lift of laughter is almost elegant.

I really need to tell him to leave, before I make this more awkward in my head.

The light in the room shifts to a burnt golden glow as the sun hangs lower in the sky outside the window. I think Yianni must have noticed too, because he exhales the last of his laughter and glances towards the window with a slight squint.

'I should get back to the restaurant. It's already time for round two.'

'They don't expect you to come back.' As soon as I say it, I know it's an obvious invitation and I feel the prick of regret stab at the back of my throat.

It's been so long since I've spent time with a man and liked him in any way like this.

He is my aunt's stepson, so what does that make him to me? Off limits. That's all.

I'm going to go ahead and guess that I'm not someone he would see himself taking out on a date anyway.

And I don't want him to.

I don't.

Plus, he is, what, maybe five or six years younger than me, and a silly sod.

His eyes flick back to mine, and we look at each other for a moment longer than is natural in the middle of a silent room.

At the same moment, we break apart, shattering the silence with motion.

He stands, and says in a husky monotone, 'I best go.'

As soon as Yianni leaves the room, I feel about for my phone in my pocket and start messaging two people about what has happened.

First off is my mum. Fortunately, Hazel hasn't already messaged her about my foot, or there would be a blizzard of worried texts from her.

Ever since Jonathan, and living on my own, Mum's done her best to silently check up on me.

I like to see it as low-key parental stalking of the sort that fourteen-year-olds have to endure when they leave the house. I put up with it because I can see it's from a place of love and it doesn't bother me to be loved.

Then there is the person I'm going to tell every stupid girly detail to: Amara.

Amara has been loving living in my house with her boyfriend, Si, and has even decided I should live in Corfu full-time so they can have holidays visiting me.

When I was debating coming here for six months, my biggest worry was where to put all my things, so Amara and her boyfriend put forward the idea of subletting my house. It's the perfect win-win situation. I didn't have to put furniture into storage, and they get to see if they can live together without having to put down a deposit.

Amara and I are in the middle of sending a million quick-fire messages back and forth when there's a little knock on my door.

An involuntary gasp makes me drop my phone on to my chest with a painful slap. I pull myself up on the bed, my attempt at moving further from the door.

'Who is it?'

'Yianni.'

Yianni? What the hell is he doing knocking at the door? I thought he was long gone.

'Oh. Come in.' Although *come in* is a statement, it comes off more like a question, because really I want to ask if he has been standing outside my door for the past fifteen minutes or so.

'I know it is not much, but, as you know, we mostly eat dinner at the restaurant, so there is less food here.' He passes me a tray with a small salad and a massive slab of feta in the middle, with a can of lemonade on the side. '*Kalinikta,* Ruby.'

He walks away.

I'm stunned and calling in his wake, 'Thank you, *efcharistó.* Have a nice evening.' Before whispering, '*Kalinikta,* Yianni. You enigma.'

Chapter Eighteen

Now

I don't do much for a few days because my foot is puffed up.

I think the bone is bruised or something, as well as the cut, because when I stand the blood rushes to my foot, and it starts to throb again like my heart has fallen down my trouser leg.

The whole thing has turned delightful shades of lilac and black and I couldn't put my pumps on if I wanted to.

It isn't long before I resent lying in the garden, however tranquil it is to watch enormous butterflies with wings of all shapes and sizes dance with bees and beetles.

Yes, I adore the shade of the olive trees that shelter me from the thirty-degree heat in the afternoon, but I'm sick of my bruised bone and of being alone. So, I tell Hazel I'm coming in and if I have to sit on a chair to prep vegetables to keep myself busy, then so be it.

As it turns out, I mostly get in the way in the kitchen and Yianni eventually gives me the role of sitting on a chair next to the till.

I'm now officially in charge of all the bills and receipts. Nico is in, and keeping me company, although Yianni has told him what I said and he is finding any opportunity to bring it up.

'I'm thinking do you think I am only meat to these girls? No?'

Nico tries his best to look sad through his doe eyes. Pressing his fingers to his lips, he tries to look dramatic and hurt at the idea of being a piece of meat.

Then he presses the back of his hand to his forehead like he might faint, before moving around the bar as though the wind is blowing and he is caught in a gust. It's a rather strange but comical skit. It's only after some tutting from me that he breaks character and laughs at himself as he tosses a glass in the air with one hand and watches it somersault into the other.

'Please don't keep doing that near me.' I flap my hands at him. 'I'm still traumatised from Yianni dropping that bloody great milk-shake on me. I don't need you chucking one at me too, thanks.'

'Poor Ruby. Do you need a cuddle?'

Nico puts the glass down on the bar and walks towards me with his arms outstretched.

'Nico.' Yianni elongates the 'O' of 'Nico' as he places his hands on the other side of the bar. 'Leave the poor girl alone. She might think the girls are only here for our good looks, but that does not mean you should be terrorising her.' He leans forwards and hisses, 'Save that for the customers. We need money in the tip jar, not Ruby crying on your shoulder. It is not good for business.'

'At least that's something we can agree on.' I give Nico a look that's just shy of poking my tongue out at him in triumph.

It's nice to just be an employee again and not worry that I'm having to set an example to other staff members. It's a completely different atmosphere here to being a maître d' for Charles.

I guess that'll all change if I can get my own place together. I'll be back to setting a good example.

Yianni and I hold a lingering smile.

It's the first night of seeing each other since the glass incident.

He has messaged to check on me, but they were all sort of formal, checking how I was healing. It's been nice so far, but it makes my body and my heart ache.

Part of me wishes we could go back to being quiet and efficient work colleagues.

Our eyes are still locked as Nico begins to chat again.

'*Naí, naí*, Yianni. You made this clear to me weeks ago. I know, I am not allowed to talk too much with Ruby. Not too cosy.' Nico wags his finger at Yianni playfully, but Yianni's eyes shift and I get the impression he is biting his jaw down hard, even under the strange smile he's plastered to his face.

I tilt my head and look between the two of them. 'What?'

'Yianni, he says, *Nico, you are being too mutz saying you will take her places. You can't date staff* . . . Blah, blah, blah.' Nico's hands circle around the space near his head as though showing me a reel of words.

Was it really Yianni who warned Nico off me then, and not Hazel after all? Why would he do that?

'Is that why I'm still waiting for that date?' I blurt out.

Their heads whip around to look at me.

Nico grins and throws the glass from the bar in the air again, this time catching it behind his back.

'I am sorry, Ruby. It is not meant to be for us. Yianni say it is so. Don't you, Yianni?'

'I just know what you are like, Nico, and I need the staff.'

I catch sight of a girl sitting taller in her chair, glancing about for someone to call over.

'Yianni,' I say, and nod towards her table. Then he is gone and so is the moment.

When he comes back, it is with a list of drinks. I add them to the bill and Nico tosses glasses before filling them.

Chapter Nineteen

Now

A few different people gather at the bar to stay and chat. Everyone else has left, apart from me, Yianni and Nico.

I'm enjoying being part of the furniture instead of doing nothing at home. There's more enjoyment to making sure every bill and receipt is in order than lying in bed.

It helps that about twenty minutes ago Yianni pushed a beer towards me – and one to Nico too.

The group at the bar are quite drunk, but in a fun and excitable way.

It's the first night of their holiday and, although they'd had every intention of an early night, excitement has taken hold. So, here they are, almost one in the morning, and still sipping tequila.

Nico is doing most of the entertaining, making jokes, being charming, catching flying glasses.

Yianni hovers over me to check the books. I can smell the sweet scent I inhaled on my sheets that first night.

The sheets smell like me now and therefore, to *my* nose at least, of nothing. I've missed inhaling Yianni at night as I close my eyes.

Slowly, I inhale another lungful of him.

The heat from his body is like a radiator. As if it isn't hot enough in Corfu. My thighs keep sticking to the stool as it is, without him making my temperature rise.

Sucking all the air into my lungs to absorb Yianni's scent makes me a little light-headed.

'This all looks good.' Yianni turns to face me.

'Of course. I *have* been doing this sort of stuff longer than you.' I flick the hair from my sticky neck and I'm glad it isn't longer than it is.

'No, no. I'm born and then I'm working for my father. Learning how it all works.'

'Come on, how old were you really?' I fold my arms and jut out my chin, knowing it can't exactly be *that* young.

He bends down and opens the chiller, not far from my feet, then stands up with two more bottles of beer. His eyes focus on a far-off point while he smoothly picks up the bottle opener and pops off both lids, all without looking down.

I gaze towards where his eyes are looking.

It's too dark to see much other than the chairs and tables or the fruit hanging from the trellis.

'Not long after my mother died, I had to learn more . . .' He slides a beer towards me but doesn't meet my gaze.

Anything he wants to say is interrupted by a chorus of *good night, kalinikta, see ya soon, bye, sleep well* among other pleasantries from the gang of smiling holidaymakers who have decided it really *is* time to call it a night now.

Nico moves across the bar towards us and says, 'Now who is cosy?' Half his face pulls into a cheeky smile. 'I am going to Athens Bar. You two coming?'

'I'm in.' I hop off my chair with genuine excitement about being invited somewhere outside of Greek Secret, only to screw my face up at the vibrations running across my foot. '*Putain!*'

'French is such a beautiful language.' Yianni grins, but I can only return a grimace.

Nico slings a tea towel over his shoulder and furrows his brow at us.

'I thought you are English. Where are you from?' Nico's face is so perplexed he almost looks concerned.

'My dad is French. I am English, mostly. I'm from a place called Suffolk. You won't have heard of it, no one ever has.'

'You are wrong.' Nico pulls the towel off his shoulder, picks up a glass and slowly twists the edge around in the towel. 'I knew a girl from there once. Her name is Alice.'

'You remember a girl's name?' Yianni feigns surprise. Nico responds by whipping the towel at him, only missing because Yianni anticipates the movement and pulls away.

'I do have girlfriends, sometimes. There are more than the ones who throw themselves at me.' Nico continues cleaning the already clean glass. 'I'm going to go now. I say I would meet some of the others when they are off work. See you down there?' Nico places the glass back under the bar on the shelf, and the towel neatly on the bar. We both nod and off he goes down the road.

'So, what's left to do before we go?' I'm still clutching the bar and gently letting the blood get used to my foot moving again after a night full of sitting.

'Finish our beers. Lock the doors.'

I reach forward to grab the beer, sipping at the light golden hops.

'You got any spare lime?'

It's as though I've asked for saffron.

Yianni makes a *tss* sound and steps away. He grabs a lime from the bowl of fruit behind the bar.

'Last one.' He shakes his head as though he is disappointed in me before picking up the knife and board that are there for the fruit needed in some cocktails.

The lime also hisses in protest as Yianni cuts into it, and a mist fills the air with its sharp and sweet scent.

Instead of passing me the wedge, he leans forwards and places it in the top of my bottle.

'Who said it was for my drink?' I lower my chin and peep out from the depths of my fringe.

Yianni twists on his heels and his hands slap down on his thighs. 'There is no pleasing some people.'

I shrug and push the lime all the way into the bottle.

Yianni busies himself putting away the remaining lime in the fridge, taking the knife and board to the kitchen, among other tasks. Then he sits himself on the other side of the bar as though he is just another customer, before standing up again, reaching over the bar for his beer and flopping back down.

'How old were you when your mum died?' The question has floated in and out of my mind many times and this time it floats out of my mouth with complete ease.

Yianni smooths his thick hair in his hands, pulling it like he's about to tie it into a low ponytail at the nape of his neck. Then he releases it again, the waves rebounding around his face. He glances at me and answers, 'Eight.'

He takes another swig of beer. Deeper than before.

Tension ripples over his face, as though drinking is suddenly hard work.

'I'm really sorry. I know loss is really hard. I can't imagine being so young and losing your mum.' I think back to the start of his sentence that was left unfinished and add, 'If you ever want to talk about her, you can.'

People pass by the bar, probably heading towards Perros Hotel or Jasmine Hotel. They're quietly laughing as they meander along the road.

Even with the narrow car park at the front, the restaurant is still open to the road. Yianni hops down from his stool, dragging his hand along the wood of the bar as he goes. With a little bit of fiddling, he begins to tug on the bifold doors to lock up the bar area.

'Sorry, if I shouldn't have asked.'

'You lost your job, I lost my mum. It is all in the past.'

I tilt my head and narrow my eyes.

Slowly, he makes his way around the doors, closing us in. I'm still waiting for the laugh, or a hint of irony or something about his comment, because that is an insane comparison.

There's nothing.

'Seriously? You're going to compare me losing my job to you losing your mum? And . . .'

I stop myself.

I've changed my mind about how much I want to divulge, although surely he knows everything about me. But then, I guess I don't really know all that much about him.

Everything I know from Hazel is the crust, but I'm sure there's a whole lot of burning magma underneath that surface. Something about Yianni says that his interior is just waiting, shifting the plates ready for an earthquake.

Unless, of course, I'm projecting my own fears about storing things up on to him. Impossible to say, really.

After falling in on myself as I so often do, I look up. He must have sensed my hesitation or my internal exploration, because he's watching me intently as he makes his way back to the bar.

All he says, though, is, 'Almost finished?' He points towards my bottle.

'Almost.' I lift it and slosh the contents a little, making the lime look like a very poor attempt at a miniature boat in a bottle.

Silence again.

I wonder if he feels awkward in these moments.

I'm hit and miss. Silence doesn't usually make me feel uncomfortable and this one isn't bothering me. But there are times around Yianni when it feels like the tip of my nose is itchy and there is no way to scratch it.

I get too aware of myself and too aware of his good looks.

It was easier when I thought he didn't like me.

Maybe he still doesn't, but he feels bad about my foot and has to be OK with me now from the pull of shame.

'What did you nearly say? Are you going to ask another question about my mother? People often ask questions.'

'They do, but no. I wasn't. She is yours. It's up to you what you want to tell me. It's no one else's business but yours. From how you feel to who you tell.'

His stubbled chin dips in a concise nod. Then he rubs his bottle between the flat palms of his hands, twisting it one way then the other, making a damp mark from condensation on the otherwise clean surface.

'And?' He looks me over.

Releasing the bottle, it's as though he wants to take hold of me instead. He presses his elbows into the bar and balances his slightly square chin on his fists.

'And?' I pout, as though I'm oblivious to anything he might be asking. Because frankly, I am.

'What were you going to say?'

I exhale hard through my nose and my incisors nip at the inside of my cheeks.

'I guess I just assumed Hazel had told you more about me. I know you're not on socials or anything like that. It's not like we've ever properly spoken in the past. It's been, what? Nine? Ten years since your dad and Hazel got married? But Hazel is always giving me those sympathetic looks. She's not subtle. I guess I'm surprised she hasn't said anything. Although I guess she's a bit more like me and she isn't a blab like my mum.'

I take a sip of my drink before looking him right in the eyes. His thick black eyebrows are pulled tightly together. His face is still and perfectly balanced on his fists. Waiting.

I don't really want to, but I feel like I've got no other way out, so I begin to talk. 'I had this boyfriend. We'd been together for years. I always thought he was the one.' I air-quote 'the one', and as I talk, I can feel myself using my hands more than normal.

Maybe if I wave them about enough, Yianni won't notice it's me talking behind them. 'He was an actor. Good-looking, talented. All the clichés. We met in London. Working.'

'And it all fell apart?'

My hands lose all momentum, and so do I.

Yianni removes his chin from his knuckles and glances towards the door. My story is too predictable to hold his attention. He works in a restaurant, and when the food service is done, he works behind the bar, listening to inebriated people tell him every story and problem under the bright Corfiot sun.

He thinks I'm just another woman with baggage. With a boring story about a boring boyfriend.

'Yeah. Something like that.'

'Sorry it didn't work out.'

I twist the ring on my right ring finger under the bar and look down at the golden band and tiny row of stones.

'Yeah,' I say, 'me too.' And I mean it.

Chapter Twenty

Now

I can't shake the feeling of Jonathan.

How things had been between us before there was no more us. The pain of it all.

I make my excuses to Yianni and head off to get my helmet. I have only had two small bottles of beer across the whole evening, and I feel fine to ride my bike home.

I'm not sure if Yianni is disappointed or surprised. His fingers stretch out as though he might catch my arm, but then he thinks twice about it and withdraws his hand.

'Nico will wonder why you have not come for another drink.' There's a playful note in his voice, yet it falls flat. Like it was never there in the first place.

'I'll see him tomorrow.' And with that, I put my helmet on and drive out of the village and up towards the house.

I skim past the now empty restaurants and glowing bars.

As I pass Athens Bar with its low-slung deckchairs and short tables, I catch sight of Nico. His head thrown back in laughter.

Soon, Yianni will be with him. Laughing.

I shouldn't dwell on the past, but sometimes it feels so close. Like things were moments ago, not years.

As the road takes me away from the streetlight, the stars become overwhelmingly distracting. Mesmerising.

Points of light so piercing that calling them diamonds seems ridiculous, because I have never been as consumed by a diamond as I am by the vast array of stars that weigh down the deep navy of the night sky. When I pull into the driveway at the house, I don't want to go inside.

It's a warm evening and I'm not ready to leave the cocoon of the cicadas and the stars – although I could do without the mosquitoes.

I meander into the garden and sit in the dark on a sunlounger. The rhythmic two notes of an owl's call sound not too far from me over the thrum of the cicadas and multitude of other insects.

I watch a satellite skirt the night sky and wonder about Jonathan.

Most days I don't let myself think about him. What's the point?

Everything that could have gone wrong went wrong. I can't go back and change anything.

Wishing it had all worked out differently consumed me for a long time, and when I think about what happened, there's a distinct feeling of suffocating myself. My oesophagus seems to close, in an attempt at holding everything in.

There never seems to be an easy way to move on.

I didn't want to be with him, but I didn't completely stop loving him either.

Emotions aren't like hitting the brakes on a car. There's no sudden stop.

Even when everything ends, the feelings carry on.

Like it or not, it takes time to heal. It doesn't matter if things end well or not. Pain lingers either way.

It doesn't matter whether I'm thinking about the good times or the bad times, it's all like torture. Like I'm having my fingernails pulled out.

Sometimes, I let myself relax into thoughts of the early days, when we were happy. He had a job in a touring theatre company, going round schools. I was so sad I couldn't watch him in that play.

I can't even think what it was now – one of Shakespeare's, but modernised to make it accessible for kids. Oh, that's right. It was *A Midsummer Night's Dream*, of course.

He loved telling me about it on my night off while we ate takeaway pizza and chatted on the floor of his room.

Even that memory stings now, though, since I found out he was sleeping with the girl who played Titania.

I'm glad Yianni didn't press me to talk about Jonathan. There isn't a sensible start point, and certainly no ending I want to talk about.

Yianni. He's like a stone that I keep tripping over. My mind trips on his name. Yianni.

As I hold his name there in the same breath as Jonathan's name, guilt traces spindly fingers along my spine. There is no reason to feel guilty. Not unless it's because Hazel is Yianni's stepmother, or because Yianni is that little bit younger than me, and of course the fact he has shown absolutely no interest in me whatsoever.

Actually, that's not strictly true. He has possibly warned Nico off me and looked almost sad I didn't go with him tonight. That might mean something. And also . . . the way he looked at me for a moment there at the bar.

The door to the house creaks softly open, but it's enough to make me sit bolt upright.

'Ruby?' Hazel's stage whisper cuts through the dark.

'Over here. On the sun lounger,' I return in an equally forced tone.

I scoot along, nearly tipping the whole thing up, but save myself and stand at the last moment before hobbling towards the shadow that is Hazel.

'Why are you on a sun lounger when it's dark?'

I can distinctly hear a sing-song laugh in her voice underneath the whisper and the shroud of night.

'I made the mistake of overthinking.'

'Uh-huh . . .' I know she knows straightaway that I'm overthinking either Jonathan or the loss of my job. 'Do you want to talk about it?' I can see her silhouette clearly. Her head tilts sympathetically.

'I'm OK, really. Why are you up, anyway?'

'I heard the bike pull up, but then I didn't hear the door go. I started to wonder where you'd got to.'

'Shit, I'm so sorry if I woke you.'

Her hand finds my elbow, then slips through the crook of my arm to link hers with mine. Together we walk slowly into the house, and away from the million glaring thoughts shining down at me from the ceiling of the earth.

'Don't be silly. I was still awake.' Hazel gives my arm another little squeeze.

I'm sure this is a lie.

She's as bad as my mum under it all, worrying about people and soaking up their problems the way other people drink water.

That's why I'm here, after all, because she wants to help. Unless July and August change things drastically, or Greek Secret magically gains a swimming pool, there is no way they *need* me at lunch.

In the evening, fine, yes, we get busy, but I'm sure adding me into the lunch rotation was just another layer of Hazel's pity and desire to make everything *right* by distracting me. Maybe she can tell I've been falling more and more into the mist of my own thoughts.

As we step into the kitchen, she switches on the light.

I almost want to shade my eyes against the trio of hanging lights above the table. The glare from their frosted glass is too much after the soft brilliance of the stars.

'Water?' Hazel wrinkles her forehead in question and read-justs her cotton dressing gown while turning towards the cupboard where the glasses live.

I nod. 'Please.'

She turns on the tap, holding her finger under it to check the temperature as she talks.

'How was your night with the boys? I thought you might be back later than this.'

'Yeah, it was OK.' I swallow back my thoughts of Yianni. 'Hazel, how did you go about buying Greek Secret? You own it, right?'

'Pericles owned it before we were married, love. You're better off asking him or Yianni about the details.' She places the water down on the table near me. 'Why do you ask?'

'Just wondering.'

Now I'm *just wondering* why Yianni has to be the one to know everything round here.

'Maybe ask Yianni. He's feeling ever so guilty about your foot, you know.'

'Is he?'

I pull out a chair at the kitchen table and sit down next to my water, pressing the palm of my hand under my fringe and into my forehead.

Letting the weight of my head and my thoughts be supported by my fist and my arm.

Although he has been a little softer with me, Yianni isn't overtly acting as though he feels particularly guilty. He clearly felt sorry at the time, and he has shifted his manner, but he hasn't continued to make a fuss about it.

Unless he has conveyed something to Hazel that I don't know about.

'Maybe on Monday he can take you somewhere to say sorry. Maybe a trip to somewhere you'd like to see. I think it might do you both some good to take a day off.'

'How? I mean, one of us taking the day off, maybe, but both?'

'I'm sure I can find someone for a day, don't you worry.'

I pull my feet back from under the table, pick up my glass of water and stand in front of Hazel.

'Honestly, Hazel, I think you might be overestimating how guilty Yianni feels. And really, he has nothing to feel guilty about. It was an accident. My foot's a lot better today, just tender, really.'

'We can talk about it tomorrow. Right, you should get off to bed. Goodnight.' And with that, she leans forward to kiss my cheek. Her night cream smells of lavender, just like my mum's.

A pang of longing for the comfort of my mum passes through me like the striking of a chime.

I have enjoyed being here though. I've always looked up to my Aunt Hazel since I was a kid, and spending time with her now is making me realise how I've been holding back from my mum, even when we're together. She's been holding on to me too tightly, trying too hard to smile, and it's left me being distant. I was actually surprised when she said coming here would be good for me. I'm glad she did support this. She knows me better than I know myself.

'Night, Hazel.' I quickly depart the kitchen, taking my water with me.

Hazel calls after me quietly, 'Sleep well. I'm always here if you need me.'

Chapter Twenty One

Now

Apparently, Yianni *does* want to take me out.

Either that, or Hazel talked him into wanting to take me out.

I text this news to Amara; I'm not sure why. Maybe I want her to think I'm having a good time and not isolating myself completely.

I know she thinks that's the case, and it's been hard to deny.

Before Monday lands at my feet, I muddle along at work, which involves another day of me sitting and doing the till before I'm on my feet more. My foot's still badly bruised and standing on it for too long makes it swell up a little.

I think it is more to do with the heat than anything. My body is used to standing about for work, but not normally in sweltering heat that exceeds that of a normal kitchen.

I haven't actually worked inside the heat of the kitchen for quite some years. Only walking in and out of them, organising.

I did a stint as a commis chef many years ago to try it out. Same as I have with every role hospitality has to offer. All in my attempt to understand every minute detail of how a restaurant works and runs when the kitchen and front-of-house teams are in perfect harmony.

It's Sunday evening, and things are starting to quieten down.

I nestle myself in a corner table with a plate of food, away from the people still finishing their meals. There is a real selection on my plate.

I wonder what I'll eat tomorrow with Yianni.

Apprehension niggles as I take my first bite of Hazel's garlic-laden tzatziki.

The screen of my phone lights up.

Amara's face flashes up on the screen. She's there, with Rob and me from a night out years ago, arms around each other's necks. We all look so young and carefree.

It feels like a lifetime ago. I barely recognise myself now.

Rob introduced me to Amara when we were all working in London. They're still friends, but I'd say I'm closer to them both. Amara moved to Suffolk before me and got me and Jonathan our jobs when we first moved back.

'Hey you,' I smile as I press the phone to my face. 'How's pretend married life going?'

'Urgh. It's all gone to shit and I nearly kicked him out.' Amara exhales. I can hear the banging of things in the background of our call.

'Are you still at work?' I ask, before taking a mouthful of my tender pork chop.

'Yep. It's been so quiet though. Good ol' Charles said I could knock off early. Thank God.'

I swallow my food, wishing I could enjoy the tang from the garlic, mint and dill in the tzatziki for a moment longer, but I need to open my mouth to ask questions.

'Last time we spoke, you two were all loved up. What the hell happened?'

'What? Me and Charles?'

'No, you fool, not Charles. Yuck! You and Si.'

I balance the phone between my shoulder and my ear so I can devour the rest of my meal – the pile of salty purple olives and the entirety of the chop – as Amara explains that Si has just started to get on her last nerve.

He leaves his socks all over the place and wants to play on his Xbox a little too much.

'None of this sounds like a reason to end a good thing. These are little niggles you've had before. Am I missing something?'

'Well, I haven't ended it. I threatened it, that's all. I just can't be bothered with him messing everything up all the time. You know? Didn't you ever feel like that with Jonathan? It can't have always been perfect.'

I know she isn't trying to be inconsiderate, and I don't want to become overly sensitive, but I've just taken a bite of pitta piled with feta and swallowing now feels like I'm trying to gulp down a balloon.

'No, it wasn't perfect, and you more than anyone know that very well. We argued, mostly about money and the future. But it was a very different situation.'

I've never gone into detail even with Amara about my internal turmoil around Jonathan.

How it took me so long to see the pattern. The ridge formed by manipulation. I'd slipped off it and deep down into a gully.

How there was never any obvious abuse; in fact, I'm loath to think of it as abuse, more that the relationship soured over time.

He soured.

He became too possessive, too controlling. Too selfish.

I change the phone from my left ear to my right.

My appetite is completely diminished, which is good, as I'm also full and that will stop me eyeing up a bowl of ice cream. I'm still impressed at how I'm now completely full and utterly empty, simultaneously.

I suppose because one is physical and the other is emotional.

Amara is apologising, agreeing, talking over herself, stopping and starting and restarting sentences.

'Let's change the subject.' I push my plate away from me. 'Are you outside now?'

'Uh huh. Now heading to my car. Are you excited about the date tomorrow? What are you doing again?'

'Please stop calling it that. He is a step away from being my cousin.'

'He isn't your cousin though. He is no relation at all, and he is taking you for a full day of just the two of you. Sounds like a damn date to me.'

'I have to get back to work. Unlike some, there's no getting out early for me. Keep me updated about you and Si, OK?'

'Shall do. Have a nice date.'

'Night.'

I relax back into my chair.

People are enjoying their food in a dreamy Greek setting. The restaurant is just the right balance of authentic and holiday cliché, with everyone sitting in the shade of the grapevines.

The room is starting to empty. There's a hum like the background sound of the cicadas, only this is the consistent murmur of human interaction – people sharing stories, food, drinks and excitement for the rest of their time on the island. Traditional Greek music plays underneath it all.

I turn my head sharply to the bar. I want to check if it's busy, if I need to hurry up with my dinner.

Instead, I catch Yianni watching me. I caught him just before he managed to avert his eyes.

He just wasn't quite quick enough.

A smile touches my lips, knowing he was watching me.

Chapter Twenty Two

Then

The sun warms my soul.

Jonathan was right. We need this, and it's so well worth eating into my restaurant savings for.

Celebrating our three-year anniversary with our first holiday was such a good idea of his.

Plus, the last-minute deal to Fuengirola in Spain means loads of sea swimming, which is my absolute favourite pastime and something I rarely get to do, living so far from the sea. I spend all my time in swimming pools back home instead. I was going to join a group, but we couldn't really afford it.

It feels like ages since it's been worth putting a bikini on, let alone lying in the sun.

'You look so good in that.' Jonathan's fingertip skims a line along my stomach down to my navel to touch the edge of my white bikini bottoms.

My eyes are shut, with the sun streaming down on my face making my skin tingle and my freckles burst into life.

Bringing my hand over my eyes, I open one a crack to find Jonathan leaning on one elbow on the sand, watching me.

'You look good too. But we're on a crowded beach, so no getting any ideas. In fact, I'm going in for a swim.'

Reaching over, I press a kiss firmly on his mouth. 'Are you coming in, or staying here?'

'I think I'll work on my tan. My agent said if I can get brown enough, there's an audition next week for some ancient Greek retelling thing.' He lies back on his towel and closes his eyes as I grab for my goggles.

I wouldn't tell him, but I'm glad to go in on my own. I'm a much stronger swimmer than Jonathan, and I like to swim properly, rather than play at it.

Bounding into the sea, I get out as far as I need to, to get deep enough for a good swim without catching my legs on the seabed.

Placing my goggles over my eyes, I set off, cutting through the waves and parting the water with the determination of an arrow.

I pass people and fish and a whole host of life living their own ways. I'm just here in passing. An extra in their show as they are an extra in mine.

I've clearly spent a lot of time with actors, with thoughts like that.

When we do manage to socialise, it often needs to be with associates of Jonathan's, to help get his name and face well known in the right circles. He always reminds me, it's not what you know, it's who you know.

The sea ahead looks clear, so I switch to a backstroke, squinting against the sun until I have to close my eyes.

My hand slaps down on something with a crack. I curl myself in to spin in the water and find out who or what I've hit.

A tall man with a thick black beard and tattooed arms – he has to be tall, because my feet can't touch the seabed but he seems to be happily standing – clutches his head.

'I'm so sorry, did I hit you?'

'A wee bit. Don't worry yourself. First I was nipped by a crab, now I've been hit by a beautiful siren. I think it's high time to get out of the water.'

'Don't leave on my account.'

A wave jostles me forward. Without any footing, and with him standing firmly, I knock straight into him again.

'God, I'm so sorry.' I do my best to swim away a little.

'If you're trying to be rid of me, you just have to say.'

I can feel my skin running cold under the water with embarrassment, laced with a tiny bit of fear.

'I best head back in myself.' I look over towards Jonathan. He's sitting up, watching us.

He can get a little jealous of other men talking to me. More protective, I guess.

A few months ago, two men were in the pub and one asked for my number. I thought Jonathan might ask Motka if he could kick them out. It was a little embarrassing.

'I'll come with you. How long are you here for?' The man's Scottish accent rolls over the 'R' beautifully. I've always liked listening to accents, just not right now.

Right now, I wish this kindly man, who I've hit twice, would leave me to escape.

'Only a week.'

'Same as me. Maybe I'll see you around for a drink? I'm here with my mother – she's not been too well.'

Jonathan's up and strolling across the sand towards us. He's still a way off as I've swum quite far, backwards and forwards.

When my toes latch on to some sand, I'm ready to run out of the sea, but this broad man is being so sweet and chatty I don't want to be rude to him. Nor do I want Jonathan to be rude to him.

'I'm so sorry to hear about your mother. Sadly, I don't think my boyfriend would like me going for a drink with a tall dark stranger.'

'You missed off handsome.' The man winks at me and it's hard not to throw him a laugh. 'I understand. How could a girl looking like you not have a boyfriend, eh? Have a nice holiday.'

The waves push us forward at a quicker pace, which I'm glad of. The Scottish man's long legs stride over the now shallow waves and off in the opposite direction.

My heart is pounding in my chest like one of those Celtic drums, a bodhrán.

By the time my feet hit the dry, powdery sand, Jonathan is there waiting for me. There's a smile glancing over his lips, but it isn't a deep, beaming smile, and I can't see his eyes behind his reflective sunglasses.

'You all right? What was he talking about?'

'Nothing. Poor guy, I accidentally hit him twice. When you're that big, you're a bit of an easy target for these things, I guess.' My laugh hits an unnatural tone that sounds nothing like me.

Jonathan hums in acknowledgement as he steps back, crushing one of the hand-made sandcastles lining the shore.

'He was just a bit chatty; his mum's sick or something. Maybe he felt lonely.'

Another hum, more of an *uh huh*, stays in his throat as he walks back along the beach, moving past sun loungers.

'You know I love you, right? Jonathan?'

'I know. I just don't think chatting to *lonely men* while you're half naked is going to give them the right idea. The way men's minds work . . .'

I swallow hard. Why did I mention the lonely part?

'Oh yeah?' I do my best to laugh it off. 'Is that how your mind works? You can't chat to a girl on a beach without getting ideas?'

'That's not what I said. *Some guys.* That's all. *Some guys.* I didn't like the way he was staring at you either. I'm protective, that's all.'

I catch Jonathan's hand, and he turns to face me.

'Please don't let some random guy upset you.'

'I'm not upset. I'm just looking out for my girl.'

Jonathan encases me in his arms. I press my cheek to his naked shoulder and relief rolls along my skin, from my toes to the tip of my nose.

It was me. I was overreacting. Worrying over absolutely nothing. Jonathan was just looking after me, that's all.

Chapter
Twenty Three

Now

Stuffing my black leather backpack with anything and everything I can think of, I dart downstairs.

Even with my mixed feelings about the day ahead with Yianni, I actually managed to get some rest last night.

I'm no sooner at the bottom of the stairs when his car pulls up.

I feel like a teenager again, back when I didn't want to introduce my date to my dad, so I'd run outside and jump in their car as fast as I could.

The difference is, this is Pericles' son, Aunt Hazel's stepson. He is seen as my cousin. My family.

I'm grateful that at least he doesn't call Hazel *Mum*. It is always *Hazel*. Always.

As I pass through the kitchen, I wash the room with pleasantries and manoeuvre around the chairs. Pericles makes it to the door first and swings it open before I can get there.

Yianni's casually walking towards the house. He doesn't seem the least bit awkward or abashed. He comes in and kisses everyone's cheeks, including mine.

In French, it is called *la bise*. The two bland kisses, one to each cheek, as robotic and unwavering as a handshake or even just a verbal *hello*.

He isn't looking at me or talking to me. It calms me.

He isn't chasing me. Instead, he's saying something to Natalia, his half-sister. My cousin. I need to keep repeating this because the stupidity inside me isn't going anywhere.

'No, sorry, little one.'

I had tuned out the conversation by accident, and instead I was focusing on my own thoughts.

I really need to stop doing that.

'Ruby wouldn't mind. Would you, Ruby?'

My mouth drops open, hoping to find an answer to an unknown question. Luckily, Hazel saves me.

'You still have to work, Natalia. Perhaps you can show Ruby around more places another day.' Hazel lifts her eyebrows high above the frames of her glasses.

Without words, her body language shifts and she manages to hurry us out of the door seamlessly. She's so much like Mum sometimes.

Only once my bum makes it on to the seat of Yianni's car do I ask what on earth we are going to be doing.

'Well,' he begins, 'I am surprised not to have you ask me this sooner.'

Momentarily, he falls silent as he turns the car around, shunting it a little forwards, a little backwards, until it's facing the right way, forcing me wait even longer to know.

He's right though. I could've asked at work, pushed him more. I asked once and he replied with *I'm not sure yet*, and I left it at that.

'Well,' he starts over, 'I asked Hazel what you have been doing. In the mornings. And what you like to do. She tells me that before you hurt your foot, you went swimming, so I went to speak to a good friend and I have hired us a boat.'

I'm not sure what to say.

There's a tickle inside of me at the thought that he's actually gone to the trouble of asking a question about me. Maybe he really does feel guilty about my foot. Before I can formulate a response, he continues, 'How is your foot now?'

I shrug. 'A lot better than it was. I'm not sure if I should go swimming yet though.'

He makes a sound like opening a can by way of disagreement. 'The sea will keep it clean and heal the bruises. You'll be fine.'

It's not long until we're parked on the beach.

People are already in rows on beach beds. One whole row is nothing but bodies with open books for faces.

In my limited experience of being in San Stefanos so far, that view means the weather will be uncomfortably hot. It'll be hot and muggy.

The line between the sea and the sky is almost invisible. It's a cornflower-blue haze that ripples between the two.

Lines are blurred.

Everything is one and the same now.

After a brief – almost non-existent – introduction to Yianni's friend, who has other people waiting for boats, he points us towards a small white one with a thin aqua-blue line running all the way around the hull.

Poles support a matching blue awning that shades about half of the boat from the sun. The boat is barely even bobbing.

The air is still and so is the water. It gently caresses the sand, lapping slowly at our toes. There is no sign of angry froth or foam, only the sensation of comfort.

Following Yianni, I remove my bag from my back, tossing it on deck along with my flip-flops, and climb aboard.

Yianni starts the engine, and we pull away towards the haze. The air rushes past, making my short hair sauté and pirouette around my face.

My fingers skim the surface of the water, which is so clear I can see the stones, fish and shapes on the seabed. Then I turn my attention to the island – Corfu Island – while my fingers continue bouncing and gliding along like a fin in the sea.

To my side, jutting rocks with layers of trees carpet every available surface. Then there are the surfaces that have been stolen from nature but are somehow just as beautiful. Some are whitewashed buildings, others are pale yellow with sunshine-coloured doors.

My favourites have traditional blue doors and look like they were made to be photographed for postcards.

All have flat roofs and windows that are like eyes looking out to sea, watching boats go by. Watching us, as we're watching them. Or I do, anyway; Yianni is looking where he is going.

I break my eye contact with the shore and gaze at him.

He continues to look straight ahead.

His hair, much longer than mine, dances even more wildly around my face. I don't know how he knows I'm looking at him, but it's as though it has initiated a cue for him to speak to me.

'Do you know why Greeks call Corfu Kerkyra?'

I shake my head and edge round to face him more, gently lifting and lowering the ring on my right hand with my thumb as I wait to find out the answer.

'Kerkyra was a nymph. Poseidon fell in love with her, and they had many children called Phaeacians, who were accomplished sailors. These sailors, they helped Odysseus on his journey to Ithaka, but there was a shipwreck and Odysseus turned up at Palaiokastritsa, not far from here. He was then gifted a boat, but Poseidon, he was angry at him and turned it to stone.'

'Why was Poseidon angry with Odysseus? What had he done to annoy him?'

'I forget this part.' Yianni shrugs and a brief smile crosses his lips as he lifts his arm to sweep his hair back to one side.

I take a deep lungful of the salty air and bite my lip at the view, which now also contains Yianni.

His muscular frame beneath his clothing . . . I really need to stop having these thoughts.

I have an urge to put my head underwater and scream at the fish, but instead I turn away to watch the cliffs and coves gliding past.

'Corfu is also where Heracles partied with Melite and – what do you English say? – knocked her up.'

I slowly turn my head back to look at Yianni. He has a grin plastered on his face.

When he said *knocked her up*, he had put on his best cockney accent. He has never been silly like this with me before. I've seen him laugh and joke with Nico and Natalia, but not really with me.

Delayed laughter splutters from my lips.

'What? These are the most random Greek myths I have ever heard. Are you just making them up?'

'Maybe. I was not so much interested in Greek history at school.'

'Natalia said the same thing.'

The mention of his sister's name brings softness to his face.

It's so long since I've had fun with someone of the opposite sex. I feel like I missed out on dating in my early twenties.

At first, spending time with Jonathan had been *fun*, but I look back and feel like I didn't go on adventures, all for the promise of a future that would be full of it. A future that only happened in our imaginations.

Yianni didn't make a big declaration of fun and adventure.

Yet here we are. Sailing off into the unknown.

More than I expected to, and more than I want to, I feel completely relaxed in Yianni's company.

Chapter Twenty Four

Now

We carry on skirting the island. Fawn-and-cream-coloured cliff edges bite down into the sea most of the way along.

The salts and the shingle have dug away small alcoves, caves and notches over time, as well as bays.

Squinting, I try to see into the darkness of one or two caves. They look magical enough to believe there is treasure hiding in there.

Our boat buzzes along now, cutting through the water, which protests with a rhythmic *ch-ch-ch* underneath us.

Since Hazel and Pericles' wedding in Corfu, I had only made it as far as Spain – most of my money had gone on rent and not on holidays abroad.

I have never hired a boat before.

I can taste the fine salt spray tracing my lips, and it tastes a lot like freedom.

The boat comes to a gentle stop and Yianni nods towards the beach, perhaps fifty or so metres away. 'Paradise Beach.' His dark eyes hold the view of the shore. 'Locals call it Chomoi.'

The sand is so white I have to squint to look at it, and the rippling water around us as clear as glass.

In fact, even with ripples it is clearer than the glass in my bathroom mirror.

Fish are darting about, some almost looking like they are nibbling at the hull.

'This is as far as we go. The rest of the way, we swim.' He hesitates. I haven't really seen him hesitate before. 'If . . . if you want to. If not, we can keep moving.'

I shrug, smiling over at him before thinking about all our belongings on the boat.

'What about the bags?' I point at the two bags and the shoes under the awning, but when I look up, Yianni is already unbuttoning his shirt to reveal his firm, almost hair-free chest. It's the richest gold tan I've ever seen, as though his skin has been painted in a dark brandy. 'So, leave them here then, I guess.'

'It is up to you. I need a swim, either way.'

He turns to face me, steps backwards on to the edge of the boat and, holding his body completely rigid, lets himself fall backwards into the sea.

The whole boat rocks and it's as though a bucket of water has been thrown in my direction.

Even though I turned my face at the last possible moment – if I could have believed what he was doing, I might have looked away sooner – water still slaps along my ear and my chest.

After the initial gasp that automatically shoots into my chest, I mutter, 'You shit,' and start pulling my celadon-green smock over my head. I'm wearing a much darker green swimsuit underneath, with high legs and cut-out sides. It's my favourite.

I don't wear bikinis any more. I have this, a plain black one and one with flamingos all over it that my mum got me before I left.

Without even thinking to tie my hair into its usual little pony-tail, or considering my make-up, I dive in after Yianni. Skimming along the sea, not down into it.

It isn't really deep enough for that. Or maybe it is.

These things can be so deceptive that I wasn't going to risk it. Instead, my aim now is to catch up with Yianni, who, after his insane backwards fall into the sea, has started swimming to shore. He is dawdling, though, and swimming is one of my favourite things to do. Not that I have had much opportunity in the past few years. Sometimes I get up early in the summer and force myself into the freezing sea at Felixstowe. At home, it's more a game of sprinting in and swimming as fast as humanly possible. Here, it's a pleasure – other than today, as now I want to prove some pointless point to Yianni.

Even as I edge towards him, I wonder what the point is. But somewhere deep inside me there is a naughty little laugh wanting to escape, as though getting ahead of him is the funniest thing in the world.

Soon, it's too shallow to kick, but I'm ahead and smiling to myself. As water drips off the tip of my nose, I desperately want to touch my face, wipe it away. But I can't.

The tingle of the saltwater makes me feel fresh and clean, other than on my face, which is itching underneath my foundation. Of course – I have put on concealing make-up that holds up against sweat and splashing, but I've never tried it fully submerged in the sea before.

There's nothing I can do now though. If my scars are on show, so be it.

He's a bloke, and not just any bloke, but Yianni. He likely won't notice and, even if he does, what's it to him? I know deep down it's nothing to anyone but me. Even if the thought of people looking at them makes my heart beat harder in my chest.

My fingers rake the ends of my hair and my fringe press like limp seaweed on my forehead. Wet strands of hair saturated with saltwater weigh on my skin, hopefully covering the scar there.

All this thinking has wiped the smile from my face and washed it away, and I wish I could sink back into the water and swim away from myself.

As long as I don't touch my face, it'll probably be fine.

I need to stop thinking.

As I make my way out of the shallows, the hot sand sticks to my feet in clumps like powdered sugar on butter. The sticky strips holding my foot together are allowing my body to form yet another scar inflicted by someone else.

My flesh is safely working its healing magic under the wrap provided at the health centre. I'm unsure how much longer the bandage will last, though.

It's almost time to expose the wound to the world now anyway. To give it fresh air to heal more quickly.

I turn to Yianni, who is equally caked in pale, sugary sand.

'Now what?' I say, my hands gripping my hips.

The sun is steaming the water from Yianni's body, leaving it glittering with lines of fine white salt crystals.

'We swim?' He takes a breath then continues. 'There are' – he waves his hand in front of his face – 'snorkels in the boat. Or we can relax on the beach. Hazel says I should treat you like you are on holiday. This is what people on holiday do.'

He's right.

If my phone hadn't been on the boat, I would have been taking a photo and sending it to everyone I know back home, just to show them how gorgeous it all is. It's no wonder it has the nickname of Paradise Beach.

'Well, do you want to swim, or stay on the beach? Or I can take you somewhere less beautiful in the boat.' He smiles at me. Straight white teeth, definitely from braces. Surely no one is born with such perfect teeth.

Yianni pushes back his black waves, which are dripping on to his shoulders, and squeezes water from them.

'Your hair is actually a lot longer than I thought.'

Turning back to me, he throws his head forward and then, much like a mermaid might, he whips it back, making a stream of water droplets dive from the tip of each strand of hair.

He then poses like a model, poking out his bottom lip a little too far and looking off into the distance through lightly squinting eyes. Not a good model, though. It's exceptionally exaggerated. I think the look is meant to be smouldering, but it's overtly camp instead.

'Do you like it?' he says, still posing like a statue.

Laughter that I've been storing up inside me since he fell off the boat rolls out, tickling my sides as it flows up from low in my abdomen. 'Very nice. You're the perfect gay icon.'

His body relaxes back into its normal frame. 'I take that as a compliment. Gay men always have good taste, no?' He winks at me, a super-cheesy wink.

My forehead wrinkles, but laughter is still slipping off my tongue. 'Who even are you and what have you done with the miserable sod I work with?'

I stomp past him into the sea. It's late in the morning now and there isn't enough breeze to be standing around under the full power of the sun. I need the relief of the sea to cool me off.

Yianni follows me and keeps pace. He is making some kind of *uh-uh-uh* sound.

I'm not looking at him, but I imagine he is shaking his head. I release my body back to the sea, where I'm sure it belongs. It's only deep enough that it comes up to my neck while sitting though. But it feels like cool silk on my burning skin.

'I am no *miserable sod*. I just like to get my work done. I am hard-working, this is all.' His fingers curl around the words *miserable sod*, as well as exaggerating them verbally.

'Maybe it's just me then. You've been better since smashing that thick milkshake glass on my foot, but before that I felt like you were avoiding me. At best.'

Yianni flops down opposite me in the water, so he is facing out to sea.

There's a pause.

His hairy knees poke out above the water and he wraps his arms loosely around them, with his fingers linked together, to hold everything in place.

I'm more free, leaning my weight back on my hands and letting the slow rocking of the sea do what it wants with me. This is how I want to be. How I've always wanted to be.

'Yes, I will admit. I'm not a fan of these overly pretty girls who don't eat food. Their minds are only on the next photo for Instagram.' My eyebrows lift so quickly I can feel the hair that was stuck to my forehead abruptly peel off. 'This is who I thought you are at the airport. I come out and there you are looking at your phone, not seeing me. Living in some daydream. Not thinking that *your* name on paper could mean *you*. Now I think maybe I'm wrong. Maybe I judged you too soon.'

'Are you saying you thought I was pretty and now maybe you don't?'

'Yes. This is exactly what I meant. I am glad I made myself clear.'

'It's the scar, isn't it?'

His face changes and the joke and laughter jar to a stop.

I don't even know why I said it.

129

That unconscious self-doubt crept out into the open and mocked itself publicly.

I suppose because the past is always there in the back of my head. Lurking. Never wanting me to fully let go. Never letting me relax with someone I might like. Not that I want to like Yianni, but he's making it almost impossible not to today.

'What scar?' His head tilts and his eyes narrow on me.

I shift and mirror his body language, pulling myself in and wrapping my arms around my knees then habitually pulling at the ring on my right hand. Slipping it up and down, twirling it around.

When I don't answer, Yianni asks again, 'What scar? The one on your foot? I am sorry. I do feel bad for hurting you.'

'No. I'm being silly. I'm just not used to you being so friendly.'

'Do not get used to it.' He laughs and, in one quick motion, flicks water at my face. My jaw drops open.

'You're such a shit, Yianni.' I don't mean it, of course. It is obvious to anyone that I'm laughing under my words. 'And, I'll have you know, the first time I saw you, you were looking at your phone. So, who is addicted to their screen *really*?'

'I was checking my messages from Hazel. It's a big shame you couldn't do the same.'

I press my lips tightly shut. There's not much I can say to that.

'And, Ruby, you are wrong. That is not the first time you saw me. The first time was the morning before my baba and Hazel were married. You came to our old house with your mother and father, and we all had drinks and English biscuits.' He looks past me towards the boat, then back to look me in the eye. 'You drank tea.'

'I'm sorry.' I don't want to be sorry, so I continue searching the files of memories in my mind. 'I don't remember that at all.'

'You spent a lot of time on your phone. Your hair was long and dark.'

Any skin that's not submerged burns in the sun overhead, or that's how it feels, because it seems like Yianni hasn't blinked in a while.

Maybe he has, but there's something so intense about this memory that he's projecting on to me. Intense for him, it seems, anyway. I can barely remember being in their house. And he is younger than me.

He was the kid.

'I can't believe you remember all that, and I don't.'

'I'm Greek. I remember everything. It was a long time ago,' he shrugs. 'Would you like to snorkel?'

Of course, the answer is yes.

We spend the next hour snorkelling, watching fish of different shapes and sizes. It's so peaceful – even though there's a handful of other people on the beach and in their boats, or like us in the water, it's still like no one else is around.

At times, it's almost like being completely alone with the sea. The difference is the comfort of knowing Yianni *is* here, experiencing it all alongside me.

He is here completely for me. He made this happen.

I haven't had that feeling since Jonathan. And even then, it felt different to this.

With Jonathan, it was always the other way around. I felt like I was there for him. I was the warm-up act and he was the main attraction.

The thought settles somewhere in the depths of my head.

It's something I normally get a tinge of guilt for thinking, but today I don't.

I let myself be consumed by the sea and all its beauty and wonder . . . And, Yianni.

Chapter Twenty Five

Now

It's only when it feels as though hungry fingers are grabbing hold of my stomach that we get back on the boat.

There's nothing much on Paradise Beach.

Yianni explained to me while we were bobbing about in the water that people are warned not to walk on the beach. Those who do, do so at their own risk, as stones and rocks often fall down from the cliff face that lines the narrow strip of sand.

If it hadn't been for this piece of information, I might have gone exploring in some of the little alcoves on the beach, but it doesn't seem like the smartest idea, given the facts. My foot injury is enough to last me for a little while.

'We can sail somewhere else for lunch, or . . .' Yianni reaches behind where I'm sitting and taps something with his open palm. I turn to see a cool box.

'Ohh!' My eyes grow wide and Yianni playfully sniggers at my reaction before standing to pick up the box and place it in front of us. 'I asked my friend to stock it for us.'

Pulling off the lid, his hand disappears into the box and comes back out with two bottles of Corfu beer. This is met with applause *and* a small cheer from me. I gladly take a bottle of beer from him, then put it down to dig into my own bag.

'Ah ha!' I pull out my keys, which are actually Pericles' keys for the bike and the house on one key ring.

Yianni reaches out to touch the key ring briefly. 'I got this for my mother on a school trip many years ago.'

It's a flip-flop that doubles as a bottle opener on a key ring.

I use it to open my bottle and then pass it to Yianni.

He runs his thumb along the shiny surface of the flip-flop before using it to open his bottle with a hiss, then he carefully hands it back. I give it one last look with a new interest, before placing it more carefully back in my bag.

'Nice that you got your mum such a useful gift.'

'The trip was on her name day. We are big on name days here. I do not know if you know this. We do name days and not so much birthdays.'

I nod. I'm aware because of Natalia. She likes to celebrate both and when she was very small, visiting us in England, she liked to tell me about how important her name day was.

'I had got her something already, but on the trip I wanted to get her another gift. I see this' – he points towards my bag – 'and it's the only thing she might like. I used the money Baba gave me for lunch to get it for her.'

'So, it turns out you're a thoughtful one when you want to be.'

He doesn't respond. Instead, his hand dives back into the cool box to pull out more items – a small loaf of bread, a tub of tzatziki, a tub of another dip that I don't recognise, and a big bag of crisps.

'We can eat on the boat, or I can take us somewhere.'

'Here's good.' I slap my hands on to my thighs and my cheeks are painfully tense from grinning.

Yianni passes me bread and we rip off small corners to dip into the pots.

'How come you and your dad never come to England with Aunt Hazel and Natalia?' It's a question I've been storing up. I have lots of them. Mostly about the restaurant, but there should be plenty of time for that. This is the only time without anyone nearby that I can find out the real dynamics.

'It's not cheap coming over to England, and it's not really how I like to spend my winter.'

'How do you spend winter here? Is there much to do?'

Yianni shrugs and scoops out more dip. 'Yes and no. I like to see my friends, go running. I prefer to spend time with Baba. Just the two of us.' This doesn't surprise me. He might not like sharing his father. 'I'd like to travel, but I've been doing things to Greek Secret at the end of the summers to make it better for the next season. The restaurant does well. It is doing better now I am taking over and changing things. But we only make money half of the year. Money is also being saved for Natalia to go to university in England.'

'Did you always want to work in Greek Secret?'

'No, when I was a kid I wanted to work like every kid does. As a superhero. Then I thought more sensibly and decided that one day I should be a rap star.'

I can't help but laugh at the idea of Yianni rapping and ending with a mic drop. 'And how did that work out for you?'

'Great! I'm a famous rap star in New York, I come here for people not to know me.' He raises an eyebrow before swigging more beer.

'OK, OK. It was a stupid question—'

'There are no stupid questions.'

I make a noise of disagreement through my nose.

'Better to be with questions than to be . . . how would you say it? . . . to be without wonder.'

'I like that.'

I spend most of my days blocked up with questions, but seeing them as wonder sounds so much better.

The boat gently rocks as we both sip our drinks and sea birds call overhead.

'As there are no stupid questions, I have another. How well do you get on with Hazel? She's been in your life for a long time now.'

'She has. No one can replace my mother, but I'm glad for my baba to find love. All of us need love. It's part of what makes us human.'

'And what about you?'

'Me?'

A small shot of adrenaline strikes me in the chest. The question fell unintentionally from my lips.

'Not love, I mean. After the rap star dreams were killed off' – I cough to give myself space to recover – 'did you go to uni?'

Yianni eyes me as he slowly tears off more bread.

'Yeah. I studied business in Athens. You?'

'Same, business studies. Not in Athens though.'

'No, your Greek is . . . not so good. How long have you been working in bars?'

'How do you know my Greek isn't so good?'

'*An boreís na to kataláveis aftó. Syngnómi.*'

I study his face before saying, 'I forgive you.'

Yianni almost spits out the bread he has just put in his mouth.

His eyebrows shoot upwards, and he searches my face for answers. There's no way I can suppress the giggle a moment longer, so I let it all out.

'All I understood was *sorry. Syngnómi.*'

His entire body relaxes now he is safe in the knowledge that I truly don't speak Greek, and anything he has said in Greek near me has indeed gone over my head.

'To answer your question . . .' Yianni gives me a confused look before the memory of asking me a question slaps him round the face and makes him nod. 'All my life I've worked in hospitality, one way or the other. Cafés, bars, restaurants, pubs, tavernas.'

As I say the last one, half my face twists into a smile, which he catches and mirrors back at me before I continue, 'I've always wanted to own my own restaurant. To run it how I want and put the food I want on the menu. Every time I've saved some money towards my dream, I've had to spend it. Rent, Christmas . . . a new car.' I take a sip of my beer. The liquid is quickly warming up, even though it's in the shade. 'You know, I've only ever told two people that.'

'I am honoured.'

'Please don't tell Hazel.'

'You are safe with me.'

There is peace in the air, a calm where the only sounds are tiny creaks from the boat, a wild goat occasionally bleating near the edge of the cliff.

Just as the haze over the sea isn't letting up, cocooning everything, mist fogs my brain.

Yianni's words linger in the thick air that rests heavy between us.

Before I let myself get trapped in the idea of him and what it might be like to have his lips on mine, I find questions to keep my mind from slipping away with him.

'What about you? Are you happy? Do you have dreams of somewhere that isn't Corfu?'

'No. I would like to travel more, but when your home is this' – he gestures towards the cliffs and out to sea with his bottle – 'then there is no reason to find a new one.'

I agree. Who wouldn't want to live here? It's paradise, for God's sake.

Even though I miss my family and my friends back home, Corfu is already holding me tightly in her grasp. As though the lush greenery is growing over me and pulling me into it.

Without thinking, I let my fingers glide through my hair, momentarily pushing the hair off my face before the sticky, salted strands fall back down, and I sip at the last of my beer.

Yianni's hand meets my face.

At first I recoil, yanking the bottle from my lips to glare at him.

He lifts his eyebrows gently at me. There is a softness about his face that makes mine relax too.

I let him push the hair away from my forehead again.

My throat becomes unbelievably dry, and I can't swallow; there seems to be nothing left to swallow. No air to breathe. Nothing.

His index finger traces down my right eyebrow, sliding along my cheekbone, and comes to rest along with his thumb on my chin. Carefully, he lifts my face towards the sun.

'This is the scar you meant, *nai*?'

Chapter Twenty Six

Now

'Yeah.' My voice is a gravelly whisper. 'It was the scar I meant.'

My pulse is raging, but I manage to maintain a steady breath.

I don't want Yianni to know that the combination of his fingers on my skin and the revelation of my scar under the pressure of his gaze are causing me to tip over into somewhere I don't want to go.

A small rock tumbles down the edge of the nearby cliff, and I feel like my heart's gone with it. Out of control, with gravity pulling it away from everything it knows.

Yianni's eyes meet mine and he releases me from his gentle grip. I take a deep breath and it catches in my chest, the way it might if I'd spent the last hour crying instead of swimming.

'How did it happen?'

I lick my lips and snatch my eyes back to a piece of bread. It's already curling in the heat, but I press it into the last of the tzatziki anyway and thrust it into my mouth.

I answer through my mouthful. 'Car accident.'

I look at Yianni. Waiting for the usual concerned look. It's there, of course. His brows are furrowed and he's now leaning a little closer to me.

He's not concerned – he hasn't been able to make out what I said. His body contracts slightly to indicate his lack of comprehension.

I swallow my mouthful of food, and say again, 'Car accident.'

'*Gamoto.* Are you OK?'

'I'm here, aren't I?' My tone is further from playfully sarcastic and closer to shitty than it should be or than I meant it to be. Quietly, I add, 'Yeah. I'm fine. Did have to buy a new car though.'

'When?'

'A few years back. It's fine, I'm fine.' I smile at him. 'These things happen, don't they? Everyone tells me I'm very lucky. I am. I'm very lucky. Not something everyone gets to walk away from. It's not something I exactly look back on fondly, though, or talk about much. What about you? You don't seem to have a mark on you, not even a birthmark.'

I pull my fringe back into place and press my lips together in an attempt at a smile while I wait for him to list scars or injuries to prove he isn't so perfect.

That isn't what I get.

'You have been noticing me.' A smile glides over his lips and despite myself the muscles in my cheekbones respond by lifting too.

'I thought you were an arrogant shit, with all of your pretty thick hair, and it turns out I'm right.'

We laugh together, but the air seems to shift around us. I don't feel comfortable any more.

My swimsuit feels too tight, like I'm being strangled by it. I want to get back and maybe to get changed too.

'Would you like to go somewhere else or to go back to San Stefanos?'

'I think I'd like to go home.'

'I don't have enough fuel for England. Maybe just San Stefanos?' He doesn't flinch, as though his answer was the most sensible response and the only one I should have expected.

'OK, I suppose that will have to do then.'

He packs the cool box away, then we are off, skimming the surface of the water again, edging around the island and around the mass of my past in the process. I spend my time questioning everything in a way that I know I shouldn't.

I can't even concentrate on the colours of the sea to mask what I'm really thinking and feeling.

Instead, everything seems to be pulsing through me along with my blood. Pain, passion, scars. Then the engine cuts out.

'Ruby, quickly, look.' Yianni pulls at my arm, tugging me up to standing. He's frantically pointing further out to sea.

'What? What am I looking at?'

He stands behind me, pressing his body into my back before reaching his arm over my shoulder and pointing out to sea, lining it up so I can follow his direction.

That's when I see it – or not it, them. Something out of the water. His arm drops but we stay stuck together for a few moments, both of us in awe of the creatures breaking through the surface of the waves.

When Yianni pulls away, it's like pulling off a plaster. I can still feel the pressure of him on my skin.

I feel raw and vulnerable without him.

It's been so long since I've had anyone pressed against me. But now he's groping under things on the boat, pulling open places I didn't expect would open until he finds a pair of binoculars.

He stares out through them for a moment, then passes them to me.

'What are they?' In the binoculars the creatures look much bigger than dolphins, but with sort of similar noses.

140

'Whales.' The click of his phone taking pictures snaps next to me.

'I thought you didn't do Instagram?'

'I don't.'

Then comes the distinctive beep from his phone as he starts to film them.

The whales are actually not that far away, and with binoculars it's like I could touch them. They're all marked with jagged scars and lines – like me. War wounds covering their bodies. They're strangely beautiful.

I pull the binoculars from my face and pass them back to Yianni as he lowers his phone.

'What sort of whale are they?'

'*Zifiós.*'

'English?'

Yianni lowers the binoculars, leaving us both squinting. The whales seem to have vanished for good under the surface.

'I'm not sure. Beaknose whale? We must report this to the research institute. They will need these photos and videos too.'

'Do you know all the different types of whales and dolphins?'

He starts up the engine and we head off again.

'Some. The *zifiós* are rare, but one washed up into Arillas not so long ago. Oil companies have been causing *seismikés* vibrations. It's thought this harms much of the sea life. Disorientating them, killing them . . .' He trails off in a soft tone, but his entire body is taut.

Arillas is the next village down from San Stefanos. It's not far at all.

'Did you see it? The beached whale?'

He shakes his head. 'No. There were enough people to help, and I didn't know until later. It is very sad to waste life in this way.'

I couldn't agree more.

Hearing Yianni like this, so emotionally involved in life, it's a new experience for me. Jonathan never showed much interest towards nature or conservation.

Yianni looks physically pained by the plight of the whales. He truly cares.

By the time we reach San Stefanos, it's mid-afternoon. The journey back has given me time to cool off, helped by the distraction of the whales and not helped by the lingering sensation of Yianni's firm chest pressed against my back.

If only the thoughts of the accident wouldn't linger along with it. I wish the breeze would take the hurt away.

I've rarely spoken about it to anyone, even when it happened.

My mum had wanted me to see a therapist because I refused to talk to her about it. I didn't go. There would be no point paying someone just to hear my silence on the subject.

She tried to use food to get me to talk about the accident. She made all my favourites and all the comforting puddings imaginable. I'm sure she knew that pressing me too hard would never work to get me to open up. It didn't work when I was a child, and it wouldn't work now. I guess that's why she spent weeks making all my favourite foods.

Silence was the only way I could process the lack of control I have over my life. To be inward and quiet is all I have.

That's all anyone has. Or maybe not. I guess other people like the idea of a problem shared being a problem halved. It's just not me.

Having others appraise my pain and compare it to their own makes me shut down.

I'm more than happy to listen to people tell me about themselves and their problems. It's one of the things I like about working behind a bar or in hospitality.

I get to listen with the focus as far away from me as it gets.

When I work, people aren't judging the validity of my issues or poking at my weaknesses. I'm just there to bring them happiness in the form of good food and scrummy drinks. I love that.

I can still remember the first time I played restaurant with my parents. I made a menu and cooked everything on it from scratch. I must have been eight or nine. They were so happy. I knew then I wanted to see more people smiling like that. Food is a place where people come together. I guess that's why Mum tried to use it to get me to open up. Eventually, I did talk to her a little about it.

When Yianni and I get out of the boat, I don't fancy people staring at my scars and I don't want to seem vain by getting my mirror out to see what I actually look like.

I wish I didn't care.

I don't want to care.

I wish I could forget they were there and feel confident that no one would stare or ask questions I don't want to answer. Instead of going along the beach with Yianni to talk to his friend, like he wants me to, I wave at him from a distance and wait at the edge of the sea while they chat.

I look away again and out to sea to catch my breath as I try to shake off the feeling that swirls around me. The smell of seaweed lingers and fuses with the smoky smell pooling down from one of the beach bars or restaurants just past Yianni.

It's delightful. It takes my mind off myself and back to the charming island that I'm lucky enough to be calling home this summer.

A child, maybe five or six years old, stomps into the sea next to me with a bright red bucket, scooping up as much water as he can before splashing away again. He probably has a moat that needs filling.

I lie back with my calves and feet in the water and my head resting on the sand. The desire to close my eyes and nap catches me off guard. 'You will have a strange tan in that swimsuit. With those holes.' Yianni's voice jolts me back into reality.

Shielding my eyes, I find him standing over me, hands linked behind his back in the same way he stands in the entrance to Greek Secret.

He's close enough that I can almost see up his khaki swim shorts.

'Well, I can see up your shorts and I'm not impressed.'

I can't *actually* see anything. Not because it isn't there, I'm sure, but because of the angle.

It is enough to make him step back, though. And shut him up, which is the whole point.

'Do you want me to take you back to the house to get washed and dressed for tonight? Or are you sleeping on the beach?'

He sits behind me on the mound of sand that's been pushed there by the sea. I roll on to my belly to face him, lifting my feet out of the water to prevent getting sand in the bandage on my foot.

'I don't mind sleeping here if you'd rather spend the rest of your day off with your friends, you know. It's kind of you to hire a boat and to take me out, but you really don't have to spend your time with me.'

He watches over me for a moment before stretching his legs out and digging his heels into the sand.

'Why do you think I do not want to spend my time with you?'

'I just meant, you have a life here and probably have better things to do.'

'No. All my friends are working. I am stuck with you.'

'You could always go into work.'

I press my top teeth into the middle of my lower lip, waiting for a response.

He subtly rolls his eyes and turns his attention to his bag, pulling out a towel and spreading it neatly on the sand.

'Drink?' He stands over me again.

'Water, please. I can see up your shorts again.'

'Lucky you.' He pulls a wallet out of the bag and stalks up the beach.

My forehead presses into my arms and my skin itches and prickles with sand and salt. My scalp and hair are caked with the stuff. I love it and hate it in equal measure. Like a painful exfoliation that's oddly satisfying.

I even take pleasure in the sun wickedly trying to set my skin on fire. Then the waves crawl up my legs to put it out.

I close my eyes to it all. I can hear people playing, a baby screaming, distant chatter, but I let the sea swallow it all up and drown it until all I can focus on is Yianni. How he makes me laugh. How he has been so thoughtful. Against my better judgement, he's making a mark on me that goes deeper than the scars on my face.

Chapter Twenty Seven

THEN

'Ready?' My shoulders lift and squeeze with anticipation.

The key twists in the front door of our first proper home together.

It took so much discussion, heartache and growing up to get here.

Jonathan wanted to be nearer his mum in Chelmsford, but being in Ipswich is so much cheaper because it's that bit further from London. It has a train line straight to London though, and it means we could afford a little two-bed place that isn't that much more money than we were paying for one bedroom just outside of central London.

I'm happy to be back in my home county and only a short drive from my parents. After almost four years away, I'm excited to see friends from school and college. It'll be nice to be able to pop round and see my parents instead of only squeezing in catch-ups a handful of times a year.

We make our way through the empty rooms. They're all white boxes ready to be filled with memories.

It sort of reminds me of the room Jonathan was renting when we first met. Only here we don't even have a mattress yet.

This was my idea, though, so I've agreed to spend more of my savings buying some furniture. If I get some second-hand, it shouldn't be too bad. Plus, Mum and Dad said we can have the bedframe and mattress from their spare room.

Apparently, Mum was looking to redecorate, so we're doing them a favour.

That's what they've said, anyway. They'll be bringing it around this evening.

I haven't managed to save much for the restaurant so far. Only three thousand and fifty-eight pounds. I don't know what I'll have left after buying sofas and things.

There's always something else we need or *have* to have. Another part on the car, or insurance or food.

It's why I've asked that we prioritise my dreams for a while. I managed to get us a job through a friend of mine called Amara. Rob introduced us when I was working with him in London. We got on well, but she likes to drift from place to place.

When I saw she was living in Suffolk, I jumped at the chance to reconnect.

'So what now?' Jonathan drags his feet from the kitchen to the living room, glancing in with disinterest.

'I know this isn't ideal, but think of the money we'll save.'

'I still don't think it'll save money, babe. Not when I have to get trains to London every other day for rehearsals.'

'You haven't got any rehearsals—'

'But I will. I will have soon enough. Something will come up.'

'After we lost the last jobs we had, this really is the best option. Anyway, I think it's time to settle. Maybe put down some roots and look for a nice place to start the restaurant.'

'Why should I settle? I'm destined for greatness, not settling. Not this.' The last part he mutters under his breath before he quickly continues, 'And don't think I can't hear you blaming me for us losing those jobs. You don't have to say anything for me to hear your judgement.'

I don't rise to it. I do blame him, because it was his fault entirely. He was the one lying about why he wasn't there then bursting in to announce he *got the part*.

That was the last straw for me.

I knew then we had to make some big changes. Smart changes. Changes that would bring our worlds together instead of tearing us apart. We love each other. We work well together.

No matter what, we always support each other's dreams, and this is the best way to do that.

'Aren't you even a little excited that we have a whole house together now?' I'm only now aware I'm still gripping the door key as I awkwardly attempt to cross my arms over my chest.

Jonathan turns to face me, leaning in the doorway into the living room.

'I guess there's one thing I'm excited about.' His eyes glance over my skin but the rest of him stays dead still.

'Oh yeah? What's that?'

'Come here and I'll show you.'

I take steps towards him, dropping the keys on the floor in our empty hall.

Jonathan wraps his fingers behind my neck and I tiptoe to kiss him.

He pulls away, looking down at me. Pale-blue eyes study my face before his finger, and eyes, trail over my neck and down to my new white blouse.

Gripping it with both hands, he rips it open, tearing the buttons and the material too.

I audibly gasp, caught completely off guard by his action.

'Jonathan! You've ripped it.'

I look down at the sad soft cotton gaping over my bra.

'If you can afford all this, you can buy a new one. Now let's christen the living room, shall we?'

Chapter Twenty Eight

Now

While I was asleep on the beach, Yianni tried to put more sun lotion on me, spritzing me with it. But overall, he's right. I've been left with a strange tan with circles on my sides. Although the tan is a little redder than I'd like to admit.

Yianni is in Natalia's room, getting himself ready for the evening.

She's already at work for the night. We're the only ones in the house.

I can hear him moving from place to place, and I wonder if I should invite him to chat to me while I redo my make-up. He's already seen the scars on my face, after all. Chances are, he won't ask any more questions about them.

Although, he might. Maybe I won't ask him in.

I've just finished getting ready, deciding on a pair of mint-green linen shorts and a white top paired with white criss-crossing sandals. It was hard to pick anything out, because I don't want to look like I'm trying too hard, but it's nice to go out in the evening wearing something other than a black skirt or black shorts for work.

With one last glance at myself, one last scrunch to the roots of my hair and ruffle of my fringe, I step out of his door, only for him to be stepping out of Natalia's at the same time.

He's sprayed some aftershave and I can smell the masculinity nipping at me, the same fragrance that lingered on his sheets when I first came to live here.

Citrus undertones, *mmm*. I catch myself because I nearly make the noise out loud.

Turning the creepy noise into words, I squeeze out, 'You look nice,' and smile a little too hard to cover the contented look that I'm sure has drifted over my face.

What I want to do is text Amara and say, *Dear God why does he have to be so hot? I can't bear to be around this man. He's so good-looking I want to cry.*

He's wearing fitted denim shorts that are almost down to his knees, but not quite, with a white shirt with a few buttons undone, displaying a black chain necklace.

There's nothing particularly fancy. He doesn't need bells and whistles to look good.

He returns my smile and looks me over with a flash of his thick eyelashes.

'You look good too. But this is normal for you.'

A choke of air escapes my chest before I pull myself together and say, 'Thank you.'

Lowering my eyeline, I desperately hope he hasn't noticed my second momentary lapse. As we make our way down the stairs and into his car, I stay in his shadow. I have to, because I'm physically shaking my head to scatter any thoughts of him that might border on sexual.

I find a new mantra: *He is your aunt's stepson, she doesn't want anyone distracting him and I can't get distracted by another pretty face.*

We go to a place called Manthos. There's a white archway into the open-air restaurant. The view across the beach and sea almost takes my breath away.

I hesitate while taking it in, giving Yianni's hand the opportunity to find the small of my back, ushering me forward.

In this one little movement, he snatches my attention. He introduces me to people, but I'm still dazzled by my surroundings, and by the sensation of his fingers lingering on my back.

Even as he moves away, I can still feel the imprint of him.

It looks like the sun is about to go for a leisurely dip in the sea. It's illuminating everything in burnt sienna with flecks of gold rippling along towards us on the waves. The entire sky is alight.

No longer blue.

No longer am I looking at the line where the sea meets the sky. Now the line is clear. The horizon is ablaze, and the sea is beginning to turn purple under the golden glitter swaying on its surface.

No more haze. In this present, there's only clarity.

By contrast, everything in the restaurant is fresh, with clean, sharp lines. White and pale blue engulf every surface, including the uniforms. Everything is just so.

There's even a couple of swinging chairs made of wicker, shaped like eggs, white with pale-blue cushions. I want to ask Yianni to take my photo in one but I'm pretty sure he would mock me.

It's worth the risk. It would be a great photo to send my parents and Amara, and I don't care what he thinks, or what anyone thinks. Two years ago, I decided I was never going to live a life for anyone but myself. I won't divert my life, my plans, my goals for anyone. Never again.

I follow Yianni to a table for two with a perfect view across the sea.

The sun dips further down into its nightly bath, letting the sea put the fire out for the day.

Yianni pulls my chair out for me and I can feel myself heat up, not just because of the sun – although it still holds a sharp heat even as it disappears – but because this feels like a romantic date.

Even though Yianni is undeniably gorgeous with his swimmer physique, designer stubble, thick beachy hair, eyes so dark they are like sinkholes – I could go on – I don't *want* to date him.

I don't *want* to fall into his sinkhole eyes.

I'm not sure I'm ready for anything like that. If in some crazy moment we did both like each other, then everyone around us would be looking at us, talking about us. I've had enough of that.

I'm going to treat him like I do Amara. Take a breath. Relax. Talk to him like a friend and nothing more. Because that's what he is, after all.

'Would you like some water for the table?' The waitress's tone is as relaxed as the breeze.

Yianni nods and begins to chat. Then she asks if we know what we would like to drink other than water. Yianni asks for a Corfu beer. *What would I have if I was with Amara for a girly meal or a night out?*

'Spiced rum and Coke, please.'

Yianni raises both eyebrows. 'I changed my mind,' he says. 'I will have the same.'

As the waitress goes off with our drinks order, Yianni's eyes stay on his menu, but even without looking at him, I get the sense that he wants to say something.

Maybe it's the way his eyes don't look like they are reading anything, as though the menu he has is completely blank. Or maybe it's something on a molecular level that's sending me signals that allude to the fact he has something he wants to say or do.

Eventually, he comes out with it. 'You surprise me.' His eyes stay fixed on the menu as he turns the page.

'Or, you don't really know me.'

I don't look up from my menu either.

My peripherals are on point from working in restaurants. I can watch patrons without them knowing, just in case they need me, or when I think they might raise a hand for the bill.

No one likes to feel like they're being watched, but staff are also meant to be attentive. I suspect that Yianni has the same skill.

'You are right.' He lets his menu slap to the table so he can look at me without pretending he isn't. 'Tonight, this will change.'

'Oh, will it?'

'Naí. Yes.'

'Good luck with that.'

I look him right in the eye, letting a small smile cross my lips.

His face screws up and he mumbles in Greek as he turns back to his menu. I can still see the smile that's tugging at his lips, even though he's trying his best to hide it in a language I can't understand.

'If we're both drinking, how am I getting home tonight?'

'I won't drink much, but there is always someone driving back to the village if this changes. It's nothing to worry about here.' I know he's right.

People are always happy to give a lift. I've seen both Yianni and Nico give lifts to customers who didn't even have that far to go.

'Would you take my picture in one of those egg things?' I know he'll tell me he was right, and I am one of the girls who just wants to take photos of themselves. I brace myself for it, holding my breath.

'Sure. It would make a beautiful photo.' His eyes flick to mine then back to the menu.

I don't want to admit it as I exhale, but now we're even. We've already both surprised each other and the night is only just beginning.

Chapter Twenty Nine

THEN

'Babe, do you have some money on you? I've got to get a train to an audition.' Jonathan's hands are in his pockets while his mouth is stuck in a wide grimace, making his dimples look more haggard than cute. His eyebrows are pulled together, making him look like a sad dog, pleading.

I know the look well.

'What about work?' The muscles in my shoulders tense and I take a deep breath to stay calm, or at least try to.

'Can you tell them I'm sick?' He's gathering together his things – a portfolio of headshots and the usual items he takes with him to auditions.

'They'll know that's not true, and I'm not lying for you again. Charles isn't stupid. You're the worst waiter we have.'

'Thanks, Ruby.' His voice and face crinkle at my comment, but I know he doesn't really care. If he did, he wouldn't duck out at any chance he gets.

'Not the worst, but the least reliable. You can be as good as you like, but if you're not there, then it's pointless, isn't it?' My fingernails find my waist and grip. 'There are a lot of tables in tonight. Please come in with me.'

Jonathan turns to me and clasps his hands together as though he is about to beg, but really, I'm the one who's pleading, not him.

I'm the one who's embarrassed when he doesn't bother showing up to work. I'm the one forced to lie, even though I hate it.

'This isn't just a regular audition, babe.' He pulls my hands away from my hips and grips them in his own. 'This is a callback for the supporting role in a feature-length drama. For the BEE-BEE-CEE.' Jonathan draws out each letter as though it's a separate word that he is explaining to some idiot who has never heard of the BBC.

His mouth stays hanging open, almost like he is gasping, even though he isn't.

This is the first time I've wanted to slap the excitement for his acting career right out of him.

At thirty-one, he's almost five years older than me and he still expects me to be gleeful about any audition, like there's nothing else in the world.

I love him, and I've supported him, but I've definitely fallen out of love with his acting since we've moved to Ipswich.

It's like he's forgotten the reasons we had to leave London.

He begged and guilted me into lying, then made it pretty obvious I had, when he excitedly ran in during the shift to tell me he had got a part in a panto.

My cheeks burnt with the heat of shame like I had a fever, to the point that my lips were chapped for a week after.

I swore I wouldn't do it again.

We got the sack and I said we needed to make changes. I thought moving here would be the change we needed. It would help us both to grow and mature.

Things don't always work out how we think they will, I guess. He's the artist and I should support him. It's all he's ever wanted, and after all, I knew this when I started going out with him.

We're lucky to have the jobs at La Salle à Manger. Amara is the sous chef and she put her neck on the line getting us these jobs. The thought of letting her down and losing a friend over a bloody audition makes my throat go completely dry. And it's not like it's the first time.

When my fingers hang loose in Jonathan's, and I don't scream with excitement that he *has* to get a train into London, he drops my hands completely and shakes his head.

'You know how much this means to me. You've always known. This could be the one, Ruby. The. One.' His hand releases his folder as he fans out his fingers and repeats the motion for emphasis. 'The one that changes it all. Changes *our* life. Come on, just smile sweetly at Charlie-boy. We all know he fancies the shit out of you. You could get away with anything.'

'I don't want to get away with anything,' I mutter, but either Jonathan doesn't hear me or he chooses to ignore me.

I take a deep breath and inhale his aftershave. He's been a bit too heavy-handed with the stuff and it's gone from attractive to choking, smothering me with sweetness.

After everything I've done to support him, I just want a little bit in return. It's taken moving here to make me see things a little differently.

This job is the first time I've been a maître d' and I don't want to lose it because he can't be bothered. 'I'm not going to lie for you. But I will tell Charles the truth and try to explain that it's a really great opportunity. He's a good man under it all. I'm sure he'll understand.'

Jonathan's face completely changes. It's almost back to the faux gasp from moments ago.

'And' – I cut across his emotions, and even this word makes him pause – 'I'm not paying for the train. We don't have the money right now. I need to save—' My hands wave to prevent his interruption, which I can feel bubbling up. 'We agreed to settle things down a little bit. If I pay for your train, I can't pay my part of the rent in full, and I know you can't, so—'

'Oh, for fuck's sake, Ruby. It's a great opportunity and you're only pretending to be supportive. What am I going to do? I swear you're always trying to hold me back.'

I bite back the upset of this comment.

He doesn't mean it.

He's angry and not thinking.

'Just call your mum. I'm sure she'll lend you the train fare.'

He slips on his coat and mutters something before he leaves, slamming the door as he goes. The one photo of us on the wall falls to the ground. The glass shatters all over the floor.

My fingers pinch the car keys from the bowl and toss the weight of them from one hand to the other with a satisfying clinking noise.

I'm not clearing it up.

I'm not.

This time, I'm not.

Charles is going to be angry, but Jonathan is as aware as I am about the way Charles looks at me.

He's probably right, and Charles won't be half as mad with me telling him as he might be if Jonathan called in.

Jonathan often jokes I only got promoted *because of your face and your tits.*

But it doesn't matter now. It'll be what it'll be.

And for the first time, I stood up and said no to Jonathan. Well, at least half a no.

158

Chapter Thirty

Now

'One last drink for the road. This one is on me.' Yianni gets a key out and unlocks the door, unfolding it partway open. 'Last drink is always tequila. You know that. Chocolate or regular?'

'Seriously?'

He hops over the bar and starts juggling two bottles, somersaulting them in the air.

'Stop showboating.'

'What?' He doesn't stop. His lips part in concentration as the bottles whizz in front of his face.

I press my hands into the cool wood of the bar and lean forwards, then slowly repeat, 'Stop showboating.'

'I don't know this one.'

I exhale and walk away from the bar. 'It means stop showing off. I don't want you dropping anything on my other foot.'

I smile as I make my way towards a table not far from the bar. It has something akin to oversized deckchairs around one side, and a bench against the wall.

'Who had chairs like this first? You or Athens Bar?'

'No, no. Don't start that debate. Same year.'

I slump on to the bench. The look of the plump blue cushions reels me in, and I have no willpower to refuse. I swat away a mosquito and relax, a sleepy haze falling over me.

'How many places did you take me to? A hundred and one?'

'No, no. It only feels that way because you have so much fun with me.'

'Surely it feels that way when you're not having fun?' I bite my lip to hold in laughter.

Yianni acts as though he doesn't notice as he brings two shot glasses and a bottle of tequila to the table. He pours tequila into the glasses, then slides one towards me before sitting down next to me.

'*Yamas.*' Yianni clinks my glass, even though it's still on the table, untouched. Then he takes the shot with ease.

I pick up the glass, lift it in Yianni's direction and sip at it. Chocolate.

'*Yamas.*'

'Don't tell Hazel, but I think the food at Manthos might actually be even better than here. That sea bass . . . And that view out to sea.' I press my hand to my chest. It's the type of place I'd love to own, right on the beach. One day.

'I'm glad you enjoyed it. And do not worry, I won't tell her. Not yet, anyway.'

'What do you mean, *yet*?'

'I have this to hold over you now. If I need you to cover a shift or—'

'Let me stop you there and point at my toe. You owe me your silence.'

Yianni's eyes roll as he grabs the bottle and pours himself another shot.

After our meal, Yianni took me for one drink in as many places as we could fit in. At first, I thought it was a bar crawl. I've never been on a bar crawl before, so I thought this was one, as he said we had to have one drink in every bar.

Halfway round, I noticed a theme. He wasn't worried about what we drank. Although he did have a cocktail in Nafsika, he had a frappé in a place called Silver Star and water in Little Prince.

It was when we were in a place called Cicala, as he walked me straight to introduce me to another lovely family, that I realised . . . he seemed more interested in people meeting me than drinking. Yianni pushed me to the front, telling people about me in more places than I can count. Silver Moon, Barras, Condor, Bar 38, Athens Bar, Aquarius, Three Ws and others. I can't remember all the names.

'It was nice to meet people. To chat and hear stories about you and Hazel and Pericles.'

'Don't believe anything anyone told you tonight.' Yianni waggles his finger at me.

'It's strange to think this thriving tourist stop started with only the Waves Taverna on the beach, I don't know, when I was a baby.'

'You're not that old.'

'I'm older than you.'

Our eye contact lingers with something unspoken. I can't hold it. It catches in my chest and I quickly return to safer ground.

'In Bar 38, who were the elegant older couple clad in vibrant prints that came over to chat to us? I've seen them in the restaurant before, but not spoken to them.'

'Paul and Jean. They've been coming here forever. As long as I remember.' Yianni beams in the same way he did earlier when I was chatting to these people he has known his whole life.

'I can't believe you were shy as a teen though. I think they must've been talking about someone else.' I sip more of my shot.

'Me? I'm shy now. I'm always shy.'

'Yeah, you're shy and Nico isn't a flirt. Sure. What was it they said? *Seeing him grow and change on their annual visits has made him as integrated with their happiest times as the beach or the salty taste of feta.* So cute.'

'They mean I'm taller. That's all.'

For a moment we both study our glasses, then I finish my shot and bang the glass down.

'What made you come here to Corfu?' Yianni asks. 'Yes, you lost your job, but there must be other jobs in England.'

My left hand gravitates to my right, my fingers automatically ready to pull at my ring.

It's gone.

There is no ring on my right hand.

I look down in astonishment, mouth open but with no words to say.

My posture suddenly becomes perfectly straight and my feet – which had been resting on tiptoes – plant themselves on the ground as though I am ready to run.

'My ring's gone,' I blurt out, almost spitting at Yianni.

'What ring? The one you are always playing with?'

'Yes!' I point aggressively at my bare finger. '*Merde!* No! It's a diamond ring. Shit!'

I can feel my eyes beginning to sting and my throat closing up. Yianni lines up a row of cliché questions that no one wants to answer when they've lost something and they're desperate to have it back.

'When did you last see it? What does it look like? Could you have left it somewhere?'

I bristle under his interrogation.

'On my hand? It's a bloody diamond ring, Yianni. I never take it off. It's like skin. Fuck!' I get up and start looking around.

Maybe I've been sitting on it, or I've dropped it on the floor.

I pace a little around the bar and Yianni gets up to look about with me. 'I've been meaning to have it resized since it was given to me. It's only a little bit too big though. Since being here, and, well, it's so hot all the time, I actually thought it was fitting a little bit better. I know I play with it, slide it up and down my finger now and then. Shit. I've lost it, haven't I? That's it. I've lost it.' I shrug and slap my hands down against my body.

It's gone.

There, in the middle of the taverna, I press my hands to shelter my face. My body is rigid as I try to hold in the tears swelling under my eyelids.

That ring was all I really had left of my relationship with Jonathan.

The good and the bad.

I'd been using it as a symbol of something for such a long time. A symbol of what, I'm not sure. Of change or hope? What I do and don't want in life? I've wanted to take it off so many times. I even tried to give it back.

There's no way I wanted it – or even thought I should have it – after everything we went through. Who else would want it when it was bought for me? I gave in and kept it.

I felt obligated to wear it. Over the past two years, it's become a part of me – a gold band lined with tiny diamonds. It sparkled at all angles.

Not any more. Not on my hand anyway.

Yianni's arms engulf me. Nothing is said.

A minute, maybe more, passes by with me silently crying in his arms.

A breeze rolls in from the open door, and the warmth of his skin pressing on mine is a comfort.

His lips find the side of my head and he gently presses against it.

'I'm sorry,' I begin. 'It's just, well, that ring meant a lot to me.' I quietly sniff under my hands, because I don't want to uncover my face yet. 'Jonathan, he . . . he bought it for me. He had to borrow the money from his mum for it and everything.'

That is enough to set me off again.

I haven't cried like this in a long time. In fact, I think I'm bloody marvellous at suppressing negative emotions these days and manifesting the positive. Yianni starts shushing me and then leads me towards his room. For this, I do uncover my face as tears slide down and drop from the scar on my chin to the floor.

In his room, Yianni turns on a little white reading lamp, and stretches out his arm to indicate the single bed.

We both sit down, next to each other. Yianni stands again and leaves the room. Moments later he's back with a loo roll tucked under his arm, the two glasses in one hand and the bottle of tequila in the other.

Taking some tissue from him, I blow my nose and dab around my cheeks and chin to remove the tears stinging my face.

'Tomorrow I will ask everywhere we have been if they have seen it.'

I shake my head and my posture crumples in on itself.

'No. I bet it's in the sea. Shit, what am I going to tell Sue? *Merde.*'

'Who is Sue?'

'It doesn't matter now. I've fucked up.'

Yianni pours me a drink and I hold the tiny glass in my hand. Instead of taking it as a shot, I sip the liquid slowly. It's sweet and it trickles down my throat, warming me in an already boiling box room.

As though he is reading my thoughts, Yianni reaches over to the set of drawers next to the bed and turns on a fan. It comes alive to whirl and creak, slowly rotating to move air around every inch of the room. Then he props the door open with a shoe to let in the cooler night air. It's enough.

'Why are you still wearing this boy's ring? You are not together. You broke up.'

Another little sniff gives me a moment to think what I want to tell him about Jonathan.

Yes, we broke up, but there is more to it than that. Much more, but my heart is still raw from losing the ring.

I'm not sure I want to tell him all about my painful past. I look into his face and it's lined with questions and concern. His skin looks even more golden in the orange glow of the lamp and the full waves of his hair cast shadows, making him look so damn intense.

He needs a slice of the truth, but I can't bear to relay any of the details of it.

'Yeah. We broke up a long time ago, but that doesn't mean I just stopped loving him. It doesn't always matter if you don't want to be with someone, or they don't want to be with you. Love doesn't always just end. Yes, I broke up with him. But I . . . Don't you have an ex?'

Yianni slips his shoes off and unbuttons his shirt. My eyebrows knit together, but he doesn't seem to notice my confusion.

Instead, he shuffles on to the bed and props the pillow up to lean it on the wall. Folding his arms over his almost completely exposed chest, he exhales in thought.

'Yes. I have many ex-girlfriends. None have my rings though. A few have necklaces.' His lips turn down at the memory of them, or perhaps the thought of girls walking around with necklaces he got them.

'Well, maybe they wear them, and maybe they love those silly necklaces. And maybe if they lost them, they would cry, even though they might not want you any more.'

'I do not think so.'

I groan in protest. 'We're all different, OK?'

'This, I can agree with.' He looks at me with his rich eyes and a gaze so intense I have to look away for fear he might see all my deepest secrets. 'I am sorry you lost the ring.' His voice is almost a whisper.

'Me too.'

I lift the glass still cupped in my hands and sip the last little bit. I try to recall the last time Jonathan and I had a drink together.

I can't remember. It was a lifetime ago.

'It's late. Do you want me to drive you home?'

My head snaps round to him so fast the ends of my hair nearly catch me in the eyes.

'What? No. You've been drinking.'

'Not that much. I feel fine.'

'No.' I lower my voice and my chin tucks itself into my chest.

I need him to know that I don't find this acceptable, even if, like me, some of his drinks were just Cokes. I know he has had rum and at least two tequila shots. I feel fine too, but I don't think I should be driving.

'You will be sleeping here, with me, then?'

'No, you said that someone would be able to give me a lift back. There's only one bed here.' I say this as though he doesn't already have this information to hand. As though he isn't sitting on – and now shuffling off – the bed in question.

He removes his shirt completely and turns to face me.

'It's much later than I thought. It's OK, I trust you.' A smile glides over his lips. 'Would you like to borrow a T-shirt?'

Chapter Thirty One

Then

'Ruby, I could never love anyone the way I love you. You know that, right?'

It's Saturday morning and we've spent most of our time watching cartoons like we're kids. Like we used to when we first met and fell in love. He strokes the hair from my face and kisses my neck.

'Of course I know.'

I look over at him on the sofa as he scrolls his phone.

'Jonathan?'

'Yep.' He briefly looks up before his eyes slip back down to the screen.

'Do you remember what you said to me, when we first met?'

He shifts his weight and pulls me along the sofa until I'm underneath him and between his legs.

'Did I tell you how gorgeous you were?'

'Sort of.'

'Did I let you know that you were always going to be mine and no one else's?'

He kisses my jawline and down my neck. 'Love you,' he whispers.

'Love you too,' I whisper in return.

It was only a few years ago, when he thought I was an actress or a model, but it feels like forever.

Jonathan's smooth cheek is pressed to mine and his fingers run the length of my arm.

'Please don't go out after work tonight,' he murmurs.

Amara has invited me to go out dancing with her and a couple of her friends that I get on well with.

Jonathan doesn't have a job any more.

He's been looking for a waiter job somewhere else since he quit working for Charles at La Salle à Manger to take on some extra work when he didn't get the part in the BBC feature-length piece. The extra work pretty much only covered the costs of him getting to London and his lunch while he was there.

Of course, this still means it was worthwhile, because *you never know who you might meet on set.*

'I've said I'll go.'

'But I'll be all alone at home, and bored.'

He's angling for an invite, but I know Amara would be irritated if he were to be invited to a girls' night out.

'It's girls only.'

'I could dress up.'

I do my best to rein in my frustration as I wiggle away from his grip to get myself ready for the long day ahead. 'I'll only have one drink and then I'll be home. OK?' I twist to face him, hoping it'll reassure him.

'No. Don't be stupid. It's fine.'

Jonathan slumps down on to our sofa, kicks his feet up over the arm and begins to play with his phone.

Either he's sulking or he's lost interest.

Based on past experience, he's sulking.

He never likes me going out without him. I guess I don't like him going out without me either. I love it when we're together.

I never used to notice in London, because we always went out with his actor friends and I never really went anywhere else other than work.

I get off the sofa and go to the hallway to collect my bag.

In moments I'm back in the room, stooping down to give him a kiss before I leave.

'What's that?' He points at my leather backpack I've bunched over one shoulder.

'My handbag.'

'No, what's hanging out of it?'

I glance over my shoulder to see the sleeve of one of my dresses poking out.

'Oh, it's the dress I'm changing into when we go out.'

'So, do you really expect me to believe you're off out for only one drink when you're getting changed to go?'

'I'm not going out in my work clothes. You have to be kidding.'

'Are you even going out with the girls? Or is it someone else? Is Charles taking you somewhere?'

His lips lock firmly closed and his eyes are like the mouths of angry dogs, ready to chew me up and spit me out.

There's so much anger.

It's the first time he has made such an accusation, and I don't even know how to react.

'You cannot be serious.'

'Well, you didn't quit the restaurant when I did, and you always seem damn cosy at that place.'

There are no words in my vocabulary to formulate an appropriate answer.

None.

I just stand aghast, my mouth open like I've been frozen mid-sentence.

'Have fun, Ruby. But I might not be here when you get back,' Jonathan says, as I turn to walk away.

His smug tone sounds like he's aimed a knife at my back with his cryptic taunt. A year or so ago, that knife would have hit me square between the shoulder blades and reeled me in, stopping me from going out with my friends. But this time, that smug tone isn't enough to reel me in. His metaphorical knife misses me completely and lands firmly in the doorframe instead.

I close the front door behind me and step out into the chill of the spring air.

I haven't seen my schoolfriends the entire time we've lived in Ipswich.

The last time I saw them was at a birthday party and everyone was there. That was just before we moved here.

When I did arrange to meet them, Jonathan took the car to an audition so I couldn't get there. He apologised profusely, of course, but now I'm wondering if he even had an audition, or whether he was controlling me.

I slip inside my car and begin to reverse off our narrow drive.

Has Jonathan been intentionally separating me from people?

We see his mum all the time compared to how often we see my parents.

There's more often than not a *legitimate* reason not to see my family. Plus, he always plays the *my mum is lonely from her divorce* card. Which works on me, because I remember how sad Aunt Hazel was when she split from her husband.

I need to try to spend more time with my friends and family. I'm not going to stay for just one drink tonight. I'm going to enjoy connecting with people again.

◆ ◆ ◆

The *ting* of my key connecting with the lock is enough. The door flies out of my hand and there is Jonathan, red-faced, with every muscle in his jaw as tense as can be.

'I've been calling you,' he snaps.

'Have you? What's wrong?' I step round him and follow my usual walking in the door routine.

Remove shoes, coat, wash hands. He follows me the entire time.

'Yes. Why haven't you checked your phone?'

'I did. There's nothing there. Maybe you were calling the wrong number.'

This is clearly the wrong thing to say, as Jonathan's neck blazes a new shade of crimson. I go to my backpack and pull my phone out, passing it to him.

'I was worried about you. But now I think maybe I was right and you *are* sleeping with Charles.'

'Seriously? This again?' Pushing past him, I creep up the stairs and continue in hushed tones, 'You were happy for him to give me unwanted attention when it benefited you.'

I'm sure Jonathan's tone is loud enough to carry into the house next door and I don't want to make it worse.

'So you admit he gives you attention.' Jonathan scowls over the screen.

'I've never denied he gives me *unwanted* attention.' I make sure to say 'unwanted' carefully, otherwise he'll skip over it. Not that he's even looking at me as we climb the stairs. He's back clicking my screen.

'Look, seven missed calls and three texts.' He pushes the phone back at me as I arrive at our bedroom door.

171

I snatch the phone back and realise it was set to *Do Not Disturb* from eleven thirty onwards.

Even though I only drank water, and have photographic evidence I stayed out laughing and dancing with Amara, the next thirty minutes of my life are spent defending myself.

Mostly the mistake of having my phone automatically flick over to *Do Not Disturb*.

Explaining that it doesn't show on my home screen when it's set to *Do Not Disturb*, so how was I to know? Over and over again.

It's no use. We end up arguing. Crying.

I'm constantly *shushing* him for the sake of our neighbours, but he doesn't listen.

He layers me in accusations and shame and, as the time passes, I sit and quietly take it. This is why I never see anyone. It had just been so long that I'd forgotten the guilt he can easily smother me in.

No, this is worse.

'Are you even listening? It's like we moved to Suffolk all for you, and now you don't even love me any more. You don't do anything with me any more.'

At this, he slams the bedroom door closed with his fist, leaving a huge crack and dent.

His hand slaps to his head as he swears about this dramatic mistake he's made, costing us more money.

He didn't use to be this way about things. Sometimes he would make me feel bad for going out with Rob without him after work all those years ago, even when he was off on tour and couldn't be there. He'd call or ask me to call him, which would cut up the night and often end it before it began. But never like this.

He must really be struggling right now.

'I'm sorry about the fucking door, I just . . . I love you and I don't want to lose you.'

'Losing me was never in question. I went out with Amara, that's all.'

After churning it all over again and again, we fall asleep, and when we wake up, Jonathan begins to cry.

'I was just so worried about you. You know that, right? I don't know what I would do if anything ever happened to you. No matter what, I will always love you.'

I want to tell him that loving me doesn't give him the right to get angry with me and berate me for hours for a mistake, but I don't have any energy left.

I accept his reasoning. I know sometimes love drives people to do much crazier things.

He loves me. I love him.

We just need to learn to grow together, that's all. That's all this comes down to.

He's sorry, and I'll learn from it. We both will.

Life isn't always going to be perfect. It takes hard work to get anything worth having.

We've muddled through this far, and so much has been so good. We're worth fighting for, we're worth growing for.

I know Jonathan knows that. It was me who brought us back to Suffolk, and I know he misses being at the heart of everything in London. He needs to find his own path, and once he does, everything will be good again.

We're both struggling to find ourselves, I guess. It's not as though I've managed to scrape together enough money to prove I'm a worthy investment to start my own business. We're both having a hard time dealing with the creeping fear of failure.

It's no wonder Jonathan is holding on so tightly to us. *Us* is all we have.

Chapter Thirty Two

Now

I have to leave my mascara on.

It's waterproof and there is nothing to remove it with, unless I painfully try to pick it off. No. I don't need sharp shards of mascara making my eyes hurt, along with everything else my body seems to be feeling.

There's a dreadful mix of my painful past and Yianni looking much too appealing without his damn shirt on.

Heading to the public toilets in the restaurant, I wash my face, exposing my scars in their entirety. I can see them in the mirror. Having them on my face is torture in itself, a constant reminder of everything I want to forget.

There's no point dwelling on them, staring at them, wishing them gone. Those silvery lines are as much a part of me now as my liver or my lungs. Like it or not.

Stretching the T-shirt Yianni has given me out at arm's length, I inspect it. One of his very own T-shirts. Plain white.

I pull it into my nose and take a deep breath. It smells like Hazel's washing powder with a hint of Yianni underneath. Masculine and citrussy.

I bite my bottom lip then press the T-shirt under my nose again for another deep inhale of his scent. Exactly the same as my bed on my first night in Corfu.

I strip down and pull it over my head. I'd have liked something baggier, or at least longer. Yianni isn't exactly the sort of person to wear baggy or ill-fitting T-shirts, though. Everything I've seen him wearing is fitted, with sleek lines.

This thing's just about long enough to cover my knickers, and it's a bit tight over my chest.

I'm tugging the hem of the T-shirt as I skulk back into the side room that is his bedroom. Yianni is lying on the bed with his hands behind his head and his legs crossed at the ankles.

As I come in, he abruptly sits up.

'I am thinking, I will sleep on the floor.' Yianni begins to shuffle along the bed until his feet meet the cool tiles. His Greek accent has popped up a little. It's not the strongest accent; it's not as strong as Nico's, I guess because Yianni's around Hazel all the time.

I look down at the hard tiles to consider his idea. At least he would be cool enough down there.

'Do you have any spare bedding?'

'No. I have a sweater I can use for a pillow. It is fine.'

'That's not enough. Don't you have anything else?'

He shakes his head and begins to ball up the jumper.

I can't let him sleep on the floor. Not really. It'd be more comfortable to sleep on the beach.

'Don't be silly. We're both adults. Move over.' I flick my hands towards him to usher him along.

Stepping back, he sits back down and moves towards the wall.

Shuffling forward, I lie down next to him.

The lamp is still on. My left shoulder is pressing against his right as we both stare up at the ceiling, completely still. The only sound is the hum of the fan.

I turn my head away from him, followed by my whole body. The little room is a strange mixture of busy and empty.

There's the set of drawers, the bed, a wooden chair, and an old cupboard near the end of the bed. That's it.

The chair has a pile of clothes on it and the drawers are piled with everything from books to aftershave.

'Was this an office before I arrived?'

His voice sounds in my ear, low, almost as simple as a vibration in his chest.

'No. It always has a bed here.'

I roll to face him, shifting around while trying to keep my T-shirt in place. I press my cheek on my hand against the pillow.

'Why?'

'Really?' His brows furrow, because we both know it's a silly question.

It's obvious why.

He works late, maybe has a drink or three and doesn't want to drive home. It makes sense to have this little space hiding in plain sight.

'Can we swap?' Yianni begins to wriggle and scan the room. 'I don't like to be near to the wall. If something happened, I can't protect you.'

'Protect me? From what?'

'There's nothing. But I like to, what's the phrase, *be on the safe side.*'

I smile up at him as he lifts his weight on to his right elbow. I don't agree, or go to move.

We just spend a moment studying each other.

Perhaps he's waiting for me to move. I don't.

This is San Stefanos – I'm not worried about anything more than Hazel and Pericles bursting through the door in the morning and getting the wrong idea.

Yianni's left index finger runs the length of my jaw and comes to rest on the scar on my chin.

I roll away as best I can, turning myself to face the pile of clothes on the chair again.

As soon as his finger touched me, I could feel the quickening of my blood pulsating around my body. The heat inside me seems to gravitate to certain areas more than others.

I close my eyes tightly shut.

In my mind's eye, I see the sea and the sky. Not the distant pinprick line I so often see in the morning, but the blaze of this evening.

'Please, can we swap?'

'Fine.'

This time I turn and scoot to sit up on the pillow, pulling my knees in. He lifts himself up, reaches his left arm over me and climbs past, his face close to mine.

He has plenty of space not to get so close to me.

I can almost feel the warmth of his breath as he passes.

We settle ourselves down on the thin sheet of the bed and this time Yianni switches off the light.

Moonlight gives enough illumination to see shapes in the black of the room.

I like sleeping on my right side, so I'm left facing him. His weight shifts and moves before settling. I'm quite sure his face is only inches from mine. I close my eyes.

'*Kalinikta*, Ruby.'

Then his lips find mine.

I don't know if he meant to kiss me right on the mouth, or if he was aiming for my cheek and misjudged it.

Either way, we've collided, and I can't bring myself to pull back.

He presses more firmly into me when I don't move away. His fingers slip around my waist and carefully grip *his* T-shirt that's wrapped around *my* body.

His mouth was no accident.

His lips part and mine follow, our bodies pressing together.

My fingers slide into his curls and our tongues slip over each other's, and soon I'm burning hot and gasping for air.

My mantra comes storming into my head. *He is your aunt's stepson.* This time I add, *If you fuck this up, you could lose everything. Aunt Hazel will never forgive you if you hurt him.*

I break the spell. I pull away.

'*Kalinikta*, Yianni.'

I roll over and clamp my eyes tightly shut. What the hell just happened? How? Why?

Thoughts scramble over me like insects, until I trap one in a web and latch on to it. I need to steady my breathing. I can hear his too as he turns to face away from me.

I'd forgotten what it felt like to have someone else's heat pressed against me like that. To have their breath burning my skin and entering my lungs as mine.

What. The. Hell. Just. Happened? It's a bit undeniable now that Yianni *does* like me too.

I need to sleep, to do my best to act as though that passionate kiss never happened. As though my blood doesn't feel like lava coursing through my veins, and as though I hadn't noticed his desire pressing against me when we were kissing.

A rush of heat pulls me out of a fever dream in the very early hours.

I'm in an embrace with Yianni and his face is pressed against my chest. I wonder if I *was* dreaming.

He's gently snoring.

My eyes adjust to the dark, or maybe it's soon to be dawn and this part of the earth is getting a little lighter. Either way, I can see a little more than shapes. Notes of colour are edging back into life.

Before trying to pull myself free, I keep wondering how we ended up like this. If in our sleep and our dreams, we have just carried on with our desire.

I wanted to. I still want to.

I've wanted to touch him from the moment he spoke to me at the airport.

It was easier to focus on him being in a grump – even when he probably wasn't – because I don't want a relationship. Particularly not with my aunt's stepson.

Carefully, I prise us apart.

I'm glad I'm the first one to wake up and find our entanglement, and that he doesn't know about it.

In part because my T-shirt has shifted to be halfway around my waist.

Slowly, I reposition us, but before I roll away from him to face the other side, I watch his breathing.

The inhale and exhale.

Steady and strong.

It reminds me of watching the sea in the mornings. Rolling in and out. Strong yet peaceful.

His dark eyebrows over his hooded lids and thick black lashes like a frill on his eyes.

He is so peaceful that he makes me feel peaceful. Carefully, I run my finger along his eyebrow.

I desperately want to kiss his velvety lips again.

Instead, I lightly skirt the line of his bottom lip with my index finger. It folds in on itself and he turns his face to the fan again. Reining in the urge to touch him more, I turn over and squeeze my eyes tightly shut until the lullaby of the fan helps me to drift back into sleep.

A tickling sensation on my stomach rouses me again, then frightens me, making me throw myself forward in the bed with a gasp, nearly knocking Yianni straight out of it.

Another scar.

He found another one of my scars and decided he could touch it the way he had with the ones on my face.

'What do you think you're doing, Yianni?'

'I am sorry. I— This scar, it surprises me. Is it from the accident?'

I answer with a sharp nod. 'That doesn't give you the right to poke at me, you know.'

Then I remember touching him in the middle of the night and wonder if he really *was* asleep. Surely he was.

A flush of guilt prickles my skin. This is also the first time we are eye to eye after our kiss.

'I am sorry. I didn't mean to wake you.'

'Did you lift my top up?'

'Fuck, no, Ruby! It was up, I just saw the scar. I . . .'

A blush runs over his cheeks.

I know from the middle of the night that the T-shirt has a mind of its own. I want to tell him off, but I can't.

I suppose I don't really want to tell him off. The feminist in me wants to tell him he should keep his hands to himself unless I say it's OK, but the other half of me wants to tell him it's OK to touch me whenever and wherever he wants to.

Perhaps if I hadn't done the same in the night, then I would have told him off more. But as it is, I'm equally in the wrong. 'I need to get back to the house.'

Chapter Thirty Three

THEN

'How was the show?' My voice is barely a croak from under the covers.

Jonathan is doing his best to sneak in, but the light from the bathroom is streaming on to my face because I forgot to fall asleep facing the other way.

My eyes blur as I open them to see him wiping away make-up from his eyes. He kneels down next to the bed and looks like something from a cartoon. Thick, dark make-up is being pushed around his face by the wipe in his hand, until it slowly fades into thinner and lighter lines.

'Fucking brill. This guy came up to me after, pushed his card into my pocket. Turns out he directs independent films. Knew this play was worth it. Didn't I say this would change our lives?'

I make a noise of agreement, or tiredness; either way, it spurs him on.

'You won't have to work in any more shitty restaurants. No serving people for us. We'll be going to them, not working in them, and picking anything we want to eat.'

I pull the cover a little further down and cross my arms over it, peering at him as the make-up dissipates until I can see him instead of a character he's been playing.

'But that's not my dream. I don't want to just follow you around. What would my job be then, to do what?'

'Have our gorgeous babies.'

Jonathan doesn't even believe I can do it any more. Maybe he's right to think I should just stay at home. My parents failed, why wouldn't I?

It's too late – or early – for this. There's no point arguing or pointing out that I have ambitions and goals when I'm no closer to them now than when we met. At least he manages to perform, and people believe in his worth.

Even I'm not sure I believe in my worth any more.

He can't think all I want to do is stay at home having children.

We've briefly said we both want children *one day*, but our ambition drives us both forward. But as I'm as far away as ever from achieving anything, I guess I've suddenly been nominated to be a stay-at-home mum. I roll away and store it all up in my head.

Asking questions I don't say out loud, like, *Why is your dream more valuable than mine? What makes you think my ultimate goal is to have* your *babies?* But it's not me who's talking out loud. It's him.

'Don't be like that.'

I don't say anything.

'Fine.'

I don't say anything.

'You'll love it when I'm famous. Then all you'll want to do is have my babies.'

The door to the bathroom is pulled closed.

In the dark, I contemplate at what point a relationship turns from fun and hopeful into a habit.

When does it go from two people enjoying each other's company to waking up next to each other and living separate lives with separate dreams? When is it that only one person learns to compromise and the other continues blindly on?

Is it the same in all relationships? For all women, perhaps?

I don't know. Maybe.

We all need to compromise, to give each other space to grow. That's all this is. Finding our new roots and growing from them.

I'm not one for making a mess, but since we moved in together in our *sensible* house away from London, I thought we were going to start being *sensible*, and maybe shift some of the focus on to my much more *sensible* ambitions.

Sometimes, I worry we've slipped into a pocket like a packet of cigarettes.

Are we a habit, or is this just a hard moment? I don't want to be the sort of person to give up on something great just because it got a little hard.

As Jonathan slips into bed next to me, I squeeze my eyes shut because even if this is a habit, I don't want it to stop. There've been so many good times together.

I'm tired and being oversensitive about nothing. I'm the one still plugging away at nothing and he's there making his dreams work. He's getting there one show at a time.

I'm projecting my insecurities on to him. That's all this is.

Jonathan's home and excited and all I can do is take it as a negative. He's talking about building a family, a life, everything we've always wanted, and I'm dragging myself down.

I'm tired and overreacting. That's all.

It's not as though he said I should give up on my life or my dreams. He was seeing a future with us and a family. We have so much to look forward to, that's all.

Now is the time to focus on the future, not just the past. Or perhaps I should focus on the here and now. We're together and that's worth holding on to.

Chapter Thirty Four

Now

The most that has happened since our kiss is Yianni's fingers grazing mine while passing drinks over the bar.

It's like it never happened. Like it was a dream.

It's work as usual. I go home at the same time as Hazel, Pericles and Natalia, leaving Yianni and Nico working behind the bar.

I don't want Hazel to catch on to my attraction to Yianni, so I've been carrying on in much the same way as I did before our one and only day together.

Luckily, there was barely a question about me staying with him that one night. We're friends. We got away with it.

Pericles' only comment was that he hoped Yianni didn't make me sleep on the floor. We all laughed and Yianni said he had given me his bed. Knowing Yianni, I don't think he wanted to tell an outright lie.

Although I'm also sure he didn't want to advertise the fact we were both in the same bed either, and no one suggested he might be in there too.

This morning, before work, Yianni came to the house to have a shower. This is pretty common unless he showers at the gym.

I don't often see him as I'm swimming in the mornings.

Yesterday, Natalia came with me. It was the first time she'd seen my scars. She asked so many questions.

She knows most of the story anyway. She told me I was brave, and it must have been dreadful, and it was all so sad.

All the normal things people say.

I want to go out. After yesterday, Natalia wanted to go with me again, but I said she couldn't. I made an excuse because I didn't want more questions.

Now I need to go out, but I can hear Yianni chatting to Hazel in Greek downstairs.

I don't really want to interrupt them as they aren't speaking English. I stay in my room, messaging Amara. She has been under the weather and hasn't been into La Salle à Manger for a few days, but she is starting to feel better. Poor girl.

I can't wait a moment more or I'll miss my pre-work walk.

It's only on emerging from my bedroom that I notice the volume of the two voices has changed.

They're talking in hushed tones.

I'm quite sure it's still Yianni and Hazel, but they are no longer chatting in a normal way about everyday things. Now that their voices have lowered, the whole house feels dark, as though the sun has hidden itself behind a black cloud.

My phone pings loudly in my hand, alerting them that I'm hovering near the top of the stairs.

Clearly, they have both heard it as they stop talking immediately.

Pretending I haven't noticed their shift in tone, I plod down the stairs with my bare feet audible to anyone in the house.

'*Kalimera*.' My voice is as bright and natural as I can conjure.

Hazel's neck and chest are a little flushed, but she smiles at me.

They both greet me in an even tone, but Yianni's tugging his hair behind his ears and doesn't look at me for more than a fraction of a second.

'I'm going for a walk along the beach before work. See you both later.' With that, I leave the house, jump on my bike and head off to the beach at San Stefanos.

I wish I could speak Greek so that I could have understood what Hazel and Yianni were talking about.

He seemed irritated, but I couldn't tell if he was irritated at Hazel, at me or at something else. Something I can't guess at because I can't speak Greek.

Hazel looked like she was trying too hard to plaster on a smile and her skin was pink under her tan.

I march along adjacent to the sea, kicking up damp sand.

I don't know why I'm steaming along like this. I meant to have a relaxing walk to absorb the sea air and to admire the line between the sea and the sky as I like to do, but now I feel that the irritation I sensed in Yianni has glued itself to my skin like a rash.

During the lunch and evening service, I'm sure that Yianni's attitude towards me is off, almost as though he's intentionally not looking at me, which is the complete opposite of our normal dance.

It makes me realise just how often we spend time trying to catch glimpses of each other.

'Have you upset the little boss?' Nico stands so close to me our arms are almost touching. He's holding a glass and rubbing a tea towel around the rim.

I glance up at him. 'Don't know what you mean.'

'Yianni. The little boss.' Nico places the glass under the bar and then leans on the bar top with his elbow, twisting his body to face me. 'Even I notice he is not looking at you. Usually he watches you more than he stands at the door.' He leans even closer to my face. 'I think he likes you,' he whispers, then winks before settling back on to his elbow.

'Apparently not today.' The flippant remark slips my lips before Nico's words really sink in. 'Anyway, no, he doesn't.'

Nico begins to chuckle at my side. 'Glad you have noticed this too. I wonder why he is not watching today.'

Nico turns away from the bar, leaving me to watch Yianni alone.

Behind Yianni, someone else catches my eye. 'Holy shit, who is that?'

Nico turns to follow my eyeline towards the entrance, then starts to laugh. 'This is Gaia's parents, Melodie and Anton.'

'Wow, what are they? Retired supermodels? Blimey.'

Still laughing at me, Nico walks around the bar towards the most beautiful and ridiculously tall couple I have ever seen. No, she is tall, but he is a giant with broad shoulders and sharp emerald eyes, just like Natalia's friend and fellow kitchen helper, Gaia.

Nico walks over, kisses Gaia's mum's cheeks, and scoops the baby she is holding right out of her arms. It's a tiny thing, perhaps only a month or two old. Nico cradles and bounces the baby in his arms as he shows the couple to a table, before handing the baby back to its mother.

Yianni walks up and touches the baby's head. He's laughing with them both. Although it can't be *that* long since the woman gave birth, she looks elegant in a loose-fitting button-down dress.

I hope that if I ever do decide to have kids, I look that good afterwards.

Gaia comes out to kiss her parents and, at different intervals, so do Natalia, Hazel and Pericles. Everyone's like family or old friends, without exception.

So often people arrive at the restaurant who have been coming on holiday here since before Greek Secret was even open, and everyone hugs hello and goodbye. Although Hazel is my aunt, and I am actually part of her family, there are times when I feel like *I'm* the odd one out and *I'm* the one who doesn't know anyone.

While Hazel is chatting to the striking pair, she turns and waves me over.

I finish putting together the drinks order that I'm working on and bring it to a nearby table before stepping towards them.

'This is my niece, Ruby. This is Melodie and Anton – oh, and I must not forget baby Lily, Gaia's new sister.'

'Lovely to meet you both. Gaia is such a great girl. A real straight talker.'

Their faces lift at the mention of Gaia and Anton's lips shift into a joking smirk.

'Yes, sorry about that.' A low, rumbling laugh emanates from him. It's almost intimidating.

'Nice to meet you too,' Melodie says. 'Hazel said you'd be coming to work here over the summer. Are you enjoying it so far?'

'Love it. What's not to love?' I narrow my eyes at her, staring at the structure of her face. 'I have to say, you're such a beautiful family. You must get that all the time. I can see the resemblance. You and Gaia are both stunning.'

'I love that, and I do wish it could be true, but she's not my birth daughter. I'm very proud of her nonetheless.'

Baby Lily wriggles in her arms, and Melodie lowers her chin to appease her while I stutter, 'I'm so sorry.' Melodie and Anton both graciously shrug off my mistake.

Yianni appears at my elbow with their starter, and we leave them to eat.

My cheeks feel hot as I meander back behind the bar. As soon as I get the chance, I stick my elbow into Nico's ribs.

'You told me they are Gaia's parents, you shit.'

'Yes, they are.'

'Melodie isn't.'

'She is adopting her.'

'Fine, but I still feel like a bloody idiot for saying that Gaia looks like Melodie.'

Nico's face lifts into a lopsided boyish smile. He has a nice smile, youthful and wide.

He's the sort of guy that girls don't often take seriously though. I'm still trying to work out if that's the façade he has built up to protect himself or whether he really is the kind of guy who shouldn't be taken too seriously, and will never have a long-term relationship with anyone.

'Nico, how come you don't have a girlfriend?'

A subdued voice comes from behind me. 'I need two pints of Mythos, draft. For table four.'

I spin around to see Yianni. He has an almost purple tone skimming the surface of his cheeks. He turns away before I can say anything more.

'I do not think Yianni liked that you want to know about my love life.' Nico can't hide the smug look adorning his face.

He picks up a pint glass and spins it on the palm of his hand before tilting it under the tap.

Keeping his chin down, he looks up from under his eyebrows at Yianni as he fills glasses with Mythos. Yianni's handing out menus to a large party that has just walked in.

As usual, he is greeting them as though he knows them, which he probably does. 'Forget my love life,' Nico continues. 'What is happening with you and Yianni?'

'Me and Yianni? *Pfft.*' As soon as the dismissive sound is out of my mouth, I know I've overplayed it.

Nico looks at me from the corner of his eye and that's enough to break down my defences.

'I have no clue. We had fun last week, a lot of fun. But now I think he's in a mood with me. *Shh*, here he comes.' I flap my fingers at Nico, and he chuckles and puts another beer on a tray as Yianni approaches.

'For you, Yianni.'

Yianni reels off the next orders. 'One bottle of house red, two cola, one apple juice and water for the table. You take it over.' Without even glancing in my direction, he gently taps the bar before walking away with his tray of beers.

'Wait,' I call after him.

He turns and meets my eyes. There might be a glimpse of hope, or a spark, or something, and now I feel like complete dirt because I'm about to ruin that hopeful softness drawn on his face. 'You didn't say how many wine glasses.'

His lips press together, pulling his mouth into a thin line. 'Four.' He turns and walks away.

I exhale and Nico glances at me before sniggering and collecting glasses for the next order.

Nothing more is said as we work around each other. He knows I'll collect the bottle of wine and I know he'll do the soft drinks.

I don't usually drink while I'm working, but I pick up a beer and snap it open on the opener attached to the back of the bar. I'm hot – and clearly bothered – and I want a cold drink to take the edge off my growing mood.

'That bad?' Nico says as he picks up the tray of drinks to walk to the table.

'I'm just thirsty.'

Even though we've only been working together for a short while, Nico and I have spent enough time together to get to know each other. But as for Yianni – do I know enough about him to potentially shock and upset our family?

He seems to be back to square one with the moodiness that he had when we first met, and it makes me question everything that happened between us. There's no way at all I want to be with someone who can't communicate or someone whose negative attitude is destructive in any way.

Stop it.

I can't keep thinking in these terms. Particularly when it's massively hypocritical of me.

It's so easy for me to hold everything in, and the hardest thing in the world to let secrets out. Communication isn't exactly my strong point.

Anyway, I can't keep wondering whether there's something more to my relationship with Yianni. It's making me slip into an emotional headspace that I don't want to be in any more.

Chapter Thirty Five

THEN

'A guy tried to grab me at work today.' The words are out of my mouth before my keys hit the sideboard.

'Hey, look at this,' Jonathan calls from the living room. The TV is blaring. He hasn't even turned to look at me as I appear in the doorway of the lounge.

'A guy grabbed me tonight.'

Jonathan snatches up the remote, turns the telly off and twists to face me. 'They did what?' He arches one eyebrow at me and points the remote at me too, as though he could use it to play the information right out of me.

'There were two men. They were drinking a lot after their meal. I was trying to be pleasant, but also move them along. You know how it is. But then one grabbed me as I was showing them out. I only went to the door with them because they were last out, and I was going to lock up. It was lucky Charles came out of the kitchen to sit and look over his papers, the way he always does.' My throat feels like it's closing up.

I snap my jaw shut, unable to tell Jonathan that one of the men pinned me to the wall and tried to put his tongue down my throat while the other bloke laughed and said *my turn next.*

Outrage burns in my core and goosebumps rise on my fore-arms like angry volcanoes.

'What did they look like? I'll deal with them. I'll make them regret ever touching you.'

'It's over now. You're not going to manage to Facebook-stalk them when I don't even know their names now, are you? Don't be silly.'

'I'm not being silly, Ruby. You're being stupid. It's important to protect what's mine.' He jumps up from the chair and walks over to put his arms around me.

My face presses against his chest, but I don't feel in the slightest bit comforted.

Mine.

I'm my own. I don't want to emasculate him, but I don't even want to be with him, let alone be spoken of like all I am is a chain around his neck, there to be looked at and possessed.

I turn my face away from the crush of his embrace and let my thoughts trickle out. 'I know it's my birthday on Thursday, and we said we would get breakfast together before work, but Amara goes to a self-defence and mixed martial arts class. I want to go with her.'

Jonathan pulls away and looks down at me, gripping my shoulders. His big hands digging into my flesh nudge in thoughts of the lecherous man at the restaurant.

'You don't need that. You have me to protect you.'

'You won't always be here, Jonathan.'

Quizzical eyes search my face and confusion seems to fill his features before he finds words. 'What's that supposed to mean?'

I twist out of his grasp and move back into the hall, towards the stairs.

What do I mean? What do I want that to mean?

My head throbs with adrenaline and fury. Carefully, I press my fingers to my temples as everything swirls around my mind.

The urge to tell him I'm done burns in my chest. I've had enough. He's pushed me to my limits. But I close my eyes and see the birthday party my mum's throwing for me. How much pain and drama there would be, and for what? Because I've given up on us? I'd have to spend the entire evening explaining to everyone why he wasn't there.

Everyone loves him.

He's always the life and soul of a party. He can tell any story. It doesn't matter whether it's true, a complete fabrication or whether he's telling a story that is actually mine. He sells it and they all lap it up.

I thought he'd been taking life seriously at last, accepting a job working for a theatre company – directing a children's production of an original script – as well as making it to a few auditions.

Maybe he deserves one more chance.

We do. We deserve one more chance.

If things don't pick up after my party, then I'm giving up.

In the meantime, I can look into room shares within his budget, based on him carrying on with the children's production. That way, if things don't pick up this week, I won't be kicking him out on to the street. I'd be able to offer him a plan. And I can avoid spending my whole party explaining to everyone I know that we're not together any more.

He might surprise me. He might really make an effort for my birthday and turn things around.

'You weren't there tonight, were you?' I say now. 'You won't always be with me.'

My feet slap against the first two steps up to our bedroom before I catch myself and tiptoe the rest of the way, trying to be considerate of the neighbours.

'Maybe I should pick you up from work.' He follows me into the bedroom.

'Don't be ridiculous. We have one car. *My* car. And I'll be using it. I want to go to this class with Amara.'

'What's the point? You're meant to be going out with me in the morning. It's bad enough you're working on your birthday. This incident . . . I bet it wasn't even that bad. Are self-defence classes really necessary? Don't you think you're overreacting?'

I glare at him, biting back the words that want to jump out of my mouth to choke him.

I don't tell him he is wrong, or that he is sort of right, but only because Charles shouted, *Get the fuck out or I'll call the police.* I have no idea what would have happened otherwise.

I was crushed against a wall, trying to duck down but failing. There's no way I want to feel so helpless again. I had no idea how to react. Not really.

'We can celebrate at the party.'

'Seriously? That's days away, and it was organised by your mum. What are you, twelve?'

Needles walk along my flesh, dancing over each nerve, and my fists contract. I snatch a breath and take my time over the exhale. He wants an argument, but if I let myself get dragged into it, he'll twist it around until I'm the bad guy.

'I just wanted to spend some time with you, Rubes. I feel like I hardly ever see you. You're always working. Now this class. When will you have any time for me?'

And here it is. I'm the bitch. Some prick tries to – God knows what he was really trying to do – kiss me or something, and *I'm* the one with a problem.

'Look, it's been a really shitty night. I'm going to sleep now. We'll just have to do lunch another time.'

'Breakfast.'

'Yes, that's what I meant.'

'See, our plans mean so little to you, you don't even know what they are.' He storms out of the bedroom, slamming the already damaged door.

A baby starts to cry and I whisper, 'Sorry,' to the neighbours.

Chapter Thirty Six

Now

'We all want chips and beers, thanks, love,' a skinny boy with freckles announces in my direction, before tapping his fist on the bar.

He's with a group of blokes who've just walked in. Youngish. They march straight to the bar.

'I'll sort the drinks first and then we can sort food. Draft or bottles?'

'Draft.'

The conversation between them concerns their wanting to be moved to a different resort, one with nightclubs. One of them, a shorter guy with spiked hair and a twisted nose, is getting the blame.

They're all quite pale still, but with a pink glow, which leads me to conclude this is their first night here.

I can almost feel Yianni and Nico prickle at them as they talk and demand things of me.

Yianni has been doing his best to keep his distance from me. He's been watching me again though, and I can't help but look at him, even when I shouldn't.

I've wondered whether he thinks I should ask what's wrong, but I'm not chasing anyone. I'm OK with holding everything in and letting everyone else get on with their own lives. Either I'm factored in or I'm not. It's that straightforward.

Tonight has been no different. Although the restaurant is heaving, I caught him looking even before this group came in. It's been so busy we've had people waiting at the bar for a table, and yet I've still caught his gaze more than once falling on me.

It's getting late and the kitchen closes soon.

Nico's chatting to a cluster of girls whose sole reason for coming to our restaurant is to get Yianni to serve them food and Nico to serve them drinks after. They're having a rainbow of cocktails and laughing at any charming or joking comment Nico can give them. He loves it.

But for now, both Yianni and Nico have half an eye on me.

Not that anyone else would know or sense this from them; they're smiling enough. I can feel them watching though. They feel what I feel, as though the breeze has switched direction and nothing feels quite right.

Yianni manages to herd the blokes to a free table that's safely away from the people who are still sitting and enjoying the last of their meals. Alongside the cluster of girls in front of Nico at the bar is a couple having 'one for the road'.

Before the group of boys arrived, they were telling me lots of fun things to do in Corfu. Now, though, I'm pulling the pints for the boys' table and the couple's eyes keep flicking in their direction. I guess they feel it too.

Yianni's watching me as I come round the bar and pick up the tray. He isn't making his usual sidelong glances; he is actively watching me while noting down another table's dessert order.

Even Pericles, who is at present chatting to a table in the far corner, seems to be keeping tabs on me. Having an audience is making me a little paranoid that I might drop the tray.

For the past few weeks, I've been wearing either reasonably short black shorts or a fitted black miniskirt because it's been too warm to wear anything else.

As I walk along, I can feel my skirt riding up, little by little.

Maybe it's something I don't normally notice because I don't normally have an audience, but as I approach the boys' table, I can see an elbow being poked into ribs and they all look up at me simultaneously and fall silent.

I've worked in this industry my entire life. Not much fazes me. I think my heart is only beating harder because of Yianni's eyes tracking me.

'Here you go, lads.' I carefully walk around the table, placing down all five beers one by one.

'What's your name?' I look over to see a man in a black polo shirt talking to my boobs across the table.

I have a strong urge to say something sarcastic like, *Which one are you asking and I'll tell you?* or *I haven't actually named them, but they like to be treated as individuals.* I refrain, and instead maintain the smile on my face.

'It's Ruby. Just let me know if you need anything else.'

'Three plates of chips, thanks, love,' another one says, and they all laugh as I walk away, inching the hem of my skirt down with my fingertips. Luckily it wasn't as high as I thought.

I'm not sure what's so damn funny. But they're elated.

Yianni rounds some tables and walks next to me. I look up at him and say, 'Do you have a drinks order for me?' It feels nice to have him so close to me again.

I can feel his warmth and smell his delightful masculine scent. Something inside me that has been quietly lying dormant for the past few weeks feels like it's just kicked me in the throat.

'No, it's for the kitchen. Desserts. Tell me if they bother you, yes?'

'Don't be silly. They're harmless. I have an order for the kitchen too, three plates of chips.' I get myself back behind the bar and Yianni makes his way into the kitchen with the dessert order and the order for chips.

It should be the last one of the night.

He comes back out moments later with bowls of chips, and takes them to the table of guys. There's the sound of tipsy laughter and I'm sure they're all looking towards the bar. As Yianni walks away from them, he has that purple glaze on his face and his lips are tightly pursed.

Nico is shaking cocktails again as Yianni comes over to the bar.

'Two more beers. Let me know when they are ready, I can take them.'

'Draft?'

Yianni nods and turns back towards the restaurant. His fingers are digging so hard into his hips that they are crinkling up his shirt.

A customer nods at Yianni, obviously wanting to get the bill. He walks over and chats to them a little while I'm pouring.

I finish and he is still talking.

What's two beers? I'm perfectly capable and I don't need Yianni or anyone else to walk them over to a group of boys for me.

I pick them up and take them myself.

As I lean forward to set them down on the table, one of the guys taps me on the bottom.

Tension ripples over me.

'Please don't do that.' I try to sound casual, but my teeth are a little more gritted than I first intended.

The lads are young, maybe in their very early twenties or late teens. Perhaps it's their first holiday without their parents.

I use these thoughts to curb my irritation. Post alcohol, they're basically toddlers who have no idea what they're touching.

I straighten up and turn to look down at the short one on my right. He puts his hands up like my eyes are guns and he's looking down the barrel.

The smile is still etched on my face.

As I turn to head back to the bar, the shitbag on my left grabs my left hand with his and pulls me on to his lap.

They all hoot and cheer. For a moment I'm taken aback.

Within a split second, my instincts kick in.

Still holding his left hand in mine, I grab it with my right hand too and spin away from him, twisting his hand down and under itself. I finish standing by his left side, rotating his hand and arm back so far that it's straight to the point of hyperextending. He bends forward as far as he can to try to escape me, but he can't.

I lean into him as his friends mostly fall silent. Apart from one who can't stop sniggering, writhing about to control laughter that wants to burst out.

The one I'm holding tries to edge away, but it only forces his face closer to the table in front of us.

'We have a look but don't touch policy here,' I say, then look up. 'I think it would be good if you all remember to respect other people's personal space before you hurt yourselves.'

I drop his arm just as Yianni, Nico and Pericles appear behind me.

As I turn to face them, it's Yianni's expression that catches me off guard.

His cheekbones are higher on his face than I've seen them in days. There's a micro-movement, an upwards twitch of his eyebrows. I think perhaps he was impressed.

The expression is so brief it's hard to say.

Then it's gone, as he asks the guys in the nicest possible way to pay up and leave.

They say loudly how they don't want to be in our *stinking restaurant* anyway and other nonsense, but the girls at the bar applaud me when I return.

My fingers creep back to where my ring used to be, but there's nothing there to remind me.

Once they leave, and only once Hazel has checked on me and Nico is deep in thought over some cocktail, Yianni comes up to me.

'I hope you are OK?' He leans his folded arms into the other side of the bar, making his shirt go taut around them. It's hard to keep my eyes on him without sighing.

At least I can keep my hands to myself unless invited. The memory of touching his silky lips ripples over me and a mixture of pleasure and guilt curdles inside me. Maybe I can't.

'I'm fine, thanks. How are you?'

Yianni opens up to me with a smile. A real one that is beautiful and charming and everything I've missed seeing.

'You're impressive.' He hesitates and takes his arms off the bar. 'Can we talk?'

'Now?'

'No. Maybe after work. Tonight?'

'Sure.' I smile at him, but he doesn't look up to notice it. Instead, he turns and heads in the direction of the kitchen.

Chapter Thirty Seven

THEN

'Jonathan?'

'Yes, Ruby.'

It's quite busy in the centre of Ipswich. Which has become a little unusual, given how much of town has closed down lately.

Rows of modern shopfronts hide beautiful old buildings either side of us.

'Where are we going?' I look up at Jonathan and a smile lifts my face as I study his dark blond mop of hair and his pale-blue eyes.

People move around us like we have a bubble holding us together. Things have been good today. Jonathan suggested a make-up shopping trip and I think maybe I jumped the gun after all, lining up ways to break up without making him homeless.

My hand feels comfortable in his. It's so damn simple.

'I thought we could go to that funny little vintage shop. You love that place. Let's see if we can get you some vintage furniture for your birthday.'

'What?' I stop walking. 'I used to love that place, but the owner was really rude to my mum. Remember?'

I can tell by the way he wrinkles his nose that he doesn't remember, but he is going to try to pretend he does.

'Oh shit, yeah. Must have been getting it confused with a different shop. Let's go to a different one then.'

'Seriously, Jonathan. You can't remember me telling you, can you? Bloody hell, she cried about it, they were so rude. You said we would never go there again. You don't remember at all, do you?'

He drops my hand and tilts his head towards the fluffy clouds drifting way above us, exhaling hard.

'No. You caught me. I'm sorry, babe. I don't remember. I'm sure it was important to you, but it can't be that bad if I don't even remember.'

He starts walking and, in a daze, I follow.

He isn't the same person I met years ago. The person I shared my secrets and dreams with. Or was he always this self-obsessed?

I was charmed by his confidence and utter enthusiasm. He pursued me like no other man had, and I liked it. Sometimes it's like I never even knew who he was, let alone knowing who he is now.

It's all just a grey area.

The fact he doesn't remember me telling him about my mum and the shop hurts me as badly as an open wound, and I feel that anything that touches me, even my clothes, is only causing more pain.

I was with my mum in the shop when the owner was rude. She was more than rude, if I'm honest. Mum's shoe caught on the floor, the rubber sole sticking, making her ankle twist, and she fell to the ground like a sack of spuds.

Instead of coming over and checking on my mum, the woman accused her of falling on purpose and said she couldn't sue her when she *clearly fell on purpose*. It was the most bizarre reaction. My mum actually apologised to the owner! Which, in hindsight, neither of us could quite believe.

I went on and on about what had happened to anyone who would listen. Clearly, Jonathan hasn't been listening.

'Come on, let's go to your favourite shop. You lead the way,' he says, and changes direction.

I stand still in the middle of the street, making someone behind me almost walk right into my back. 'What's my favourite shop, Jonathan?'

His fists turn into rocks by his sides and his nose does that thing again, crinkling up. Under his breath, he says, 'I don't know, Ruby. One with shoes?'

I shake my head. 'It's the bookshop, Dial Lane.'

My arms lock together in front of my chest and we start weaving through the streets of Ipswich again, only now our bubble has well and truly popped.

'Hold on, Rubes. I need to get you more than just a book for your birthday. If that's all I get, it doesn't look great, does it?'

I don't even bother to stop walking.

I don't even bother to think of a response.

It's all about what it looks like to other people. That's all he cares about. Not me.

Maybe that's all it's ever been. To him I looked like a model, and maybe that's what was important.

He doesn't know me; he hasn't got me anything for my birthday. I'm going to have to pick a present and eventually pay for it when the credit card bill rolls in.

Probably a good thing, because when he does surprise me, the surprise is, it's something even more expensive that I'll end up paying for.

I exhale through my teeth. It's hard to manifest positivity when my lungs feel like they've shattered along the lines of their alveoli, making it impossible to breathe.

I hold my breath to keep the waves of emotion in check. I can't let this get out. Not now, not yet. Soon.

After the party my mum has organised. I'll tell him it's over.

That gives me enough time to get all my ducks in a row and to figure out how I can say goodbye to him without making him homeless.

'It's not really a party, it's a gathering. Anyway, it's nice. We haven't exactly been able to do anything for the past couple of years.' I hook a pair of diamante earrings in my earlobes and watch Jonathan pull up his jeans in the mirror.

'Yeah, I know, I know. I just prefer it when it's just us.' Under his breath, he adds, 'But we didn't even get to do that on the big day, did we?'

He has brought up the fact that I chose going to a class with Amara over a cheap fry-up with him at least three times a day from then to now.

'You went out with your friends on *my* birthday.' This has become my standard counter-argument since finding out through a mutual friend that he was out dancing with groups of girls while I was serving people dinner.

'Come on, we've been over this. You didn't want to be with *me*.' I can't deny that part. 'I needed a couple of beers with my mates. What was I going to do? Wait at home and watch crappy TV?'

I don't rise to it.

Part of me wants to point out that one minute he insists on picking me up from work to *keep me safe* and the next he's out without me on my birthday.

It's just another nail in the coffin of us. Another step down the funeral aisle.

Tomorrow morning, I'll explain it all to him. I'll tell him that it hasn't been working, and that I need to focus on myself, because no one else can or does.

He certainly doesn't, and I'm getting lost. No. I'm not getting lost. I *was* lost, but lately I've been finding myself and I'm not going to play his games any more.

I nod my head to the girl in the mirror. *You're strong. It's not unkind to leave someone when you don't love them any more. It would be unkind to carry on. You are brave and strong.*

'What you smiling at?'

His voice behind me slaps the smile off my face, and guilt at being pleased to be free pours over me.

I can't hate him. A part of me still loves him. But I think I'm in love with the idea and the memories of good times, and not the person behind me in the mirror. I know being alone and gaining space is what I need now.

'Nothing. I'm just looking forward to the party.' I pick up my perfume and spritz a cloud of coconut and pear before swiftly walking through it.

'God, do you have to do it like that?' Jonathan frantically waves his hand in front of his face, squinting deep creases around his eyes. 'I don't fancy smelling like a fruit salad, thanks.'

He squares his shoulders and storms past me and down the stairs.

'It's what you got me for my birthday, actually,' I whisper. 'Nice to know you chose it with love . . .'

He got me two books that I picked out and this perfume. He said he needed some new razorheads and sprinted back to the shop while I was heading to the car.

The bottle that contains the fruit salad is very attractive, and to be honest I don't mind the smell, but I know he just saw a pretty container and didn't really care about the contents.

Maybe that's what I am to him. I know the rest of his life is about show. About what people see and what people think of him. About being perceived as the best.

I hang my head in frustration.

I wish I could do it now, break up with him now, but the performance would be unbearable. The *show*. I would never make it to my own birthday party.

Chapter Thirty Eight

Now

'We're off now. Are you coming?' Hazel leans across the bar and cups my face in her hand.

'I think it's still busy enough that I'll stay and help the boys for a bit. Yianni mentioned having a drink after too.' My left hand covers her hand on my cheek. 'Don't wait up.'

As she walks away, I blow a kiss at Natalia, who is waving and yawning. Then the two of them depart behind Pericles and it's only me, the guys and a handful of customers.

Nico and Yianni slip into Greek.

I'm not sure who initiates it, but soon after Nico is telling me to have a nice night and is leaving too, much to the dismay of our lovely customers.

The people left at the bar are fun and chatty. Normally, they would be perfect for creating a lively night while I'm working, but tonight, even though I'm laughing about the fact they've known Yianni since he was a sulky teen, I can feel time slowly dripping away, like Chinese water torture.

It's past midnight when they leave.

We wave. We smile.

Then it's just Yianni and me.

I almost hear my heart beating to the sound of the music that's playing around the empty restaurant. Yianni pulls the fold-out shutter partway across to make it clear we aren't open, even though a light is still on.

'Beer?' Yianni doesn't look at me. He just makes his way back around the bar.

'Rum and Coke.'

'Yes, I suppose you did almost break a man's arm today. I think you need a good drink after that.' I catch the smug look on his face.

Not that he's looking at me.

He's grabbing two glasses and the bottle of rum from the shelf behind his head.

'I didn't almost break his arm. I just . . . caught him off guard. But he caught me off guard first, so it's only fair.'

Yianni chuckles to himself and the sound – even though it's low and quiet – fills me. My entire face shifts to reflect the weight of missing him being discarded from my body.

'Where did you learn how to do this?' Yianni proceeds to sort of act out the moves, twisting up his arms.

'Me and my friend Amara have been going to different classes for a couple of years.'

Yianni passes me a short tumbler and I raise it briefly in his direction before taking a deep sip of the sweet vanilla-laced drink.

I make my way from behind the bar and to the same place we were sitting together only a few weeks ago. It's as though things have happened between us since then, but they're all unspoken and I'm in the dark as to what they are.

It's not the sort of game I'm used to playing. With Jonathan, it was emotional blackmail and guilt trips overlaid with a slick charm.

Albeit the charm only appeared when he wanted something or when other people were about.

With Yianni, it's thoughtful gestures or radio silence and nothing in between. Perhaps he came to the conclusion the kiss was a bad idea and that's all there is to it. Perhaps his quiet little chat with Hazel was nothing to do with me.

Yianni sits down next to me on the pale-blue cushions of the bench and we both study our glasses for a moment.

Then, like buses, it all happens at once, and we both go to speak at the same time, then awkwardly laugh.

Our eyes meet in the middle of it all, and we're left with hints of smiles on our lips, but something far from laughter in our eyes.

I let Yianni go first. 'Why didn't you tell me? About Jonathan?'

So that's what this has all been about. Jonathan.

That's what Hazel had been whispering with him about.

I shrug.

It's not as though I open up to many people anyway, and I don't know why he would expect me to just spill my whole life out in his direction now. Even when I thought I might, he didn't make it that easy.

Silence lingers.

Yianni could patiently wait for decades for an answer. At first, I think I can wait him out, but then I cave. 'I started to tell you, months ago, but you thought you knew it all, and that was that. It's not important anyway.'

'You said to me that you broke up.'

'I did say that.'

'Hazel tells me that is not true.'

'Well, I guess Hazel knows everything then.' I pick up my glass and sip before putting it down a little harder than intended. 'It's not like you've been open and chatty about your life.'

I shift to face him a little better on the bench and he automatically slides away an inch or two. 'You've never told me much about your mum, or what it was like when you gained a stepmum. One minute you're ignoring me, the next you're kissing me in the dark and then you're back to ignoring me again. I don't get it.'

His mouth opens, then slams shut again as though his teeth were made of magnets.

'After what Hazel tells me, I didn't know how to talk to you. I felt like you lied to me. Or that you don't want to talk to me. Then tonight, I see the way you are. I see more of who you are, and I know I *do* want to talk to you. I do want to know you more.'

Music's still quietly playing all around us. It's a song I don't really know, but it is painfully positive to the point of being sickly and I wonder if it's irritating Yianni too. He's so still, like a carefully crafted statue, one that comes back to life as he makes eye contact with me.

'What do you mean,' he says, 'about Hazel knowing everything?'

'I was being sarcastic. Not everything is always as simple as it seems. Life is a lot more complicated than the bullet points someone tells you about someone else's life. Surely you know that? Surely, you've gone through some kind of shit in your life?'

'Then tell me what it *really* is. Not the bullet points. Tell me what is truly in your mind.'

'No.'

'No?'

'No.'

Yianni exhales hard and slides his legs out straight, crossing his ankles as well as his arms.

He completely locks himself off in thought. He stays that way for the longest minute, to the point where I get up, make us some more drinks and come back with them.

When I arrive back from the bar, he has changed position and has both elbows on the table and his chin resting on his fists.

'What if I tell you about me? Things I don't tell anyone. Would you tell me things then?'

I push his drink towards him on the table then sip mine as I think about this proposition.

I do want to know more about Yianni. So far, the things I know are all in the present. How he can be deeply thoughtful, perhaps to the point of overthinking, but I have no idea what has made him the man he is.

'Maybe.' My eyes flick to his to gauge his response.

He exhales with a shake of his head, making his hair gently sway around his ears.

'I will take your maybe. You want to know about my mother. Well, she was the Greek Hazel.' This brings a smile to both our faces. 'She was kind and efficient but also fun and passionate about many things. Food, painting. She was never afraid of anything.' Yianni pauses before continuing. 'Not even at the end.'

'How did she . . .' For some reason, I can't bring myself to actually say the word *die* out loud. It seems so harsh.

I sort of know the answer already anyway. She went into a coma and died. I think she had some kind of surgery, and it went wrong. Something like that.

'She was hit by a car.' I didn't expect him to say that. 'She seemed fine. She was shaken, but she was walking and talking like nothing happened. Everyone tells her she must go to hospital to be looked over. She was smiling and hardly a mark on her, only bruises. She kept saying there was too much to do at the restaurant. Mama could wrap Baba around her finger. He looked so worried, almost green. Even as a kid, his face made me scared. I held her hand and begged her to go. Eventually, she agreed. On the way to the hospital, she started to repeat herself and slur like she had been drinking.' Yianni pauses, snatching a breath before continuing. 'She started saying she was tired. Everything was, *I'm tired, why am I so tired?* The last thing she said translates like, *You be good, Yianni, Mama needs a sleep.* We tried to keep her awake, but we couldn't. She went into a coma and never came out.'

I audibly swallow, trying to push down the emotions that are threatening to overflow.

'I'm so sorry.' My voice is so quiet I'm not sure Yianni even hears me.

He looks so vulnerable as he picks up his drink and holds it a centimetre from his lips.

I've never felt obliged to tell anyone anything much before, but I open my mouth prepared to at least give him something. But then he continues.

'We had to go on as though she is nothing. Baba was so broken he couldn't even speak to me. I am lucky; everyone here is family. I have cousins and uncles – you know, you've met them.' I nod and he nods to acknowledge me. 'But my mother was the one to hold us together. I understand why he fell in love with Hazel. I think my mother sent her to us, but I still find it hard how similar they can be. Hazel never pushed me to love her, she was patient when I hated her. And I did.' He chuckles and leans his forearms on the table, elongating his body over it slightly and twirling his glass in his fingers. 'I put them both through hell with my silence when I was younger, but they are hard to hate, and I love my little sister. Even when she is so annoying.'

Grinning, he takes a deep breath, then sits up in his chair again before turning to face me, still cupping but not actually drinking his rum and Coke.

The laughter rolls along with him as he continues. 'I also had a controlling girlfriend and always saying she will kill herself if I don't stay with her, but I don't find that as hard to talk about. Talking about my mother . . .' He tilts his head and sips his drink as though his actions are the end of the sentence and words aren't possible.

'I understand. I mean, I understand that it's hard to talk about things.'

Our eyes lock together.

I tuck my lips in because I know he is going to say it's my turn to tell painful truths and I really don't want to.

'You don't have to tell me things, Ruby.' His hand reaches across the table and rests on top of mine. The heat of his skin permeates mine and I let his fingers knot around my hand.

My heart's bounding like the bass of the music that's still droning on around our bubble. I can feel it in my chest, but I can't unpick the reasons for it. Is it because I want to tell Yianni everything that happened? Or because we are now holding hands?

'The problem is,' I begin, 'there are things I haven't told anyone. Whenever I've opened my mouth to tell anyone, I just can't bring myself to continue. I'm not good at opening up.'

His face changes, but not in the way I expect.

Instead of shock, fear or intrigue, he softens. His deep chocolate eyes melt me down and I start to wonder if I could tell him part of the story.

I grit my teeth and close my eyes, remembering that night.

'How about you just tell me what you would tell anyone? Or what you have told people so far? If you do not want to, I understand.'

I take a deep breath through my nose and inhale the comforting scent of Yianni next to me.

I open my eyes. I fix them on his and warmth spreads through my chest in the same way a shot would at the end of the night. I try to think where to start.

'So, you know you said about your girlfriend? The one who was always saying she would hurt herself if you left? Well, Jonathan was more subtle than that, but over the years I started to see that he was controlling every part of our life. *My* life with him. He was the only person I've ever told that I wanted to own my own restaurant—'

'He was the only other person you told? Now me.' His full lips hint at a smile and his eyes gleefully narrow on mine.

'Yeah.' I didn't mean to let that one slip.

That's for me to achieve on my own one day. To see my ideas come to life and to run a restaurant how I want to run it. To serve the food I think people will like.

'Anyway,' I continue, ignoring his gleeful face, 'Jonathan was always putting his acting career before everything else and making *me* pay all the bills, so I could never save up for my dreams. Then he started making it hard for me to see friends and family, then I had fewer and fewer people to talk to. It sounds silly now, but it was everything layering on top of me constantly. He was so different when people were there compared to when we were alone. Charming one minute, shouting at me the next. I started to see who he really was and . . .' My breath catches.

I haven't even said this much to my mum or dad, or anyone.

I never wanted people to think less of Jonathan, or less of me for staying with him for so long.

If they caught a glimpse of what our relationship had really degraded into, what would they think?

'. . . and I knew I had to break up with him. The problem was, he had nothing. No money of his own, and his mum had downsized to a place with no spare room. I just wanted to line some stuff up first so he might be able to get a place straightaway. I couldn't stand the idea of breaking up with someone then being forced to live in that emotion every day until someone moved out. Looking back, I also don't think I wanted another argument. I just wanted to plod along, ignoring it all for as long as I could. But he was always so persuasive and managed to do this mixture of putting me down and building me up to keep me feeling like I might need him or something. Does that even make sense?'

Yianni's nodding – not in a polite general way, but like he actually understands the experience and examples.

My feelings and thoughts seem to have shattered like glass, and I feel like I'm picking up small pieces of memories and emotions, cutting myself to tell Yianni what they are, and none of them link together.

They're just there, laid out all higgledy-piggledy, and I barely know what's about to slip out of my mouth, so I can't imagine how it is that Yianni seems to agree with me so fervently.

'My girlfriend, Angelika, she was like this too. Compliments that she would take back. She would say, *You try so hard, Yianni, I'm so proud of you. It is a shame you aren't better at math, I will help you, I am here.*' He puts on a stupid girl voice when talking as her, and I have to giggle.

'Is it bad to say I'm glad you understand?'

'A little.' He laughs, though, and sips his drink.

Thoughts creep over me like a cloud. How much do I really want to tell him about what happened with Jonathan?

Chapter Thirty Nine

THEN

This isn't where I wanted to be when it came out of me, but this is where it's going to happen. Here in the car, on our way home. I can feel it. It's creeping its way up my throat and sitting in my mouth, lurking, waiting to be released.

I barely saw Jonathan at the party, which was a good thing.

He worked the room. I could hear the laughter and chatter follow him around.

The thing is, I saw him drinking. It's lucky that I did notice because there was me thinking, *It's my birthday party, I'll have a couple of glasses of wine, maybe a cheeky rum and Coke because Jonathan will be driving home.* Apparently, he had other plans.

Even when I went up and said, in front of my dad, 'I thought you were driving?'

'Oh shit, sorry! I totally forgot. Your dad got me this, couldn't say no, could I?'

Yes, actually, you could.

I'm sure Jonathan didn't pay for one drink all night, and now he is drunk; not so drunk anyone else would know, but drunk enough for me to notice.

He's being snide. Making comments that I was talking to Rob for too long – and he keeps it up when we get in the car to go home. I'm having to drive, of course.

'Bloody hell, Jonathan, he's gay!'

'He's bi. I'm pretty fucking sure I saw him looking at your tits.'

'Yes, he did compliment my outfit. I'm sure in your mind that constitutes staring at my *tits*.'

'I just don't trust him.'

Tension ripples over me as the ties that Jonathan has enforced on me begin to crush every muscle.

I can't take it. I can't let him consume my life in this way any more. He's drowning me and I can't live this way for a moment longer.

He's still talking about some imaginary crap that he thinks he saw, or that he thinks I did.

'Shut up.'

I grip the steering wheel of the car. The leather's still cold from the night air and my fingers are so cold they feel almost crisp.

'What did you say to me?'

I'm not looking at him. I'm looking at the road being swallowed by our headlights, the A14 disappearing underneath us.

Through gritted teeth, I repeat myself. 'I said, shut up.'

Trees are rushing past us in the dark. The wipers automatically awake with a screech, as rain speckles the windscreen.

I snatch a breath and speak without letting myself think about the words. I had some planned, soft and gentle words, but they're being washed away with the rain as it begins to increase.

'I can't do this any more. It's over. I'm sorry, but look, I've worked it out and I can pay rent without you, so we don't have to worry about that, and I paid the deposit anyway. I've put together a list of places that are looking for flatmates. Before you dropped your job this morning, you could afford them all. Maybe if you ask for the job back, it might work out.'

'Stop. This is how you break up with me after all these years? You're money-obsessed, Ruby. Listen to you, you heartless bitch. Is that all you care about after all this time? How much money I earn and if you can afford to live without me?'

I didn't mean for it to come out that way, but I've been storing this all up and I've already had time to process things in my head. Even after sacrificing so much to support him for all these years, I was trying to help him.

The thoughts that I've been processing and ironing out in my mind probably seem to him like an ice-cold mess.

'You know that's not it. I've paid for everything over the years and sacrificed my savings to support you and us. I just—'

'I only took that directing job on for you. Surely that proves I'm willing to do anything?'

'You quit!' My voice matches the sound of the wipers in tone and my head snaps to look at him.

He curls in on himself as if the rain outside is directly pummelling his skin, and he holds his face in his hands.

He's crying.

Waves of pain crash into me. I should have waited and told him at home. Got my words out right. Made it softer, more amicable.

'I can't believe you're being so heartless, selfish. Fuck's sake. Just think about it for a minute, you can't do this to us. I can't live without you, Rubes. I'll do anything.'

He places his hand over mine on the wheel. His thumb gently glancing along my skin, thawing it.

So comfortable.

Then his words hit back into my brain: *You're money-obsessed, Ruby. Listen to you, you heartless bitch.*

No, I'm not. I am, on the other hand, desperate to be free, desperate to not have someone draining my energy and preventing me from fulfilling the dreams I've held for so long.

If I'm obsessed with anything, it would be security and peace.

I can't get that from him. There's no peace of mind, there's no security. On my own, I can have those things. With him it's all turmoil, a roller coaster, because each day I don't know what surprise – or shock – will come next.

Is there enough money to pay the bills today? Is he going to accuse me of something I haven't done? Well, no more.

'I don't believe you.' My words were meant to be soft, but they come out defiant, because I don't believe he will change or that he will do anything to keep me with him.

I'm ready to step away from him and his delusions. Tears slip down my cheeks because I'm pushing away someone who was once my best friend. The person I've shared all of me with.

The person I used to chat to until sunrise about dreams and ideas, the person I thought I would marry one day.

'Why are you doing this? Is there someone else? There is, isn't there? Is it that new waiter at work? Fucking tell me, Ruby!'

'No. You don't know me at all, do you?' My eyes cloud with tears so everything in the road becomes blurred shapes between my tears and the rain. I do my best to blink to clear my sight, but everything is foggy and deranged.

Jonathan's fingers crush mine and jerk down on the steering wheel.

He is howling like a wild animal in my left ear. I can't understand what he's saying, if they're words at all.

It's slow motion but somehow incredibly fast at the same time.

Trees, grass, headlights only showing us a snippet of the world around us as the car dances along, almost gracefully hurtling us towards the side of the road. As though it's relaxed, in contrast to my body, which is braced, tugging the steering wheel almost out of the column and pressing my feet as hard as I can to the pedals.

I awake from tormented dreams of pixies slicing up my skin and feasting on it.

My head's pounding in time with the music in the distance. Where the hell is that coming from? My eyes flicker.

It's not music.

It's sirens, creeping closer.

Everything stings and something's in my face.

Then the jagged memory of the car spinning off the road comes back to me.

'Jonathan?' My voice seems disembodied, searching in the dim light.

Something's clawing at my skin, pressing into my face.

A branch?

What the hell is a branch doing in the car?

Focus is coming back to me. I can see an empty field stretching out that is being illuminated by my headlights. But inside, a branch is pressing into my face and my abdomen.

I try to turn my head to Jonathan, but I'm pinned in place.

'Jonathan? Are you OK?' At least I can hear him breathing next to me.

Heavy, laboured breaths, long and slow.

Engines and voices swirl around not far from the car. I try to call out, but it hurts. I try again. 'Help. We're over here,' I call. 'It's OK, Jonathan, help is here.'

Still no reply, only the sound of breathing. It's so slow.

The fingers of my left hand crawl along the rough bark of the branch and over to Jonathan.

His side is wet. Really wet.

More light fills the space around us, and a man appears at the windscreen.

I'm squinting, but he seems relieved when he sees me make eye contact with him.

'Hello, I'm Byron. I'm a fireman.' He doesn't move around the car. He stands in front of the windscreen . . . Wait, there's no windscreen. Where's the damn windscreen? 'What's your name?'

'Ruby.'

'Hi, Ruby. What I need you to do for me is keep looking at my hand. Can you see my hand?'

He holds his hand up in front of the car and I nod.

'Don't nod, OK? Just answer me.'

'Yes.'

He keeps his hand in front of the car as he moves to the side.

'Keep looking forward, keep looking at my hand, OK?'

'OK.'

A voice, noises, crowd the left side of the car.

He's still breathing.

We need to get him out now.

Get the cutting equipment.

We need to cut away the car, and the tree.

If we don't get him out soon . . .

'Ruby? Did you hear me? I said: can you tell me where it hurts?'

I squeeze my eyes shut and tears burn in cuts on my skin.

'Everywhere.'

Chapter Forty

Now

I close my eyes. I can vividly recall the day Jonathan died, but only in snapshots.

Nothing's fluid.

It's almost like a picture book. How we argued.

How he pulled the wheel as hard as he could.

How he sealed both of our fates.

If he had lived, all the anger I felt would still be with me, but as it is, he died because of a stupid, angry reaction to news he didn't like. It was my fault.

I shouldn't have told him in the car when he was drunk. I knew he had a temper, a flair for the dramatic. He always had. He seemed to be able to absorb other people's emotions and regurgitate them perfectly.

He could store them up and let them out for stage and screen too. Each moment of extreme drama was something he felt every grain of and relished.

I knew that. So, it was my fault.

I may as well have been the one to turn the wheel. I did, I suppose – just with my words and not my hands.

But do I tell this to Yianni? I've never told anyone before. That it was Jonathan who made us crash.

I've never told anyone because I'm to blame anyway and I knew my silence would protect his memory. It's the least I can do. If I'd been able to see clearly, if his hand hadn't been on the wheel . . . we'll never know. All I do know is, I started it. I could've waited.

There's a pull to Yianni though, like he might listen and take it in, but he is also far enough away from the situation to be objective, unlike everyone who met Jonathan and knew him . . . and loved him. Yianni never knew Jonathan, so I wouldn't be ruining his memory of him the way I would for everyone else.

I don't know; I'm still not sure.

I remove my hand from underneath Yianni's, where it had been quietly enjoying his touch, and it retreats to my lap.

'I was driving my car in the rain back from a party. My birthday party. He, Jonathan, was in the passenger seat.'

'That is how you got your scars? It was that car accident?'

It's obvious, but I silently dip my head to acknowledge that he is correct. The last rum and Coke I made was a little stronger than I would normally pour. It's as though my skin is resonating like the cicadas and turning me lightly numb.

'I loved him, but I wasn't *in* love with him any more. I miss him now and then. We were together so long and then he wasn't there. Death is so final. That's a stupid thing to say. It's just— I'd prepared myself to not have him there every day, but death meant he left on his terms and I can't do a damn thing to change it.'

'It was an accident. He did not really leave on his terms.'

My eyes flick to Yianni.

Perhaps it's the physical loosening that comes with the consumption of alcohol, even in small doses, or perhaps my mouth folded in on itself in a certain way, or the way I shifted my weight signalled something to him, but Yianni's frowning, leaning in towards me.

His fingers stretch towards mine and he steals them from the security of my lap, placing my hand back on the table and lightly gripping it.

'Ruby?'

That's it. That's all he says.

It's not like my mum knocking on my door to check on me twice a day for months and asking me to talk to her about what happened.

It's simple.

His deep voice vibrates through me and the way he says my name rattles something loose inside me. I have to squeeze my eyes closed again.

'He grabbed the wheel. He pulled it down . . . my eyes were blurry with tears and he was screaming. I— I don't know if he saw something or if he did it in a fit of rage. I'll never know.' The words are barely audible.

They don't even sound like they came from my lips, but I felt my lips move.

I've never told anyone this part of the story – or even that we broke up right before the accident – and now the words are floating on the warm Greek breeze that sweeps in through the doors and I can't take them back.

I'm too afraid to open my eyes to see Yianni's thoughts written all over his face.

I feel the fingers of his other hand curl under my chin, and his thumb skims my cheek.

'Ruby, this is not your fault. You are not to blame for this.'

My eyes are still closed, but I shake my head.

My lung capacity seems to have ripped in half as I snatch in minuscule breaths that shrink with each inhale.

Yianni pulls me in and wraps me in his arms.

Our knees press together awkwardly under the table, but the hug is comforting, with the feel of his solid clavicle against my forehead.

I bite back the thought of tears. I will not let them fall.

There have been so many tears over Jonathan and so many people have treated me differently since it happened. It's taken a long time to get to this point, to one where I feel closer to myself and my dreams without the nightmare of our ending and his death constantly on my mind.

Not that it's completely gone. It's always lingering nearby.

'You can talk to me, Ruby. I will not tell anyone your secrets. They are yours, and if you want to share them with me, I will keep them safe for you, locked inside my chest. You can trust me, I promise.'

'Thank you.' My voice is muffled against the soft fabric of his black shirt.

I pull away slightly to look up at him. Our faces are so close together I can feel the warmth of his breath on my cheek, and the sweet scent of vanilla from the rum lingers between us.

I want to tell him that Jonathan wasn't trying to kill me, or himself.

Maybe he was, but I like to think that it was more of an impulsive act.

He had said many times he couldn't live without me, that he would die. Not exactly that he'd kill himself – like Yianni's ex – more that he would just stop living. Or that's what I thought he meant.

I'd never believed him; he was always being overly dramatic. I still like to believe that if Jonathan had thought about it, there was no way he would have done what he did. Or maybe he saved me from something I didn't see? There's no way to find out, but I like to think it's possible.

But I can't say it. I can't say any of it.

My lips edge towards Yianni's. I carefully press them to the side of his mouth.

'Thank you,' I repeat.

Then he turns and kisses my mouth fully. His right hand slips round to the back of my neck and his fingers get lost in my hair. *Don't get distracted, don't distract him* flashes into my head, and I snatch myself away from him.

'I shouldn't have done that.' I touch my lips, as though by removing the warmth of his mouth on mine, I've removed a layer of my skin.

As though my lips are burning and stinging, knowing the only antidote is for him to kiss me again.

To soothe me with the soft touch of his lips and the prickle of his stubble.

He doesn't say anything.

Instead, he dips his face towards mine again and kisses the scar on my chin. The sensation makes me almost wince as though the scar is an open wound, and he is sprinkling it with salt.

'It is not your fault, Ruby.' He kisses along my jaw. 'You cannot punish yourself because of what he did to you. He was a man with his own freedom, and he nearly stole yours. You did nothing wrong.'

I pull away from him, but he catches my hands in his.

'That's not true. I shouldn't have told him it was over while we were in the car. That was a stupid thing to do.'

'You could not know he would do this.'

Yianni's fingers glance over my scar.

'It was stupid of me not to pick a better time. If my eyes hadn't been blurred with tears, if he hadn't had his hand over mine on the wheel . . .' I snatch my hands from Yianni and go to twist the imaginary ring on my finger.

But that's all it is now, imaginary.

It's another lost part of my past, like a bad dream.

That ring was my reminder to be kind, my reminder of how we once were, and my reminder to be cautious with my heart and my actions.

But it was also my constant reminder of Jonathan. As though he was there, watching every decision I've made since he died. Without his presence pressing into my skin and imprisoning my finger, maybe I can let myself be free to step out of his shadow.

I look up to see Yianni's eyes focused on the same spot on my bare right ring finger.

He's squinting and I can almost see the words bubbling up towards his lips before he says, 'What is the real story about that ring?'

Chapter Forty One

Sue keeps hugging me and crying.

She keeps almost touching the stitches on my chin with her shoulder when she pulls me in. She apologises to me, then I apologise to her.

Neither of us has anything to apologise for, but we both feel sorry.

So, so sorry.

I'm sorry she's lost her son; she's sorry I've lost my boyfriend.

I said that now I'm out of hospital and back on my feet, she could come round and go through Jonathan's things with me. She'll want to keep things, and I already know that I want almost nothing.

It all hurts too much.

I haven't told anyone he pulled the steering wheel from my hands. I can't understand it.

I replay the moment over and over again as best I can, but it always feels like it's just out of reach. Was there something in the road I couldn't see through my blurred vision? Or was he having a reckless moment of anger?

I can't ask him now. I can't ever truly know. Even if I could ask him, I don't know whether I could trust his version of the truth anyway.

Everyone thinks it was an aquaplaning issue in the rain, and I play dumb.

The professionals say it's shock and injury. That's why I can't remember anything.

That loads of people can't remember the moments just before impact.

It's partly true: I can't remember the moments right before, only the sensation of Jonathan's fingers digging into mine on the steering wheel and pulling the car off course.

As far as Sue knows, it's all my fault that her son is dead.

I was the one driving, after all.

She hasn't blamed me though. I blame me instead.

If I'd kept my mouth shut for even twenty more minutes that night, then it would be him packing up his things and moving out to carry on living.

Now it's as though we both died in the accident.

Everything feels irreparably shattered. Picking up the pieces of my life is like dropping a packet of glitter on the floor and trying to pick up every last piece. I can't. Then, when I try, I realise it's not even glitter, it's glass – and each memory, each part of me cuts deep into my flesh, leaving more and more scars on my heart.

Even if I managed to pick up all the pieces of my broken life and try to stick them back together, the cracks would still show, and everyone would still be able to see how broken I am. It's written on my skin now.

So why am I even bothering to be alive?

The whole morning has consisted of blurred vision and tissues with every shirt pulled from our shared cupboard.

I guess it's just my cupboard now.

I sniff and pass Jonathan's backpack to Sue. There are a few scripts and headshots inside. I let her look through it while sitting on our bed. My bed.

It's only me who lives here now.

I start opening my drawers too, to look for cufflinks that have been thrown in with my jewellery. I know there were some that had been his grandad's and I'm sure she'll want to keep them.

I silently ask Jonathan how we let it all come to this. Why did he do this? Was he trying to save us, or kill us?

I find the little silver discs. They're so simple, about the size of a penny, highly polished, with a tiny ruby in the centre.

He thought it was fate that we met, that his grandad had sent me to him.

I rub along the red dot at the centre of one with my thumb. I wonder whether he's with his grandad now. Whether they're both blaming me.

I blame me.

I never met Jonathan's grandad, but I'm sure he would have hated me and there's no way he sent me to ruin Jonathan's life. To accidentally murder him.

I'm still eyeing the cufflinks and I'm about to tell Sue I've found them when I hear the sharp inhale of horror in her lungs.

'Oh my God,' she adds on the exhale.

It's as though the air has been completely snatched from her, making her words high-pitched. 'Ruby, I'm so sorry. I'm so sorry.'

There's a new layer of grief hanging in her voice, and I feel it in the cut along my stomach as though I've been freshly jousted by that damn tree.

My whole body shudders and I press my hand to the healing wounds on my abdomen.

I turn to look at her and see she is holding a small green box in her nimble fingers. Fresh tears fall down her already raw cheeks.

It's only as I step forward that I understand what it is, and the horror on her narrow face makes sense.

An engagement ring.

He was preparing to marry me, as I was preparing to leave him.

Maybe he did want me dead.

Chapter Forty Two

Now

'His mum, Sue, she found the ring after he died. She wanted me to keep it, to wear it . . . to keep his spirit alive. Apparently, he'd borrowed some money from her and that's what he'd got with it. I'm terrified to tell her I've lost it. Mum thinks it's best I don't tell her. For the past couple of years, she's wanted to see me on his birthday. Luckily, it's in a couple of weeks and I'll be here, so that breaks that painful tradition . . . unless, of course, she takes a holiday here just to see me. Honestly, I wouldn't put it past her. We got on well enough, but only because I always kept my mouth shut and went along with things to maintain a peaceful life. Same way I did with Jonathan, really.'

'When Hazel told me it was your engagement ring, and you chose not to tell me that when it was lost, I thought I should step back. When I kissed you in the dark, you pulled away, but I understand why. You have been through so much.' Yianni's eyes somehow look rounder, tinged with sadness.

'Do you know what I'm fed up with?' He arches his eyebrow at me, and I continue. 'I'm so fed up with everyone seeing me as broken. I liked not telling you everything because I didn't want you to feel sorry for me. I've always told myself I didn't tell people what he did to protect his memory, but maybe I was protecting me a little too. Think how they would look at me then. How you're looking at me now.'

Both of his fluffy eyebrows shoot up at this and his hand comes to his chest. 'Me?' he says. 'How am I looking at you?'

I gesture towards his face. 'You're sorry for me because I'm the girl whose boyfriend tried to kill her and ended up killing himself. And since then, it's like I've been cursed with everyone keeping their distance. I'm damaged goods.'

Yianni starts to laugh, and my eyebrows pull together at the sound of it.

Folding my arms over my chest, I wait for him to calm a little.

'Do you want to know what *I* see, Ruby?'

I shrug, because even though I do want to know what he sees, I don't like that he's been laughing at my pathetic life for the past ten seconds.

I'm not about to smile about it and tell him I'm desperate to find out every thought he has ever had about me.

'Not damaged goods. Not people keeping away. A girl who is loved by family and friends and people who come up to the bar at night. A girl who doesn't see her own face when she looks in the mirror. I see an independent thinker, a girl who doesn't share herself easily. You are guarded, but you are not afraid. You hide behind this past, but it does not have to *be* you. You do not have a curse on you. You are always trying to protect yourself. Hiding. But this *curse* . . . It doesn't change the way I feel when I'm near you. Am I sad this happened to you? Yes and no.' His fingers confidently lift my fringe to look for my scar there.

235

It's the worse of the two, but my make-up will be covering it in the dim light, I'm confident of that.

I hold my face and body taut under his gaze.

As his eyes meander over me, his smile deepens. 'I would never want anyone to feel such pain, but if this is why Hazel pushed you to come here and help when we did not need it, then I am glad.'

All my nerves tingle, as though each and every one has been touched by his words.

In all the time he has spent glancing at me at work, it's like he has seen more of me than I do. Maybe he is right in thinking I can't see my own face in the mirror.

Sometimes, I can't even understand who I've become. I don't dare to dwell on the emotions he's brought up from the depths of my chest. Instead, I focus on the last part, about Hazel.

'She said someone left to go to uni.'

'Then she lied.'

'Proving that everyone pities me.'

'Good. It brought you here, and I will never be sad about this.'

'Do you know what I don't understand?'

Yianni tilts his head and crosses his arms over his chest to mirror me.

'Why Hazel didn't tell you sooner. I thought everyone knew. She's not the sort of person not to tell you all about it when it happened. She can keep a secret, but what happened wasn't a secret.'

'No, she did. Only, it was years ago and she kept talking about this Jonathan guy. I don't know any Jonathan and I was at uni, going through things with Angelika. I didn't realise her stories were about you. Somehow, I miss this part. Then when she is saying, *We need to be kind to Ruby, we need to be gentle with Ruby*, I thought you were some delicate princess now. I was foolish.'

'We all make mistakes.'

Yianni rolls his eyes to the ceiling and pushes his fingers through his wavy curls.

'You know, when I told Hazel about you losing your ring, she says to me how important that ring would be to you, it all made sense to realise *you* are the girl who lost her boyfriend. Hazel tells me you *lost the love of your life, no one can compete with that.*'

'She doesn't know what she's talking about. He wasn't the love of my life.' A breeze rolls in and against the warm night I shiver, and goosebumps explode across my skin.

As I say this, Yianni's face changes into something much more serious.

The cool breeze rolls around us, making my hair shimmy around my cheeks.

He smooths it down, then his fingers linger on my face again.

My breathing starts to weigh me down and I'm much too aware of everything – the music still playing to itself, the breeze, my heart screaming in my chest.

His face moves towards me, but I can't wait a moment more and I meet him halfway.

Our lips collide and his tongue finds mine, and we melt together in the fiery night's heat.

Or at least my body feels like it's alight as he presses into me. His right hand slips behind me on the bench to support his weight as his left hand tickles under my shirt and round my waist before it's his turn to pull away, but only a centimetre.

'You won't break my arm, will you?'

I laugh into his warm mouth, then pull away long enough to say, 'No, you're safe.'

Yianni pulls me harder towards him and slips his hand further up and along my ribs.

I breathe into his mouth as I adjust myself to bring my right leg around him, pinning it between the wall and his side.

His weight lowers between my thighs and my head falls back as he kisses my jaw and the length of my neck. He skims the scar on my chin with his lips.

I don't feel pain this time. Instead, everything inside me has shifted. He has seen it all, all my suffering, everything I've hidden from the world, and instead of walking away or pitying me, he laughed.

It was the last thing I expected, but it was what I needed.

I can see straight out to the road. It's dimly lit in the restaurant with most of the lights out, and we are as far from the road as we can get, but I don't like the idea of someone walking back late from one of the bars and seeing us like this.

'Yianni?' I lift my head and shift my weight on to my elbow to sit up. 'Everything is open to the street, and you haven't even locked the bar.'

His head flops back down between my breasts.

A moment later, he bounces up and runs round closing the doors and turning the music off.

While he finishes sorting things out, I go to the ladies' toilets.

A knot forms as I think about what's unfolding. Every fibre is telling me this is a stupid idea.

I should go and say goodnight now and go back to the house.

There's no way Hazel would be OK with me and Yianni, even if she did bring me here under false pretences.

As I leave the toilets, everything is dark except a stream of light like an arrow leading towards Yianni's bedroom.

I have no choice but to go in.

Chapter
Forty Three

Now

'Anyone interesting?' I hover in the doorway.

Yianni switches off the screen to his phone and places it next to the lamp.

I consider closing the door behind me, but I don't because I know I should be walking straight back out of it. I shouldn't have even engaged in a question.

'Nico.'

'Messaging this late?'

Yianni shrugs and begins to shuffle towards the edge of the neatly made bed – pale-blue sheets tucked in perfectly, in a way I can never quite achieve myself.

'You've got air-con in here now!'

A little machine hums in the corner of the room. It's free-standing and only small, but it's enough to make the room comfortable.

'It's for when I have guests,' he laughs, and he gets up to walk past me and close the door.

Perhaps he can sense my thoughts and my uncertainty, but as he steps towards me, he has no such hesitation.

He tilts his head down towards me and his hand wraps around the back of my neck as his lips meet mine.

My skin tingles all over and I let out an involuntary low sigh into his mouth, making his lips smile against mine.

We hold on to each other, our hands skimming each other's bodies, our feet edging one by one towards the bed until we lower ourselves on to it. We fall on to our sides and Yianni begins to slowly unbutton my shirt.

It's been so long since I've had someone's face and eyes so close to mine.

Seeing me in close-up, seeing into every part of me.

When Yianni and I were last pressed against each other in this room, it was dark and clumsy. It was nothing like this. Now it feels like I'm watching him under a magnifying glass as we press together.

I pull away to see him more clearly, but my fingers linger, clinging to his shirt, looping my fingers in between two buttons.

I don't want to pull away any further, but I also need a moment to think. Yianni's quietly gasping for air, my air, straight from my lips as our foreheads press together.

A thought escapes my brain and falls from my mouth.

'How can I trust you?'

He cups my face and his eyes search mine, from one to the other. In the shadowy room, his eyes look almost black, but even so, I can see the kindness that resides in them.

'We do not have to rush.' The corners of his lips tug upwards and he releases me from his grasp. 'In truth, I do not want to rush.'

I can't help but lower an eyebrow at him and pull on my open blouse.

'I didn't say I don't want you, just that it's nice not to rush. We have all the time.'

Yianni's eyes linger on my abdomen now it's exposed.

'Do you have to stare at my scars?'

I wrap my blouse back around my torso and hunch forwards over my knees, turning away from him.

Outside of doctors, he's the only person to have seen them. I haven't shown them to anyone. Why would I? It's not the sort of thing anyone would ask to see.

My mum helped me with them when they were wounds and I needed her to, but since then she hasn't seen them.

A small part of me wants to put my hand over the jagged line where the branch of a tree tore into my skin.

I fight the urge.

This is me.

I can't change my past. It's written all over me in silver lines, freckles, tan lines, and I'm sure, soon enough, in laughter lines and age spots. They will never change, even if they have changed me. It's fixed. The past is fixed. The future isn't though. It's open and full of anything I want it to be.

'No. I like to stare at you though.' Yianni shuffles back in the single bed and presses his back against the wall, before he pulls his legs up to stop them dangling over the side. 'Hey, would you like to see my scar?'

I twist to look at him, now that he's behind me. His fingers are in his hair and his elbow is resting on one knee. 'My stories are not so impressive, but . . .' His lips turn down in thought. 'Maybe you still like to see them?'

'Go on then, impress me.' Still clutching my blouse, I sit up and twist to face him.

His cheeky face lights up, ready for the show-and-tell session to commence.

His fingers dive deeper into his hair, and he tilts his head forward.

'Here, look.' His finger jabs at a thick scar, thicker than any of mine and a good inch long.

'How the hell did you get that?'

'A good friend throws a rock at me. Not his fault—'

'How is that not his fault?'

'We were, what do you call it?' He folds his leg underneath himself then slices with his right arm.

'Oh, skimming stones?' I jump my finger along, acting out the motion in a similar way to Yianni. 'So they bounce.'

'Yes, I duck down to pick up a stone, he throws, but I stand up too fast and his stone hits me. I shouldn't have gone in front of him, but there was a good stone.' He is grinning at the memory while rubbing his head. 'I got stitches.'

'But that's a nice story. Mine ends with a dead boyfriend and a tree in my side.' Yianni stops laughing and his lips press together. 'Sorry, that was a bit . . . abrupt.'

The air-con unit next to the chair hums along under the silence I've caused.

Yianni says, 'You can tell me. You don't always have to be alone.'

I look about his box room. It's a lot tidier than last time I was in here.

All the clothes have been put away, the bed is neat-freak perfect and even the items on the bedside have been organised in rows. I'm going to assume this effort is for me. Because he invited me to talk to him tonight. It's strangely comforting, the effort he has put in for me.

'I'm not sure I'm ready to give you all the gory details. It's been two years and it's stayed between me and Byron the whole time.'

'Byron?'

A smile crosses my lips at the memory of the fireman who talked to me – for what felt like days – while they cut the car and tree away from us and did their best to save Jonathan.

'Yeah, he's a fireman.'

'A sexy fireman?' Yianni almost looks jealous – that is, until my face cracks and I burst into laughter.

'No! He was twice my age and reminded me of my dad. But, the Suffolk version.' My abdomen relaxes and I think back to that time. How hard the responders worked, and it still ended with a funeral. 'Do you know what? There *is* something I can tell you.'

Yianni leans in a little bit, ready to give me his full attention.

To be honest, when I'm with Yianni, I always feel like I have his full attention. He never seems half-hearted. He's present with me. Not picking up his phone halfway through a conversation or looking off into the distance.

Other than one time, when I was on the verge of telling him a little bit about Jonathan.

'No, wait – why did you look so distant that time I was going to tell you that Jonathan had died? You kind of brushed it under the carpet.'

'In the bar?'

I nod. Where else? We're always in the damn bar.

'I was . . .' He hesitates before continuing. 'Jealous, maybe. You dwelling on a boyfriend. It's not what I was wanting to hear.'

I nibble my lip. Makes sense that he was different to his usual, focused self.

'What were you going to tell me?'

'At Jonathan's funeral, there was this girl I didn't recognise. A tiny little thing, but held herself like she was a giant, you know? Shoulders pulled back, chin in the air like she was looking down at people, but with a soft face that didn't match her body. Anyway, at the wake she comes up to me and does the usual *I'm so sorry for your loss* bit. I asked her how she knew Jonathan. She said that she was a performer, and they used to work together. She heard about his passing through a friend and wanted to pay her respects. She told me they even dated for a little while when they were touring around schools performing *A Midsummer Night's Dream*. I asked her when, but I knew when before she answered. We hadn't been together that long, and he was seeing her at the same time. I didn't tell her. I think she would have been mortified. The thing is, I just wanted to laugh. It all made sense, how controlling he was, how he would accuse me of cheating. That's because he was reflecting what he had done himself. In that moment I was kind of glad he was dead, but feeling that way burdened me with so much guilt. Just because he was controlling and cheated on me doesn't mean I wish him dead.'

'This Jonathan, he sounds lovely.'

I'd been looking at my fingers and the space where Jonathan's ring once gripped my finger, but Yianni's comment makes my head snap up so fast I'm surprised I don't have whiplash.

Yianni's eyes are bulging in his head they're so wide, and he's baring his teeth in an exaggerated grimace. He looks like a maniac.

Laughter tickles my sides. It bubbles out until I flop back on to the bed. Yianni's laughing too, looking down at me. Then his face slowly falls serious.

'He did not deserve you.'

'No, perhaps not. We were young when we got together. I think I was a bit naive and sort of star-struck with the actor-boy-friend bit. He could be so charming and funny when he wanted to be. But that's not enough, is it? Just to be pretty and charming. There was no care, no kindness . . . No, that's not fair, there just wasn't enough. Not for me, anyway. I'm sure he loved me, but only as much as a narcissist can love anyone other than the mirror.'

Yianni exhales through his teeth and hangs his head before sliding down next to me on the bed. He's still watching over me as he props himself on his elbow.

'You've changed. I guess he changed you. Or perhaps the car crash changed you?'

'How do you know I've changed?' I screw my face up, but this only makes Yianni laugh and etch his finger along the creases I've formed in my forehead.

'I remember you. How could I not? This beautiful creature with long dark hair. Softly spoken and kind to everyone. My friend, who throws the rock at my head?' I nod, as he says it like a question. 'Well, he was at Hazel and Baba's wedding too, everyone was at the wedding. We were maybe fourteen? And you were, I don't know, maybe eighteen or nineteen?'

'Nineteen,' I confirm.

'To us, you were a woman and we were nothing. But my friend – he is called Yianni too, by the way – he says he will ask you to dance. I burnt with anger at the idea that he will hold your hands and have your attention and I never could.'

'I don't remember anyone asking me to dance.'

'Oh no, he didn't ask. He was all bravado.'

'It's funny to think of you watching me back then. In my eyes, you were just another kid.' I brush my fringe out of my eyes to look up at him a little bit better.

'You wound me. I'm Greek, I was born as a man. At that age I had already been helping in the restaurant for years, learning the family business.' He falters, looking towards the door. 'I thought I was a man, but I already knew you were too good for me. I didn't really know what it was to get the attention of a woman.'

'I can't believe you've been harbouring feelings for me for all these years.' My fingers press to my lips and I gently shake my head at the thought of it, but I can't shake off the smile that's hidden under my fingertips. 'In what way have I changed? Other than chopping off and bleaching my hair.'

'You're more confident. At nineteen you didn't say much, or get involved in much of the dancing—'

'Seriously? All I remember was the constant dancing at that wedding.'

I roll my eyes in jest as Yianni continues, 'You liked watching from the sides, clapping your hands. Now, not so much. Now you want to talk to people, you smile at them, ask them questions. Yes, sometimes I see you falling into your head full of thoughts, but you can get involved now too. And, of course, now you can break a man's arm as well as his heart.'

My lips open in laughter and ready to dispute this claim, but before I can form words, Yianni cuts across the sound.

'*Nai, nai, nai.* Yes, you can. Don't you pretend. I think you could break a man's arm.'

'Oh yeah, I'm sure I can. It's the *heart* part I'm laughing at.'

'I wouldn't be so sure.'

We lie smiling at each other for a moment before I tilt my chin up, signalling to him my intentions.

He slides lower on the bed and kisses me slowly. His lips are firm yet delightfully smooth. His hands glide over my back to gather me in.

He snatches his lips away and breathes, 'I am still safe, yes? You won't break my hand?' His eyes glint in the reflection of the lamp and his face is taut with suppressed giggles.

'Honestly, with me, who knows?'

We are so close I can feel the vibration of his laughter in my own chest as though we exist in the same space and are already fusing together as our lips collide again, and we search each other for answers to questions we're too afraid to ask.

Chapter Forty Four

Now

Five hours of sleep is better than no sleep.

We kissed all night – well, until maybe four in the morning, maybe five. I'm not really sure any more.

It was like being in high school again, like we were both a little too nervous to take it any further than kissing. Our hands were everywhere, like shadows following each other's bodies from place to place.

Being with Yianni makes me feel like I get to live things I missed out on with Jonathan. We didn't have adventure or fun, it was all hard work and scrimping. It's like Jonathan snatched away my youth and Yianni is handing it back.

We didn't discuss that we wouldn't take it any further. If we take this further, we can't undo it and we have no idea how the rest of the family will react.

To them we are cousins and, to us, we're just two people who really like each other. We weren't brought up together – we're not even related – but it's still tricky to know what people will say.

I didn't come to Corfu just to upset people and ruin their lives. I guess I came because I was looking for something I knew I wouldn't find on my doorstep. There were plenty of jobs I *could* have applied for, but I just kept finding reasons why they weren't good enough.

I guess, deep down, I was fed up. Fed up with having to be sad and everyone thinking I should be sad. As far as they were concerned, I lost the love of my life. After all, I hadn't told anyone about my intentions to break it off with Jonathan. Now I never can.

People expect me to move on eventually, but with the burden of sadness someone has when they lose their forever love. For two years, I've worn an engagement ring that was never actually given to me by a man I've since found out used to cheat on me.

I've never wanted to drag Jonathan's name through the dirt; what would be the point? He can't defend himself. I had to escape England and all the nails that were pinning me to the spot.

I needed adventure on my terms, and this was right at my feet, waiting to be scooped up.

I wonder if Mum knew that the whole time, but gave me the space to figure it out on my own.

Yianni messages Hazel and Pericles to say that we had a late night and won't be in for the lunch shift, that Nico will be there instead. They don't mind.

We are walking to get pancakes – or maybe waffles – from Silver Star, our little fingers glancing each other with each step.

It's only a short walk down the road. Everyone who passes us says hello.

It makes me want to burst into a shower of giggles knowing we are together, wishing we could hold hands while everyone else goes about their day completely unaware.

Maybe they are questioning why we're together at nine in the morning.

I'm sure they're not. I don't care either way. My heart pounds with excitement in my chest just to be close to Yianni.

I feel pretty grim in yesterday's clothes, though. They're so plain, and I wear variations of the same every day, so I hope it's not obvious to anyone but me.

The sun sinks into my all-black outfit and suddenly I feel drenched in sweat.

'I can't bear this. I'll meet you in there, OK?'

Yianni mumbles an 'OK' but looks puzzled as I begin to jog away.

I'm in my little ballet pumps. It's still a little painful on my foot to jog, so after a short distance I stick with very fast walking, going up the incline towards a clothes shop I've seen further up on the left all on its own, Peli & Maria. I've often admired the dresses and sarongs as I pass on my bike, but I haven't actually gone inside. There's a mixture of floaty outfits, children's toys and keepsakes all under one roof.

I whip my fingers along the clothing, one item to the next, occasionally pulling something forward. I settle on a dark-purple loose-fitting dress that's gathered at the bust.

I'm making my way to the till when something else catches my eye.

Like the pull of gravity, I move towards it without thinking or choosing. I pick it up from its resting place and look it over, swaying it this way and that.

I swallow hard and take a deep breath. *You are brave. You are strong.*

I come into Silver Star at the side entrance that's level with the street instead of walking around and climbing the stairs. After saying hello to the owners, I scan the open terrace for Yianni.

I can't see him, so I keep moving around. There are only a few tables taken, and I start to think he's turned around and gone back to Greek Secret when I find him as far away from where I walked in as possible.

Past all the round tables circled in wicker chairs and brightly coloured cushions, he's sitting on a long swing chair with cream cushions, and he's slowly rocking back and forth with his heels.

'I thought I'd lost you.' I stand over him as he lowers the menu he's hiding behind.

'I thought you ran away.' He looks me up and down. 'That's where you went. You look lovely.'

'Thank you.'

I want to sit next to him, but I'm not sure if that will look too coupley and cosy.

I don't care. If I want to sit next to Yianni then I'll sit next to Yianni.

I plonk myself down right next to him, making the swing chair shoot backwards a little harder than I meant to.

Yianni chuckles and watches me from the corner of his eye.

'I cannot believe you put face wipes and make-up in your bag.' He passes me his menu to peruse.

'And a toothbrush. Don't be so shocked. You tidied your room and got air-con. Anyway, after the last time, I wanted to have them in my bag just in case. It's no big deal.'

Yianni makes a low growling noise in the back of his throat like he doesn't believe me. He shouldn't believe me. We all live in hope, I guess.

We order waffles with ice cream for breakfast and greedily scoff our way through it all. Mine has sticky chocolate sauce too, with a few slices of tangy strawberries to top it off. Delicious.

When we're done, I don't want to rush back to the house for showers, although I don't think anyone will be there. I'm not ready to break this little bubble. We might not be holding hands or kissing, but being in Yianni's company is as warm as being in the Corfu sun.

'Can we go for a walk along the beach? Instead of straight back to the house?'

'Of course.'

We meander along the road, waving to everyone, smiling at everyone.

Anywhere else, it might feel like some sort of celebrity status. Not here. It's just saying hello to all your friends. More for Yianni, of course, and some of them are his family too.

We walk all the way to the beach, talking about nothing and everything, enjoying the slow, delightful pace of life.

I lead us all the way to the water's edge and kick off my shoes to let the foam tickle my toes.

In silence, we look out to sea and the line that is the meeting of two entities. It's like the crux of where the past and present meet, and that almost-invisible line is the present. As soon as you focus in on it, it's already gone and melted into the past.

All we have is now.

Everything else is just the shades of blue that encase us on this planet.

We're standing close enough together that when I stretch my little finger in Yianni's direction, it glances his.

My heart is like a drum, so loud I feel it in my chest.

The present is now. There's nothing else.

I turn to face him then take two steps past him, away from the sea, and I remove my dress.

In the shop, I also purchased a bikini, the first bikini I've worn since the accident.

I subdue the urge to put my hands over my stomach and I turn towards the sea. Yianni doesn't look at my scars this time. He looks me in the eye and in a low voice says, 'I really want to kiss you.'

My lips press together in what I can only imagine looks like a nervous smile, because that's how I feel, tinged red with anxiety.

It's not enough to stop me. Not enough to worry or care.

It is not so much that I needed anyone else's approval to get me to this place, but I needed to find someone I could tell the truth to before I could show the world the end result – the jagged scar of an injury that, if it had been only an inch or so further across, would have killed me.

Lucky. So I was told, anyway.

Over and over I was told I was lucky, when I really didn't feel lucky at all.

But I was. I am.

I'm here on this beautiful island, surrounded by happy voices and the calm crawling of the sea along the sand.

Then there's Yianni, someone I like. I don't want to think further than that. One step at a time. And that's exactly what I do, take one step at a time into the sea, into the all-encompassing blue.

It's taken two years to get me here: a ton of alone time, staring into space and trying to connect with something and reaffirming everything in my head.

Jonathan took more than his life that day.

Yianni pulls off his top and throws it down with my dress. He's not wearing swim shorts, but his shorts are sporty and made of breathable material. He doesn't even question it, he just strides into the sea behind me with his pants and shorts on.

I shake my head and a laugh splutters past my lips. He says, 'What made you change?'

I don't know if he wants me to say that it was him. 'That.' I point out to sea and into the distance.

Yianni squints, looking for something he'll never find.

To him it's turquoise seas and cloudless skies.

We continue walking into the sea until it's skimming along under my fingertips then past my scars above my belly button.

'Do you want me to explain?' I smile over at him.

He has raised one hand to shade his eyes while he continues to look out into the wide open expanse of blue.

'It might help.'

'I've stood here looking out to sea for weeks now, and it's helped me to focus. It's helped to put everything I've been doing over the past few years into perspective. I haven't really been living. I've been existing somewhere between the past and the future, but never in the present. I'd be wrenching my neck in one direction or the other, but never seeing the now. Looking at the place where the sea and the sky come together, it's not really a line – I mean, it is to look at, but the Earth is a globe and the sky is all around us, so the line is this fleeting thing. I see it as the present, the here and now. The sea is a reflection, so it's like the past, it's who we were, and the sky is the future, wide and infinite. I sound stupid, don't I? Like I've spent way too long on my own.'

'Not stupid. Perhaps, alone to think. But I like this idea of the line, and if it helps you, this is no bad thing.'

'It has helped. It's made me want to live in the present. It's forced me to focus on it and what's important. Then there's you. You're the catalyst I didn't know I needed, but not how you might think. You were staring at my scars, and it didn't make them hurt any more or any less. I didn't need a man – even one I really like – to tell me I look OK. Or even that they don't look OK. What I needed was for someone to see them before I could walk around with them for the world to see, because I needed to know that I would be all right. That I wouldn't fall apart at the thought of the accident. That people seeing my scar wouldn't make me instantly see Jonathan illuminated under artificial lights with the shadow of the tree over his face as his life slipped away. His head pressing against the tree, and—' I stop myself, because the memory is much too gruesome.

My wet hands are pressing to my head as I'm acting out the memory, but the water dripping over my face makes me think of the blood trickling over Jonathan's skin.

I saw a lot before they could get a screen between us. He died soon after.

There was no hope of him living, not really, but the firemen and women and the paramedics did everything they could anyway. They didn't want to give up, but it was too late.

Yianni's hands carefully wrap around my wrists and remove my hands from my face.

My body's shivering like I've been in a bath too long and the water's gone cold. He brings me into him and my wet face sticks to the soft skin of his chest.

'You really like me. It's too late, you've said it now.' And with his words, we both begin to vibrate in laughter.

He brings the light back on to my skin again and it penetrates my soul, illuminating the pain, but letting it dissolve a little into the shadows. I don't give him the satisfaction of a response.

Instead, I step back out of his embrace and splash him, before diving into the blue.

Chapter Forty Five

Now

Of course, we had to get to work eventually.

Although we did find time to kiss some more on my bed – that is, Yianni's bed – at the house, until we heard the door swing open downstairs as Pericles called up to Yianni.

We jumped apart so quickly that Yianni was out of the room and jogging down the stairs to speak to his dad in a nanosecond.

I feel like my heart might never stop speeding. It's like being a teenager again. With Jonathan, I felt like I was old and that was that.

Even now, Yianni's actually looking at me less than normal. Usually, I catch him gawping at me all the time. Today it's the opposite – it's like he knows he can't look at me, because if he does, it'll all fall apart, and everyone will see right through us.

Or we won't be able to keep ourselves apart and gravity will pull us together.

Nico, on the other hand, has been toying with me.

He hasn't actually said anything or asked what happened, but he's being very suggestive, which is designed to get me to a breaking point of snapping and saying something about Yianni without Nico having to ask.

I have no intention of snapping, so it's a waiting game.

'Yianni looks very mutz happier today, no? Do you not think so?' Nico's pouring a glass of wine while watching Yianni.

Yianni's brimming with smiles at an elderly couple he's helping up from their table for two underneath the hanging vines. It's the time of evening where it all starts to thin out and people who are still here are moving on to desserts.

'You would have to ask him whether he's happy. I'm sure I couldn't comment.'

'Oh, so, you would not know any reason or any events that might put smiles over his face?'

'Nothing I'm aware of. Although, he did get to see me in a bikini earlier.'

Nico makes a noise that sounds a little like a hi-hat as a reproach to my comment.

'A bikini? Everyone is wearing a bikini. Some not even that. You went swimming with him before, what is so special about a bikini?' Nico laughs as he places the wine on a tray along with a bottle of beer and a glass.

He turns to face me because I'm in the way. He stops to assess me.

'What's wrong?'

'Nothing. Just, it was a big deal actually. I haven't worn a bikini for quite some years. I was in a car accident, and I have some scars. It's silly really.'

'No, it is never silly to have scars. These accidents, they can change lives for ever and leave you with pains worse than scars. But I am glad you're in a bikini again.' He brushes past me and

256

continues, 'You should never hide who you are, especially when you have a body like yours.'

He smirks and walks away. I know he said it for two reasons: one, because he is the biggest damn flirt on the island, and two, because Yianni had appeared, so he complimented my body in an exaggerated voice to try to get a rise out of him.

It didn't work. Not this time.

'I almost thought Nico was going to be sensitive or mature then.' I do my best not to beam at Yianni coming over to chat to me.

'He is underneath it all. He just likes to hide it.' Yianni scans the room then turns back to me. 'It should start settling down in here soon.' He leans on the bar with both his forearms flat to the wood, leaving him looking up at me for a change.

'Correct. I was thinking of getting an early night.'

His face changes, and he stutters something about that being a good idea and it's important to get rest after a busy day.

'I'm kidding. Can I stay?'

'You're staying here again?' I hear Hazel's voice at my elbow, and she comes to stand over the books next to the till.

My heart launches itself into my throat.

'Only if it's all right with Yianni.'

Hazel pulls her glasses down off her head and on to her nose as she peers at the books in front of her.

My eyes widen at Yianni because I feel a little trapped in this conversation. We haven't really been quizzed on the sleeping arrangements when I've stayed here, but I have a feeling it's about to come up.

'Well, I'm glad he lets you sleep on the bed. You're a gentleman, aren't you, Yianni?' Hazel reaches over the bar and pinches his chin.

'I do my best.' Yianni playfully rolls his eyes as she releases him.

'I hope you don't *really* sleep on the floor, though. Not when you have comfy chairs out here.'

'No, no. Not the floor.'

My palms feel clammy and it's not just the fact that there's no breeze tonight. I hope no one puts a drink order in or I might end up being the one to drop it on my foot this time.

'I can't believe it's my turn to check the receipts again. I hate this part of the job, don't you? I think we're due someone coming in to do a spot check though. It seems like ages since the last one.' Hazel glances between us, her eyes looking even wider under her glasses.

We both begin to agree. I don't mind too much; I like taking in everything there is to know about owning a restaurant anywhere in the world.

'I'm happy to help.'

'I best get back to work.' Yianni taps the bar and begins to turn around, only Hazel makes a rhythmical *uh-uh* sound and looks at him over her glasses.

'You didn't answer the poor girl, Yianni. Can she kick you out of another one of your beds for the night? She's a cheeky one, isn't she?' Hazel's elbow finds my ribs.

There's a funny tone about her and my clammy palms are no longer my biggest worry; my face is feeling hot. To make matters worse, I sort of snort at her little joke about me being cheeky.

'I wouldn't kick him out of his bed.'

'Oh really?' Her bright-blue eyes shine their light on me, and I wish I could go back and swallow my words.

I'd probably only choke on them though.

'I mean . . . You know what I mean.'

From the corner of my eye, I can see Yianni cringing, and sweat is weaving down my spine as Hazel looks between us.

'Well, it's good to see you're getting on.'

Pericles strolls over and mildly berates Yianni in Greek.

I'm pretty sure Hazel speaks in his defence, maybe blaming herself for his pause in his duties. I'm going by body language alone.

Pericles softens at Hazel's tone and Yianni moves away. Nico scoots behind Hazel and me and begins to clean down the bar. More people vacate the restaurant, and another group leave their table in favour of bar stools.

I watch as Yianni disappears.

'I can do the books if you like,' I offer again. Happy to take everything in.

'Would you, dear?'

I bob my head, and Hazel cups my face. 'Are you happy here, Ruby? You seem happy.'

'I am.'

She pulls me in for a hug and I see Yianni watching us as he takes a dessert order. As he walks away from the table, he gives me the briefest wink before pushing his hair off his face.

Hazel kisses my cheek. 'Right, looks like Yianni has some work for me. Thanks for doing the books tonight, sweetheart.'

'No worries.'

I smile in her wake then turn around to Nico, only a short distance away from me.

He says, 'Don't think I didn't see that wink. Were you telling Hazel her stepson is your new boyfriend?' His grin engulfs his whole face, but I ignore him.

I have no interest in letting anyone else's excitement layer on top of my own. Yianni and I are still finding out who we are. I'm not going to start thinking about what we are, or what we could be. That's a little too much future, and not enough present.

Chapter Forty Six

Now

'*Yamas,*' we all chime – not quite in unison – and we knock back the smooth liquid.

As the night draws to a close, Nico takes too much satisfaction in hanging around and having a drink while everyone else is leaving.

I don't mind particularly; I like Nico. Yianni seems to be amused by how amusing Nico finds himself to be too.

It's a completely relaxed evening and the scent of honeysuckle floats on the air from a plant growing beside the restaurant. I've never noticed it much before, but tonight the sickly-sweet fragrance being carried in reminds me of my childhood.

There was honeysuckle in my parents' garden, and it was always smothered in butterflies. I wish I could tell my mum about Yianni and the bikini and how much I've pushed myself lately. I miss seeing my parents face to face. Even FaceTime isn't the same.

Yianni gets behind the bar and serves me and Nico as we take seats on the stools. He doesn't quite have Nico's finesse when it comes to putting on a show with glasses and bottles, but he's still bloody good.

Not like me.

I flinch and close my eyes every time they juggle bottles and glasses near me, let alone trying it for myself. Yianni fills our three glasses again with chocolate tequila and slides two of them over to Nico and me.

'I'm not interrupting your alone time, am I?' Nico glances between us, his eyes glinting.

'Piss off.' Yianni's glass knocks against the bar to punctuate his words. There's no malice though, only jest.

'When will you tell your parents, Yianni?' Nico then turns to me. 'Sorry, sorry, your *theía* and *theíos*? What is it?' Nico snaps his fingers as though this will help him remember.

'Aunt and uncle,' Yianni and I both reply, this time in perfect unison.

'Nico, there really isn't anything to tell yet. We aren't thinking in those terms. Let's just see what life brings our way.' I do my best to give him a sweet smile, one that might soften him up and make him back off a little about Yianni and me.

'Fine, fine. I have mutz to do in the morning. I need to help my mother. Be good. *Kalinikta.*'

We both watch as Nico struts his way out of the bifold doors, which are halfway shut.

As soon as he's gone, I lean my forearms on the bar and Yianni does the same until our faces are only inches apart.

He removes the space between us with a lingering kiss that lands on my lips with a taste of chocolate.

'Would you like to go for a walk? Condor Bar has live music tonight,' Yianni says, but he stays inches away from me.

'Nah, I'm good, thanks. I quite like the music here.' We both grin as the most clichéd Greek music quietly chimes around us, with the traditional bouzouki taking pride of place.

'We could dance here,' Yianni says. 'Practise for next week.'

'Oh damn, I'd forgotten it was a special Greek Night next week.'

'Yes, for the height of the season we will have our very own dancers and set menu once every two weeks.'

'Who are the dancers?'

'Are you sure you want to know?' His dark eyebrows lift but he lowers his chin.

My head bobs enthusiastically.

'Just some kids from Natalia's school. We join in too.'

'We? Who's we?' I'm suddenly giddy at the idea of Yianni dancing.

'Me, Nico, Baba. Then Natalia and Gaia sing.'

'What?' I pull myself up straight and press my fingers over my mouth. 'You have to be kidding. How did I not know this?'

Yianni shrugs and collects our shot glasses ready for washing.

'Seriously, you dance?'

'We all dance.'

'Teach me.'

As soon as I've said the words a niggle of regret fills my belly, but it's right there next to excitement. Living in the present has to include doing new things.

Yianni looks over the bar at me with doubt written all over his face. Looking me up and down, he considers his options.

Maybe he thinks I'll be too rubbish. He's probably right, if that *is* what he's thinking.

His hand swipes over the bar and he goes towards the little iPod behind it which connects to the sound system of small speakers concealed in the vines and corners of the room. He changes the track, although the music is still Greek in style.

I move back from the bar, waiting for instruction.

Yianni looks at me from under his curls with a serious expression. His wrist starts to curl around itself and he clicks his fingers. I'm not really sure what to expect. The only Greek dancing I've seen has been groups of people walking in a circle and crossing over their legs as they go, or men kneeling and getting back up again. That's all I remember.

This is different.

The air seems to shift and part of me wants to giggle, while another part feels distinctly like I'm about to fall into something I'll never be able to escape from – a perfectly woven spider's web with glittering threads that I'll never want to leave.

My fingers twitch by my sides as Yianni edges towards me, then moves to stand behind me. He places his hands on my hips and begins to move them in a rolling figure-of-eight motion.

'Lightly step your feet to the music. On the spot.' His voice trickles down from above my ear.

I step my feet lightly like a happy cat as my hips swirl. 'Like this?' I feel mildly ridiculous and intoxicated in equal measure.

'*Naí, naí.* That's it.'

His hands run along my waist, my ribs, then along the inside of my arms to lift them away from my sides. Then he stops touching me completely.

He moves like a shadow only inches from my body, slowly weaving around me, so close, but as if we are magnets that can never meet.

He moves in front of me with small steps, holding his arms out and somehow encasing me within them. His chin lowers; his face is right there, above mine.

I look up and our eyes meet as our hips twist in perfect synchronicity, so close but still not touching.

Yianni moves lower on my body, still without touching me. He licks his lower lip and all I want is for him to kiss me.

Full lips edge a millimetre closer to my face and his heat fuses with mine.

Yianni's hips stop moving and his arms drop as he leans down and presses our lips together.

He pulls me in, almost lifting me off my feet. Then that's exactly what he does. My legs wrap around his waist as we explore each other's mouths and cling together. He carries me like this all the way to his room and places me on his bed on my back.

His hair's so silky my fingers get lost in the curls, while his fingers masterfully unbutton my blouse.

When it's completely unbuttoned, he presses his forehead to mine and looks across me and makes a soft sound of appreciation. I'm still aware of my scars, but it's like they've become invisible to him.

I press my lips hard to Yianni's, and hold him to me with my legs, wrapping them around his buttocks. In the small space of his bed, we twist around one another until I'm straddling him, and I undo his buttons at an even faster rate than he undid mine.

Sitting straight on top of him, I make the same kind of sound that he did as I admire him.

He laughs, and I feel it in my thighs – and that's not all I can feel there. I bite my lip as we make eye contact.

Is he too good to be true? He is not perfect; no one's perfect, I'm under no illusions there. But from his smooth golden-brown skin to his handsome face and intense eyes, to his thoughtful and caring soul, he seems as close as anyone could possibly get.

Then the imperfection of the situation floods my brain. If we take this any further, there's no going back.

'We shouldn't be doing this.' My voice is wispy like smoke, fine and almost transparent.

He either doesn't hear me or he chooses to ignore me, sitting up to meet my mouth with his. He starts to kiss my neck while he carefully peels off my blouse and undoes the clasp of my bra.

The bra falls away to the floor, discarded along with my blouse. His tongue glides along my skin and his mouth covers my nipple.

A ripple of pleasure nibbles all the way through my spine down to my toes, which curl with pleasurable tension.

My mind completely empties of everything that exists outside of this moment. It's just me and Yianni. One of my hands continues to coil around his hair as the other grips his shoulder, firm and grounding.

'Yianni, how have we gone from you being such a grumpy shit to this?' My voice is still floating and fine like smoke.

Yianni looks up and laughs before murmuring, 'I was never this *grumpy shit*. It is much more complicated than this, and you know it. You would not be with me if you thought I was only a *grumpy shit*.' His tongue cautiously teases me again, then he adds, 'Or maybe it is because I thought you were here to torment me, to show me all that I wanted but could never have.' His warm mouth finds me, making me gasp. 'Until now, perhaps,' he mumbles as his mouth moves over my body.

His hands push my fitted skirt up and now it's just a belt around my hips and waist.

Every muscle in Yianni's body becomes solid under my touch. In one move, he manages to place me on my back again and removes the last items of my clothing and more of his.

I'm completely exposed, and even with my scars, I'm more confident than I was before them.

This is who I am now. This is all of me and I'm not changing for anyone but me.

Sitting over me, taking me in for a moment, Yianni's face glows with a wash of red and he licks his lips as his fingers slide and dance over my thighs, my hips, my breasts, making goosebumps appear in rebellion against my body heat.

'You are perfect, you know that?' He smooths my hair off my cheek where it has stuck to my burning skin. I grab his hand, hold it to my face for a moment more and close my eyes.

Opening them, I look down at the area still covered in his tight black boxers. 'Your turn.' My fingers stretch out, but he moves away.

'What was it you said to Hazel?' He is trying to suppress his laughter. 'You wouldn't kick me out of bed . . . ?' He lowers one eyebrow with this reminder.

I roll my eyes and momentarily cover my face at the memory of it.

I expect him to take off his boxers, but he doesn't.

Instead, he places his hands either side of my waist and kisses me. He kisses all of me, every inch of me. I feel his lips like a branding iron hot on my skin, burning me with the need for more until I can feel my hips gently lifting, rising to him as he takes me.

Sweat springs on my skin and my chest feels like it might explode as I gasp for air. It's all I can do to stop myself from screaming his name, until I don't stop myself, and I'm just saying it over and over.

My whole body trembles and I realise I'm holding fistfuls of the bed sheets.

'Oh my God,' is all I say, and it's like I've lost my entire vocabulary.

Yianni smiles. 'Yes, you may call me Zeus now.'

'I'm going to need a moment.' I put my finger up and that's about all I can manage.

Yianni slides his arm under me and pulls me in to hold me close.

I close my eyes against his chest. When my breath finally begins to steady itself, I let my fingers travel down his body, feeling the rise and fall of each individual muscle across his stomach, and his deep groan of pleasure vibrates in my ear.

My mouth finds and nibbles his earlobe, then slips down his neck, enjoying the light salty taste and the smell of his citrus after-shave warming me as I nuzzle my face around his collarbone.

I let my fingers tease him, then I manoeuvre myself down his body and devour him in his entirety. His fingers find their way into my hair, and he's swearing in Greek – I know that because Nico taught me words and phrases. I laugh a little and the vibration spurs him on.

'Wait . . .' There's a rasp in his voice that doesn't usually belong there, but I do as he wants, and I make my way back along his perfectly tanned body and straddle him.

He reaches across to his drawer and hunts out the protection. I take it from his hand and do it for him.

We move slowly, cautiously, as though we both know that this changes everything now.

We can't go back to playing a game of chess around each other.

We can't pretend we don't need or want each other any more. It's officially gone too far.

We sit up together, one of his arms around my waist and the other behind him, holding his weight. His lips begin to caress my nipple, but I take his face in my hands and run my thumbs lightly over the stubble on his cheeks.

We look into one another's eyes as we breathe each other in. We consume one another slowly.

I can feel every sensation – every moment is vivid, as though we were designed to be together. Our lips meet, and all too soon I can't catch my breath again.

I'm not used to feeling so out of control and so easily pushed to the edge of a cliff by anyone; yet here I am, ready to fall all over again.

His name is on my lips and his breath is in my lungs and then together we fall. Deeply, painfully, perfectly. We fall. Over and over again, we fall.

Chapter Forty Seven

Now

If I wasn't still tingling from the night before, I would be too exhausted to function.

All I've had is two hours' sleep. Yianni and I stayed awake for hours talking, before deciding to relive our passion all over again.

Now I'm dressed in yesterday's clothes, waiting for him to bring me back a pain au chocolat from the bakery as well as a black coffee to keep me awake for the rest of the day.

During our long discussions, we agreed that we still aren't ready to tell anyone else yet, although Yianni did point out that Nico will be impossible about the situation – which I completely agree with.

We both use Nico as a sounding board, and he just loves to use what he knows to wind us up. We decide to give ourselves a couple of weeks and then we will find a way to tell everyone.

Underneath it all, I feel sure about us. There's something here, something real.

Yianni says he feels sure about us too, enough to tell people now, but he agrees that waiting is probably the right choice because we need to figure out how to word it.

Plus, I'm only here for the summer, and then what happens? He knows I want my own restaurant, and I don't know if I can do that here, or if I've saved enough money yet.

There's a lot to figure out, and while my last relationship still haunts me, we are going to do our best to stay in that impossible place – the present.

My phone vibrates from Yianni's bedside. I've got it on charge there. Leaning up on to my elbow, I can see it's a message from Amara.

How's life in paradise? It's shit here. I just broke it off with Si. Don't worry. I'll still pay your rent. Call when you can. Miss you. xx

'Oh my God,' I say out loud to my phone screen. I hit the screen to call her right away.

Her face next to Rob's sweaty one brightens my screen as it calls. Without bothering with *hello*, I'm asking questions. 'What happened? How're you feeling? I thought it was all going so well?'

'It was.' I can tell she's been crying. There's a wobble in her voice. It's tiny, but it's there, an echo of recent pain becoming audible all over again.

'I don't know, I just got so fed up and I wasn't very well at all last week and he was barely sympathetic. He got me chocolates.' Her voice is incredulous at the idea.

'So? Isn't that a nice thing to do?'

'No,' she snaps, 'not if someone is feeling sicky. How will chocolate help with that? And dairy always makes my migraines worse.'

Jumping up, I start pacing around Yianni's small room. Two paces then turn, two paces then turn. I must look like one of those big cats that are shut in zoos, going round and round all day.

'Sorry,' I begin. 'It's hard to gauge. It's not like I'm there to see it all and assess it all.'

'Wish you were.'

Yianni carefully opens the door and I instantly smile at him. A white plastic bag hangs from his wrist, and he has a takeaway cup in each hand. He passes me one of the cups and stoops to kiss my neck while Amara continues.

She explains how she felt like she was snapping at Si every day and that he begged her to change her mind, but she was feeling much too miserable around him.

'What's the time there?' Amara cuts herself off with a question to me.

'Nine-ish, I think.'

'It's still early here. I've said I'll meet the girls from work for breakfast. They want to cheer me up. Wish you were coming.'

'Me too.'

'No, you don't.'

I don't. I really don't.

I wish Amara could appear in Corfu for me to comfort her, but if I'm being completely honest, I don't want to leave Greece any time soon.

'I do wish you were here though.'

'Me too. I best go. Call me later?'

'Of course.'

'*Ciao.*'

'Call me anytime. *Salut.* Bye.'

Then she's gone and it's just Yianni and me.

We chat over our breakfast, but we both know we need to get back to the house to shower, and we have to hope we don't get quizzed when we're there.

Back at the house, everything's normal. We are normal.

Our past normal, anyway. Other than turning up at the same time, which has only happened once before.

In front of Hazel and Pericles, I thank Yianni for a lovely evening – and I'm pretty sure it comes off a lot more stilted than I intended.

In passing, I tell them that we stayed up chatting and Yianni adds with a scowl that I ended up taking over his bed again.

I have to nip my tongue with my teeth to suppress my laughter. It's like I'm a kid again. I haven't felt this way in so long. Yianni brings out the fun in things.

They don't seem to notice; they're on their way out the door to do everyday chores and Natalia is already at her boyfriend's house for the morning.

No sooner are we in the door than we're alone again. The last words from Hazel were, *See you at the restaurant.* Which will probably be in a couple of hours at least. I follow Yianni up the stairs. He turns in to my room, then stops in the doorway.

'Sorry. I'm forgetting—'

'It's OK. It is technically your room.'

We edge around each other in the doorway, our bodies so close but, like the wrong end of two magnets again, we make sure we don't actually touch each other.

We've already agreed we should be *normal* in the house. We need to get ourselves ready for work. That's all. He leaves and I close the door and go straight to the bathroom to shower.

I don't even make eye contact with myself in the mirror. My head is down, and I get myself ready for the day.

I need to call my mum at some point. She tried to call while I was on the bike, and now I have two missed calls from her. Steam fills the room and my body drips with sweat that muddles with the water. The taste of Yianni's skin is on the tip of my tongue and his fingers searching my body for answers plays in my memory.

I *really* like him.

There's no way I would do anything that might rock the boat with Hazel unless it was worth it, and I know in the pit of my stomach that Yianni is worth it. He is the first person since Jonathan that I like. I've been asked out a few times by men who seemed nice enough, but I wasn't interested in even giving them a chance. Not until Yianni.

The spark isn't something I can explain, it's just there. Burning embers that won't quit.

It doesn't really matter that I didn't bloody well want to like him this way. There's no choice in the matter now.

Every fibre of my body decided on it without my brain and, even when my brain caught up, I just liked him more.

Dread seeps in as I lather my hair. I know I'm trying to live in the now, but some questions can't be ignored, not when they're screaming at the back of my head.

How will we tell Hazel, Pericles, my mum and dad – Natalia? Shit, she's going to think I'm dreadful. She adores her big brother and she's included me like a sister.

My eyes clamp shut at the thought of it, and I do my best to move away from the negativity. We'll work it out.

Do I want to move to Corfu? I'd miss my parents and Amara and a couple of other friends. It's mostly my parents though.

Since Jonathan died, I've been talking to my mum almost every other day and seeing them at least once a week, and sometimes more. I can't see Yianni moving to England; in fact, I can't see it being possible at all. And what about my dream restaurant? I never imagined for it to be here in Corfu.

I turn the shower off and step out to grab my towel, wrapping myself up in its fluffy white cotton threads.

Stepping into my room, steam lifts off my skin. A quiet knock sounds at the door.

It can only be Yianni.

I hesitate, wondering whether I should try to get dressed before answering, but I'm soaking wet still. There isn't much choice but to let him in; it is his room, after all.

'Come in.'

The door creaks and Yianni is standing there with one towel around his waist and one rolled-up towel around his shoulders, catching the drips from his thick mop of hair.

He looks me over and I'm aware how short my towel is, grazing my thighs.

'I have been thinking. Maybe we break one rule? It is only one.'

He walks into the room and stands an inch or so away from me.

'It depends which one, I suppose.' I want to touch him, but I refrain.

'The one that says I can't touch you in this house. This is my bedroom, after all.'

He hooks my chin with his index finger and lifts it up towards him, pulling me into him. Our towels melt away to the floor.

'You're all wet.'

I laugh into his mouth, and he makes a little noise of acknowledgement as though he hadn't realised what he was saying when he said it.

We flop back on the bed in our heated embrace and our flesh is sticking, fusing together, but we know we shouldn't take it further.

We just enjoy each other's hands and mouths before we really *do* have to get ready for work.

Chapter
Forty Eight

Now

'I want you to stay all night tonight, no more leaving before the sun is up. I want to hold you the whole night.' Yianni's voice softly touches my ear as he leans over the bar.

I've been staying as late as I can get away with each night for over a week. We don't want to draw attention to ourselves. So far no one has questioned it, because no one knows how late the patrons are leaving, and sometimes it's pretty late.

'Do you have an order for me?' I press my hands to my hips.

'Yes. That is my order. I order you to stay here tonight and f—'

'Ruby? What are you up to tomorrow morning?' Natalia slides up to the bar from the side and wraps her arm around her brother's neck.

We were too wrapped up in our close conversation to notice her skipping over to us from the kitchen.

'Am I invisible to you?' Yianni continues in Greek for a few sharp sentences that I don't understand. 'I was here making my *orders* first,' he finishes in English.

Yianni's eyes flick towards me, with an unnatural slant to the word *orders*.

My heart rattles in my chest like a woodpecker is making its nest there.

'A bottle of house white, half a pint of Mythos and a frozen daiquiri. There. Your turn.' Yianni twists himself off the bar and out of Natalia's grip before sauntering away from us.

'Well? What are you up to? Do you want to go swimming or shopping? Mama says we should do something fun. I asked that we could skip lunch service.' Natalia rests her cheek on her fist and her big dark eyes are gleaming over her smile.

'Sounds good. I'm staying here tonight, I think. Nico said something about going out for drinks.' I dip my head towards the other end of the bar, where Nico is out of earshot, putting on his usual performance for a small crowd of girls.

'Nico!' Natalia calls out.

Nico holds up a finger before cocking his head towards Natalia.

At times like this, Natalia fizzes with a bouncy energy that would be impossible to contain. She waves him over. Before he leaves his adoring public, he apologises for the inconvenience of his departure from the conversation.

'How can I help the most beautiful girl in Greek Secret?' Nico leans on his forearms over the bar towards her.

The playful look he gives to all the women who order cocktails from him appears on his face. The raised eyebrow, the nip of his lip.

The thing that catches my attention more is the blush that rushes along Natalia's cheek and the way she tries to play up to him, wriggling herself on to a stool to get a little closer.

'Can I come tonight? If Mama says yes? I can have a beer and stay late with you all.'

'Tonight?' Nico recoils under his heavy eyebrows.

I jump in, doing my best not to seem too forward. 'Yeah, we were going to stay later, for a drink? I thought I'd stay here tonight if we were drinking. Remember? We were talking about it earlier.'

There's only the slightest widening of his eyes to give away his recognition of what's really going on.

'Oh, yes, yes. Well, it is not up to me. You know this. You will need to speak to Pericles. Pericles? Pericles!' Nico starts calling to the other end of the bar, where he just came from.

He knows as well as I do that where Hazel might say yes, Pericles will probably say no. I'll have to thank him later . . . and make it up to Natalia tomorrow.

'Nico, no! Stop.' Natalia grits her teeth at Nico, but it's too late.

Within moments, her dad has called off the whole idea of her going out with us – in particular, with Nico.

'We'll do something fun tomorrow, to make up for it,' I prom-ise her before she skulks back to the kitchen to retrieve her phone and probably beg Hazel to overturn her father's decision.

Placing the wine, half a pint and the freshly made cocktail on a tray, I grab Nico's arm before he disappears to his waiting audience.

'Why were you flirting with Natalia? She's way too young for you and she has a boyfriend. Yianni would fly off the handle if you went near his sister.'

Nico folds his arms over his chest and dips his chin in gentle laughter.

'Yes, this is all true. But you forget, she would be . . . what is the word? . . . offended, if I don't talk to her this way. Did you never like someone older than you to flirt with? Isn't this where Yianni's obsession with you starts? He saw this beautiful older girl and he wants her.' Nico leans in closer. 'And now he has her. But don't worry, Natalia is safe with me. I have no such intentions.' He shrugs. 'All the girls like me. I'm too kind to break their hearts, this is all.'

As Nico slides back towards the other end of the bar, his words fall heavy in my head like the dropping of stones into water. Yianni told me before that he liked me back when he first saw me. I didn't think much of it. We all have crushes. Clearly, he told Nico too.

I'm not sure how I feel about that being our start. That all I am is an image or an obsession. Does he like me for me? Or the idea of me?

Jonathan asked if I was an actress or a model when he first met me. Things like that were important to him. That I looked right on his arm. My tongue twists in my head as I roll over too many conflicting thoughts of the past.

Taking the drinks over to a table under the hanging vines, I track Yianni as he moves from the opposite back corner to where I'm putting down the glasses.

Without too much thought, I skip to get in step with him, barely acknowledging the chime of *thank you*s from around the table.

'Yianni, can I talk to you?'

It takes all my willpower not to catch his arm and twist him to face me. I want to ask him outright, right now. Am I some childhood conquest of his? Are we even real?

'Now?' Yianni keeps moving, scanning tables to check for anyone else who might need him.

'I mean . . . no. No.'

Pericles narrows his eyes on us from the end of the bar, where he's chatting to an older couple. With me working here, he's more like the host of his own party each night than much else. If he's keeping an eye on us now, there's no way to stop and have a chat in the middle of dinner service.

My shoulders round under the weight of my full head. 'It can wait.'

Yianni pauses between the tables and scans my face. For a moment, I think he might actually reach out and take it in his hand.

'No. We can talk now. Come.' Yianni sharply tilts his head towards the door to the side room. To his bedroom.

As we pass the bar, I leave the tray on it and do my best to keep up with Yianni's long strides.

I'm barely in the room before he's closing the door behind me.

'Should we be in here? Alone? Won't everyone be suspicious?' My hands lock into my hips.

'I do not care. Your face— Something's wrong? Has something happened?'

'No, I'm being stupid—'

'Nothing you say is *stupid*. What is it?'

Yianni reduces the space between us and curls his fingers around the back of my neck and into my hair.

'Something Nico said. About you having a crush on me all those years ago. It got me in a tailspin. Like . . . is this real or just you proving you could have me?'

'Is that a serious question?'

Yianni raises an eyebrow at me before lowering his head to rest it against mine.

In truth, the way he read my face and ushered me in here to check on me told me I was overreacting.

More remnants from a painful past repeating on me and dragging down the present. I want to trust Yianni, but certain things feel like being jabbed in the ribs with a hot poker and I don't have the skill set to deal with them.

'I guess, Jonathan chased me, you know? And how much did he really want me for me, or just to place on his arm because I was what he thought he wanted?'

'I am not Jonathan. Yes, I have eyes in my head. Even all those years ago I could see your beautiful face, even when you would hide it behind all that long dark hair you used to have. But that isn't why I want to spend time with you.' His lips move over my jawline like a feather. 'I like how you challenge me. Your strength, the way you try so hard not to laugh at my very funny jokes.'

Yianni's mouth meets mine as I do my best to suppress the laugh he so badly wants from me.

I pull away no more than an inch. 'We need to get out of here. People will wonder where we are.'

Yianni steps his legs between mine and twists us to press me against the wall.

My mouth falls slack as a gasp rattles through me. His mouth pulls at my bottom lip as his fingers trail up my ribs.

A knock rattles the door as the handle moves to open it.

My heart almost rips from my chest and my bones turn to jelly.

We split apart in a rapid motion as the door creaks open and time feels like it's tearing at the seams. I can't handle this. I can't have anyone know.

Nico pokes his head in around the door. A cold sweat soaks me in an instant.

'You are lucky it's me. Pericles was on his way, marzing here to find you. Wanting to know what the problem is. This is a work day. Yes?'

Relief washes over me, but in the same way as getting knocked over by a big wave and being pulled under the water momentarily. The salt stings my eyes and the relief of not drowning is short-lived against the fear of drowning.

We need to be more careful.

The weight of Yianni's head presses down on my shoulder and a nervous laugh ripples through both of us.

If nothing else, tonight has made me realise how far away from ready I am to tell anyone about us.

Chapter Forty Nine

Now

'I can't believe we nearly got caught tonight. What the hell would we even say?' I sit down on Yianni's bed and watch him close the door to an empty restaurant. 'We need to be more careful.'

'Or we tell everyone.' Yianni pushes his thick hair off his face.

I snatch a breath, hoping it'll give me time to formulate words. It doesn't.

Every molecule tingles with fear at this idea of holding hands, strolling back to the house and standing there waiting for their appraisal.

Yianni fills the silence for me. 'I know it is too soon. We need to find ourselves before we share this with everyone. I know what we said. For now, we have to live with this possibility of getting caught.'

Yianni's fingers move down the buttons on his shirt, undoing them one by one.

I slide myself back along the bed in anticipation of him meeting me here. Feeling the weight of him, holding him. That's what

I need to push these thoughts away. I roll my shoulders to try to tease out some of the tension, ready to relax and forget everything from the past that's holding me back.

When Yianni reaches the last button, he stops and sits at the other end of the bed.

'I know waiting is also because of him. Because of Jonathan. For me too, I've made mistakes, trusted the wrong girl. I don't feel like this with you. This is . . . different. As long as we are open with each other. That counts to me.'

'I've never been more open with anyone.' I shuffle a little further away, not wanting to add *other than with Jonathan*. 'I've shared my scars, my body. My strange musing about the convergence of the past and the future.' My hands hang awkwardly in the air at the imagined line before slapping down to my thighs.

I was open with Jonathan, too, and look how that worked out. That was before the scars though. It was easier to share myself back then. Yianni's managed to pull me in when I wasn't even sure it was possible any more. Slowly edging around me until I was dizzy for him.

'The present.' Yianni's eyebrows flick up.

'I mean, you've kind of oversimplified it, but yeah. The present.'

There's a shared warmth. Not laughter exactly, but an acknowledgement of being content in our own world of understanding.

This understanding is what was missing with Jonathan. With him, if it wasn't spelt out, it wasn't there. With Yianni, we have subtlety born of sneaking around. We can read chapters from each other's minds where everyone else sees only a look.

Like tonight – he could see me unravelling without more than me asking for a quick chat.

Yianni's hand slides towards my foot and rests on top of it.

'It's not just Jonathan still holding me back, you know. Hazel told me she worries about you. *With girls.*'

Yianni raises an eyebrow and settles towards me, placing my foot on his leg.

'Hazel worries about everything.' His eyes roll over this half-truth.

I actually think she's quite laid back, compared to my mum anyway.

'I really worry that she'll think I'm bad for you.'

'No, I'm not worried what people think.' He begins to massage the arch of my foot, making my head slump back on to his wall.

'This isn't people,' I say to the mosquito biding its time on the ceiling, 'this is family.' I return my gaze to Yianni. 'And trust me, it's hard when everyone has an opinion on *your* life and how *you* feel. And everyone *will* have an opinion, one way or another. They always do. I'm so sick of everyone having an opinion on my life. Talking about me like I'm not there or making assumptions on how I must feel. Or, my favourite, saying they understand. As though they too were in a car and had someone they care about die inches from their face.'

I bite my lips together and Yianni's hand stops dead.

Even with the air-con trying its best, sweat trickles down my skin and I want to go outside and run to the sea, where everything will be shades of black and blue, like the angry bruises that linger inside me.

Gently lifting my foot off his leg, Yianni moves up along the bed and tucks me into his arms. With his shirt falling open, my cheek presses against his skin.

'You're going to have a make-up imprint of my cheek on your chest.'

'I don't care about that. I care about you.' His lips cautiously press against the back of my neck.

'People like to talk and talk. It's how they all connect. We will be old news as soon as they know about us.'

He doesn't understand. How can he? My life really was in the news.

When Jonathan died, everyone was posting on social media and sharing articles about the accident. His mum even paid for a piece in a national newspaper about his life and his career that featured brief details of me and the car crash.

'The thing I've come to realise – I guess accept more than realise – is that I had to mourn Jonathan according to everyone else. Everyone thought we were still *so* in love that I'd have said yes if he asked me to marry him and that I should wear his ring and, and . . . all I felt was guilt.' I unfurl away from Yianni's embrace a little. 'I've missed him; he was there almost every day before he died. By my side for years, but I wasn't in love with him any more. No one knew that I was about to end it, so everyone expected me to mourn in a certain way. A way I then felt I had to meet.'

'Everyone except me.'

I tilt my head up to face him.

'I know the truth. You tell me everything.'

'That's true, but I'm not ready to find out whether our relationship meets everyone else's expectations. Hazel thinks you need to have space away from women or whatever. She might take against the whole idea of us. What if this doesn't work out, with everyone watching our every move? I don't want to lose her, or you, or anyone. At least keeping it secret means we can protect what we have while we figure everything out. Without the pressure of everyone else. I had to hide how I felt about Jonathan's death for so long. I still do. I just want to be free of all that for a little bit longer.'

'I would hide this for ever as long as I can be with you.'

Chapter Fifty

Now

Days merge together in the same way dreams flow from one idea to the next. Like waves crashing against rock. We stay up together and steal as much time as we can before I have to go back to the house.

Whenever Yianni passes me behind the bar, his fingers graze mine, unseen by the world around us, and electricity runs through me, burning so hot I wouldn't be surprised if sparks caught light in the golden heat of the island.

Sneaking about suits us. Each shift at Greek Secret is like a pulse building towards our time together alone. Nico sometimes passes comments and winks, but never within earshot of anyone else. He's actually been tamer than I gave him credit for. He might like to wind people up now and then, but for whatever reason, I think he knows how important his silence is to us.

Tonight, traditional bouzouki music blares out of the speakers at a volume I haven't heard at Greek Secret before, and Yianni's little bedroom has a bunch of boys from Natalia and Gaia's school in there, including their boyfriends.

I've only met Natalia's boyfriend a couple of times. He doesn't speak English – not to me, anyway – and my Greek is mostly rude words, thanks to Nico.

Everyone's smiling and the taverna vibrates with clapping hands as the lads, all dressed in black with white sashes around the waist, exit the little side room and dance in a circle. Yianni and Nico sit out this round of side-stepping and circling.

Then one boy, who I think might be Gaia's boyfriend, steps forward to do a little solo that consists of impressive kicks and dropping to his knees.

Gaia's parents and family have booked a table, and they stand up and clap until their little baby cries and has to be joggled about just outside of the restaurant.

Yianni comes to the bar to place an order for another round of drinks and I see Gaia bring out plates of food, but really she wants to see her boyfriend's big finale. As soon as the plates of food leave her hands, she's frantically clapping him.

'When's it your turn?'

'Not long; another dance in ten minutes perhaps.' Yianni looks at an invisible watch on his wrist. 'I forgot to put it back on.' He laughs at himself before giving me the slightest wink and moving back to help with the serving of food and general running of the place.

Drinks orders flow easier than the wine itself and soon the music kicks up another notch and it's Yianni, Nico and Pericles who step forward for their turn on the floor.

More stepping and stamping ensue, and Pericles even smothers the floor in lighter fluid, igniting it in front of them. Flames lick at their heels as they kick and twist over them.

I'm clapping along so hard my palms sting and my cheeks ache from giggling.

Yianni glances at me a couple of times, but he's a good little performer; they all are. I guess they've been doing it long enough.

I'm sure Yianni said they learn some of the dances in school.

Just as they're really going for it, I hear – and feel – my phone in the back pocket of my shorts. I pull it out and glance at the screen. Amara.

I hesitate over the answer button. She'll call back – she probably forgot the time difference, she's all over the place at the moment – but even if I answered her, I don't think I'd hear her over the music filling the room.

As soon as the ringing stops, I place the phone back in the pocket of my shorts and carry on enjoying the dancing.

When they finish, whooping and clapping from the tables takes over, but Yianni isn't taking it in; he isn't even bothered. He's pulled Nico close to whisper in his ear. Nico's forehead collapses into a frown but he bobs his head in some kind of agreement. Yianni then does the same to his dad as Nico jogs towards the bar.

'All done?' I enquire as Nico gropes for the little iPod.

He doesn't answer me, but there's a lingering smile as he hits play. I recognise the song just as he grabs my wrist.

'No, Nico, no, please,' I hiss.

I try to look calm because I don't want people to know how much I don't want to be pulled forward into the clearing they've made for the event.

Nico passes me to Yianni as Pericles pulls Hazel forward. By the looks of it, she has basically been pushed out of the kitchen behind me.

She delicately pushes her glasses on top of her head and tucks loose strands of hair behind her ears as she spies the people watching us.

Nico steps forward and points to a woman not too far in front and invites her up to dance with him.

She looks thrilled to get involved and they take centre stage with Yianni and me framing one side and Hazel with Pericles framing the other.

Yianni moves around me and I do my best to steady my pulse, because my hands are shaking. It's impossible to hide with my arms out at the sides.

'It is just me and you,' Yianni whispers in my ear as he glances around me.

I look up at him and for a moment I can almost believe him from the way he's looking at me. It's so intense.

Our hips sway but we never touch, not even a graze.

I'm losing myself to him and this island. Maybe this is him telling me he wants everyone to know about us?

Maybe I want that too.

My chest rocks in erratic breaths while I do my best to plaster a coy smile on my face to fit with the dance and the sensual swaying.

My phone blares out in my pocket again. I physically jump at the sensation of it vibrating and my hip collides with Yianni's hand, ruining the illusion of a forcefield around my shape.

We continue to dance awkwardly despite the phone, as Nico and his audience partner repeatedly glance in our direction until it stops.

Moments later it starts again, and this time I can't ignore it.

'I have to answer it, I'm sorry.'

I break from the bubble and let my hand glance Yianni's stubbled cheek before running off to answer the phone. I catch a glimpse of his hurt eyes watching me before he merges with the people watching the sensual dancing from the others.

The picture of Amara and Rob from a night out is there on the screen as it carries on ringing.

'Can you hear me, Amara?'

I weave my way into the kitchen for some quiet. The cook who works alongside Hazel nods as I come in but carries on with what she's doing.

'Is everything OK?'

'Erm, yes, but you sound a little wired. Is everything all right?' It's not Amara's voice, but a man's.

I look back at the screen. I've used the same photo for Rob when he calls as I have for Amara.

'Rob? I thought you were Amara.'

'Amara? I wish I had her skin, but I'm sure we don't sound at all similar, *ma chérie.*'

'Is everything OK?'

Natalia appears in the kitchen, swinging an empty tray at her side. She starts talking to me before she realises I'm on the phone, making me miss what Rob is saying. 'You look like you've done this dance before—' She interrupts herself, clamping her lips shut when she sees the phone pressed to my ear and covering her mouth with her hand. She then mimes the word *syngnómi* – sorry.

'Rob, say that again.'

'I said, I'm calling about a promise you made me a few years ago. I heard you were working in Ipswich, so I came all the way to England to ask you, but you're not here. It seems my information is a little past tense. Thanks for the updates, by the way. I'm heart-broken to be so out of the loop. Anyway, what's bad for Charlie-boy could be good for me. Amara tells me you're visiting your aunt in Corfu for work. I thought you were just on vacation.'

Aunt Hazel moves around me with sweat-drenched hair and rosy cheeks as she gets plates ready for the last of the night's orders.

I shudder as I can almost hear Jonathan in the back of my head calling Charles Charlie-boy in the same tone as Rob.

'I'm confused.' My fingers press into the bridge of my nose and I lower my head to concentrate on Rob's voice in the speaker.

'I need a good maître d' in Rouen.' He says the words uncharacteristically slowly. 'I've gone through two girls and one chap in the past six months and they've all been useless. It's a busy position all year round and we need someone who can keep everything running smoothly. You'd be working with the best, aka me.' I can almost hear Rob fluttering his always curled eyelashes. 'I know you're meant to be in Corfu with your aunt, but I need you, and you did promise.'

My breath catches in my chest. This is big. Really big.

I've saved almost enough to apply for a loan already, but the experience of working in a chic city restaurant in France could seal the deal.

'I'm at work right now,' I splutter, changing the phone from one ear to the other. 'Can I call later? Maybe in the morning?'

'I had expected an instant yes, but sure. You think about it and I'll email some details. *Bisous, ma belle.*'

'*Bisous, à bientôt.*'

The line goes dead and I lock the screen as my arm falls slack by my side. Between Amara and Rob, I'm left completely still and in shock as the kitchen around me swirls with steam, releasing a new wave of garlic and dill.

'You and Yianni looked good together,' Natalia says as she makes her way past me with two fresh plates of food. 'You should do it again next time.'

I swallow the sudden urge to cry and smile instead. 'No, thank you. I was terrified. I'll leave the performing to you lot.'

I briefly squeeze her shoulder as she slides past and take a step to follow her back through the staggered corridor and out towards the bar.

'Ruby!' Hazel's voice echoes along the corridor.

She appears, wiping her hands over her apron. 'Ruby, are you all right? You look pale.'

'No, yeah. It was Rob. Do you remember Rob? He got me my first job in London years ago. You met him at my birthday thing. The night . . .' I snatch a breath and steady myself into being brave and finishing the sentence. 'The night Jonathan died.'

'Yes, I remember him. The one with lip fillers he said he'd modelled on your full lips.'

A short laugh hits out of my chest. I can see him saying it, and it's impossible not to smile. 'Yeah, he always says that. He's offered me a job as a maître d' in France.'

'Oh my! Are you going to take it?'

'I have no idea.' My shoulders rise and fall as another wave of confusion threatens to drown me.

'You're so multi-talented, he'd be lucky to have you and we'd be sad to lose you. You can tell me all about it later.' Hazel squeezes my arm before turning towards the clattering of pans in the kitchen. 'I'm so proud of you.'

I float back to the bar on legs I can't even feel.

'You've broken Yianni,' Nico laughs, as I slip behind the bar. He glances at me, then back towards the draft beer he's pouring. 'Can you do two house white?'

'Of course.' I sound like a robot and then move like one around him. 'How have I broken him?'

'The dance. It was his idea and you left him to the sharks.'

'Sharks?'

Nico's shoulders bounce before he flashes me a wicked smile and nods towards Yianni, who's chatting to a woman, perhaps in her fifties, in a very low-cut dress.

Yianni's smiling, and charming. He's used to all the attention. The woman reaches to squeeze his bicep. She's attractive and slim, but I'm in no way jealous. If anything, I'm amused because even from here I can see the fear lingering in his eyes.

What would happen if I went to France? Are we strong enough to last with distance between us?

Things are so early, so new, and I'm still not ready to deal with everyone's thoughts on yet another part of my life.

I have so much to talk to him about, so much to process.

'Where is the wine?' Nico snaps me out of my reverie.

I can't do this. I'm more lost than ever. I've let a man distract me from my goals and I can't let that happen all over again.

I pull a cool bottle of white from the chiller and watch as Yianni and Pericles take to the floor, clapping their hands together harder than before. Yianni fills the floor with flames and smashes a plate behind it to cheers of *Opa!*

My heart burns in those flames.

I'm in love with Yianni, but I can't give up everything I've worked so hard for.

Tears want to pour out of me faster than the wine glugging into the glasses.

I watch on as Yianni jumps over flames in a way I could never have imagined from him before tonight.

Will he support me? Or are we going to both get burnt?

Chapter Fifty One

Now

'You want to leave.' Yianni's on the floor opposite the side of the bed where I'm sitting, his back pressing into the wall and arms resting on his knees.

His chin is still lowered but he looks up at me under his hooded eyes. They look so dark, like lumps of freshly split coal.

'I don't know what I want.'

We've never spoken of the future. Not in any real terms. Only the space between here and telling people about us.

We've been running around enjoying ourselves like we're twenty-one. Only now does it hit me that Yianni's only a few years past twenty-one. It's me who's close to thirty.

When I was twenty-four, I thought Jonathan and I would be together for ever.

I was so deeply in love with his enthusiasm and dimples that nothing else mattered. Not even me.

Rob followed up our call with an email. There's a place where I could live and more money than I'm getting here. Plus, the opportunity to prove I can run a place that isn't owned by my family or someone who wants to get in my knickers.

'You said you want to run your own place. Why not here? With me?'

'We don't even know if Hazel and Pericles would go for that. This is their taverna.'

'One day it will be mine.'

'And Natalia's. Not just yours.'

Silence ensues. One more formidable than the swell of the humid air around us.

'I do not want you to leave like this, off to France with this Rob.'

'Rob's gay, if that helps.'

'A little.' Yianni shrugs and we share in the warmth of smiles for a moment.

'Don't you trust me?'

Jonathan never trusted me. He was a cheat and he would always judge me by his low standards. It eroded what we had. Or at least, what I thought we had.

'I do. If you want to go, I would never stop you. This is your life and I'm lucky to be a part of it. But I need you to know, I want you to stay.'

Yianni moves to his knees, resting his arms on my thighs and his hands on my hips. The lamp dipped at our side casts a harsh shadow over the door.

'We need to talk about the future. About us.'

'I want to be in your future, but my life is here in Corfu. I want to run Greek Secret with you by my side.'

'I want my own restaurant, something I've created from scratch. You know that, I've told you that.'

'Could you do this here? Find a place of your own in Corfu?'

A lump travels slowly down my throat. It's too soon to know. Too soon to ask these questions.

I thought I had time to work all this out.

I've been avoiding thinking too far ahead. I thought I had over a month to figure out the next step.

I've saved more than I thought since being here. Each day my dreams become closer and closer to reality. I could put a business plan together now, if I knew where I wanted to be, and I could probably get a loan for anything else I needed.

All because Hazel won't even let me pay for my drinks at Greek Secret, let alone anything else. Everything I earn here is mine. I never thought I'd be in this position so quickly.

I still don't feel ready.

I've wanted this for so long and now I'm not even sure I'm strong enough to carry the weight of it. At least going to France and running a busy restaurant there would push me to see if I still have it in me.

I've paused too long, and I still have nothing to say that will help.

'I don't know; I don't know where I want to be.' My voice is hushed but it still hits him hard enough for sadness to crush down on his forehead before he bows his head completely into my lap.

My fingers lace into his hair, tilting his head back to look up at me again.

'I love you, Yianni. But I've put someone else first before and it ended . . .' I could say in disaster, or heartbreak. But really, all that's important now is that it ended. 'We've only just begun.'

The corners of his eyes crease and the corner of his mouth twitches up. 'I love you too, Ruby *mou*.'

We've never said this before.

The L word.

The last person I said it to and meant it like this was Jonathan.

Elation and fear curdle inside me and all I want to do is run. *What if* echoes in my head and all the reasons we shouldn't be together course through me.

I trusted Jonathan and there's a niggling possibility that he tried to kill me, or himself. I'll never know. The numb sensation from my scars radiates out from my stomach, leaving me hollow and lost.

Yianni's thumbs rub over my hip bones. 'I have never felt this for anyone. I don't want you to go to France.'

'I don't know what to do.' I open my mouth to continue but I stop.

I don't want to tell him I'm afraid I'm too broken to make anything last.

I'm afraid that everything I went through with Jonathan might mean I'm never ready to tell anyone about us, because if we do, then *us* is a real thing. Our relationship will be alive in other people's minds and it'll be out of control. I can't stop what they think or how that might change things.

Sometimes I feel like I'm back in that car, sliding around with my foot pressed on the brake, but nothing stops no matter how hard I try. I just want things to freeze and for me to find the air around me again.

People thought Jonathan was so wonderful, but he was so flawed. We all are, and that terrifies me. What flaws might Yianni reveal over time, what flaws might I reveal to him? Ones that we can't overcome or ones that hurt the other?

'Then do nothing. Stay here. If you're not sure of the job, be sure of me.'

His hand reaches up to my cheek and I can feel his desperation to keep me here pulling me in.

I do love him, but is love ever really enough? Love can shatter and break. I've seen it, like the glass of a car windscreen broken and glittering all over the dashboard.

Cupping my hand over his, my lips find his palm. I press my eyes tightly shut to hold in the tears that are biting in the corners.

Yianni's velvet lips seek out mine and I press hard against him, pulling him in with one hand still wrapped in his hair.

I lie back on his bed as we grip each other almost painfully tightly, our hands trying to hold on to all that we have.

Our hands pull at buttons, prising them open one by one. Yianni's mouth begins to weave down my neck, my collarbone, the scar on my stomach, until he's back kneeling on the floor in front of me.

His firm grip rolls up my skirt and tugs down my underwear.

Closing my eyes, I do my best to clear away all the things I don't want to think about and enjoy the heat of Yianni pressing against me. To feel the rise and fall of air in my chest and the pulsing of pleasure rolling over me, swirling and consuming.

The air catches in my chest and I can't breathe. It's all too much.

All the blood rushes away from my head and my hands claw into Yianni's thick hair.

It's sweet torture.

One that drives pulses of shallow breath and screams held in for so long that they throw themselves out into the world like angry curse words.

When the outpouring of pleasure ends, the cloud in my mind opens up to the light. I'm hurting myself over a future that hasn't happened, because I'm terrified it *can't* happen.

I'm lucky even to have a future to pick from. It's more than Jonathan has.

Yianni climbs on to the bed and we hold each other for a moment.

I need to put me first and I need to find the right words, because I don't want to lose Yianni to find myself. But if I don't find myself, my voice, my dreams, how can it really be me here with him?

He's helped me so much to gain back some of my light, some of my confidence, but it feels like the first step, not the last.

Yianni buries his face into my neck as my fingers trace lines over the swell of his bicep.

I close my eyes. If I open them and look around this room full of his clothes and knick-knacks, where we fell in love, I might not be able to do this.

'What about this: I work for Rob for one year. I'll have more than enough money to pick what I want to do next, whether that's here or France or England . . . but in a year I can challenge myself, maybe train someone up for Rob while I'm there, and we'll know if this, us, is serious. If all we've done is think of the other and if all we want to do is tell everyone . . . then we'll know. But I need to prove I can succeed without it being my aunt telling me I'm good enough or someone who fancies me.'

'I know two things. This, *us*, this is serious, and you are ready to have your own restaurant.' Yianni runs a finger over the scars on my abdomen. A strange and numb sensation where the nerves will never quite be the same again. 'No matter what you do, I am here to support your dreams. Take your year in France, and at the end, I'll be waiting.'

'I promise, I will come back.'

I owe him that. I owe us that.

There's no way to know what a year might bring. All I do know is, until I'm sure of myself, how can I be sure of us?

Chapter Fifty Two

Now

After very little sleep, I head back alone to the house.

Even when we eventually decided it would be a good time to sleep, I couldn't.

Instead, I watched the gentle rise and fall of Yianni's chest and wondered why life has to be so complex. And whether I'll ever actually stop being afraid of the vast past and future.

While Yianni lay dreaming, hot tears burnt my cheeks. I wish I knew how other people lived their lives. How they could progress without fear looming over them.

It feels like a lifetime ago that I built the confidence to walk on the beach in a bikini. Now that triumph is overshadowed by my inability to face people's opinions on something new.

It's taken me two years to accept my new body. Will it be another two years of hiding Yianni before I feel we can be seen in the sun too?

I need to stop going over it all in my head, because what I have to do now is talk everything through with Hazel.

Not everything. Not my feelings for Yianni, but I do need to talk to her about France and Rob.

She's the one that offered me the job and has been so supportive of everything. I don't want to let her down. I can't accept Rob's offer without knowing Greek Secret will be OK without me.

◆ ◆ ◆

'You're back early. Natalia's still in bed. I think all that singing tired her out.' Hazel nurses a cup of tea at the kitchen table. She gets the teabags from a shop in Corfu Town so she can maintain that one little English habit in the morning.

'She has such a beautiful voice.'

'She does. No idea where she gets it from, must be the Greek side. I can't sing a note.'

'Me neither.' I slide out a chair and sit opposite Hazel at the table. 'I need to talk to you.'

'About the job in France? And how you want to take it, right?'

I nod my head, curling my hands together under the table.

'We'll miss you, you know.'

'I'll miss you too.'

I want to add, *I don't know how I'll live without seeing Yianni's secret smiles every day.* But I don't. I hold it in. I bite back the emotions swelling in my head. The ones that threaten to overwhelm me.

'Don't worry about Greek Secret, we'll just about manage. If you ever get bored of France, you're welcome here any time.'

'I guess I'd best book a flight then.'

That was even easier than I expected.

Aunt Hazel has always supported me. Even pushing for me to come and stay here and be a part of things because she believed in me.

One of the heavy loads that has been compressing my spine lifts in the knowledge that she supports my choices. I can't quite believe how easy that was.

Hazel removes her glasses and discards them on the table, studying my face before her cool hand reaches out and holds my chin.

'You've been wearing a little less make-up lately. It's nice to see your freckles coming through.' Her hand drops to the table and she slides it back to lean on it. 'You're so impressive, you know that? Your mum worries, how could she not? But you've come so far since getting here. At first, I felt like you would slip into a dream world and you were a million miles off. Now you seem like the old you, but with a new twist.' She taps the table to punctuate her words. 'I mean, you could run the place single-handedly with the ease and grace of a seasoned professional. And not to mention that time with those lads.' Hazel slaps her hand harder on the table and begins to laugh. 'You should've heard Pericles and Yianni raving about you after that.'

'Seriously?' I shift in my seat at the thought of them all talking about me.

'Oh yeah! Yianni kept saying you could've broken that bloke's arm and Pericles said he'd never seen anything like it. You really are one in a million, sweetheart.'

A new kind of light burns in my chest. The echoes of pride rebounding from her to me, making me feel a glow. One that I've desperately needed.

I've always looked up to Hazel and her inspiring life in paradise. She's always done things her own way and been so brave, starting life over again and doing an amazing job of it.

Now she's looking at me with the admiration I've always felt for her.

'Thanks, Aunt Hazel.' I swallow back the emotions, holding them in just how I've always done. 'Guess I'd better book some flights.'

I pull out my phone, while Hazel potters around the kitchen near me.

I concentrate on travel arrangements and not the loss of the people I've loved being near to for the past few months. Already it feels like my roots have attached to theirs and it's going to hurt to cut myself free.

I'll be back soon enough. In a year.

Within minutes, it's all booked. First to England, to see my parents and get clothes more suited to northern France, and then I've booked the ferry to France.

On the screen, it all looks so simple. Exciting, according to the confirmation emails littering my inbox.

I leave tomorrow.

Excusing myself from the kitchen, I walk out into the garden to sit on the sun lounger.

In the burning light of the morning sun, I type out a message to Yianni.

Tonight is our last night together. Xx

I really hope those words aren't true. I hope I can find what I need to in Rouen.

Closing my eyes, I lie back, ready to contemplate the line again, the elusive line of the present and what the hell I'm doing with it. Whether or not I'm wasting it or if my focus is too heavy on the long game, even though no one knows if they've even got a long game.

The buzz of my phone cuts up my thought.

The photo of Rob and Amara is there again. This time, it really is Amara.

'*Kalimera!*' I close my eyes and settle myself back down on the lounger to tell Amara everything that's happened. 'Sorry I didn't pick up last night. Rob called me and offered me a job and it's completely thrown me.'

'I'm pregnant.'

My eyes snap open to be blinded by the sun, with painful blotches left to stain my retinas.

Amara's voice cracks and she sniffs before letting out a huge moaning sound into the phone. 'I don't know what to do, Ruby. I can't have a baby. I just can't. I'd be a useless mum, and I don't want that. It wouldn't be fair on the baby.' Then there's more words, but I can't understand them through the sound of snot and tears.

'Slow down, slow down. Firstly, you would be the best mum. You've always put up with me, haven't you? Worrying about your ability to be a mum is not a reason to not want a baby. Not for you, anyway.' A flash of fear burns like the sun's rays. What if Si doesn't want it, and she's feeling pressured to give it up? Or if she thinks this will be the way to get him back? 'And what about Si? What does he want?'

My spare hand scrubs at my hair as worry throbs deep in my skull.

'I've taken a test. Cried. Taken another test. Cried some more. Called you. You didn't answer, fell asleep crying and now we're here. That's it. I've only told you.'

My feet connect with the dry grass as I sit up on the lounger, nearly tipping the whole thing up.

'I think my hormones could be why he was getting on my last nerve. He never wanted things to end.'

'I know my mum said when she was pregnant my dad couldn't do anything right for the first few months.'

It's true, she has told me that loads of times, and how he used to make her favourite raspberry macarons and rub her feet to keep her happy.

But most relationships don't go that way, and who knows how Si might react.

Muted sniffing fills my phone. 'I don't know . . .'

'You two were good together. But do you think he'll be OK? You don't think he'll think you've been hiding it from him or something? Or say it's someone else's.'

'Ruby! It can't be anyone else's.'

'I know that—'

'We've only been apart a few weeks, Ruby. Jeez. There's no way he would think that.' She lets out a sharp, jagged breath from crying.

'You're right. I'm sure you're right. If there's even a chance you want this baby, you need to speak to Si. It's his baby too.'

'What if I've ruined everything? What if he's already moved on?'

I can't imagine the fear Amara must be feeling right now. I wish I could wrap my arms around her and get her a hot drink and a chocolate biscuit.

'There's only one way to find out. You'll have to be brave. You have to take a chance.'

Amara releases all the air in her lungs into the phone.

'I know. Do you think . . .' Amara hesitates. 'Do you think he would've moved on already? I can't bear the thought of him with somebody else. I've missed him so much. I just didn't want to admit it before.' Gulping sobs erupt again.

The fact is, I don't know.

I never thought Jonathan would've cheated on me, but I know he did. There's lots of things I never thought could be true between two people who say *I love you*, but I know differently.

I want to reassure her, but I don't want to lie.

'There's only one way to find out. I wish I could hug you right now.'

'Me too.'

'You need to contact him now. Tell me what happens, OK? Love you.'

'Love you too, but do me a favour and take your own advice. Take a chance. And tell me about this job later, OK?'

'Deal.'

It's still morning, but the temperature is climbing. My phone is hot in my hand and my cheek tingles from the memory of it being pressed there.

The screen is caked in foundation and blusher.

I toss it into the shade under the lounger. There's still no message from Yianni on it anyway and I don't want to sit and stare at it, waiting for a reply.

I sit on my hands because there's nothing useful they can achieve right now. They're desperate to do something to help Amara, but there's nothing I can do.

It's up to her to decide if she can trust Si, if she wants to keep this baby and how she'll bring it up. I'm finding it hard enough to search through the jungle in my own head right now; I'd hate to be in Amara's position.

I let the sun energise me. I need to recharge. As if I wasn't finding the thought of today taxing enough, Amara just took the last slice of my energy with her.

I need something to get me through my last day here for a year. The sun on my face will have to suffice.

As I scrunch my toes into the golden grass, I close my eyes and consider Amara telling me to take my own advice. Take a chance.

That's what I'm doing. I'm taking a chance on me, on my dreams and my future.

I can't rely on anyone else. People leave or they die or they grow and change and things fall apart. I have to make this move to France for myself.

However much I want to take a chance on Yianni too, I'm not ready to hear what everyone else thinks about us when I don't even know what *I* think about us.

I know I love him, but I've seen what letting love in too deeply can do. I've seen how it can corrode everything with time, like rust deep in the hull of a boat.

I don't want that for us.

Chapter Fifty Three

Now

Dust pools up around my bike in the car park of Greek Secret. Before my helmet is off, Hazel is marching towards me.

Amara spoke to Si and ended up telling him everything about the baby. We had a long phone call about it and now I'm running late for work.

Si wanted to keep the baby and proposed to her then and there. I've never heard anyone cry so much while trying to tell me a happy story.

I'm over the moon for her, but a part of me can't help but question it all. I hope for her this is the real thing, and that Si won't let her down, and I really hope she isn't having the baby because she feels she has to.

I don't think it's that. It's impossible not to worry for her, though, knowing how worried she's always felt about the idea of being a parent after hers were barely in her life, and when they were, they weren't worth having.

I did reassure her about it. Her grandparents on her dad's side were always wonderful. Apparently, Si pointed that out to her too. I'm sure that's a good sign.

Chatting to her this afternoon was a good distraction from Yianni not replying to me. I didn't have to go into work for the lunch shift, as Natalia and Gaia were both there. Even though he was working, I still thought he would reply.

Hazel nearly misses her footing as she descends on me.

She already looks a little wired, with strands of blonde hair sticking out and her mascara a little smudged from the heat. Her slender arms work overtime with her legs, as though she couldn't keep her legs moving without her arms working in time.

Fear rolls along my spine. She has a look that reminds me of my mum when she told me off in the past for doing something wrong or for being late home from a party.

'Yianni and Pericles have been held up. You have to run the place – that's OK, right? All the bookings are written down. It's going to be a busy one. Yianni said you could handle it?'

I march along beside her and towards the bar. Fear twists into nerves that tickle low inside me.

'Sure, it's fine. Who's working tonight?' My maître d' voice comes back in. The one with a matter-of-fact edge.

'Natalia, Gaia, Nico, then us two cooks, as always.'

Opening the folder with the bookings, I scan along them.

At eight, we have four bookings. One table of six, one of eight and two of two. We have five other bookings spread throughout the evening.

'We can manage this. Where are they anyway?' I try to ask casually, without even looking up from the book.

'It's not really my place to say. I'm sure Yianni will tell you all about it later.' Hazel kisses my cheek. 'Let me know anything you need.'

As she bustles back to the kitchen, I give myself a moment to catch my breath. I have to focus my mind away from Yianni and wondering what he might be up to. This is my moment to shine.

I get everyone working as a team, the way I used to back at La Salle à Manger. I welcome people, decide where to place them and how we can accommodate the numbers.

Typically, it's even busier than the average August night, with people arriving all at once looking for space that isn't really there.

Chatter rises above the sound of cicadas and the airs swirls with every flavour from our menu.

I do my best not to turn anyone away, but I do have to explain there might be a short wait or it might be good to grab a cocktail and relax with some complimentary bread and dips.

Natalia and Gaia take orders and help behind the bar when it's needed or bring out food at Hazel's or my request. The night passes quicker than ever as we all move around each other with the elegance of ballerinas whirling on stage.

My mum always used to say, *You're like a swan – above the water you look so elegant, but I know those legs of yours are working hard under it all.* Those words follow me with every casual smile and nod to the staff to keep things going.

By the time eleven hits, and there's only four tables left, I snatch a moment next to Nico.

I've barely said hello to him all night.

'You're good at this, Ruby. Bossing us all about. Maybe better than little boss.'

'Do you know where Yianni is? All Hazel said was he got delayed.'

Nico shrugs as he pours out a pineapple juice. 'I know it's the— what is the word?' Nico stops pouring to look off into the distance. '*An-ee-vesy*, of his mother's passing.'

'Anniversary?' My hands grip into my hips. 'He never said anything.'

Why wouldn't he mention such an important thing to me? Why would he hide this of all things, when I've opened up so much to him?

Yianni's car pulls up in the car park.

'Speaking of the donkey.'

I almost do a double take at Nico. '*Donkey?*'

Nico chuckles. 'Your eyes! So wide. Donkey, yes. It must be a Greek thing.'

He picks up the glass of juice and a large bottle of water and takes it around the bar.

As soon as I see Yianni, I want to hold him. To press his lips to mine and keep him with me. All while wanting to stamp my feet and demand he tells me what's going on and why he's been hiding things from me.

I do my best to play it natural, walking over to Pericles first, welcoming him, asking if he was all right, then the same to Yianni.

The difference is, with Yianni I squeeze his arm and take in his smell. It's different to normal. There's a note of something floral. I whisper in his ear after I press my lips to his cheek, 'What's going on? Is everything all right?'

He gives me a wink and smoothly whispers, 'Later,' before heading to the kitchen to let Hazel know they're back.

I fold in my lips, biting them in. My stomach pulls taut, as though all my tension is being pulled inwards through my scars and crushing my bones.

I guess we'll talk later then.

Two more tables pay then leave and the rest follow on not too long after, thankfully.

We all sit together, like we did that very first night. Only now with the addition of Gaia and Nico. The other cook went home after the rush.

'It's all arranged,' Hazel begins. 'You're staying here tonight, as discussed, and I've arranged for you to be picked up bright and early.'

It was my idea to get a taxi. Gaia and Natalia can't help tomorrow, and I didn't want to risk someone taking me and not getting back in time for the lunch shift.

I need to leave earlyish in the morning and it's easier to leave from here in San Stefanos, and not the village where Hazel and Pericles live, which gives me the perfect excuse for one last night with Yianni.

'Yianni, you can take up your own bed again. *Nai?*' Pericles says through his thick accent as he leans back in his chair.

'Maybe tomorrow. Not tonight, I don't like Ruby being here alone.'

'Always the gentleman,' Hazel beams, reaching over to squeeze his arm. 'You were amazing today, Ruby. I know I've already said, but you really did us all proud. Yianni said you would be brilliant, and I had no doubts, but you were so swift, smooth. You're such a natural.'

'Did Yianni tell you to say that?' I snort, and I pick up my beer, pressing it to my lips.

Hazel tilts her head and wrinkles her nose.

'No? Not at all. Why would he?'

I drink deeply into my bottle, catching Yianni frowning from the corner of my eye.

'No reason. Thank you. I enjoyed it. I've missed organising everyone.'

We all share in a strange shot Nico puts together and then continue to chat about the last few months, and the months to come.

The whole time, I feel like there's a volcano ready to burst out of my chest as I can't wait for my time alone with Yianni. My skin itches with questions. I haven't felt this on edge in years.

Not since Jonathan was alive.

When Hazel, Pericles and Natalia say goodnight, I get a little tearful. It's been such a long time since I've lived as a little family, and I know I'll miss them terribly.

The idea of living with a stranger in France, the way Rob has arranged, fills me with regret.

We all embrace and kiss cheeks, and Hazel tells me to have a safe journey while she squeezes my hands and then my face.

'I wish I was taking you to the airport myself. Promise you'll call as soon as you're there.' Hazel has said something along these lines at least six times. That, or how she feels terrible for not taking me herself. It's OK though; they have so much to do every minute of every single day in the summer that I would almost be annoyed if they did insist on taking me to the airport.

'I promise.'

Even Pericles squeezes me so tightly I think I might pop, and Natalia demands I come back as soon as I'm able. Telling me I should come over for a week in the winter, if not sooner.

Gaia gives me a hug and wishes me luck in France, then Nico wraps his arms around my neck and exhales in my ear. Nico, my partner in crime, the one keeping me entertained behind the bar for the past few months. From being warned off each other, to becoming good friends, I'll miss his silly jokes and somersaulting glasses.

'You will visit?' Nico steps back, pushing his shaggy hair off his face.

'Of course.

'Then this is, as you French say, *à bientôt.*' He reaches to squeeze my arm one last time and pats my back.

'Yes, soon. Hopefully very soon. *Kalinikta*, Nico.'

Then we're alone. Yianni puts things away, and I hover where Nico left me, with one foot in and the other outside of the entrance.

It's only the sound of cicadas that surrounds us now.

We're so far apart.

Yianni stops shuffling things away and hovers a few metres away from me.

Locking my arms over my chest, I try to keep myself steady. 'Where were you today?'

'I asked Baba to Mama's grave, a meal in her honour. This day is the anniversary of her death.'

'Nico told me. I just don't know why you didn't.'

'I did this for you. To show you I trust you, that you fit here, that I would sit back, let you take it over. That I will give you all you want here. Now you have all the proof you need.'

My head sways one way, then the other, and my hands fall to my hips.

Jonathan would never have even thought far enough ahead to do something like this for me. Maybe I was wrong to let fear crawl in and make a nest in the back of my mind all night. 'I've already accepted the job. I have to go.' I take a step towards Yianni.

His jaw locks, his fingers twitch at his sides, then he tilts his head back and mumbles to himself. He takes three big strides towards me and pulls my hands from my hips.

'Then I want you to think of this night while you are gone. How you can be happy here, and have it all, here with me. I will do anything to make your dreams real.'

I heave in shallow breaths as I search his golden skin and deep dark eyes, almost covered by his hair. I brush some of the unruly waves out of his eyes.

'I'm still upset you didn't tell me about your mum.'

'And I'm still upset you are leaving.'

We press together, then stumble along undoing each other's buttons as though this is it. As though this is the last time, and we only have minutes before everything turns to dust and floats away on the warm breeze of the night.

He manages to undo all my buttons first and tugs the shirt from my shoulders and down my arms as we edge into his room. Our lips stay locked together, determined not to separate.

I pull at his shirt and the last button rips off completely, making a tinny sound as it bounces to the floor. Neither of us cares. I don't even apologise.

His right hand unclasps my bra as his left disappears into the right cup, before that item of clothing joins my shirt and his button on the floor.

It's not long until our mouths are everywhere. Then I pull away and step back. Then another step.

For a moment, he's confused.

His eyebrows knit together so tightly they almost join before he sees what I'm doing.

I want to take all of him in. To imprint him on my memory in this moment.

His dark eyes, strong cheekbones, thick curly waves, firm muscular frame, dark tan. At first, he shifts his weight from one foot to the other, subtly contracting one muscle then the next.

It takes a moment for him to relax before he watches me too.

My chest heaves at the sight of him and I don't want to spend another second not pressed against him. I almost lunge at him and nearly knock him off his feet.

We laugh and kiss and fall on the bed together and spend most of the night awake, knotted as one.

Chapter Fifty Four

Now

My alarm rattles me out of a dream about Yianni and our time on the boat together.

I blink through blurry eyes to find Yianni is already awake and gently stroking the scar on my abdomen.

'How long have you been awake?' I croak.

He shrugs in response.

My fists gravitate to my eyes to rub away the blur before I open them again to marvel at how handsome he is, even with almost no sleep inside him.

My fingers run along his stubbled face. It's as though his beard never grows; it's always just perfectly trimmed to a millimetre or two.

Stretching over Yianni, I grab my phone and turn off the alarm, which is still making a high-pitched tinkling noise next to his head.

'*Merde!* I set the wrong time! *Merde!*'

Flying from his bed, I begin putting things where they should go. I'd set my alarm an hour later than I meant to.

Yianni jumps up too and grabs boxers and shorts. 'How long before they are here?'

'Twenty minutes, maybe? Shit.'

There's no time to think. I just grab the day's clothes and sprint towards the loos. I hear Yianni call after me, but I don't catch what he says. Then he repeats it, shouting it towards me.

'I'll go get you breakfast. You must eat.'

Then he's gone and I'm already halfway to ready.

Six minutes later and I'm washed and dressed and have dragged my suitcases out towards the car park.

Placing my make-up on the bar, I begin the task of covering my scars while I wait for Yianni to return.

A rustling pricks at my ears. A tugging on the unlocked door. I don't bother to look away from my mirror.

'Don't rush off like that again, Yianni. I missed you.'

When there's no reply, I look up from my compact to see the silhouette of a girl standing in the doorway. Her head is tilted and she seems to be watching me.

'Oh, *kalimera*. Can I help you?'

'You mutz be . . . Rubay? Cousin? Err, is Yianni?' She flicks her heavy black hair over her shoulder as her eyes dart past me.

She walks towards me and smiles. Her accent is very strong and her English is slow but understandable.

It's not even nine in the morning, but she's perfectly put together in silver pumps and a very baggy, but equally short, black dress. 'Yes, I'm Ruby. Hazel's niece.' I do my best to keep my words a little slower than normal. Her eyes narrow and she tilts her head again, searching for understanding. I reword my meaning and tap my hand on my chest, 'I'm Natalia's cousin.'

'*Naí, naí*, Natalia and Yianni cousin.'

I physically recoil when she says I'm Yianni's cousin, and I have to correct her immediately.

'Natalia's cousin.'

She smiles and says, 'Daphne,' and touches her chest.

There's a pause and I feel the need to fill it. I'm not usually sucked into feeling awkward in a pause, but her eyes are almost unblinking as she comes to stand next to me at the bar.

'So, Daphne, why are you here so early?'

'I am early. *Naí*. Yes. Mutz of the time. Today, I have the, the good news for Yianni.' She leans in and lowers her voice. 'I am having baby.' A wide grin shows a mouthful of small, gappy teeth. 'Yianni baby. He will be very please. Very happy.'

Behind her head, I can see my car pulling up.

My entire mouth is dry, and I have no words.

That's when it hits me.

I recognise her.

She was here early once before. I saw her being let out by Yianni on my first morning here, when he got me making him an early-morning mojito and showing me where everything went. It was her.

'Yianni baby?' I repeat, and point at her stomach.

'*Naí*, yes. I tell Yianni about *my* Yianni baby.'

'So' – I stutter over my words as my tongue feels twice its normal size – 'Yianni is going to be a dad, a baba?'

'*Naí*, Yianni. My Yianni baby.'

While I'm scooping up my make-up, I manage to say congratulations, because what else do you say when someone says they're pregnant with the child of the man you love?

My mascara rolls to the other side of the bar as the driver gets out of the car. I have to leave it because I can't be here a moment longer.

This woman, this Daphne, nods to me and almost skips as she wanders off into the depths of Greek Secret like she owns the place.

This isn't her first time swanning around here.

How can this be true?

My throat feels like a hornet has attacked it and sweat covers me like a thousand minuscule spiders running over me.

What was he really doing yesterday? Did he take her somewhere? Maybe she was a one-night stand and she's come to share her good news.

I can't deal with this, no matter what. I can't handle any of it.

My emotions shatter across the floor and as I gather everything up to escape to the taxi, each step feels like I'm stepping on the broken shards of *us*.

I can't trust anyone. I was a fool to think even for a moment that anything I touch could end in anything less than disaster.

As I slip into the car, I'm sure I hear Yianni call my name.

It doesn't stop me.

The car door slams behind me and the vehicle pulls away out of the dusty car park.

My eyes start to sting, but I hold it together, because if there is one thing I'm good at, it's keeping everything locked up inside.

As soon as we're out of the village, doubt seeps out of my bones.

What if it's all in my head? Am I completely irrational?

It's like my brain has been saturated in fear and now I can see through the fog of it.

Jonathan used to sleep around, but I guess that doesn't mean Yianni would do the same. They're so different.

The only time he could see someone else would be in the mornings, maybe, when I swim.

I have no idea how good he might be at hiding things from Pericles or Hazel. We've managed to fool everyone. Maybe this is normal for him.

Maybe this is why Hazel worries about him with girls, because this is what he's like.

Or maybe Daphne was talking about a different Yianni. She probably was. There's so many of them. She was probably talking about another Yianni. It's such a common name here.

It can't be possible, Yianni isn't like that, but then . . . I didn't think Jonathan was like that.

I don't know what to think.

I have to speak to Yianni, I need to know the truth. He owes me that.

I begin to go through my bags, trawling through all the contents to find my phone.

It's not here. It's not in my make-up bag, my handbag or my backpack, and it can't be in the suitcases because they were already packed and locked.

We're halfway to the airport when I remember where it is. I've left my phone in Yianni's bedroom, on charge.

Without caring, I rub my forehead, leaving my fingers sticky with make-up.

There's nothing I can do about it now.

I bury my face in my hands as the wash of green Corfu runs past the window.

A stab of pain nearly splits me open from my belly button to my teeth.

If I'm wrong, and he's done nothing to hurt me, I'll be lucky if he even wants to speak to me after this.

I might never even find out the truth if he won't speak to me about it.

I don't have his number anyway. It was saved in my phone, and he isn't on social media.

My fingers tug at the roots of my hair and I could scream until my lungs collapse.

The only positive is that Hazel printed out my boarding pass because she doesn't *trust all these apps*. I'd laughed at her, but now I'm grateful for her organisation.

I'm sure this is my confusion, but fear pools in a thick layer on my skin. Perhaps this is why he agreed that we shouldn't tell anyone about us. He *could* be another charming Jonathan all over again.

No.

It's a misunderstanding.

It has to be.

It has to be.

It has to be.

Have I picked the wrong person all over again? I wish I could feel sure of him, but I don't.

I don't believe in myself enough to believe in him.

As soon as I'm home and I can get hold of him, I'm sure it'll all be smoothed out.

The flight gets delayed by two hours and my luggage is the last off the belt.

My finger feels raw from fiddling with the place that used to be home to Jonathan's engagement ring.

By the time I round the doors at Gatwick, my nails have never been shorter and my hair is a tangled mess from constantly pushing it off my face.

When my eyes meet Mum and Dad, they look elated and concerned in equal measure. Instead of hello or *salut*, my dad's first words are, 'Bad flight?'

'Something like that. I left my phone in Corfu.'

'Don't worry about that now,' Mum coos. 'You're here safe and sound and I've missed you terribly.' She wraps her arms around me and rests her chin on my shoulder.

She smells sweet, like Hazel.

'Not just your mum, me too,' Dad adds, as he kisses the top of my head. Mum then squeezes me until I can feel my cheeks flushing red.

We chat as we walk to the car, but my mind isn't on it. I'm not listening. The words are going in my ears and other words are coming out of my mouth, but my brain isn't engaged.

At what point can I borrow a phone and call Hazel to tease out information from her?

I wait until we are settled into the car to bring it up.

'Can I borrow your phone to call Aunt Hazel and tell her I'm here? With the delay, she'll probably be worrying.'

'Of course.' Mum digs in her fat pink handbag for what feels like twenty years as the car's air conditioning cools off my sweaty nerves. 'Here.'

She passes the phone to me over her shoulder and I scroll the names to find Hazel. As soon as the phone presses to my ear, acid burns at my insides and I remember I haven't had anything to eat all day.

Even on the plane, I felt too sick with worry to eat.

'Fern? Is everything all right with Ruby? Yianni says she left her phone behind.'

'It's me, I'm fine. The flight was delayed, but I'm in the car with Mum and Dad. I just wanted to let you know I'm safe.'

'Oh, thank goodness. Thank you for letting me know.'

'That's all right.' I hesitate as I try to formulate a way of asking this naturally. 'I heard about Daphne's baby. Please say another congratulations for me, won't you?'

'Well, good news really does travel fast! How did you know? Oh, I suppose you were here this morning. We couldn't be more pleased for them.'

'What did Yianni say?'

'Oh, he was thrilled. How could he not be? He adores Daphne. We all do. She and Yianni are such a beautiful couple too. Have you seen them together?'

I close my eyes, and all I can hear is my own voice in my head wondering why the hell I'm so incapable. How it is I've got this far, and on the one hand I can't imagine Yianni being anything but good, but on the other I don't trust my own judgement any more. 'No, no, I haven't.' My voice is a shadow.

'Sorry, Ruby, I've got to go. I'll make sure to pass on good wishes. Natalia's got a big dinner order for me. Love you, sweetheart. Bye.'

'Love you too.'

I hang up.

I pass the phone to my mum.

I bite my cheeks hard enough to taste metal to try to stop the tears from stinging in my eyes and the lump swelling inside me.

That told me nothing. I need to find a way to get hold of Yianni.

Chapter Fifty Five

Now

Mum and Dad wanted to know every detail of Corfu – even though we spoke on the phone regularly and they've seen photos, they wanted me to tell them everything all over again.

I couldn't tell them the most important thing, of course. That I've fallen in love with someone but I don't even trust my instincts to know whether they are what I think they are.

It's hours before I manage to ask Mum casually if I can use her laptop to get on my Instagram to tell people I don't have my phone.

Before telling anyone anything, I message Nico. *Hey, Nico. I was wondering if you have Yianni's number. I don't have it and I need to speak with him. Thanks xx*

I tap the keys lightly with my fingertips, praying he has his phone on him and that he will reply in the next three minutes before I have to sign out and wait to check again later.

It could be hours. Nico isn't on his phone much.

The laptop loudly *bings* and there's Yianni's phone number plus the words, *You owe me big kisses. Don't tell little boss xx*

Little boss brings a smile to my face. *Thank you, please tell him I'll call as soon as I can. xx* A new waiting game begins. This one has to last until Mum and Dad are in bed and I can sneak downstairs and use their landline to ring Yianni.

I wait until I can hear gentle snoring from their room before sneaking downstairs.

It's like being a teen again. It seems it doesn't matter what country I'm in, when it comes to Yianni, I'm always sneaking around.

The phone rings and rings.

I'm sure the line will go unanswered, until there it is. His voice. His mouth with my name in it once more.

'Ruby.'

They're two hours ahead of England; it must be past midnight there.

'Hi.'

'What happened? You left. There was no goodbye. I have your phone.'

'I need to know something. Is some girl having your baby?'

The line is so clear that the silence on the other end is even more cutting. I look at the screen to check the line is still live.

'What?' There's a trace of laughter in his question. 'A baby? Not unless this is how you tell me you're pregnant?'

'No! No. I'm not. No. It's just some girl came in telling me she was having *Yianni baby* and I freaked out. I called Hazel and she didn't make it clear . . .'

'My friend Yianni, the one who hit me with the stone, he's married to Daphne. Daphne is Maria's daughter. You've met Maria many times.'

I have. She is the cleaner at Greek Secret, an older woman who speaks almost no English at all. She would smile at me and wave if

323

she saw me. She was in five nights a week for about thirty minutes to clean the toilets and empty the bins. That was it.

I didn't know she had a daughter.

'Daphne comes in two mornings a week to give her mum two nights off. So, when she told you she was pregnant, you thought—?'

'Yeah.'

'You really thought I was with some other woman?'

After everything with Jonathan, it's not outside of possibility to think I might spend my life with someone one minute and find out they've been cheating and lying the next.

That's not what I think of Yianni, but it's a notion that's hard to shake.

It's not so much him that I don't trust, it's me. My ability to know when someone is being honest.

Maybe it's because I spend so much time hiding parts of myself from everyone around me – why wouldn't they do the same to me?

'I don't know what I thought. I felt scared. Lost. I never thought Jonathan would've cheated on me. Not until I found out he had. I thought maybe I got it all wrong, like I'm not able to read people any more.'

'I'm not Jonathan.'

'I know.' I curl up on my parents' soft leather sofa, burying my forehead into my knees.

'I love you.' Yianni's voice feels so close that with my eyes closed, sitting in the dark, I could be there with him in Corfu.

'I love you too.'

'Book flights. I'll pay. Anything. Just come back to me, *nai?*'

'I can't. I leave for France in two days. I think we need to take some time apart. All this . . .' My voice trails off because I can't really explain what *this* was all about. Fear, I suppose. 'You'll be busy all summer anyway . . . We need space and I need to clear my head.'

Even though he's done nothing wrong, even though he's still the man I shared so much with, all my feelings are bunched together and I can't understand how everything inside me has got so tangled up.

Fear has put razor-sharp claws into me, and I need space to find myself again.

This is my first new relationship since Jonathan, and I'm already tripping over myself to find flaws, to sabotage it when it gets a little scary.

The only way to save what we have, and make this work, is to find a way to trust myself again. Without fixing me, there will be no way to fix us. I need space to figure out if I can ever truly trust someone again.

'I'll come back to Corfu this time next year, OK? Like I promised. And if you still feel the same, and I do, then we'll figure out how to make this work. I've spent too much time hiding my fears, my scars, everything that *really* happened with Jonathan, not to mention my aspiration. I guess I've started to believe everyone around is hiding things from me too. I've been burying whole chunks of my life from everyone I'm closest to . . . I need to sort myself out before this can really work. Right now, I don't even know if I believe any relationship could survive me.'

'I want you to come back to me. But I know this means I will have to wait for you.' He pauses, and all I want to do is wrap my fingers into his. 'One year?' Yianni doesn't sound like Yianni. He sounds deflated and weak.

'One year to figure my life out and I'll come back to you. I promise.'

'Then I will hold our secret until then. I love you, Ruby *mou*.'

'I love you too.'

I can't bear to say goodbye, so I say goodnight instead.

'*Kalinikta*, Yianni.'

'*Kalinikta*, Ruby.'

The line falls dead, and so does my heart.

If this is the right thing to do, to fix myself and pursue my dreams, then why does it hurt so damn much?

Chapter Fifty Six

Now

'What . . . ? What are you doing here?' Stepping away, my hands clutch the leather menus hard enough to leave nail marks.

I haven't seen Hazel for almost four months, since I left Corfu for France.

'Well, that's not much of a welcome, now, is it?' Hazel nudges into my mum. They both bubble with so much energy they're bouncing on their toes and bumping into each other playfully.

This looks like a planned ambush. Both sisters are dressed ready for a night out in the city with smart dresses that cut off just past their knees and kitten heels. They've even adorned themselves in elegant wraps instead of coats. They must be freezing. December has been bitter.

Mum often moans she needs to shed a few pounds, but she doesn't. The bold floral pattern suits her. They both look well put together and ready for a glass of champagne.

'I just can't believe you're really here.' I kiss their cheeks and embrace them with one arm, still pressing the menus to my chest. 'Do you have a reservation?'

'Of course! We know how busy you can get. It's under H and F.'

The booking *H et F* had caught my eye, but I had no inkling it could mean Hazel and Fern.

'Gosh, you two are such little devils, surprising me like this . . . Oh, wait one moment. *Bonsoir, madame.*' I switch to French to welcome Noelle back to the restaurant.

Noelle is an elegant widow who comes in once a week. It's her grandson's flat that I'm living in. Technically, I'm living *with* him, but he's hardly ever there. He's always off travelling the world.

She's usually on her own, but when he's back she'll come in with him.

In French, I introduce her to Mum and Aunt Hazel before going into English to them to explain.

'Let me show Noelle to her normal table before seeing you two to yours. Does Rob know you're here?'

They both nod and grin.

After having my weekly chat with Noelle, I come back to find Mum and Hazel have been shown to their table by my head waitress, Louise.

'I still can't believe you're both here. I'm off tomorrow though, if you want to do something? I can show you both around Rouen. How long are you here for?'

'Only a few days to mooch around the Christmas market, before heading back to our respective homes.' Mum bunches her shoulders up like an excited toddler as she peers at me over her menu.

Catching Louise's arm as she passes me, I whisper to her to fetch a bottle of champagne. Not that I think Mum or Hazel's

French is good enough to understand much conversation, but I know they'd understand the word 'champagne'.

'I must get on, but I'm looking forward to a proper catch-up. If you need anything, do not hesitate to ask me or one of my lovely wait staff.'

'*My wait staff.* I love this confidence, you're positively glowing.' Aunt Hazel presses her hands to her chest and gently shakes her head – I hope with pride, not disbelief.

Louise brings the champagne in a silver bucket on a trolley that gets placed next to the table.

'We didn't order this.' Mum waves her menu between the bottle and the glasses, wide eyes darting from my waitress to me.

'No, it's on me.'

They both coo and aww like they're purring cats as I leave them in the capable hands of my staff.

Aunt Hazel's right, I do shine here.

I've been left to manage front of house however I like. Rob and I make a good team, linking everything from the kitchen to the polished square tables seamlessly.

I love my time working here. It's my spare time that's been tough.

With only two other tables left polishing off wine, Rob orders me to sit down with my mum and Hazel. He'll join us soon enough.

Snatching a chair from a nearby table, I pull it over to sit with them. It's the first time I've sat down all day and the sensation of sitting makes every muscle in my back cry out with relief.

'How was everything?' I glance from one to the other as I begin kneading the muscles of my lower back.

'Perfect,' they both chime in unison, before laughing to themselves.

Today, they look even more similar than usual. Maybe it's because they're wearing dresses of a similar style, or that they've both let their fine blonde hair be free around their faces. The biggest difference is always Hazel's tan and her naturally narrower frame.

'It's been lovely watching you gliding around and keeping the show running. You were a wasted talent at Greek Secret.' Hazel rests her bronzed cheek into the palm of her hand, pressing previously unnoticeable wrinkles into the skin around her eyes.

'As long as she's happy,' Mum proclaims with a tap to the table, 'that's what matters.'

'How much have you two had to drink?' I stop kneading my back and lean to see what's left in the bottle in the champagne bucket.

I slip my shoes off under the table and pray no one needs my help. Glancing over my shoulder, I see one of the couples is getting up to leave and the other is writing out a cheque for the bill.

Cheques are something I've had to get used to again in France. They seem so old-fashioned in England. I don't remember ever writing one out myself.

'Well,' Mum begins, 'we saved you a glass of champagne, but we need a glass.'

Louise is still here, standing in for me now I've sat down. I indicate for a fresh glass and she's on it right away. It's on the table before a minute has passed.

Mum fills my flute to the brim, something I've told her time and again not to do as the champagne needs air.

'Gosh, there's still some more.' Mum wiggles the bottle to and fro before pouring some into Hazel's flute, then her own.

'How have you two been sitting here all this time and not even polished off one bottle of champagne?'

'Don't be ridiculous, this is the second bottle.' Hazel pushes her glasses back into her hair, making it wild. Just how I always see her in my mind's eye.

'*Santé.*' Mum raises her glass.

'*Yamas.*' Hazel raises hers.

I pick up mine, clinking against theirs. 'Cheers.' I take a sip and let the cool liquid refresh my palate with its bubbles. 'How's everyone in Corfu?'

My chest pulls tight. This is where I hear someone else say his name again.

I haven't let myself say his name out loud. He's only been allowed to live in my imagination. Coming alive when I'm alone in drawn-out memories that could never match up to the real thing.

I've spent every moment I'm not at work thinking about him, wondering what he's doing and if he still wants me to come back to him.

We promised to take a year away from each other so I could figure things out and try to leave my Jonathan baggage in the past.

So far, all I've managed to do is throw myself into a job I adore and pine after Yianni when I'm not here. It's more like torture than self-improvement.

We're not allowed any contact, not until August. So far, I've hated every moment of not hearing his voice.

However much my feet ache and my lower back throbs from a long day, I really do love it here. The biggest thing I've learnt so far is that Yianni and Hazel were right – I am capable.

It's every moment without Yianni I find truly tiring.

'Very good,' Hazel says in response to my question, 'although I'm sure Natalia's told you already, she's having boyfriend troubles. I thought it was bad enough worrying about Yianni, but now Natalia's single and miserable.'

'Yeah, she has.' I press my glass to my lip and speak before sipping, 'And Yianni, how is he?'

Hazel takes her glasses off her head and rolls her eyes as she places them down.

'I'm always surprised you two don't talk more. But I guess boys like Yianni are never big talkers unless they're in front of you. He's off travelling around Europe. He got a bee in his bonnet about seeing the world and – what was his word? Not maturing. Actually, he was saying it in Greek.' Her lips press together in thought. 'Anyway, I think he's doing well, from what we can gather. He's in Italy at the moment, and apparently he's been off making lots of friends.'

Travelling? He said that's what he wanted to do. It's what I told him to do, once. To grow, to see the world and to be sure of himself and of us.

Whenever I imagine him, he's pottering around Greek Secret, making improvements for the next season.

Suddenly, my bones ache more than before, but now with the longing to ask questions. I want to know how he's getting on, whether he thinks of me or if his feelings have changed.

Has he been swept up in the arms of some beautiful Italian girl and is now glad I'm out of the picture?

Whenever Jonathan was touring in one play or another, he'd say he missed me, but I know differently now.

I have to stop comparing Yianni to a ghost. He deserves to be happy, with or without me.

A smile lifts my face. 'Good for him. I know that's something he really wanted to do.'

'And he's moved out and in with Nico. So when he's home, he won't be coming home at all.'

The fact things are happening in his life and I don't know about them makes me nervous. What else has changed?

'That reminds me.' Hazel picks her handbag up from next to her feet. 'Yianni said if I did come to visit you, I should give you this.'

She passes me my old phone, the one I left in his room back in August.

I'd needed an upgrade and have a French number now. At least now I can look at all the photos of us that hadn't automatically uploaded to the cloud.

'Thanks. I don't really need it now. Do you think Natalia would like it? Once I've got everything off it?'

'I guess she told you she's smashed her screen, didn't she? That's so kind of you, Ruby. She'll be thrilled.'

With the last patrons out the door, Rob bursts out of the kitchen and lights up the room with his zest for life and another bottle of champagne for us all to share.

I'm glad they surprised me. Seeing their faces and having some fun after hours is just what I needed.

Chapter
Fifty Seven

Now

'Sorry, there's not much open. At least now it's December, more things will open up at some point.' I pull my thick army-green coat around me as the white sky threatens snow.

Squeezing it makes me think of Yianni's warm arms holding me at night.

Everything makes me think of him.

A shiver does its best to shake away the thoughts of his hot bare skin pressing to mine.

'Why are you apologising?' Hazel's boots hit the cobbles hard; the sound echoes down the empty streets. 'Did you tell everyone to be closed on a Monday morning?'

'Of course she did,' Mum joins in, 'you know what she's like.'

'Not everywhere.' I roll my eyes. 'I can take you out for breakfast with a nice side view of the cathedral.'

Rouen is a beautiful city, one of my favourites in France. It's filled with narrow winding streets and crooked centuries-old buildings. It's also filled with churches spanning the ages, with bells that chime and give it a unique character. Victor Hugo dubbed it 'the city of one hundred bells', although the bell towers are somewhat depleted now.

We meander through the closed Christmas market, made up of white wooden chalet-style huts. They look so romantic with the sheets of fairy lights linking them together that I usually try to avoid them.

Everywhere's kitted out with golden Christmas lights and festive pines taller than houses, which look small compared to the Gothic cathedral that dominates the central square.

A few people mill about from place to place, but Monday morning is quiet, even in a city like Rouen.

'Do you have many friends here? Other than Rob and his boyfriend, of course.' Hazel links her arm in mine.

I've missed talking to Hazel in the mornings. We message now and then with updates, but nothing beats being in someone's company.

'You met her yesterday,' my mum interjects.

Mum and I talk on the phone at least once a week, the same as we did when I was in Corfu. She's always tried to keep up to date with everything I'm doing.

'How much champagne did I have that I don't remember meeting anyone new that wasn't Rob's boyfriend?' Hazel twists to look at me as we carry on. Her eyes bulge behind her glasses.

'It was the little old lady with the black and red cape. Noelle. Ruby adores little old Noelle.'

'I do, actually. She's very interesting. There's Pierre too, her grandson. He's all right, when he's about. Other than that . . .' I shrug. 'It's hard to make friends in a city when all you do is work.'

I don't like to tell them I spend my spare time in a little white box room riddled with beautiful dark wooden beams, and furniture that rests at all angles on uneven floorboards.

I'm often on my own.

The building I live in is beautiful though. The front looks modern; it hides what I assume is the original entrance. The tiny walkway makes me think of a tunnel into history.

It even smells musty and old, but how I imagine it smelt when it was new too, as though the smell is caught in a capsule along with the thick beams and peeling paint.

It feels like a place where I can go back in time, long before my time. Long before I caused myself misery by leaving Yianni and *doing the right thing by finding myself.*

I can't tell them any of that. They'd think I was unhinged.

'Not that any of that matters, I didn't come here to make friends. I came here to work with Rob again and gain some more experience so I can be the best I possibly can be.'

'Ruby, you've been working in hospitality your whole life. How much experience do you need? Surely you should be finding a job you love in a restaurant you love, and you can work there happily?'

'Maybe it's about finding adventure,' Hazel cuts in as we all fall in step. 'First Greece, now France. Why not?' We arrive outside the boulangerie I know will be open. It has a scattering of black metal tables and chairs outside. Only one is taken. An old French boy with a hand-rolled cigarette in the corner of his mouth and an espresso cup between his fingers sits reading a newspaper.

I nip inside and order us all pains au chocolat and hot chocolates as Mum and Hazel grab a table looking towards the side of the cathedral and its large round stained-glass window.

Balancing a trayful with ease, I sit snugly with them at the table. It's really designed for two, but we can sit happily around it elbow to elbow.

'Ruby, your mum and I got talking after all that champagne last night—'

'Please don't say "champagne",' Mum interrupts.

I bite my bottom lip to keep in a snigger at the memory of them both tottering out late last night, laughing.

'Anyway, I have a question and I know it's hard, but I have to ask it. I suppose it goes with what your mum was saying about finding a job where you can be happy . . . Do you think Jonathan is still affecting your choices?'

It's as though the morning's ice has spread its fingers and caught on to me, sticking me still.

I begin to stumble over my words, stunned by how blunt she is. Mostly, people edge into any Jonathan conversation; even Hazel has never jumped in so hard before.

'I mean' – my hands come up into an empty shrug – 'how could he not? It's my fault he's dead, after all.'

If only they knew how much it was my fault, and not just because my hands were on the wheel, but because my words drove us off course.

'I can't believe you're actually worse than me.' Hazel presses her hand over her mouth as she shakes her head. 'Or maybe I can see it clearly in you and not in the mirror. You can't blame yourself for an accident.'

'What do you mean, *worse than you?*' The chill in the morning air seems to be rising from the ground and swallowing me up, and now my legs are juddering under the table.

'Well, that brings me nicely to what I've wanted to tell you for some time. It's only, it can be hard sharing the past. You know that better than anyone.' Hazel grips her hot chocolate – the steam looks like the cup has its own lingering cloud. 'Which is rather handy, as I had no idea how I was ever going to talk about it before. Things your mum has hinted at, things you've said, probably without even knowing, have left a deep scratch in my mind. I've been left thinking about my relationship with Tim, and yours with Jonathan.'

I push my fringe out of my eyes, only for it to fall back in place. From feeling the frostbitten morning on my toes, my cheeks now blaze like a log fire.

'I know you avoid talking about him . . . I guess that was the first red flag. The lengths you've gone to sometimes to avoid anyone even saying his name.' Hazel shakes her head in disbelief. 'Then all this wanting to be the best you can be . . . it makes me think of me after Tim. When he first left, I was a shell of a person because I didn't believe in myself any more, and yet part of me was still relieved. Even at the time, I could barely untangle my own thoughts. I know it might make you feel guilty, because Jonathan didn't leave you, but feeling relieved to be free is OK. I know you don't like to talk much, but you can talk to us. Or you can tell me I'm wrong. Tell me you're competitive and that's why you want to be the best maître d' instead of forming new bonds with people your own age. Or tell me that he was the love of your life, like you've told us all in the past.'

It's impossible to take a deep breath. If I do, I'll break my chest and all I'll be able to do is cry. 'I'm trying to get better. I want to talk to people. It's just, every time I open my mouth, I don't know how to tell them . . .' I think of Yianni and our conversations late into the night. I could talk to him for hours, snuggled into his arms on that hard single bed.

It was easy to separate out all the different parts of me with him. I just couldn't work out how to put them back together, and that's what drove me away from him.

I need to be brave now and let them know the truth, however hard it is to say.

Chapter Fifty Eight

Now

Carefree sparrows nip crumbs from next to our feet. Their dowdy feathers are puffed up against the cold.

They're not even put off by my knocking knees under the table.

Their little hearts race at least twice as fast as ours. That's normal for them. It's not normal for mine, but I'm sure I'm keeping up with them right now.

'It . . . it didn't end how everyone thinks.' My mouth is dry and even sitting I feel light-headed. The only way I can grow and change is by opening up. I have to do this. 'It really *was* my fault.' My voice sinks into the ground and I can't pull it out.

Mum and Hazel lean in closer to hear me, even though there's almost no space between us as it is.

'I broke up with him, in the car that night. I'd had enough of putting myself last and being overlooked. I'd been talking myself out of it for ages, telling myself it was a phase because of the move to Suffolk and that things would get better. But seeing him that night, parading around and drinking and ignoring me . . . It was meant to be *my* night with *my* family. It felt like another episode of the Jonathan show. He never supported the things I wanted, and I'd started to realise how on edge I felt even talking to another man, with him accusing me of things. I'd had enough and I snapped.'

Both women nod intently for me to continue. Mum has deep lines accumulating on her forehead and around her pursed lips, and so does Hazel.

My eyes begin to blur, just how they did on that rainy, miserable Saturday night.

My fingers twist around the soft skin where Jonathan's ring used to keep me in check.

'We began to argue. I was so upset. We both were. My eyes filled with tears, I couldn't see the road properly then . . . Jonathan pulled the wheel. I don't know why. I'll never know whether it was out of spite or if he saw something in front of us that I didn't. It's all my fault.'

A tear rolls over my cheek and Hazel passes me a napkin to carefully dab it with.

'It's not your fault.' My mum can't control her tears from streaming down her rosy cheeks. She snatches up two napkins to press to her face. 'You would never have hurt him on purpose. You're my beautiful, wonderful, kind girl. This is not your fault.'

Mum drops the napkins and takes my hand. Aunt Hazel puts her hand on top of both.

The man with the espresso clears his throat and stands to leave. I think we've ruined the view across to the stained glass of the cathedral.

Hazel's face turns hard, lined with anger in a way I've never seen. 'Your mum is right. This is not your fault. He pushed you too far, and never, ever think you did something wrong. You didn't. The problem here is one I have some understanding of. Jonathan is still affecting you. Not just the big dramatic end to it all, but the way he treated you before he died. I'm sure you won't be telling us the half of it—'

'I've blocked out the half of it.'

She's right though. Jonathan's tendrils, even in death, have wrapped around my future with Yianni and pulled it away before it began. My fears cast evening shadows that are hard to shake.

'I wish I'd done more. I could see you slipping away and I was so afraid of losing you completely.' Mum's face looks as crumpled as her discarded napkins. 'You spoke to me less and less while he was alive, and you seemed to shrink away behind him. Before Jonathan, you were always laughing.'

It's all cutting too close to the bone – it hurts too much to know how this was hurting Mum too. My mind slips back into the past and all the bad times. All the times I paid for Jonathan's mistakes, all the times I trusted him and he was cheating, all the times he told me I was the one overreacting, when I couldn't see it was him.

'Come on, these pains au chocolat are getting cold.' I slip my hand from their grasp and scoop mine up to take a bite, sending flakes of buttery pastry like confetti across the table.

Mum picks up a fresh white napkin and does her best to compose herself and wipe away her remaining tears without leaving pastry or mascara on her face.

Hazel takes a thoughtful bite of her breakfast, chewing carefully.

People are starting to move around the street a little more now and I'd rather not continue to make a scene where people can see us. 'Before you worked at Greek Secret, I'd never seen you working,' Hazel begins. 'I remember chatting to your mum on the phone before you arrived and her telling me how good you were and how you loved the social aspect of hospitality. It then surprised me that you seemed to use it to avoid real connections. I know the antisocial hours make it even easier for you to hide. It took a long time for you to shine with us. I'm grateful to Yianni and Nico for that. Those two boys really took you under their wing and you began to really shine.'

'I miss them both, so much.'

I miss Yianni more than words could ever allow, but I don't want to hurt him by dragging him down with me when I'm like a torn-up rag doll inside.

'Yianni really helped me to get the confidence to show my scars.' The words stick in my throat, and I have to quickly gulp back some of the thick, sugary hot chocolate to burn away whatever is stuck there.

'He's a very caring boy, just like his father. With everything he went through, losing his mum the way he did . . . I think he had to grow up a lot, which makes him such a good listener and a caring soul. It's why I'm always worried about him getting hurt.' Hazel sits back in her chair, her lips pressed into a distant smile.

'It's nice you've got men in your life showing you how to be strong. When Jonathan put you down or told you—'

'Mum—' I need her to stop, because the wobble in her voice makes me want to cry all over again.

'No, let me finish. If he ever put you down, he was only doing it to make himself feel bigger and better. Not because you weren't good enough, but because he knew he never would be. It was the same with Tim and Hazel. They think they can slowly make you feel bad about yourself as a way of controlling you. I know the type, Ruby. I saw it in time.'

Hazel takes her stare and presses it on my mum.

'You never said anything to me, Fern.'

'How could I? I didn't like to admit it to myself, but I could see a bit of Tim in Jonathan. We didn't spend all that much time with you when you were with Tim. Ruby probably barely remembers him. You pulled yourself away from me, just how Ruby did. Tim was always full of smiles when people were around. I was fooled too, for a long time. Stupidly, I thought he was bloody brilliant, in fact. He was such a charmer.'

Hazel glances back at me and her words descend into my mind, that Tim could put on charm and take it off like a necklace. I remember her saying it when we were eating ice creams back in Corfu Town. I wonder if that's what she's thinking too.

'What made you realise he wasn't?' Hazel switches back to my mum, with her arms tightly wrapped around her chest.

Mum lowers her eyes, and her fingers begin twisting around each other again.

'One New Year's Eve, he had too much to drink when we were all out at a friend's party in this big country house. Do you remember?' Aunt Hazel nods. 'Anyway, it was almost midnight, and I went to find you both. You didn't know I was coming up behind you, so he didn't know I could hear him. He was pointing his beer towards some woman, and I heard him say something like, *You used to look that good. You still could if you put some effort in.* It was something like that.' My mum's face flushes a dark crimson and she rushes over her words. 'There was more to it all, but it made me see him differently. It opened my eyes to how much you were shrinking away.' Mum takes Hazel's hand in her own. 'You were heartbroken when he left, but honestly, I was relieved too.'

I can't imagine Hazel putting up with anyone like that.

She always seems so put together and strong. She might be behind the scenes in the kitchen of Greek Secret, but she's a big part of its driving force. She's there at the heart, making sure everyone's happy and well fed.

Plus, Pericles is so loving. I can't imagine her with anyone else now.

That's not to say I haven't seen them have the odd heated debate, but the way he looks at her says it all. It's the same way Yianni would look at me.

Watching me from across the room with a contented curl on his lips.

I swallow back the thought and the image in my head. I hope to have him look at me like that again. I hope I don't ruin what we had, all because I ran away to find some kind of peace or closure.

'I can't imagine you letting anyone talk to you like that.'

'These people wear you down so you don't notice it happen. You can start off as the strongest oak tree, but they can whittle you down to a toothpick and you won't even remember being rooted to the ground by the time they're finished. I think you need to find your roots again, Ruby.' Hazel's blue eyes sparkle with tears that she's holding back. She sniffs, and a fresh smile lifts her face. 'You know, when I first met Pericles, it took a lot for me to trust him. Well, we had a bit of a funny start really, and I often wonder, if I hadn't got pregnant, would I have stayed. I don't think I felt like I deserved him. Tim used to put me down a lot. It made it hard to believe Pericles was the real deal. For years I was waiting to find out what was wrong with him. Turns out his biggest flaw is spending too much time gossiping at the bar instead of working behind it. But I can forgive him that.'

Words don't come easily to me in response to this outpouring. I've already said more in the past twenty minutes than I have for the past three years.

I want to open up and tell her I agree and she's right. That that's exactly what Jonathan did to me, with his constant backhanded compliments and his roller coaster of emotions. And that I've fallen for Yianni, and I just need to work through everything and find my way back to him.

'It's OK, Ruby.' Hazel nods to emphasise her words. 'You don't have to say anything more if you don't want to. We're always here for you. Just think about who you want to be and what you want.

Start holding that beautiful head of yours up again. I know you can be that oak tree again.'

'We can be your roots in the meantime.' Mum smiles, but her chin wobbles again.

'Exactly. It's all still inside you and I don't want your confidence to be defined by anyone but you. Or your ability to trust people, including your family.'

I hold eye contact with the two women who mean the most to me in the world. The two women I shut out for so long but who have always stood patiently waiting for me to come back to them.

There is one thing I know they'll understand and that'll make them smile.

'I wore a bikini in Corfu for the first time since the accident.' I can feel my cheeks lift at the memory.

They turn back into bookends, little wrinkles in the corners of their eyes deepening with tender smiles.

Mum's fingers move over my cheek as she smooths the hair from my eyes.

'I know that's a big step, showing people your scars. I'm so proud of you, Ruby.'

'We both are,' Hazel adds.

'Thanks.'

'And you were shining again last night. You're finding yourself at long last.' Mum squeezes my arm over the table before picking up her drink.

She's right, I do shine at work. I've gained so much from being here already, and Rob has said he'll write anything I need to help show anyone I have the skills to run my own restaurant or brasserie, or whatever I want to do next.

This needs to be a turning point.

I might not be able to change completely, but I recognise the importance of talking to someone about pain.

I feel a little lighter.

After all these years, maybe I should talk to someone else about these problems. In France, it's quite normal to speak to a therapist, and I think it would be better to talk to someone here. Someone who is as far away from it all as I can get. Someone who doesn't know the road, didn't see the report in the newspapers.

Maybe here in France, I will finally heal.

Mum leans over and kisses me on the forehead in the same way she always has, before wrapping me up in her slender arms.

'Love you, Ruby. Thank you for talking to us.' Then she says, 'Even if it has taken your whole life.'

A comforting laugh shudders through us all.

'Right,' I announce as I pick up the rest of my pain au chocolat. 'Now I want us to have a happy day. The rest of the day is all about retail therapy!'

Chapter
Fifty Nine

Now

Being on my feet and working is what I need. It's the only thing that has stopped me dwelling on my loneliness for the past few months. At work, I'm back to feeling real connections and enjoying meeting people again and hearing their stories.

Even when we have an awkward customer, or if someone has double-booked a table, I can take it all in my stride now. Everything is getting easier. I can take the small failings and they don't over-whelm me.

It feels good to have put myself first after all these years and to hold my head up and say I'm trying and know that I can do this.

Loving my job so much does make Mondays tougher for me. Everything is a little too quiet when I'm not at work. It's been positive to talk to a therapist though. It was the right thing to do. I've been able to see that I'm not at fault, and that we all have flaws.

I've also been able to talk to Hazel and Mum more. I even managed to talk to Dad about it all on the phone. I wanted it to come from me, and not from Mum.

We all used to be so close. And for the first time in a long time, I feel like we are again.

I've even made sure to hold on to other connections, messaging some of the people I went to uni with and talking to Nico on socials here and there. We never mention Yianni, though.

I think Nico knows not to.

It's like our relationship never happened, as though it was just a dream.

I saw a photo of the two of them out in a group at one of the clubs in Corfu. Their arms were all woven together like a tapestry of smiles, taunting me. Pretty girls and handsome guys all slotted in and sharing in a joke that I wasn't told. His eyes were creased in the corners and his head was thrown back in open-mouthed laughter.

I could almost hear the two of them.

I didn't go on social media for a week after that.

It's good to know Yianni is safely back from his travels at least. It's so hard though, living in a world where everyone is so connected. It feels so broken not to talk to him every day when all it would take is a message.

I've typed them out to him. Telling him simple things about my day, or if things happen at work that would make him laugh. They're all there in a note on my phone, like letters without stamps.

We decided to give each other a year. I guess, really, *I* decided. So that's what I'm doing.

I decided to be here and not there. Now, instead of staring into the impossible line that is the curve of the Earth and seeing it as the elusive present, I lie in bed in the mornings and stare at the point where my white wall meets my white ceiling.

It really isn't the same as having warm, wet sand cocooning my toes and the breeze moving through my hair as the sun drenches my soul and tans my skin, and knowing I'll be pressed to Yianni each night.

Since Hazel and Mum came to stay, I have photos of us to look at on my phone of the times we were pressed together. My favourite is a selfie Yianni took of us lying in his bed. We're laughing, because just as he went to take it, a mosquito buzzed in my ear and I screamed. The first photo is dreadful, but the second is bursting toothy laughter. I love it.

Natalia has that phone now. I asked Hazel to wipe it for me because I was in a rush at work when I gave it to her. I trust her though. When I handed it to her, she told me Tim used to read her messages, so she'd never do that to anyone else.

Strolling down the cobbles, I make my way to Maison Vatelier. It's open on a Monday and it's a patisserie that I adore. They have award-winning brioches, but that's not why I go there. I'm in it for the giant raspberry macarons with a petal on top. They're one of Mum's and my favourite things in the world.

Aunt Hazel made us go in when she and Mum visited, and I've been obsessed ever since.

I don't allow myself to come here often, because it's not cheap, but when I do go, it's worth every penny.

Once my treat is in its box in a pale pink paper bag, I make my way towards the cathedral.

With the Christmas market dismantled months ago, I can sit outside the front of the imposing edifice while contemplating everything that has brought me to this point – sitting alone on a stone step in the cold, eating giant macarons.

I count down the days until I can see Yianni again, and hope that all this work I've done on myself will leave me in his arms and with my own little taverna in Corfu.

I settle into my daydreaming while studying the rows and rows of statues that decorate the façade of the cathedral. They all look down their stone noses at me, as though they know something I don't.

I scoop the first macaron out of the box and inhale the fresh tang of the raspberries and the vanilla in the centre.

As I take a deep lungful of the delicious scent, a man to my left catches my eye. He's watching me sniff my food.

He's also sitting on the steps not far from the cathedral and he's sprinkling little crumbs from what looks like a brioche for the birds near his feet.

He's holding a pink bag from the same shop as I am.

'*Très bon choix.*' Good choice. He gestures towards the pink bag by my feet.

He's good-looking, with character to his face – wide lips, tidy hair – and he's well dressed in a smart overcoat. I smile and nod.

'Do you speak French?' he asks in heavily accented English.

I suppose I must look confused. Or perhaps sitting around sniffing macarons is more of a tourist pastime. '*Oui,*' I say, and look out across the empty square in front of us and the row of restaurants with chairs spilling out on to the street. All empty and ready for the evening.

The man scoots closer to me and asks me if I live far from here.

I glance away from him as he shuffles nearer, and then I stiffen. '*Merde,*' I say under my breath.

The stranger begins to apologise.

'No, not you.' I wave a hand towards him, then repeat in French, '*Non, pas vous.*'

I stand as he continues to gawp at me.

Pulling my long coat up and open, I pull my vibrating phone from the back pocket of my jeans.

The stranger's attention only reaffirms to me how much I only want Yianni's attention. Something tugs in my heart at the ringing of my phone – I hope that it might be Yianni calling, telling me he can't wait another day to see me.

'Hello?'

'It's a girl!' Amara's voice sings down the line.

'Congratulations!' I spend a moment squealing on her behalf before asking how she is. 'And how's the baby? What's her name?'

The man next to me continues to wait for me to talk to him, so I pick up my things and begin to walk away down the high street filled with centuries-old beams and smart shopfronts.

'I'm not telling you until you meet her. It went well . . . OK, that's not true. It was shit. Episiotomy level of shit. They said I'll get to leave once they've seen her latch on well to my boob. Then home. When will you come and see us?'

'I'll be there as soon as I can book a train. You couldn't stop me. Do you want me to bring you anything from France?'

'Not that I can think of. Just you.'

'I'll be there soon. Give that gorgeous baby of yours a kiss from me. And send a photo, so I can confirm she is as gorgeous as I'm sure she is.'

'Nope. If I send you a photo now, you might not rush to see her.' She laughs, and I know she wouldn't be so mean as to not send one. 'My tea has arrived. I can't wait to see you.'

'Me either. I'm so proud of you.'

'I haven't done anything yet, I've only pushed her out. The hard work starts now.'

'You're amazing, and you'll be the best mum. Congratulations, Amara.'

'*Ciao.*'

'*À bientôt.*' See you soon.

And with that statement, I hop down the street with joy for my friend.

One of the deals I made with Rob before agreeing to work in Rouen was that when I needed to, I could visit Amara when she had her baby. I wanted at least a month off to be in England.

He agreed, even though he moaned he'd want to see her too.

I take another bite of my hefty but light macaron and stare up at the big golden clock Rouen is famous for. *Le Gros-Horloge.* It's one of the oldest working clocks in Europe, dating back to the Renaissance. It's passed time and watched people wander underneath the bridge it sits on for so long.

It'll be here when I'm not, bringing the future to us, one tick at a time.

It'll stop one day, and so will I, but there's no point wondering when. It ticks now, and so do I.

When an overwhelming thought comes to mind, like it is right now, my therapist said I should take a breath and try to take one step at a time.

I'm grateful to have time. I wish I could know why Jonathan pulled the wheel from my hands that night and put an end to his time.

I'm doing better now, though. I spend more time being grateful for what I do have than thinking about what he doesn't.

Chapter Sixty One

Now

Corfu. Back at long last.

I've hired a little car from the airport and can almost taste the synthetic scent of pine needles hanging from the air freshener on the mirror.

Driving along the winding roads, I'm consumed by the real pine trees all over again. Just like last year when Yianni picked me up from the airport.

The vivid greens that carpet the rolling landscape. Passing through villages with terracotta-and-white houses and jutting balconies, the hot-pink bougainvillea in full bloom. Nothing's changed.

Except me.

It's crazy to think this could be my home. Another wave of adrenaline pulses under my skin. What if Yianni's changed his mind?

It's mid-afternoon by the time I pull up outside the taverna and park next to Yianni's car. It's almost exactly a year since I first arrived at Greek Secret with him.

So much has happened.

I've lived here in Corfu and been happier than I can ever remember, then France where I was lonelier than I could've imagined. It was the right thing to do though. To sort through the past and give myself the space to believe in a future. The seven months, however hard they were without Yianni, have changed me for the better.

It was something I needed rather than something I wanted.

I wanted Yianni and I needed time.

I've learnt to trust myself, I got myself this far. It's taken time, but I believe in myself now and I know that without risk, there's nothing worth risking. I'd rather have a life filled with people worth losing than four blank walls.

At last, I feel like I might be able to deal with problems if they come my way. It's like Amara and Si – they know they have flaws, but they still love each other. And Yianni has always accepted me for all of mine.

My body tingles and my heart hammers in my chest as I make my way through the dusty car park.

The restaurant looks empty but the sign to say it's closed isn't up at the entrance.

His car is here, though. So he must be too. Unless he's walked down into the village or to the sea.

I suspect everyone will be back at the house now, probably getting ready for dinner service. The vines still weave beautifully along the terrace and the chairs and tables are all perfectly laid. Nothing has changed, except me and maybe Yianni . . .

'*Kalispera?* Is anyone here?' My voice sounds strangled and strange.

'One moment.'

Chapter Sixty

Now

Our old house is officially Amara and Si's.

It used to smell like Jonathan, and even after he died I would catch the sweet smell of his body spray in the furniture.

Now it smells of flowers, and there's already a hint of baby lotion in the air.

I kiss Si's stubbled cheek in the hall and he apologises for not having managed to wash as he smooths his hand over his soft Afro hair.

Going through my walking-through-the-door-routine feels strange, with the memory of these walls being mine. Remove shoes, jacket, wash hands . . . but not because I'm home. Now I wash them to hold a baby. They've painted the living room purple and there's a Moses basket in the corner where the TV used to be. There's no baby in it; instead, it's brimming with cuddly toys.

I've brought a little soft pink bunny to add to the collection.

None of it is mine now. We changed over the lease and I sold off anything Mum and Dad couldn't fit in their garage.

Amara's always-wild hair looks like it'll turn to braids if she doesn't brush it soon, and Si looks like he hasn't slept, possibly ever.

He leaves us in my old living room to get tea.

Amara's peachy cheeks glow and her unruly cape of black hair coils around her.

'Meet Lola,' she coos as I step towards where she's sitting on a velvet sofa.

I look over to see a squishy red face wrapped in a pink fluffy blanket. Lola's eyes are tightly shut. She's perfect. I sit next to her and Amara proceeds to tell me her birth story, which might be enough to put anyone off having children ever.

She admits to being overjoyed and overwhelmed in equal measure, and I'm envious of her ability always to be honest about her feelings.

'How do you do that?'

'What?' She isn't looking at me; she's watching Lola and slowly rocking.

'Be so open about how you feel? It took me months to say to Jonathan that I loved him and even longer to tell him I didn't any more. I couldn't even tell you or Mum or Hazel what *actually* happened in the end for years.'

Amara looks up at me and smiles. 'It's simple. You just open your mouth and say what's in your head. It's not a big deal. If you let go of the fear of hurting yourself or the people around you, you can pretty much say anything you like.'

I make a *tsk* sound.

She's right, but it's completely unhelpful. It's just not that easy for me.

It leaves everything too open. Although I know Jonathan made me even more guarded, there's no way to magically change that now.

'Here.' Amara passes me Lola and I'm suddenly overwhelmed with the fear of dropping her, even though I'm sitting.

I've never held a brand-new baby before.

As I scoop her out of Amara's arms, she chuckles at me. 'I didn't know your eyes could get that big. She's a baby, not a rabid dog.'

I glance at Amara, but only for a second. I'm too afraid to take my eyes off the creature in my arms.

She barely weighs as much as a doll. Her eyes stay closed and her mouth puckers into a tiny 'O'.

'When are you going to see Yianni?'

I groan, ignoring her question completely.

'What made you forgive Si and ask him back?' I say in my best taunting tone.

'Well, this is bad timing.' Si brings in two teas, placing mine on the sideboard and Amara's in her outstretched hands.

'I didn't mean it like that.' I do my best to backtrack. 'I mean . . . things weren't going well and you got over it. Both of you. How do you do that?'

Si slumps down close to Amara and places his hand on her knee, waiting to hear her answer even more eagerly than me.

'Other than you told me to tell him?' Amara shifts, tucking one foot underneath her. 'There was a reason for the problems and there were solutions. Sometimes, two people come together and the initial spark is enough to burn them. They bring out the worst in each other, or one of them's toxic. That's not us. I was being overly sensitive, and Si was being lazy. We talked it through. At the end of the day, we both want to be together. We're happier together. It's not perfect. We both have issues, but we work on them. Together.'

'She's bang on. I was miserable when we broke up. It made it even clearer.' Si leans to kiss Amara's shoulder.

'I know that Si believes in me. You know how afraid I was to have kids. My parents—' She shakes her head and her flowing hair moves over the place Si just kissed. 'They were dreadful and selfish. Si helped me to feel confident that that's not me.'

They've had ups and downs, broken up and come back together. Now they have Lola to cherish too.

Maybe it is possible, maybe I can be happy and have a future with Yianni without ruining it.

I look at Lola's state of unburdened peace.

'And you're not afraid of it all falling apart?'

'What? Of course! I'm a new mum, I'm afraid of everything and I cry at everything,' Amara snaps at a louder volume than the rest of our conversation, and baby Lola disapprovingly exhales and wriggles in my arms. 'But if we weren't together because we were afraid of it not working out, what sort of life is that? That's running, not living. I'd rather pick being happy in the here and now than worrying about mistakes we haven't even made.'

Amara tilts her head and draws her eyebrows together.

She's right, and seeing them in blissful happiness, I know that's what I want.

'I'm so happy for you both. I'm happy you've found a way to stop letting the past hold you back.'

'Yeah?' Amara clenches her jaw and leans over Si, with her tea precariously aimed towards me and Lola. 'Well, now it's your turn.'

Chapter Sixty One

Now

Corfu. Back at long last.

I've hired a little car from the airport and can almost taste the synthetic scent of pine needles hanging from the air freshener on the mirror.

Driving along the winding roads, I'm consumed by the real pine trees all over again. Just like last year when Yianni picked me up from the airport.

The vivid greens that carpet the rolling landscape. Passing through villages with terracotta-and-white houses and jutting balconies, the hot-pink bougainvillea in full bloom. Nothing's changed.

Except me.

It's crazy to think this could be my home. Another wave of adrenaline pulses under my skin. What if Yianni's changed his mind?

It's mid-afternoon by the time I pull up outside the taverna and park next to Yianni's car. It's almost exactly a year since I first arrived at Greek Secret with him.

So much has happened.

I've lived here in Corfu and been happier than I can ever remember, then France where I was lonelier than I could've imagined. It was the right thing to do though. To sort through the past and give myself the space to believe in a future. The seven months, however hard they were without Yianni, have changed me for the better.

It was something I needed rather than something I wanted.

I wanted Yianni and I needed time.

I've learnt to trust myself, I got myself this far. It's taken time, but I believe in myself now and I know that without risk, there's nothing worth risking. I'd rather have a life filled with people worth losing than four blank walls.

At last, I feel like I might be able to deal with problems if they come my way. It's like Amara and Si – they know they have flaws, but they still love each other. And Yianni has always accepted me for all of mine.

My body tingles and my heart hammers in my chest as I make my way through the dusty car park.

The restaurant looks empty but the sign to say it's closed isn't up at the entrance.

His car is here, though. So he must be too. Unless he's walked down into the village or to the sea.

I suspect everyone will be back at the house now, probably getting ready for dinner service. The vines still weave beautifully along the terrace and the chairs and tables are all perfectly laid. Nothing has changed, except me and maybe Yianni . . .

'*Kalispera?* Is anyone here?' My voice sounds strangled and strange.

'One moment.'

Hearing his voice again makes my skin tingle.

It's coming from the side room, the one he used as a bedroom while I was staying in his room at Hazel and Pericles' house. The one where this all began.

Footsteps come echoing from the hall to the kitchen and Natalia appears.

'Ruby?' Her chocolate eyes shine as she bounds towards me. 'How are you here?' She grabs my arms and bounces before hugging me. Yianni appears in his doorway.

Nothing has outwardly changed since I saw him leaving that room to get us breakfast. He's still in his black fitted short-sleeve shirt and tight trousers. It could be the same day and everything else was a nightmare.

As I eye him, his face gives nothing away, only perhaps the briefest note of surprise.

I clutch Natalia's slim frame against my own, more to steady myself than anything else.

All I want to do is run into Yianni's arms and tell him I'm ready to start living.

I want to tell him I'm sorry if I hurt him, but it had to happen.

But I can't, not with Natalia here.

Maybe it's good that she's here. It delays me finding out whether he has moved on without me. The thought causes stomach acid to burn the back of my throat. If he turns me away, I need to hold it together.

I swallow back the stinging sensation and try to stay focused.

Natalia releases me from her grasp. 'Look, Yianni, it's Ruby!'

'*Kalispera*, Ruby.' His tone is stone cold.

At best, I could call it neutral.

His arms knit together over his broad chest and he smiles politely, but I swear it's only because Natalia's beaming.

'Where is everyone?' I glance at the empty restaurant in an attempt to seem natural.

To seem calm.

Nothing feels natural or calm right now. I can even feel my pulse in my fingertips.

I nip at the sides of my skirt to give my hands something to do.

'Mama and Baba left after the last customers,' Natalia says. 'They'll be back later for dinner. Yianni promised to take me into Sidari to meet friends. I can call and cancel, and we can all go to the house.'

'No, no. Please don't cancel for me. I'll be staying for at least a week. We'll have plenty of time together. I'll go to the house and surprise them.'

'At least come in the car with us. I have so much to tell you. Please?' Natalia momentarily reminds me of her younger self, back when she was ten and she followed me about and wanted to do anything I did.

I take a breath and look back at Yianni, who has kept his distance in the doorway of his room. Or what was his room here at the taverna. 'It's up to Yianni. He might have things to do after dropping you off.'

'Oh yes, he has big plans to be helping Baba in the garden before having a nap. So, he can take you there after taking me to Sidari. Let me get my bag.' Natalia bounds back towards the kitchen, leaving Yianni and me alone.

'Yianni, I . . .'

But before I can even start, Natalia is back from the kitchen and marching us off towards Yianni's car.

Chapter Sixty Two

Now

'So how come you're here?' Natalia quizzes me in the car.

'Erm.' I look back at her, twisting in my seat.

She has politely insisted I sit in the front of the car next to Yianni.

Now he's backing the car out into the road, sitting only inches from me. Heat burns from my pores so hot it might mix with the air conditioning and cause a cyclone.

Does he feel it too? So far, he won't even look at me, avoiding my gaze as though I'm Medusa.

He's probably moved on and wishes I wasn't here. Maybe he's figuring out how he'll tell me this is well and truly over.

'I was in England, visiting Amara and Lola, and I just wanted to see you all.'

It's true. Seeing Natalia's face light up when she saw me made me realise all over again how much I missed being here and being a part of a family unit. But I came back for Yianni, because I don't want to be away any more.

I've even handed my notice in with Rob. Louise has been shadowing me now for months and I trust her to do a great job.

I already know what I want to do in the next phase of my working life, and how I want to go about it. I just need to know if I'll have Yianni by my side when I take those next steps.

'Will you stay for Easter too? I know you said you always wanted to visit for a Greek Easter.'

'I'd forgotten you haven't had Easter yet.'

'Forgotten? Isn't that why you are here?' It's the most Yianni has said to me. His eyes dart towards me then back at the road.

I swallow hard, knowing I need to be honest, but I don't really want to include Natalia in the conversation.

'No, actually, it's not.' I openly study Yianni's reaction. The twitch of his fingers on the steering wheel and the way he sucks in his top lip in concentration.

The car bounces over a pothole and I look away.

I can't have another big conversation like this, with someone sitting behind the wheel. I lock my eyes back on the road.

I've missed watching him, being near him, breathing in the same air as him. But I need to stay focused and wait until we're safely away from a moving vehicle.

It's Natalia who breaks the moment of silence, clearly oblivious to any tension between me and Yianni.

'If not for Easter, then why? Not that I'm unhappy. It is always good to have you to stay.'

There's a couple walking along the road holding hands, and it takes all my effort not to take Yianni's in mine.

'Because I made a promise to return.'

Natalia tells me about the plans for Easter and hopes I'll be about to enjoy it all. She asks if I'll be staying at the house and I explain that I've booked a room at Perros Hotel for the week. It's not far from Greek Secret.

Her chatter consumes the journey into Sidari.

Then she's gone and it's just the two of us.

We're alone.

Yianni drives out of town and into the bloom of Corfu, all to the sound of our silence.

The air-con is freezing and my throat is completely dry when I try to speak.

'Why are you here months early?' Yianni's voice is low and husky over the smooth cool air.

'Not here. I can't have a conversation like this in the car.'

He pulls the car over in a lay-by next to high grasses and reeds.

The engine abruptly shuts off and Yianni pulls on the handbrake before he gets out of the car, slamming his door.

I follow suit and watch as he looks up at the sparse clouds, like froth in the sky.

He begins to stride down a narrow side road and I follow alongside him. I snatch a breath, trying to figure out my words.

'You've moved on, haven't you? It's too late, isn't it?' Tears catch in my throat and my hands clutch my stomach as pain shoots through my body. 'Jonathan was right about one thing: I really am stupid. I should never have left, but I had to. I had to heal.'

Yianni's fists contract into balls at his sides and his broad shoulders round.

'Don't. Don't ever say that about yourself.' His hand cuts the air. 'You are not stupid. Don't talk to yourself that way. Never use words like that to talk about someone who is trying so hard all the time to do the right thing. To think how everyone else will feel and think about her. Someone who cares so deep.' His tone is hard to read – it's like Natalia is still with us and he's still trying to hide what we have.

What we had.

Yianni's eyes narrow on mine and he pushes a thick curl out of his face and behind his ear before mirroring my body language by placing his hands on his hips.

'I thought you came back early to tell me the same. That you were staying in France without me.' A smile tugs at the corner of his mouth before an exhale of laughter follows.

His hand glances his chin then covers his mouth, before more laughter ripples along his chest. He exhales hard again and doubles over.

'What? Why would you think that?'

'I've been worrying ever since I came back from my travels. Hazel tells me all about how well you are doing and how France suits you and she's never seen you stronger or happier. For me' – he places his hand on his chest – 'I've never felt more proud and more scared.'

Yianni pulls himself upright. I take a step towards him and he grabs my hand, pulling me in on my tiptoes to meet him.

His fingers wind into my hair, tilting my head back.

My body reacts and my pulse quickens.

'You told me I couldn't see you again for another few months and no one was to know about us.' Yianni brushes his bottom lip over mine.

He doesn't kiss me.

'It all just . . .' My breath catches as his lips skim my neck. 'I missed you and—'

'But you said this wasn't allowed. That we had to talk first.'

'Shut up and kiss me.'

Laughter waves over him as he presses his lips to my throat.

I can't take any more. My body is alight in the heat of his arm and the Corfiot sun.

Taking his face in my hand, I press my lips against his, making him stumble back.

His laughter stops as we find our rhythm. Pulling each other in.

Our hands glide over each other's clothes, grasping at fabric, wishing it wasn't there.

Yianni pulls away, resting his forehead on mine.

'I take it this is a sign? That you are ready?'

All I manage to say is *mmm-hmm* as his mouth descends towards mine again, warm and inviting.

I pull back, only an inch. 'I'm not good at talking about everything I think and feel, but I am better with you. I've worked through my past and I am ready to move to the future. I can promise I'll try to be better, and I won't leave again.'

'You can leave, to the shops or the beach, but not to another country. *Naí?* Not without taking me with you.'

'I think I can manage that.'

'And what about your restaurant? Are we staying here?' I'm sure that my palpitations must be visible in my throat as I tilt my head further back to see him clearly again. My breath and my heart feel like a skipping record. 'Will Greek Secret do for now?'

The months we were apart were a gaping void, but in his arms I have found someone I can talk to, someone I want to be with. Someone I love.

We hold each other so tightly I think our cells might fuse together as his aftershave fills my lungs.

'I have enough money to put towards something now, and I have an idea that I think might work. But I want your help with it.'

Yianni looks down at me, gently shaking his head. His hand comes to rest on the line of my jaw. 'For you, I would do anything.'

'Now we have to tell everyone.'

We still have so much to work out, more than just telling everyone.

I still have to stop myself falling into the traps that Jonathan laid for me. But I'm a stronger person than I was last year. And I can grow by surrounding myself with better people, like Yianni. Like the supportive family I'm so lucky to have. Just how Hazel did after Tim.

'There's something I should tell you . . .' Yianni's fingers trace a line down my neck. 'Natalia knows.'

'What?' Now my eyebrows shoot up.

'You gave a fifteen-year-old girl your phone without deleting anything. What did you think would happen? The same day she was knocking at my door asking question, question, question. A thousand questions.'

'Oh, bloody hell. I told Hazel to delete everything.' I squeeze my eyes tightly shut to suppress the thought of Natalia reading texts that Yianni and I had sent one another.

'She didn't know how to, so she told Natalia to do it . . . It's good. She's so excited. I am surprised you couldn't see how crazy she was in the car.'

'I was too worried about you.'

'It's time for us to tell everyone. No more secrets. Are you ready?'

I weave my fingers into the curls around Yianni's neck. 'Not even a Greek Secret?' I let a cheeky grin spread across my face.

Yianni groans and rolls his eyes before pulling me into his chest and pressing his lips to mine.

Epilogue

THE FUTURE NOW

It all needs to be perfect.

Every napkin needs to be just right, every glass. Everything's white and fresh, from the wedding dress itself to the chairs.

The only pop of colour is the bougainvillea over the curve of the arch. There will be nothing else to distract from the view of golden sand and the setting sun over the sea when the time comes.

Right now, the sun is still high in the sky as it blazes into mid-afternoon.

I move frantically from table to table, polishing knives, adjusting the well-placed linen swans until they're perfect, and picking up wedding favours only to put them back down again in the same position.

My heart pounds in my chest and adrenaline pulses, crashing over me like sea on rocks.

I smooth my hands along my dress and step back.

It's all ready.

I turn and glance around, only to remember I'm alone and my phone is nowhere to be seen for me to take a photo of it all. Soon, the whole place will throb with people and napkins will be shaken out and placed on laps.

There'll be no trace of the hard work that went into it all.

It's worth it though.

I couldn't be more excited for this moment. It's as though my whole life has been leading me here.

'It is perfect. Like you.' Yianni's voice carries on the sea breeze and a smile touches my lips.

Turning back towards the entrance, I catch sight of him. White linen trousers and matching shirt unbuttoned just enough to see more of his silky tanned skin. The only embellishment of sorts is the sprig of gypsophila for his buttonhole. His dark curls dance around the smile on his face.

'You're not meant to be here. Not yet.'

I do my best to purse my lips. He isn't fazed. He strolls towards me with a cheeky look on his face.

'Something arrived, and I thought it was important to bring it before the guests arrive.'

'It's here? They finished in time?'

My fingers dig into the thick muscles on his upper arms and I almost hop with anticipation. A laugh pulses from his chest as he nods.

'Show me. No, wait, I need to take a photo before a breeze comes and changes everything. I can't find my phone though.'

'Ah.' He slips his hand into a back pocket, and it reappears with my phone in it. 'You left it at home on charge. You don't change.'

'Do you want me to change?'

He passes me the phone but doesn't let go of it when I try to take it.

Instead, he pulls me in. Instinctively, my chin tilts up for a lingering kiss, enjoying his soft lips and the graze of his stubble on my chin. It's the perfect moment of peace before the inevitable madness descends.

Yianni's mouth leaves mine and he studies my face before saying, 'No. It's too late for that now. I'm used to picking up after you.' He grins, then hops away as I swat at him.

'*Espèce de—*'

'Oh, yes? You know I know this one now. I'm some kind of . . . ? What?' He narrows his eyes at me, but he's still there with a broad smile plastered on his face. 'It is all right. I forgive you. You take your picture and stay there. I will soon have a smile back on your face.'

'Be careful you don't get dirty,' I call as Yianni moves away, his feet padding back towards the entrance and out on to the beach beyond.

Pushing my hair back over my shoulder, I begin to snap photos of the neatly laid tables stretching out in front of me.

From the corner of my eye, I'm aware of Yianni putting out a stepladder and I listen as he begins banging about at the entrance.

It isn't long before I can't wait a moment more. I march over, ducking under where he is working to watch him make the final adjustments.

Stepping back into the sand, I look up as he hangs the hand-painted and sculpted sign we commissioned only a month ago. We spent so long struggling to pick a name for our new venture, I thought there wasn't going to be one.

'It's beautiful, just how I imagined. And just in time too. The caterers and staff will be here soon.' I press my thumbs to my temples. 'God. You know, I think I'm more stressed about this than I will be when *we* get married.'

I got the idea to have a wedding venue when Amara announced her and Si's engagement before I left for Corfu; I just had to find the right place. Hosting weddings is the ultimate in hospitality.

It's perfect, because we can still work at Greek Secret when there aren't weddings booked. I've loved every minute of working there since first coming to Corfu, and enjoyed travelling with Yianni in the winter months.

Last year, Yianni came home with a story about a little lonely beach taverna for sale in another part of Corfu. It was tiny and falling apart. It had mostly been used for local families and, even then, not for some time, not since the head of the family died and no one wanted to take it on.

It needed everything done and there wasn't much else nearby, so it hadn't turned a profit in a long time. The family wanted it gone.

Yianni knew I'd want it, knew the potential it had for the events and weddings I'd started dreaming up.

We've put everything we have into it. Every last penny of savings, every spare moment of time fixing things and building it up from scratch.

Today is the day. The first wedding reception.

Amara and Si's wedding reception, no less.

I check the time on my phone. I need to get back to have my make-up done. Amara has given me strict instructions not to be late getting my bridesmaid dress on. She knows I will be checking every detail of the reception up until the last moment. She knows I just want everything to be right for her.

It's a dream venue, nestled back into the curve of a little alcove of rocks and sand, with no one nearby. The guests will be able to dance all night if they want to. I want the whole reception to be a dream for Amara, and Si too. They deserve to have this big celebration of their love.

'It's Amara. She would forgive us if we get it all wrong.' Yianni edges the sign a little to the left as he speaks.

'*I* wouldn't.'

Yianni laughs as he studies the sign again from his vantage point on the stepladder. 'I am very proud of you, Ruby *mou*.'

With my thumb, I spin the white-gold ring encrusted with diamonds on my left hand and smile. 'I'm proud of us.' I continue to look up at him as he steadily aligns the sign, taking as much care as I had with the tables. '*We've* done this. All of it. And there's going to be so many more.'

I'm so grateful for everyone who helped to get me here. To a place where I can see it's OK not to do everything alone, it's OK to trust others. In fact, they deserve my trust and I deserve their love. Yianni's love.

Yianni jumps off his stepladder and down into the soft golden sand.

'There,' he says, 'now we are ready.'

Yianni's arm wraps around me and he squeezes me in, tucking me into the curve of his arms before pressing a kiss on to the top of my head.

Over the entrance and under the swag of sweet pink bougainvillea, our whitewashed sign reads 'Secret Love'. Only, it's not much of a secret any more.

ACKNOWLEDGEMENTS

I would like to thank my good friend Brian Hawes QFSM for talking to me about his experiences.

I would like to acknowledge and thank my editors. *Greek Secret* has had different editors along the way and I'm grateful for them all. Firstly, thank you to Debra for helping me in the very first airing of this book and for always pushing me to be better. Next, I would like to thank Victoria and Lindsey for all their insight, and for helping me to find the confidence to build on my ideas. I'm grateful for all the developmental, copy editors and proofreaders for their hard work.

I would like to thank my ARC readers, in particular Gemma, who always sends me lots of helpful feedback.

Last, but never least, my mum and my husband. I think we make a nice little team. We still have some growing to do, but my success thus far wouldn't have happened without you working alongside me. Love always.

ABOUT THE AUTHOR

Photo © 2023 Samuel Thomas

Francesca Catlow writes bestselling fiction filled with passionate love stories that feature flawed and sometimes broken characters as they face a crossroads in their life. She often explores heartbreaking themes while also whisking readers off to beautiful locations.

Francesca loves to travel. Born and raised in the heart of Suffolk, England, she has travelled extensively in Europe with her French husband and, more recently, their two children. In 2024 she relocated to France, where she spends her days dreaming up stories and her evenings sitting in her garden relaxing with her family.

In 2023 Francesca was a finalist for the prestigious Kindle Storyteller Award and was nominated for an Innovation Award for her work with libraries in Suffolk.

Francesca loves to hear from her readers. If you would like to contact her, you can do so on her social pages, or subscribe to her newsletter.

To stay up to date, and for free content, please visit https://francescacatlow.co.uk/subscribe

Facebook and Instagram: @francescacatlowofficial

X and TikTok: @francescacatlow

For trigger warnings, visit: francescacatlow.co.uk/trigger-warnings/

Follow the Author on Amazon

If you enjoyed this book, follow Francesca Catlow on Amazon to be notified when the author releases a new book!
To do this, please follow these instructions:

Desktop:

1) Search for the author's name on Amazon or in the Amazon App.
2) Click on the author's name to arrive on their Amazon page.
3) Click the 'Follow' button.

Mobile and Tablet:

1) Search for the author's name on Amazon or in the Amazon App.
2) Click on one of the author's books.
3) Click on the author's name to arrive on their Amazon page.
4) Click the 'Follow' button.

Kindle eReader and Kindle App:

If you enjoyed this book on a Kindle eReader or in the Kindle App, you will find the author 'Follow' button after the last page.

Printed in Great Britain
by Amazon

63312715R00221